Forbidden HEART

THE HEARTS OF SAWYERS BEND
BOOK NINE

IVY LAYNE

GINGER QUILL PRESS, LLC

Forbidden Heart

Editing by:
Samamntha Skal, samanthaskal.com
Julia Ganis, juliaedits.com
Olivia Zugay, storyflowsolutions.com

Find out more about the author and upcoming books online at www.ivylayne.com

Also by Ivy Layne

Don't Miss Out on New Releases, Exclusive Giveaways, and More!!

Join Ivy's Readers Group @ ivylayne.com/readers

WHERE PROMISES LIE

Fractured Promise (July 2026)

Deadly Promise (November 2026)

Dark Promise (2027)

Shattered Promise (2027)

Last Promise (2028)

THE HEARTS OF SAWYERS BEND

Stolen Heart

Sweet Heart

Scheming Heart

Rebel Heart

Wicked Heart

Wild Heart

Broken Heart

Reckless Heart

Forbidden Heart

THE UNTANGLED SERIES

Unraveled

Undone

Uncovered

THE WINTERS SAGA

The Billionaire's Secret Heart (Novella)

The Billionaire's Secret Love (Novella)

The Billionaire's Pet

The Billionaire's Promise

The Rebel Billionaire

The Billionaire's Secret Kiss (Novella)

The Billionaire's Angel

Engaging the Billionaire

Compromising the Billionaire

The Counterfeit Billionaire

THE BILLIONAIRE CLUB

The Wedding Rescue

The Courtship Maneuver

The Temptation Trap

Chapter One

PAIGE

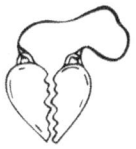

ONE YEAR AGO

I stared into the cold dregs of my coffee and let out a sigh. I wanted to curl up in a ball and sleep for a million years. Slouching back in my chair, I tried a deep breath, hoping some oxygen in my brain would wake me up. I hadn't slept well in months. At night, I'd lain in my childhood bedroom listening to the rattle of my mother's breaths as she struggled for air, dying a little more every day. Now, the silence was oppressive, every creak of the house as loud as a gunshot.

I was alone. I'd thought it was all I wanted.

I hated this house. The walls were a sick mustard shade, stained by years of cigarette smoke. The linoleum in the kitchen was faded and worn through in spots. My mother had refused to update any of it. Decorations were a waste of money, she'd insisted, and waste was sinful.

I'd escaped this house as soon as I could figure out

how, leaving at eighteen for college, paying my way by working as a nanny, a job I'd found out of pure luck. I'd arrived on campus knowing my scholarships would only go so far, and I needed to find a job fast. Then a professor had a friend who had lost their nanny last minute. They were desperate. I was desperate. I didn't have a ton of experience with kids, but neither of us was in a position to quibble. I took the position, and within six months I'd moved out of the dorms and into their home, changing my major to early childhood education. Who knew I'd love taking care of someone else's kids?

I didn't want my own—not anytime soon—but for the first time in my life I'd seen what a family was supposed to be like. For so many years it had just been my mother and me, after my father had walked out on us. Nothing about growing up with Harriet McKenna brought to mind the concept of family. Constant criticism and a liberal smack of her palm on my cheek when she was displeased had left me feeling like the only point of family was to escape them.

But at eighteen, a freshman in college warmly enfolded into the Bellingham family, I saw what it could be. A husband and wife who loved each other, who made time even though they both had busy careers. Who doted on their children despite their packed schedules. The kids were easy to love. Abby, an infant, fussy at nap time and not a fan of the bottle, but otherwise the cutest thing I'd ever seen. And Joshua—a spirited two-year-old. We did well enough once he learned he couldn't charm me, though deep inside I had to fight not to give in when he flashed those dimples.

I stayed with the Bellinghams through college and two years of grad school, intending to leave and find a teaching job from there. The kids were old enough to go to school, and I needed to make a decision. I had the degrees. I'd acquired some in-class experience. What did I want?

I'd been headed to the classroom when a friend of the Bellinghams made me an offer I couldn't refuse: follow their family as they traveled, minding two young children. It was a chance to see Europe on someone else's dime. I'd met the Smiths in the course of my years with the Bellinghams—they were kind and fun, their kids boisterous but good-hearted. I said yes, packed my bags, and off we went.

Another four years passed that way. I could have gone on like that forever. Halfway through my twenty-ninth year, I got the call. My mother—who I'd barely spoken to in almost a decade—was sick, dying, and alone. Reluctantly, I went home, though "home" hardly seemed the word to describe this place. I looked around again and sighed. What a waste. What a sad house she'd lived in— *we'd* lived in. Now that I'd seen the world and knew how things could be, the stark contrast was all the more apparent.

I'd gone back and forth, organizing things here for my mother, trying to ease her suffering without becoming her servant—which, I realized, was exactly what she'd wanted. Me at her beck and call, cut off from the rest of the world. Catering to her every whim. This was the life she'd envisioned for me, and she'd only needed to contract a fatal illness to get it.

I took care of her, but I wouldn't lie and say I liked it. Every moment under her roof was one too many. I always felt like a faker when I flew back to the Smiths and was welcomed into their family again, caring for the kids, laughing with Janice at the end of a long day. They thought I was torn, that what I really wanted was to be with my dying mother. They couldn't have been more wrong.

I never told them how bad things were at home. It was embarrassing to admit that my own mother didn't love me. Duty was the only thing between us. Harriet McKenna had raised me to understand that I owed her for my very existence, and she expected compensation for her sacrifice.

Intellectually, I got it. It wasn't me, or rather, it wasn't anything I'd done. I had the bad luck to look exactly like my father, right down to my oddly light blue eyes. I'd never met the man. He'd run off with another woman while my mother had been pregnant with me. And when I'd been born with his eyes, his dark curls, and his olive skin, she'd hated me.

I think if I'd been a little replica of Harriet—willowy with cornflower-blue eyes and wispy blonde hair—maybe then she would have loved me. I could have been a little mini-me for her to mold. Instead, as she told me over and over, I was a replica of him, sent to remind her of her failure as a wife and a woman. I was the visual representation of everything she'd lost, and she'd never forgiven me for it.

She had a heavy hand and high expectations. Some of them I'd lived up to. I'd been a good student, kept my room clean, knew how to speak respectfully. The flat of her hand taught me to keep my tongue under control. I didn't know if my father ran off because Harriet didn't have love in her, or if he'd taken her heart with him when he disappeared. Either way, there'd been none left for me.

The first few years my mother was sick, I helped without living under her roof for more than a week at a time. I arranged rides to and from chemo and coordinated with kind ladies from her church who brought over food a few times a week. My mother knew I didn't want any of this. So, of course, my presence was what she demanded. Eventually, she reached a point where I was the only one who could care for her. I left the Smiths, my heart breaking as I packed my bags, my tears matching those of the children.

My nanny families had been the only true family I'd ever known, and going home to take care of Harriet felt like a cell door clanging shut, locking me away from warm embraces and steaming cocoa, sealing me into this shadowed house that reeked of stale smoke. I was left wondering if time had stood still in these walls; the clock stopped in the early eighties, the avocado countertops cracked, and a phone bolted to the wall in the kitchen, the long curly cord trailing on the floor.

Time didn't exist in this house. For a woman who seemed to hate everything about life, my mother held on to it with a steely grip, fading slowly, day by day, dragging it out. If she'd been another kind of parent, I would have been grateful for every day we had together. But she was Harriet McKenna, and though I'd never say it out loud, in my heart I wished she'd hurry the fuck up and set me free.

And now she was gone. The house was empty, and I answered to no one. If you'd asked me before she died, I would have told you that freedom was all I wanted. Now that it was here, I didn't feel free—I felt hollowed out and empty. Alone.

She'd left me everything. Not that "everything" was much: this house, her car, a small retirement account. I'd buried her quietly in the plot she'd purchased, foregoing a wake, letting the ladies from her church set up a quiet service. I had stacks of frozen casseroles in the freezer and empty boxes everywhere. All I had to do was pack up the house, put it on the market, and take a step into the future.

I picked up the cold coffee cup and tilted it. Still empty, and it was too late in the day for more coffee. What I wanted was an ice-cold soda. Soda had been forbidden in this house, along with any other sweets.

Sugar lets the devil in. I didn't know who told her that, but she'd said it often enough.

When she got too sick to come downstairs, I stocked the fridge with whatever I wanted, including ice-cold cans of ginger ale and my favorite, orange soda. I pushed back from the table, the chair legs scraping the worn linoleum, swung open the door of the ancient refrigerator, and grabbed a can. The sugar went straight to my brain, tasting vaguely of oranges and exactly like heaven.

I needed to make a list, a plan. When she first got sick, I was twenty-nine, still in the figuring-it-all-out phase of life, feeling like I had an eternity stretching before me to settle on what I wanted. A career? My own family? Taking care of other people's children had allowed me to see the world with people I loved, while saving almost all of my salary.

I liked clothes, but I was frugal when it came to everything else. My families paid for room and board and supplied a vehicle when I'd needed one. My expenses were low. I had a nest egg—a good one. I had degrees and just enough classroom experience that I could find a job if I was willing to be flexible on location. I thought I'd be ready to jump into a new life the moment Harriet was gone.

Instead, I was still here, the weight of this house crushing my ambitions. In Harriet's last months, I'd begun to clean out the closets, knowing the inevitable was coming. We both knew. The doctors had been kind but clear. There was no last-minute reprieve on the way—she was sick, and she would die. Their concern was making her comfortable. Not that Harriet McKenna could ever be made comfortable. She was too demanding for that. In my opinion, she thrived in a state of complaint. She didn't want to be comfortable. She wanted to harangue, to order, to criticize—and she did all three in abundance.

I managed to sort through the garage and the guest room closet while she was dying, and it felt like I'd made great progress. But now, looking around, there was so much left. The furniture. Paintings on the walls. Boxes and boxes in the attic, all waiting for me to deal with them. So many decisions.

I hadn't expected to feel so apathetic. I didn't want to sort through the detritus of Harriet's life. I wanted to blink and have it all disappear, to be back in Paris, in my little room next to the children, waiting for them to wake up so I could get them dressed and take them to the park or drop them off at school.

I let out another self-pitying sigh and drained the last of my soda. The truth was, I didn't know if that was what I wanted. The Smiths didn't need me back. As always happened, the kids were old enough now—attending school full-time—that they didn't need a live-in nanny. Janice had emailed a week before.

> So sorry to hear about your mom, Paige. I wish I could be there to give you a hug. We miss you so much, but the kids are loving school. I don't know what you have planned, but I got word from a friend of a friend who's looking for a live-in. Not quite what you're used to, a small town in the mountains, but the family is lovely and a little desperate—they haven't been able to find anyone. Are you interested? Just let me know, and I'll pass your information along.
>   - <3 Janice

Was I interested? I'd spent six years traveling the world, and the last eighteen months in a small town in Ohio. I wasn't enjoying the contrast. Did I want to bury myself in another small town? Did I want another family? Or did I want the classroom? That was what I'd trained for, where I'd always intended to end up. In theory, teaching was the goal. But when I closed my eyes and tried to envision it, the picture wouldn't gel.

I hadn't answered Janice. I knew time was running

out, and at this point, I was just being rude. She'd called, and I'd let it go to voicemail, stuck in this listless state, hating where I was, unable to move on.

I squeezed the empty can of orange soda and dropped it in the recycling bin. I didn't have to decide today. I did have to pack at least a box or two and load the back of my mother's car with things to take to the donation site. I had to do something or I'd spend the rest of my life here, in this relic of a house, watching the linoleum curl at the corners, staring at the phone on the wall that never rang.

I let out another sigh, disgusted at my own self-pity. Dragging myself up the stairs, I pulled the cord to drop the ladder to the attic. It was less of a disaster up there than I'd remembered. Half of the boxes were old clothes. I tossed them through the ladder hole and watched them bounce down to the second-floor hallway, destined for the donation pile.

There was a bin of Christmas decorations that hadn't been hung in my lifetime. Another contained my mother's wedding dress. I stopped on that for a moment, unfolding it, trying to envision her as a bride—glowing and filled with joy. I couldn't see it. In my memories, her face was twisted into a scowl, her lips pursed so hard they'd been deeply grooved with wrinkles long before her hair had begun to gray.

I folded the wedding dress back up and dropped it through the hole to land with the other items I was donating. Maybe some bride could give it a new life with new love. But she wouldn't be me.

I'd cleared half of the space, a tinge of relief lightening my heart as I looked around and saw progress. I picked up the pace, carrying down boxes of books to donate. I didn't know whose they'd been. Maybe my father's. I didn't think I'd ever seen my mother read anything but the Bible or prayer books.

A few hours later, I was down to the last third of the attic. Most of it was straight-up trash. A broken lamp. A cracked aquarium. And behind everything, an old trunk shoved in the corner, *WILLIAMS* stenciled on the side.

Williams. I didn't know a Williams. We were McKennas. Why would my mother have a trunk belonging to a Williams?

The trunk was secured with a padlock. I didn't have the key. Based on the dust and the pile of crap around it, I guessed that if there had ever been a key, it was long gone.

I grabbed one of the handles on the side and dragged it out of the corner. I couldn't get through the lock, but the hinges on the back—those were a different matter. Curiosity gave me a burst of energy. I grabbed the broken lamp, lowered it in front of me, and then climbed down the ladder to the second floor. Picking my way through the piles of stuff I'd tossed down, I jogged to the garage for a crowbar and a drill. Between the two, I'd force my way into that trunk.

I wanted to know who Williams was, and why their trunk was in our attic.

I couldn't get enough leverage with the crowbar, but the drill did the job. I slapped a bit on and drilled hole after hole around the hinges. When I thought I'd done enough, I grabbed the crowbar and swung. A few good thwacks later, the hinges fell off the trunk. I opened the top, flipping it back, where it hung loosely by the padlock that had tried to keep me out.

Here was a treasure trove. A neatly folded US Army uniform, a file on top—discharge papers. Paul Williams. I sat in shock. I knew that face. Paul Williams was my father. The black-and-white snapshot of the young man in dress uniform looked like me—same eyes, same hair. I'd thought his name was McKenna. She told me we had his name, but clearly she'd lied. Because here he was, Paul Williams, who'd served in the army. Another thing I hadn't known.

Carefully, I set aside the uniform and the file folder. I found their marriage certificate on top of the suit I imagined he might have worn at their wedding. A small collection of fishing lures that looked hand-tied. A baseball with signatures. Here was a life that looked well-lived, right up until the moment it stopped because Paul had chosen to continue that life with another woman. Had he created a new family with her? I didn't know. He'd disappeared completely. He'd never reached out. Never checked in. He'd known Harriet was pregnant—at least, I thought he had—but he'd never come back.

It used to make me sad that he'd abandoned me that way, abandoned us. Now, so many years later, it was down to a dull ache. And always, questions. Why had he cared about me so little? Why hadn't I mattered?

I sighed, pushed the feelings down, and moved farther into the trunk.

I found books: Rudyard Kipling, Salinger, Fitzgerald. Was this where I'd gotten my love of reading? It felt like there were answers here, if only I knew how to interpret them.

And then, underneath an old Cincinnati Reds baseball cap, was a manila envelope. No label, address, or postage; the top flap sealed by metal prongs folded flat. I worked them open with my fingernail and tipped the envelope down. A half circle of metal fell into my hand, gleaming gold. Setting the envelope aside, I held it up to the light. It was a pendant, gold and missing its chain, designed as half of a heart. The kind of thing you'd split with a best friend. Or a lover. There was no engraving or other sign of who might hold the other half. I picked up the envelope and reached inside. It was stuffed with letters, handwritten, in a curly, feminine script. I wasn't surprised to see a woman's signature at the bottom. *Sarah.*

Sarah had written to my father,

> *Dearest Paul, my heart breaks at our separation. I wish there was a way we could be together. It seems unfair that we should both be so unhappy, but so happy together. I can't go on like this. I don't want to.*

There was a date at the top, the week before he disappeared. This was the woman. This was the one he'd left us for. If he was still out there, somewhere, could I find him through her? Had he married her? Grown old with her?

It occurred to me, for the thousandth time, that he

hadn't ever looked for me. Maybe he didn't want to be found. But Harriet was dead. Who knew if he still lived? If he was well, how much time did I have left to find him?

Maybe he didn't want to see me. But I wanted to see him, to find this man who'd left me before I was born—not to demand an explanation or unleash my anger. I wanted to look into those eyes so like mine.

And the only clue I had was *Sarah*.

I flipped through the rest of the letters. A photograph slipped out and landed in my lap. A woman, young and beautiful, with pale eyes, and a precisely curled sandy blonde bob that made me think of the sixties. She was lovely. Her eyes looked kind, with a spark of mischief. I turned over the photograph. At the bottom, in that same curly script, was written *Sarah Elizabeth Fordham*.

I didn't recognize the name. Tucking the letters and photograph back in the envelope, I set it in my lap and pulled out my phone to see what the internet knew of Sarah Elizabeth Fordham. I scrolled through the first few results. A teenage volleyball player who'd scored the winning shot in a game—definitely not her. An obituary for a ninety-eight-year-old woman—probably not.

And then—a link to a marriage certificate from North Carolina. In 1980, Sarah Elizabeth Fordham had married Prentice Braxton Sawyer. *Sawyer*. The name jolted down my spine. Why did I know that name? It sparked in my brain, and I tapped the screen of my phone, flipping to my email.

The email from Janice Smith. The family in the mountains of North Carolina who were looking for a nanny. Hope and Griffen Sawyer.

My heart pounded. My breath sped up. And a few frantic searches told me it had to be a sign. I'd been waiting for direction, and now I had one.

A goal, a job, and a mystery to solve—all of them in Sawyers Bend.

Chapter Two

FORD

NOW

"Thanks, man. See ya."

I answered with a nod as the tourist pulled the three-pint glasses into a triangle, bracing his fingers around them to carry his beers to the table.

My sister Avery worked the bar in her taproom with a wide, welcoming smile. Not me. Don't get me wrong—I liked working Avery's bar. I liked being out of Heartstone Manor. Finally free, or as free as it seemed I was going to get. Now that Cole Haywood, my former lawyer and the man who'd set me up to take the fall for my father's murder, was safely in jail, I could pick up the reins of my life. The problem was that life was gone.

My brother Griffen had my former job running Sawyer Enterprises, and for so many reasons, there wasn't a place there for me anymore. I had to do something with my life. I couldn't spend the next few decades lurking in the family home, haunting the library, reading biography after biography of people who'd managed to do better than betray everyone who loved them in the service of ambition and ego.

I was halfway through my life, if I was lucky, and all I'd managed to do was drive away most of my family, kiss my father's ass, and make money—a huge chunk of which had gone to paying the aforementioned attorney who'd double-crossed me. Not much of a legacy. I'd been given everything, and I'd squandered it.

So here I was, tending bar for my sister. I caught the pitying looks of the locals when they came in: the great Ford Sawyer reduced to pulling pints and making change. Oh, how I'd come down in the world. I wouldn't lie—there were times when it grated. I was Ford Sawyer, goddammit, not an object of pity.

Except that I was.

I grabbed a damp rag and wiped the top of the bar. Maybe every once in a while I felt sorry for myself, but it never lasted long. I always ended up remembering two things. First, I deserved all of this. I wasn't the king of the castle anymore. I never would be, because it wasn't my castle, and I deserved far worse than the year I'd spent in prison. And second, most of the time, I liked being exactly where I was. Tending bar in my sister's brewery, watching my brother set up the kitchen so they could combine forces, serving Finn's amazing food with Avery's fantastic beer. As much as a part of me yearned for the throne again, the rest of me just wanted this.

The job was straightforward: serve people beer.

Avery might have liked it if I made polite chit-chat, but we both accepted that wasn't going to happen. She seemed to like having me around. I liked helping out. The employee I'd replaced had stabbed Avery in the back, stealing from her and sleeping with her ex—all sorts of crap my sister didn't deserve. Filling in took a weight off her shoulders. God knew I needed to help. I'd caused too much harm in the years before my father died.

It had started way back when I was fresh out of college and jealous of my older brother's position in the family, his gorgeous fiancée, our father's approval, and his knack for business. I'd masterminded Griffen's exile and taken everything that had been his. I'd thought the triumph would feel so good that it would erase the pain of losing my brother.

I'd been wrong. By the time I figured it out, it was too late. I had the power. I had the position. I had the woman, the sports car, the bank account bursting at the seams. And in the end, I still wasn't much more than my father's lackey.

If I'd stayed at Griffen's side, if we'd worked together...could we have shifted things? Taken the company in a different direction? Shared the glory? I'd never know.

"Hey, Ford." A local whose name I couldn't remember bellied up to the bar. "A stout and an IPA," he said, his eyes bright with interest. "Helping out Avery?"

"For now," I said with a nod and turned my back to fill his order. I recognized the gleam in his eye. While Avery's beer was more than enough to draw in locals and tourists alike, we all knew my presence behind the bar was its own attraction, at least until the novelty wore off. The great Ford Sawyer tending bar in the smallest brewery in town. More than a few people had come in just for the fun of having Ford Sawyer serve their beer. I hadn't thought I had much of an ego left to poke after a year in state prison, but it turned out I had just enough for it to sting. Still, it wasn't enough to drive me away from my new job. Not yet.

I slid the pints across the bar, ran his card, and handed him the receipt without a word. I served beer, and I was polite, but friendly and chatty weren't on the menu. If they wanted that, they'd have to come in when Dave or Avery were working. The local left, shoulders rounding in disappointment that he hadn't gotten more out of me than his beer. Eventually, everyone would get used to the new normal. I could wait them out.

The door pushed open, and West Garfield, our police chief, walked in. He met my eyes, lifting his chin in greeting. I lifted mine back. West and I weren't buddy-buddy. He was Griffen's closest friend and had never forgiven me for the way things went down back in the day. Fair enough, especially when I hadn't forgiven myself. But he was head over heels in love with Avery, and he was a good man. I couldn't have picked a better one for my sister.

He crossed the taproom, headed for the door that led to the brewery. "Avery in her office?"

"She's back there somewhere," I said, and with a grin, he disappeared.

I didn't have friends like West. When we were kids, everyone loved Griffen just a little more than me. Or a lot more, depending. I'd always wondered if the other kids had sensed the seed of darkness in my heart. The envy that led me to betray my own brother. After Griffen was gone, I'd had a boatload of acquaintances and a million people who were happy to pretend to be my friend in the hopes of a favor—a job, a referral, a tip, anything that could benefit them. And like my father, I'd used them, getting as much as I could before doling out stingy bits of the Sawyer influence. I'd convinced myself it was enough.

Now, surrounded by family, who these days were as much friends as relations, in a house brimming with love and laughter, I finally understood how deeply I'd erred. I had money in the bank, I lived in a castle, and yet I was one of the poorest people I knew.

I rolled my shoulders to loosen the tension and went back to cleaning the bar. This self-pity bullshit was at the top of my list of post-prison fears. I was not going to turn into some useless whiner, sitting alone in the dark, bemoaning everything I'd lost. I needed to find a purpose.

I couldn't forget what Cole had said to Avery not long before West arrested him. *I'm not fucking done with Ford, but he'll know exactly where we stand before the end.*

Cole Haywood was in prison. He'd confessed to a lot, including setting me up to go down for my father's murder. Officially, my name was cleared. But there was a big fucking difference between clearing my name legally and people believing I was innocent. Most of the locals thought I'd gotten off because I was a Sawyer. Many still thought I'd murdered my father in cold blood.

It was nice to know that my family never thought I did it. Avery had looked me in the eye and said, "I could believe you'd kill Dad. But not like that. You're way too smart."

She was right.

If I'd been planning to kill Prentice, I sure as hell wouldn't have walked into his office after a big argument the whole household had heard, shot him in the middle of the forehead, then tromped around in the dirt outside his office windows, leaving my shoe prints everywhere. I definitely wouldn't have gone home afterward and put both the shoes and the gun in my own closet. If I'd been that stupid, I would have deserved to get caught.

Instead, I'd argued with my father. Artwork had been disappearing from Heartstone Manor. Most of it didn't matter, but some pieces were family heirlooms. In my mind, they didn't belong to Prentice any more than they belonged to me or Griffen. They belonged to the family as a whole, had been passed down through generations, and were meant to continue to be passed to children and grandchildren, not secreted away in the night and sold off.

Prentice had refused to tell me what he was doing—where the money was going, where the art was—and, furious, I'd lost my temper. Generally, I could hold it together, but my father's knowing smirk always got under my skin. I'd stormed out, pounding my foot into the gas pedal and roaring down the country road that led to town. Unfortunately, I'd passed a number of witnesses. Whoever had killed Prentice had come in right after, unseen by anyone except my now-dead father. And my angry drive had placed me just close enough to the time of death to make it look like I did it.

If I'd killed my father, I would have been a lot more subtle. Slow poisoning, maybe, or a hunting accident. I wouldn't say the thought had never crossed my mind. Prentice Sawyer could be an evil bastard, and until his final moments, he'd evaded any kind of accountability.

I'd thought so often, *if only he were out of the way*, but I'd been imagining a heart attack or a car accident, some intervention of fate that could save me from my father.

Fate had indeed intervened, in the form of a killer's bullet. And until we found out who the killer was, I'd always be presumed guilty.

There were days when I thought it was no more than I deserved—that I should just put my head down and move forward, try to figure out what I was going to do with the rest of my life. I had to make amends to my family, to this town. It was time I put some thought into what kind of man I wanted to be. Not who I'd been, that was for sure.

But that was just more self-pitying bullshit. Maybe I did deserve for everyone to think I was guilty, but the fact was I hadn't killed my father. Someone else had done that. They might have solved a lot of problems for a lot of people when they did, but that didn't make it right. I'd paid with a year of my life for something I hadn't done. Maybe the penance felt good—a balm on my guilt—but I knew my family, the people I owed the most, hadn't wanted that kind of penance. Suffering under a false accusation wouldn't ease the pain I'd caused. It wouldn't make things right, and if I couldn't truly clear my name, I'd never really be able to move on.

As much as I loved being here in Avery's taproom with flames merrily crackling in the stone fireplace at one end of the room, the golden light making the wooden beams, walls, and floor glow, the comforting sound of happy people talking, drinking, playing games—I had to figure out what came next. I couldn't do that with my father's murder hanging over my head.

The thought had been spinning in my brain for weeks. My siblings weren't convinced that the killer was still out there. They thought there was a good chance Cole had done it, despite his denials. I was one of the few who believed him when he'd said he was guilty of everything except killing our father.

I knew Cole Haywood—not as well as I thought I did, considering I hadn't pegged him for setting me up for murder, but better than the rest of them. I thought if Cole had killed Prentice, he would have admitted it when he admitted everything else, if only so he could brag about how he'd outsmarted the wily fox that had been my father.

I needed to talk to Cole.

At the thought, my skin crawled. He was locked in the same state prison I'd spent a year in. And as much as I despised my own cowardice, I couldn't bring myself to walk through those gates again, even as a free man. Just the thought of it sent clammy sweat to my palms, dripping down my spine. I'd survived incarceration, but now that I was out, I didn't think I could bring myself to go back, even to get answers from Cole.

I pushed the question to the back of my mind and watched Avery and West leave, Avery sending me a wave, miming that I should call if I ran into any trouble. I'd closed the taproom more than once. Everything would be fine. And it was nice to see Avery happy and rested, the shadows under her eyes gone now that she wasn't working herself to the bone and had West to lean on.

Business picked up as it usually did in the evenings, the cold bite of winter's air sending locals and tourists alike inside for the fire and the company—and for Avery's excellent beer. I imagined when Finn got the kitchen opened, we'd be even more packed in the evenings. I liked being busy, the monotony of it. Filling beers, changing kegs, running cards, wiping the counter. I even liked putting the chairs up and sweeping the floor at the end of the night. It gave me a sense of immediate gratification, something that was sorely lacking in the rest of my life.

Heartstone Manor was dark and silent when I arrived home just before midnight, everyone tucked into their rooms. I made my way to the second floor with quiet footsteps. The hallway sconces in the guest wing were turned low, giving just enough light to make my way to my door at the far end of the hall.

This wasn't the room I grew up in. Traditionally, the master of the house took the suite currently occupied by my brother Griffen and his wife Hope—a sprawling apartment in the central section of the house. It was luxurious and private, as it should be. Wings extended in a V off each side of the central part of Heartstone Manor—one for family, one for guests. The rest of my siblings lived in the family wing and would for another three years, until the terms of my father's will were up.

After I was released from prison, Griffen had offered me my old room, but I couldn't take it. The idea of being surrounded by my siblings was untenable. I didn't know if I'd been more afraid of love or accusations. Either way, I didn't want it. I just wanted to be alone.

This isolated guest room at the end of the hall seemed like the answer. I'd forgotten about the electrical and plumbing problems that plagued this wing of the house. I didn't know when they'd started, only that it was sometime after I'd moved out a few years before.

What I did know was that the plumbing knocked and banged and sputtered, and sometimes didn't work at all. Ditto for the electrical. It was a flip of a coin whether a light switch would illuminate or merely click uselessly as I flipped it back and forth. Sometimes I plugged things in, and the outlet sparked. Sometimes it worked. We'd had every electrician and plumber in the county come through, and every time they thought they had it fixed— boom, another disaster.

I'd been told our family had been having problems in the entire wing since they'd moved in after the will was read, and we were forced to cohabitate. In the months I'd been home, it seemed the issues had isolated themselves to the two rooms at the far end of the guest wing: mine and the one occupied by Griffen and Hope's nanny, Paige.

Paige was a good sport about the conditions. As far as I could see, she was a good sport about everything. She needed to be, considering that in addition to caring for

Griffen and Hope's infant daughter, she also ran herd on a six-year-old, a seven-year-old, and a teenager.

I let myself into my room, crossed my fingers, and turned on the shower. Hot water steamed, and I stripped quickly, knowing it might not last. I showered off the long day and was just about finished rinsing the shampoo from my hair when everything went dark and the pipes sputtered.

Turning off what was left of the water, I felt in the dark for my towel. Sometimes a flip of the breaker did the trick. I ran the towel over my hair to remove the worst of the damp, then slung it around my waist.

Pulling open the door of my room, I was surprised to see that the lights were still on in the hall. Turning, I flicked the switch at my door experimentally. Nothing, which was fucking weird. The breaker affected the whole half of this wing, not just my bedroom.

The door across the hall opened and out stepped Paige, bundled in a fuzzy pink robe, her hair—usually constrained in a braid or a bun—falling down her back in a riot of dark, shiny curls. Her unusual light-blue eyes, icy like a husky's with an intriguing rim of navy blue, fixed on me, and she went still. In the dim glow of the sconces, I caught pink flares of color washing across her cheeks.

She met my eyes for a split second, then looked away. "I was going to flip the breaker," she said.

"Your power's out too?" I asked.

She answered with a sharp nod, her eyes fixed on the floorboards at my feet.

"I've got it," I said. The breaker box was in the back

of a closet at the end of the hall. It would be dark and cramped with brooms and mops. "Stay right there."

It was quick work to duck into the closet, pry open the breaker box, and feel for the two switches flipped the wrong way. Hoping this worked, I flipped them back. By the time I stepped into the hall, Paige was already disappearing into her room, her quiet "Thanks" floating behind her as her door shut with a decisive click.

I didn't have to guess if Paige thought I'd murdered my father. The way she couldn't meet my eyes or force out more than a word or two in my company told me all I needed to know. And why should it burn, coming from Paige? I barely knew her. I didn't think we'd spoken more than a sentence to each other since I'd come home. Why would we?

It was better if Paige McKenna thought I was a killer. I didn't need to know her well to know she deserved far better than me. And I had no business thinking about any woman until I figured out the rest of my life. Maybe not even then. God knew, so far, I hadn't had much luck picking women.

I closed my door, tossed the towel into the bathroom, and slid between my sheets. Sleep didn't come. I lay there looking at the plaster ceiling, watching the light fixture above sway in a breeze I couldn't feel. I wanted to be free —free of the past, free of my father's murder. I just didn't know how to get there. Not yet. But I would. And once I was free, I could figure out what I really wanted.

The image of Paige McKenna flashed into my mind. Those dark curls that looked so soft. Her haunting ice-blue eyes surrounded by thick, dark lashes. Her long legs.

I tried to banish her image from my mind. I was not going to lay a finger on my brother's nanny. I didn't know her exact age, but the innocence in her eyes told me it didn't matter. She was way too young for me. So many reasons I couldn't have Paige McKenna. But as sleep finally took me under, it was her I reached for in my dreams.

Chapter Three

FORD

I paused outside the door to Griffen's office, my hand raised to knock and my gut clenching in a quick pulse of nerves. Growing up, this had been my father's office. For a brief period, before I'd gotten him exiled, our father had shared it with Griffen and me. Once Griffen was gone, my father knew he had me exactly where he wanted me. After all, I'd gotten rid of my only ally. And if I wanted to keep all I'd gained, I needed Prentice's goodwill. Unfortunate that I hadn't seen the trap until I'd walked into it. Over the years, I'd learned to hate this room.

Now, this office was Griffen's, Hope's, and Royal's. But really, it was Griffen's. Everything was Griffen's, as it was always meant to be. I'd once dreamed of running Sawyer Enterprises from the big desk. I didn't want that anymore, and by all reports, Griffen, Hope, and Royal were doing a bang-up job. I was happy for them. I was. But something about walking into this office as an interloper burned, and I swallowed hard to drive the feeling away.

I knocked on the door, a quick triple rap that left my knuckles stinging and my spine a little straighter. I was not a coward. Yes, I'd fucked up, but I wasn't running from my mistakes. It was time I took back the reins of my life. Even if I wasn't exactly sure where I was going with it.

"Come in," Griffen called.

I turned the handle and pushed open the heavy door, surprised to find Griffen pacing in front of the fireplace. His daughter Stella, a year old this past week, was cradled in his arms, both their faces flushed. Stella was missing her usual sweet expression, her little face twisted in a bright red scowl, eyes glassy with angry tears.

"Ford, hey," Griffen said distractedly. "Awesome, come here."

"What?" I asked, crossing the room to meet him in front of the fireplace.

He shoved Stella into my arms. "Take her."

"No— I can't—" My words fell on deaf ears. Before I was done sputtering them out, Stella was in my arms, and Griffen was disappearing out the door of his office. I would have called after him, but the jogging thumps of his feet on the floor told me he was long gone.

Fuck.

I didn't think I'd ever held a baby before. Was I even doing it right? Stella sucked in a shuddering breath and expelled it in an ear-splitting wail. Oh, poor kid. I didn't know what was wrong, but whatever it was, she was miserable. I gave an exploratory sniff, but all I got was lavender and baby powder, so—not her diaper.

Making sure my arm was secure under her butt, I leaned her into my shoulder. Her teary cheeks were hot and wet on my collarbone, forehead pressed against my neck as I patted her back uselessly. "It's okay. It's okay, kid. Whatever it is, your dad's going to work it out." I hoped. Because while she wasn't fighting, she hadn't stopped screaming either.

I patted and soothed, surprised by how much she weighed. After what seemed like an eternity, she let out a snuffling sigh, the volume of her wail fading. After a few shuddering breaths, she stopped crying completely, her little back rising and falling under my patting hand.

Was she asleep? I didn't know. But I was going to stand here for as long as it took, rocking side to side, patting her back, and praying that whatever I'd done to calm her down kept working. How could Griffen have just left me with a baby? I couldn't have been less confident.

The door flew open, and Griffen burst back in, his eyes a little frantic, a bright pink thing clutched in his hand. "Teething," he said as he crossed the room toward me.

At the sound of her father's voice, Stella stirred, whimpering, one little hand reaching out in his direction. Griffen thrust the pink thing at Stella and me. She closed her little fingers around it and shoved it in her mouth, stretching her lips around the frosty plastic as she gnawed so aggressively that I wondered if she was trying to chew through it. I shifted my hold to hand her back to Griffen. With a tight grin, he evaded me.

"She stopped screaming," he said. "My ears need a break. Hang on to her for a few minutes, would you? I'll take her if she gets restless."

"What is that?" I asked, watching my niece work her gums on the pink thing.

"Frozen teething ring. Her first tooth is coming in, and she's miserable with it," he replied. "Thanks. The ring usually settles her down, but I put it back in the freezer and forgot to grab it."

"No problem," I lied. "We're fine." That part wasn't a lie. We were. Shockingly.

Stella cuddled into my chest, seemingly content and unaware that I was totally unqualified to hold a baby. Or maybe she sensed my connection to her father and was comforted.

"It's weird," I said, stroking a hand down her back. "Seeing you with a baby. She looks like a perfect little mishmash of you and Hope." Stella's hair was a mass of white-blonde curls, exactly like Griffen's had been when he was a kid. Her eyes were Hope's whiskey-shaded hazel. She had a little pink rosebud mouth and rounded cheeks.

Griffen grinned at his daughter, a fierce love in his eyes. "I know. She's perfect. Life is funny," he started. "I wasn't planning on any of this, but—" Maybe realizing who he was talking to, he stopped abruptly and shifted his weight on his feet.

I could feel the tension filling the room. "I know what you mean," I said quickly. "This wasn't exactly my plan either. But it worked out for you—" Griffen started to say something, and I shook my head. "I didn't mean it like that. I meant, despite everything that came before, you're where you were supposed to be the whole time."

Griffen looked like he wasn't sure how to take that. God, I sucked at making amends. I didn't know how to say what I needed to say. I didn't know what Griffen needed to hear—or, if I did know, whether I had what it took to tell him. We stared at each other in awkward silence for too long.

Footsteps sounded in the hall, and we both turned to see Paige come in.

"Griffen," she said, her eyes going straight to Stella, her face draining of color as she realized I was holding the baby. "I'll take her," she said, coming close enough to snatch Stella from my arms before drawing her a safe distance away.

I didn't blame her. Whether or not she thought I was a murderer, she knew I'd recently been released from prison. And I'd spent most of my time since avoiding my family, especially the kids.

Ignoring me, she said to Griffen, "I'm sorry. I couldn't find the teething gel. I looked everywhere. I'll run into town and get more. Maybe Stella wants to go for a ride?"

I'd swear Stella smiled up at Paige around the frozen pink teething ring jammed in her mouth. Did she want to go for a ride? Or did she just love being snuggled up to Paige?

If it was the second, I could relate. I did my best to stay away from Paige. Her hair was pulled back in a bun, unlike last night when it had spilled over her shoulders in shining dark curls. She wore jeans and a blue sweater that brought out the unusual icy blue of her eyes. Griffen didn't expect his staff to dress in uniform—though Savannah, my sister-in-law and our housekeeper, insisted on one. Paige was more comfortable in her own clothes.

I shouldn't have had any trouble avoiding her. She kept to herself and stuck with the kids. Yet lately it seemed like everywhere I turned, there was Paige McKenna, tormenting me. Not that she knew it. She could barely meet my eyes.

Every cell in my body yearned to touch her, to get closer, to see if her hair smelled as good as it looked—or if her skin was as soft as it seemed. I'd been living like a monk in the months before my father died, and prison sure as hell hadn't helped. Somewhere in there, my libido had gone on vacation. It had roared back to life the first time I saw Paige McKenna, the day I'd been released from prison and come home to Heartstone Manor.

Why her? It was inconvenient at best and disastrous at worst to lust after my brother's nanny. Even forgetting that it was completely inappropriate, given that she worked in Heartstone, it was also the last thing I wanted to do if I had any hope of healing my relationship with Griffen. She was too young, too sweet, too innocent, and I had no business getting involved with any woman. Not now. Maybe not ever. I could put together a list of reasons a mile long of why I couldn't—and shouldn't—want Paige McKenna. Yet, as I watched her leave the room, Stella cradled in her arms, all I wanted to do was follow.

Not for you, I reminded myself. I had enough trouble. I didn't need to go out and buy myself more.

"Sorry about that," Griffen said. "Hope is out with Royal at a meeting. Paige and I are trying to manage the teething."

"Teething sounds like torture," I said, following Griffen across the room to his desk. I took a chair on the opposite side, deliberately picking the one I'd never used back when Prentice had sat behind that desk. This was now, and it wasn't Prentice's desk anymore—it was Griffen's.

"So? What's up?" Griffen asked, his tone holding a hint of hesitation.

"I've been thinking," I said. "I need to do something. With the rest of my life."

"It's kind of a big swing," Griffen said. "I don't know that you have to figure out the rest of your life right now."

I nodded. "Good point. Maybe just the next few months?" I raised an eyebrow. "I'm helping Avery out at the brewery, but—"

"That's not a career choice," Griffen finished for me.

"No," I agreed. "I need to do some thinking before I figure out what I want, where a career is concerned."

"Are you—" Griffen picked up a pen, looked at it as if he'd never seen it before, set it back down, and tapped his fingers on the desk. "Are you okay for money?" he asked.

The shame of the question curdled in my gut. "I'm fine," I said truthfully, though I didn't want to talk money with Griffen. Even after Cole's exorbitant fees, I still had plenty of cash in the bank. "It's not the money," I said. "I need to figure out what I want to do with myself. But that's not your problem," I finished, cutting off the worry I saw on his face.

Griffen was afraid I was going to ask for my place in the family business. And while I wanted it—sometimes desperately—that wasn't my future anymore. It couldn't be. I'd lost the right.

But there was something I could do. "I want to find out who killed Dad," I said to Griffen. His eyes widened, and I went on. "Before he died, I was digging into some of Dad's business deals. I was looking for leverage."

Chapter Four

FORD

"Leverage for what?" Griffen asked, sitting back in the chair, picking up the pen again, and flicking it through his fingers.

"Leverage I could use to get Dad to step back from the business. To rein in some of his more predatory behavior. I wanted to do better—for our business partners, for this town."

"And did you find anything?" Griffen asked, his head tilted to the side.

"Not enough before time ran out, and someone shot him. I know you found my notes on the contracts related to Finn's kidnapping. All I uncovered were more questions."

"Do you think your research had something to do with Dad's murder?" Griffen asked. "Cole admitted to framing you, but you don't think he killed Dad?"

I shook my head, then asked, "What does West think?"

"West thinks he's telling the truth. That he set you

up, sent people to screw with us, but that he didn't kill Dad."

"I'd believe he did it," I said, "if Dad had died right after Caro Haywood died."

Caro had been Cole's beloved wife. She'd died along with her baby during childbirth. After Cole had discovered the baby was Prentice's—and so was his wife. He'd been devastated but had sat on his rage, cold and calculating, until Prentice's fresh corpse provided an opportunity to take his vengeance. We'd learned Cole was capable of crimes of passion. He'd murdered a jewelry designer only months before for, as he'd put it, having a smart mouth. But generally, Cole Haywood was deliberate and contained.

"I think if he wanted to kill Dad," I said, "he would have done it closer to Caro's death. He wouldn't have waited two whole years after she died. And he would have done it..." Images flashed through my mind, and I shook my head. "I don't think it would have been as painless as a bullet through the forehead."

It was the simplest way I could sum up my thoughts.

Griffen's jaw set, and he nodded. "Agreed. Even with the bonus of pinning a murder on you," Griffen said, "I don't think he could have restrained himself to a single shot." He set the pen down and sat forward, bracing his elbows on his desk. "So, who do you think is good for it?" he asked.

"I don't know," I admitted. "But I want to go back through business associates, contracts, deals we were working on. I have my notes from before Dad was killed. Paperwork up in the attic that I was going through."

"What do you want from me?" Griffen asked.

I shrugged. "Permission, I guess. It's your house, your attic, and technically your storage bins full of paperwork."

If I were any of my siblings, I was pretty sure Griffen would have said something like, *It's your house too.* But he didn't, because I wasn't one of our siblings. I was the one who'd had him exiled. I was lucky he'd let me back in the Manor. It was too much to expect free rein of the place.

"It's fine with me," he said after a hesitation. "But, uh, Ford?" He raised an eyebrow.

"Yeah?" I answered.

"Be careful. I know Cole is in jail, but if we really think he didn't kill Dad, then someone else did. Right now, everything's nice and quiet. Your name's been cleared, the investigation's technically reopened, but West doesn't have new evidence, so it's not going anywhere. Whoever pulled that trigger is probably feeling pretty safe right now. They've already killed once. They might not hesitate to do it again if they feel that safety is threatened."

His eyes locked on mine, boring into me, and I nodded. "I know."

"If you're doing this because you feel like you have to prove something," Griffen said, "think about what you're risking."

I shoved out of the chair, needing to move. "Don't you want to know who killed him?" I asked.

Griffen leaned back and crossed his arms over his chest, watching me pace the carpet in front of his desk.

After a long pause, he said, "I do. I'd be lying if I said I didn't. I want to know who killed him so we can close the door. So I can be sure my family is out of danger. That this is over. But that's not why you want to know."

He was right, and it irked me.

"It's part of why I want to know," I argued. "Of course it's part. But yeah, I also have something to prove."

"Not to me," Griffen said. "Not to your family."

I thought of the look in Paige's eyes. The suspicion and fear.

"And if I was never planning on leaving Heartstone Manor, that would be fine," I said. "But Griffen, you should see people's faces when they come into the brewery. So many of them think I did it. I'm not going to put any of you in danger—" *You can't promise that,* a little voice in my head whispered. I ignored it. "But I need to know who did this. I need to clear my name once and for all. I want to do better," I admitted, my stomach rolling, uneasy with the look of compassion, of pity, on Griffen's face. "I want to start over."

Griffen started to speak, and I interrupted.

"I know I can't change the past. And I know there's nothing I can do to make up for what I've done. But I can't start over until we know who killed our father."

Griffen crossed his arms over his chest and gave a short nod. "Go for it," he said. "Just keep your eyes open. And be careful."

I forced out a curt "Thanks," and escaped his office.

I took the stairs to the attic two at a time, only a little out of breath as I reached the top. My father hadn't been one for going through files and had never ventured into the attic, as far as I could remember. Which was why, in the months before his death, I'd taken to hiding my research up here.

By then, I was living in a suite in the Inn at Sawyers Bend, unable to tolerate sharing a roof with Prentice any longer. But his office had remained here, and he'd grown hermit-like in his refusal to leave Heartstone. He'd fired staff, even Miss Martha, Savannah's mother and our long-time housekeeper. Artwork had been disappearing, the house growing dusty, cobwebs springing up in the corners.

I hadn't known he'd been grieving the loss of Caro, the woman he'd hoped to make his wife, and the child he'd expected her to give him. I didn't know how much sympathy I would have had if I had known. In a million years, when I'd suggested they co-sponsor that charity event, I'd never imagined it would end the way it had. Caro was another man's wife. Our friend's wife.

Not that my father had ever cared for other people's marriage vows—or his own. It hadn't occurred to me that he had enough heart to grieve anyone. Back then, I'd thought the decline of the Manor said something about his mental state. I'd thought if I could find anything compromising in his business records, maybe that, along with the state of the house, could be used to wrest control of the company from Prentice.

When I'd conspired to get rid of Griffen, it had been about envy. I could admit it now. But in the years before Prentice had been killed, I hadn't been driven by envy or greed. It had been about my family. After far too long, I finally saw Prentice with clear eyes: the manipulations, the lack of ethics. He knew how to stay just inside the law while rarely doing what was right, and I was tired of it. I wanted to have collaborative relationships with our business partners. I wanted to support my siblings in finding their dreams. I wanted to sleep well at night. And for any of that to happen, I had to get rid of Prentice—or at least neutralize him.

I'd gone through everything I could find, looking for the proverbial smoking gun. Now I had to wonder if buried somewhere in those papers was the answer to who killed my father. Had I been getting too close? What had I missed?

The only way to find out was to restart my investigation.

I remembered where I'd stopped, more than a year ago, only days before Prentice had been shot and I'd been arrested. I'd been going through a banker's box stuffed with files I'd hidden in an antique wardrobe in a corner of the attic. It was still exactly where I'd left it, the wardrobe too bulky and dated for Savannah to have tried to put to use.

I pulled over a threadbare bench and opened the box. Hours disappeared as I leafed through files, contracts, and pages of notes. A real estate deal for some strip malls in the upstate of South Carolina. We'd done well on that one. The seller, not as much, but there wasn't anything here to inspire murder, and I set it aside. Stacks of leases for businesses in town. I saved a few that were worth looking into. For the most part, nothing there either.

Below that, a legal-sized envelope. When I unfastened the flap, invoices flowed through my hands, thin and crinkly with age. A plumber, an electrician—but these looked old. I checked the date and did a double-take. Really old. 1986. I'd been an infant. I didn't remember this much work done on the Manor—but would a child really note that? I sorted through the stack of papers in my lap—concrete, gravel, the garage. Prentice had been the one to tear down the old carriage house and convert the second ballroom beneath the guest wing into garages—less gracious, but much more convenient. But that had been done prior to my birth, so why had he done more work in '86? I didn't know.

I shuffled the invoices back into the envelope and set it aside to ask Griffen. Maybe Miss Martha knew. Savannah's mother remembered everything. Steps sounded in the hall outside the door. The attic was divided into different rooms, most of which were stuffed with furniture. I caught sight of a small blond head of hair by the doorway.

"Is somebody in here?" a thready child's voice asked.

"Back here," I called out. "Just going through some papers."

Judging by the size and the hair color, I'd have to say August, my brother Tenn's and his wife Scarlett's son. I didn't interact with the kids much, but I knew them by sight.

"What are you doing up here?" I asked as August tentatively entered the room.

"Hide and seek," he answered simply.

That was enough. Hide and seek in Heartstone Manor was an Olympic-level event. "What's off-limits?" I asked.

"Everything on the kitchen level," he answered promptly. "Dumbwaiter, garage, cars, people's bedrooms, and Griffen's office. Also," he added, "no hiding behind the curtains in the art gallery because Mom's afraid we'll knock something over."

I nodded sagely. "Solid rules," I said. We'd had similar ones growing up. "But the attic's not off-limits?"

August shook his head.

"You want a suggestion?" I offered.

He stared at me, wary but not afraid. "Sure," he said.

I crooked my finger, and he closed the distance between us. Leaning down, I whispered in his ear. When he heard my idea, August gave a quick whoop of glee and disappeared.

It wasn't long before I heard more steps in the hall. I looked up, expecting to see Nicky or Thatcher, and was surprised to see Paige, her pale blue eyes scanning the room, jolting as they landed on me. For a second, our gazes locked. Nerves swirled across her face, and she took a step back, wrenching her eyes from mine to scan the room again.

"Have you seen August?" she asked.

I didn't want to lie, but I wasn't going to rat the kid out either—not when he had such a stellar hiding place, courtesy of yours truly.

"Well," I said, sitting up and putting the box to the side, "I've been really focused on going through this paperwork. I'm not sure I was paying attention."

Her eyes narrowed on mine. "Uh-huh," she said. "So, you don't know where he is?"

"I'm sure he's around somewhere," I said, "but if I knew, telling would be cheating."

Paige huffed out a breath of annoyance. "True," she said, "but Finn is putting out tea with fresh-baked shortbread, and I didn't want August to miss it. So, if you see him, could you let him know?"

"If I see him," I agreed.

She backed out of the room and carried on down the hall. I wanted to ask her to stay, or to follow and invite myself to tea, but talking to me wasn't part of her job description. I listened to August's lighter steps following her down to tea as the late afternoon sun shifted, casting the attic in shadow.

In a house full of family and warmth, I was alone in the dark. It was exactly what I deserved, no matter how much I might wish for more.

Chapter Five

PAIGE

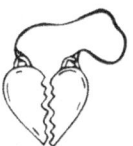

I pulled the covers up tight around my shoulders, trying not to shiver. With every exhale, my breath came out in a cloud of ghostly white. I knew if I braved the chill in the air and turned on the taps in my bathroom, they'd sputter. The light switch on the wall would click uselessly. When it happened, it happened like this. Electricity out. Plumbing dry. And my room so very cold.

Some nights, I could ignore it and fall back asleep. I'd wake in the morning to bright sunshine, running water, and working lights, as if the icy cold and dark had never happened. Other nights, I slid from bed, pulling my robe tight around me, and braved the dark hall to flip the breakers. Why flipping the breakers would fix the plumbing along with the electricity, I couldn't say. But sometimes it did. None of it made sense.

I never thought of Heartstone Manor as creepy—until times like this, in the dark of night, when I could see my breath in the moonlight. Heartstone was unlike any nannying job I'd had before, and exactly like the others in one specific way: my nanny family was great. I liked the Sawyers. I trusted Hope and Griffen. They loved their family and adored their daughter.

I'd picked up some of the family lore in the last year and knew what had happened to the patriarch, Prentice. Griffen's younger brother, Ford, had been in prison for a year for killing his own father. You could have knocked me over with a feather when Griffen let Ford move right back into the Manor after his release. It seemed none of his siblings thought he'd done it, but love could be blind.

I couldn't say I was thrilled when Ford took up residence in the room opposite mine in the guest wing. If I'd known I'd be sharing a hallway with a killer, I don't know that I would have agreed to live in the Manor. But now that I was here, it was too awkward to ask to move. It would be obvious why I wanted to leave. And hadn't getting into the house been part of my goal? It would be a lot harder to track down the mysterious *Sarah Sawyer* if I were living in town.

Not that I'd gotten far with that anyway. The Sawyers were fairly open about their recent history. Everything since the day their father had died seemed to be fair game for conversation, but their lives before that were a dead subject. I'd managed to learn that Sarah Sawyer had been Griffen and Ford's mother, and that she'd run off when they were young. Given the timing, I was almost positive their missing mother was the woman who'd written those letters to my father. As far as I could tell, no one had any idea where Sarah was, and I'd never heard any mention of my father.

Maybe if I'd approached the Sawyers openly, I could have found out more, but now I was stuck. I liked my job, and I liked the family. I'd wondered if I'd feel isolated in this small town in the mountains, or if I'd miss being in the classroom. I'd spent the last few years with my mother substituting kindergarten at the local elementary school, and I'd loved it. But now I wondered if part of that love had been the escape from my mother's house. Because now, running herd on four kids, one of them an infant, I wasn't feeling the urge to go back to the classroom.

I'd come here to find Sarah and my father. But if I asked openly, they'd throw me out. Now that I under-stood how security-conscious they were, I knew that for a fact. I hadn't bothered to hide my connection to my father, nor would I have known how to do so. And clearly, they hadn't made the connection to Sarah Sawyer either, because I was here. It helped that I was who I said I was; my résumé was filled with the truth, so I'd passed the background checks.

So here I was, the fox in the henhouse. And though I was keeping my eyes open for any further information about Sarah and my father, I was at a stalemate. I could ask openly for what I wanted and risk being booted out, or give up on my quest and carry on as I was, in a job I loved, while I figured out the rest of my future. So far, I was sticking with option number two.

Everything would have been great—except for the puffs of frozen air coming from my mouth with every exhalation, and the killer sleeping across the hall.

I had to keep reminding myself that Ford Sawyer was

IVY LAYNE

dangerous. This house was filled with dangerous men. Despite his charm and good humor, I knew Griffen's background. I wouldn't want him to consider me an enemy. And Hawk, our head of security, was considerably less good-humored and charming and obviously chock-full of danger. Every single member of the security team could take me apart with their pinky fingers.

None of them made me nervous like Ford Sawyer.

His family was convinced he hadn't pulled the trigger on Prentice, but from what I'd heard, there'd been little love between them by the time Prentice died. Ford had gotten his brother Griffen exiled in an attempt to take everything that should have been Griffen's. Why wouldn't he take the second step of eliminating his father and take the crown for himself? I'd heard enough town gossip to know Prentice Sawyer had forcibly retired his own father and taken over the company. Wouldn't Ford follow his example?

I didn't fully understand how Ford's name had been cleared. I was the nanny, not family. I caught whatever crumbs of information fell by my ears, but I rarely got the full picture—unless something was related to one of the kids. Fair enough. It was their family business, after all, not mine.

Griffen was so concerned with everyone's safety, I doubted he had a blind spot big enough to move a killer in down the hall from his wife and infant daughter. But people could be weird when it came to family. Griffen was human. His judgment couldn't be perfect all the time.

I clenched my toes under the blanket, trying to will

warmth back into the little icy blocks at the end of my feet. The tip of my nose felt like it was covered in frost. That was it. I shoved the covers back and rolled, slamming my frozen feet onto the chilly carpet at the side of my bed as I snatched up my robe. I was tired. Tomorrow would be busy, and I needed my sleep. Whatever was turning this end of the guest wing into an icebox, I wasn't going to take it lying down, shivering under the covers. Maybe flipping the breaker wouldn't work—it wasn't a guarantee—but I had to try.

The hall was dark when I opened my door, the sconces off. That could be the power failure. Or it could be that the last person up had flicked the switch. Either way, I didn't need them. I took a deep breath and stepped out into the darkened hallway. I knew my way to the storage closet at the end of the hall by feel. I shuffled along the smooth, polished hardwood—so cold under my bare feet—and felt in front of me, my fingers catching the trim around the door, the cold metal of the handle as it turned beneath my fingers.

The door swung open into pitch black. Before I could take a step, hands closed over my arms and yanked me inside.

I stumbled, coming up hard against a body. Tall, broad, male. That was all I registered before I was turned, swung around, and shoved. My back hit the wall, alarm spiking down my spine, and I let out a shriek, too scared to be embarrassed by the sound.

The figure holding me went still. "Paige." I heard my name growled.

"Let go of me," I spat out. I knew that voice. Ford.

"I'm sorry," he said, his fingers tight around my upper arms—not hurting, but not letting go.

I yanked back, my head bumping off the wall behind me. I wanted to pull away, but there wasn't anywhere to go. "Let go."

"I'm sorry, Paige. I didn't realize it was you." His voice was a low, rumbly growl. I was suddenly glad I couldn't see his face.

"Yeah, I got that," I said, my heart thundering in my chest, my mouth suddenly dry.

I was in this dark, tiny closet with Ford Sawyer, his hands on me, and I was frozen—not from the cold this time, but with indecision. My brain was screaming. *Run, run, run. Throw up my knee, nail him in the balls, and get away.* It wouldn't be the first time I'd dissuaded someone who wouldn't let go of me.

But I didn't do it. I stood there, silent, his hands on my arms like iron bands. When he moved in, closing the distance between us, I let out a slow, shuddering breath. I should run, but my legs wouldn't obey. My brain was telling me to get away from Ford Sawyer, but the rest of me was happy exactly where I was. Pressed to his long, lean body, the woodsy, male scent of him teasing me. I didn't want to want him, but I did.

"Paige," was all he said. Half a question, half a statement.

I didn't know what to say.

His hands loosened a fraction, and my brain shouted: *This is it. Run!* I stayed where I was. When his fingers renewed their grip, I didn't pull away. I let him draw me closer, my skin heating up, my heartbeat quickening in anticipation, not fear.

"Paige," he said again.

And this time I said, "Ford?" But that was all I got out.

The heat of his breath grazed my cheek. His lips followed, sipping at my skin, finding my mouth in the dark. That first kiss—so soft, gentle, nothing I would have expected from a man who carried darkness like Ford Sawyer.

One hand dropped from my arm and came up, fingers sliding into my loose hair, his palm cupping my chin. "Paige," he breathed and tilted his head to deepen the kiss.

The second kiss wasn't gentle. There was demand, and I gave, letting my head tip back, my lips part, my tongue stroke against his. So much passion. Heat. His mouth was hard and hot on mine. His other hand dropped from my chin, winding around my waist, pulling me tight to his body. He kissed me as if I'd disappear from his arms if he stopped.

My brain stopped shouting for me to run as my arms slid up, pulling him closer. I'd lost the ability to reason. I could only feel his mouth, setting me on fire.

I wanted more.

It had been a long time since I'd been kissed—life too complicated to make room for this kind of indulgence— but I knew my long drought had nothing to do with how I was responding to this kiss. In a house filled with good-looking men, why this one? The one I should most want nothing to do with.

I didn't know. But my arms wound around him, my breath coming in gasps as he kissed me as if madness had taken over us both. I knew only wanting—couldn't, shouldn't, but did.

The lights flared on, the single incandescent bulb above us swaying lightly, illuminating the room in a flickering golden glow. With that, my brain took over again, and I stumbled, reaching up to swipe the back of my hand over my damp mouth. My eyes stretched impossibly wide as I stared up at Ford. His cheekbones were sharp, his sea-green eyes burning in the sudden light.

"I... I..." I couldn't form a coherent thought.

Snapping my mouth shut, I ducked under his raised arm, disappearing into the hall and my room. I slammed the door and turned the lock behind me before diving under the covers, my heart still pounding, head spinning, trying to make sense of what I'd just done.

Ford Sawyer might be a killer, but he was a hell of a kisser. I could still feel his hands on me like a brand, still taste him on my tongue. And while I should be glad I'd escaped him, I couldn't help wondering if I'd get the chance to kiss him again.

Chapter Six

PAIGE

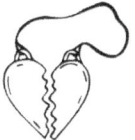

Asmile stretched wide across my face as I strode down Main Street in Sawyers Bend. I held in my hands a pretty shopping bag with twine handles and an artfully designed logo. Inside was a stash of cookies from Sweetheart Bakery for Hope and a raspberry oatmeal bar for me. Along with treats, I was carrying another small bag, an even smaller box inside, containing a gorgeous pair of garnet earrings I couldn't resist from one of the local shops.

It wasn't my day off, but the older kids were in school and I wasn't on deck for pickup. Baby Stella was with Hope, who had a light day of work—no meetings—and wanted to spend it keeping her daughter close. I'd had a few errands to run in town, and when they were done, I couldn't resist playing tourist and doing a little shopping.

I was on my way back to my car, feeling rather pleased with myself. All was right in my world. Mostly. I was ping-ponging between denial about that white-hot kiss with Ford Sawyer the night before and wondering if it was going to happen again. It shouldn't. I knew that. Absolutely not, of course. It had been completely inappropriate. He was my employer's brother. Possibly a murderer.

I'd told myself all of this a million times, and they were all excellent reasons why a repeat was off the table. Except weighing heavily on the other side of the scale was the previously mentioned white-hotness of that kiss. I was having a hard time putting that part aside.

But this afternoon I had promised myself I wasn't going to think about kissing anyone. I was shopping and enjoying the pretty town and the gorgeous winter weather. I'd thought the mountains of Western North Carolina would be cold, and I'd been told they would be. But on a sunny day in early December, the chill in the air was merely brisk, the skies an electric blue, the evergreens vibrant, and I had the feeling that I was exactly where I belonged. Finally. It had been a long time since I was genuinely happy. Not since Paris, before my mother got sick.

I'd parked on a side street, enjoying that while the town was still busy enough to keep the shop owners happy, tourism had dwindled just enough that finding a parking spot wasn't a headache. I slid behind the wheel, dropped my parcels on the passenger seat, and hit the start button.

The engine made a strangled coughing sound and fell silent. No welcoming rumble. No heat blasting from the vents. Just that sad, abrupt cough. I tried again. This time, I got nothing.

I sat there for a long minute, staring at the dashboard.

I didn't know anything about cars. I thought about getting out and lifting the hood—but really, what was the point? All I'd see was an engine, and I had no clue what to do with one of those.

Fuck.

I'd bought the car used without a roadside assistance package and had meant to sign up for AAA or something similar, but I'd never gotten around to doing it. I tried one more time, putting my foot on the brake and pressing the start button. Again, nothing. Picking up my phone, I called Hope. She answered on the second ring.

"Paige, what's up? Everything okay?"

"Not exactly. My car won't start. I'm parked on Chestnut, and when I got back and tried to start the engine... I don't know what's wrong, but it's dead. Any chance I could get a ride home?"

"Of course," Hope said, reminding me of one of the many reasons I loved working for the Sawyers. "Let me think for a second. I'm stuck here for the moment. A call got rescheduled, and it's starting in a few minutes. Let me see who I can send to pick you up. I'll call you right back."

"Perfect, thanks."

The call disconnected, and I waited, knowing I probably wouldn't have to wait long. Hope and Griffen were two of the most considerate people I'd ever worked for. They wouldn't leave me stranded. The phone rang a few minutes later. Hope again.

"Hey Paige, sorry about this. It turns out we're a little shorthanded around here, but Ford and Finn are at Sawyers Bend Brewing. Ford said he's scheduled to head back to the Manor in about forty-five minutes or so. You're only a few blocks away if you're parked on Chestnut. Do you mind walking over there and hitching a ride with them? Hawk said he's sorry he can't get you himself, and if you give him your keys when you get back here, he'll send somebody to bring your car into the shop to make up for the trouble."

"That's so thoughtful. Yeah, I don't mind catching a ride with Ford and Finn," I lied. I did mind, but I wasn't going to tell Hope why, and it was sweet of her to be concerned about the inconvenience. I didn't want to make it worse. "Thanks, Hope. Are you okay with having Stella for your call?"

"I'm sure it'll be fine," Hope said. "At the moment, she's out cold. And if she wakes up, I'll figure it out. Don't give it another thought. I'll see you in a bit."

I hung up, locked my car, and headed down the street to Sawyers Bend Brewing. I hadn't seen Ford since that kiss in the utility closet. My stomach squeezed at the thought of facing him. We hadn't had a lot of full-on conversations. What would I say to him? Was I going to make a thing about the kiss? Talk to him about it? Or was it better to just pretend it never happened?

Whatever. I'd have to deal with it.

I pushed open the door of the taproom to find it about a third full—more than I'd expected for a weekday afternoon in December. Ford was behind the bar, his face set in his usual serious expression, though his lack of welcome didn't seem to be chasing off the beer drinkers. He was the opposite of Dave, Avery's other bartender, whom I knew from previous trips to the brewery, was all smiles and friendly conversation. Ford looked like he manned the bar the way he did everything else: eyes hard, mouth in a tight line, the world locked out, and everything that was Ford Sawyer sealed up tight inside.

I didn't think anyone could break through that shell. I was under no illusion that I was any different. He'd kissed me—it didn't mean he'd tell me his secrets. That was fine. I wasn't telling him mine either.

Those moments in the dark utility closet haunted me. His strong hands closing over my hips, his mouth hot and demanding. Those stolen moments felt a million miles away from Sawyers Bend Brewing. In here, the fire was roaring, golden light flickering on the pine walls, friendly conversation filling the room.

I straightened my shoulders and approached the bar. Ford's eyes flicked to mine, one dark eyebrow raising a fraction.

"Hope called," he said. "Dave should be here in thirty."

I nodded, climbed onto a stool, and set my packages on the bar. "Thanks for the ride," I said.

He nodded once, his eyes landing on my shopping bags. "Sweetheart and jewelry?"

I nodded. "Cookies for Hope and something for me. I can't resist Daisy and Grams's baking."

"Few can," Ford agreed. "What else did you get?" he asked, nodding to the bag from the jewelry store.

"Earrings." I pulled the box out of the bag to show him, half thinking he wouldn't care. But he'd asked, hadn't he? Sort of. I opened the box and showed him the gold wire wrapped around rough-cut garnet.

He looked from the earrings to me. "They suit you," he said. "Good choice."

I nodded, not sure what to say. They did suit me—at least I'd thought so when I bought them. I didn't need Ford's approval on my jewelry, but I had to admit, if only to myself, that I liked it. *Ugh*.

"What can I get you while you wait?" he asked, lifting a pint glass from beneath the bar.

"Oh, I'm good," I said. "It's a little early in the day for me to have a drink." I'd been about to say I was driving, but I wasn't. I hesitated, eyeing the taps. "I... Maybe..."

Before I could make up my mind, Ford asked, "How do you feel about a stout?"

I tilted my head to the side, considering. "I like a stout."

"All right, then," he said. "I won't give you a whole pint, but try this." He pulled a lever, and dark liquid the color of molasses filled the pint glass about halfway.

I waited for him to slide it across the bar, but instead he turned, glass in hand, doing something I couldn't see behind the counter. When he turned back, there was a long toothpick lying across the top of the glass, skewering one donut hole.

"Try it," he said, sliding it toward me. "It's Avery's donut hole stout."

I shook my head but took the glass from him, picking up the donut hole before dipping my nose for a sniff. The stout didn't smell like a donut hole. It smelled like stout. Maybe a little yeasty. A hint of sweetness.

"Take a sip," Ford said. "Avery's a genius."

I followed his instructions and tilted the glass. The

second the stout hit my tongue, I knew he was right—there was the faintest undertone of yeasty sweetness. The drink itself wasn't sweet; it was more like an impression of a freshly baked cake doughnut woven through the dense flavor of the stout.

"Now take a bite of the donut hole," Ford ordered.

I took a nibble, letting it melt across my tongue. "Did Daisy or Grams make this?"

"Daisy dropped them off a few hours ago."

"It's amazing." I took another sip of stout, savoring. The flavors complemented each other perfectly. "Wow, Avery really is a genius," I agreed. "How do you work here and not spend your whole shift drinking?"

I hadn't meant to sit here and pepper Ford with questions, but it felt natural to talk to him. Far more than I'd expected, especially after that kiss.

The faintest hint of a smile curved the side of Ford's mouth, bringing a light to his sea-green eyes. For a moment, I saw a glimpse of a Ford I hadn't met—maybe a Ford who'd existed before he'd gone to prison.

"I have a drink or two some days," he said, "but I space them out. I've never been much of a drinker. One or two in an evening is enough for me. But Avery's taught me to appreciate every drop. She really found her calling here."

"She definitely did," I agreed, finishing the last of the donut hole.

Before the silence could get awkward, someone walked up to the bar, claiming Ford's attention. I pulled out my phone to browse. Off at the far end of the bar, an open doorway led to the small kitchen that Finn would use when he started serving food here. I'd heard getting it ready to use was a bigger job than he'd expected, and he was still cleaning it up. I couldn't see what he was doing, but heard him rattling around, banging metallic things, and occasionally swearing.

Ford pulled pints to fill his order, ran a credit card, and made his way back to the middle of the bar where I sat. He stood there, sliding a wet towel across the top of the bar. His eyes rested on me, considering, before he said, "Are we going to talk about it?"

Chapter Seven

PAIGE

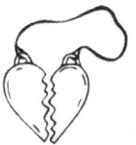

I felt heat hit my cheeks and shook my head before I could think too much about the answer. I didn't want to talk about it. What I really wanted was to do it again, and never, ever talk about it. Because talking about it would be awkward and weird, and I didn't even know how I felt or what I wanted—except to kiss Ford Sawyer again.

How did I get myself into this situation? I was always professional. And that was what spilled from my lips. "I'm always professional," I said. "And that was very much not. I work for your brother. It shouldn't have happened."

Ford nodded. "Probably not," he agreed, "because you're a professional and you work for my brother. And I don't want to take advantage of your position in our household."

"Okay," I said, both relieved and oddly bereft, as if something I hadn't decided I wanted had been snatched away. "Then we're in agreement."

Ford was already shaking his head. "What do you think we've agreed on?"

"That it's not going to happen again," I said, pushing away the empty pint glass in front of me.

Ford took it, poured me another very short pint, and handed it back. I accepted the glass but didn't drink.

"I'm not agreeing to that," he said in an annoyingly reasonable tone.

"What if I don't want to kiss you again?" I said, my eyebrows drawing together, cheeks still hot. This conversation was awkward as hell, but at the same time, intriguing.

"You do," he said, something sparking in the depths of his green eyes.

"You don't know that," I said, wanting to be annoyed but instead finding myself oddly charmed. I did not want to be charmed by Ford Sawyer.

That tiny grin curved the side of his mouth again, the light I was coming to like so much hitting his eyes for a flash.

"Paige," he said quietly, "I was there. You definitely want to kiss me again."

Damn it. I couldn't deny it. He hadn't just kissed me. I'd kissed him back. I'd kissed him back with everything I had because the kiss had been that good.

I let out a long sigh, my shoulders slumping forward. "Fine," I admitted. "I do want to kiss you again, but I also have self-control, and it's a terrible idea. I don't want to lose my job."

"Griffen is not going to fire you," he said. "Not for that. He'd get rid of me before he'd get rid of you."

I stared at him, my brows drawn together, wondering if he was crazy. "You're his brother! Of course, he'd choose you over me. He barely knows me."

"Clearly you haven't heard enough of the family lore," Ford said dryly. "We're not close, haven't been for a very long time, and it's entirely my fault. I'm his brother, and family is important, but if it came down to you versus me, he'd keep you and boot me. No question."

That didn't make sense to me in the slightest. I was just the nanny. I liked Griffen and Hope an awful lot, but I was still an employee, one they didn't even know that well, certainly not compared to their relationship with Ford.

I drummed my fingers on the top of the bar, thinking.

"You need to trust me," he said. "Dave will be here soon, and telling you the whole story would take a lot longer than we have. Ask me later and I'll give you the gory details. But for now, you need to understand that Griffen is far more likely to get rid of me than you."

"Even if that's true and I'm not risking my job, it's still unprofessional," I challenged, leaning forward, my voice low.

Ford leaned in until his face was only inches from mine. "I'm not going to kiss you while you're working, Paige. But you aren't working all the time."

"That's not the point," I whispered, feeling the conversation sliding out of my control. He was so close, his breath warm on my lips, his eyes so green.

"It's exactly the point," he said, his voice quiet and smooth, flowing over me, erasing my objections. "I don't want to interfere with your responsibilities with the kids,

IVY LAYNE

and I'm not your employer. I have no power over your job."

"Okay," I said, my heart thudding behind my ribs. "Assuming that's true, what do you see happening here?"

Ford straightened, leaving me feeling cold in his absence. "I don't know," he said. "I know that it's been a long time since I kissed a woman. And longer—if ever—since I've had a kiss like that. I think you're smart and warm and beautiful, and I really liked kissing you. I didn't plan it, but it happened. And now that it has..."

That slight eyebrow lift again, that light flashing through his eyes.

Dammit. I was on the same page. I'd been kissed before, but not like Ford Sawyer had kissed me.

"Now that it has," he said, "I want it to happen again. If you don't, all you have to do is say so. And if you do, then I guess we'll see. I'm not offering a relationship, Paige. I don't know if I have that in me anymore. I'm still trying to figure out how to be whatever this new version of me is. I have a lot of mistakes to atone for and a life to figure out. I've got nothing to offer a woman like you."

"That's not a great sales pitch," I said, fighting a smile.

"Just being honest," he said. "I'm not going to bullshit you. You deserve better than that, and you're smart enough to see through a lie."

"True." I let out a sigh, searching my heart for the resolve to tell him to try his luck somewhere else. "I should tell you absolutely not, never again."

"Maybe," he agreed. "But you're not going to."

"No, I'm not," I admitted. "It's been a long time since

66

I've kissed anyone, either. And I'm not sure I've ever had a kiss like that." He had given me the truth. I owed him the same back. Or at least as much of the truth as I could. "It's worth seeing if the second kiss is as good as the first. Maybe you'll be a dud."

"Possibly. We'll just have to find out."

His eyes flicked to his right as the door between the brewery and the taproom swung open, giving me a glimpse of high ceilings and stainless steel as Dave pushed through.

Ford sighed under his breath. He raised a hand in Dave's direction in a silent hello before turning to give a low shout. "Finn, Dave's here."

Finn emerged from the kitchen in a dusty, grease-stained T-shirt, his dark hair pulled back in an ancient bandana, his faded jeans threadbare. "Goddamn, that kitchen is filthy. It's going to take me at least another two days to get it cleaned properly." His eyes scanned the bar and landed on me. "Hey, Paige. What's up?"

More flustered than I wanted to admit by the conversation with Ford, I put on my professional face. "You guys are giving me a ride home. My car conked out on me," I said.

"Oh, good timing at least. You had one of Avery's donut hole stouts?" he asked, his eyes landing on the half-finished refill in front of me. "Fantastic, right?"

"Absolutely," I agreed.

"Let me wash my hands, and then we can head out." Finn glanced at the newcomer. "Hey, Dave."

Dave raised a hand and flashed a grin at Finn before

he went back to talking to Ford about the status of the kegs and the cash register.

A few minutes later, they were both ready to go. I rounded the bar, following them through the door to the brewery.

"I parked on the side," Ford said over his shoulder, "so we don't use up spots for customers."

"Have you ever been back here?" Finn asked me.

"No," I said slowly, looking around, my eyes absorbing the business end of the brewery: clean concrete floors and high ceilings in the warehouse-style room, Avery's shiny stainless-steel vat and copper kettle, crates of bottles, the smell of hops. It was ruthlessly organized and squeaky clean but still somehow warm and welcoming. "It's so cool back here."

"I know," Finn agreed. "So different from the taproom, but somehow not."

"Yeah," I said, following Ford out the side door, looking back over my shoulder for a last glimpse of the brewery.

Finn led us to a Jeep parked a few spaces from the door. "Take the front," Ford said, opening the passenger door and holding it for me.

I looked at the length of his legs and started to shake my head, but he was already moving to open the back door. He didn't need to be a gentleman about it. I would have been fine in the back, but I appreciated the thought. I had to wonder how much his chivalry had to do with wanting to kiss me again. And if that was what it was about, was it working?

Nope, I decided, because I was going to kiss him again anyway. But a little chivalry didn't hurt.

I was so wrapped up in my deliberations, I didn't hear feet pounding the pavement until it was too late. Ford let out a shout, and I turned to see a man dressed in black from head to toe launch himself at Ford. Something dark was in his hand—a gun?

Was that a gun?

What the hell was going on?

Ford leapt at the man, bellowing, "Paige, get down!"

My body followed his direction before my brain had time to catch up, and I hit the ground, my palms and forearms breaking my dive with a raw scrape of flesh on asphalt. My bun unraveled into my eyes, blocking my view with a tangled, dark curtain of hair. The packages fell from my hand as I scrambled under the Jeep, which seemed like the safest place to hide. I tried to see what was happening through the hair in my face, but all I caught were feet moving on the asphalt, Ford's and the attacker's. It looked like they were fighting, but I couldn't tell who was winning.

From the other side of the Jeep, I heard Finn calling 911, calmly explaining what was happening.

How was he so calm?

A gunshot blasted, far too close, and my heart stopped in my chest. I squeezed my eyes shut, waiting to feel pain, but if the bullet had hit someone, it wasn't me.

I wanted to scream Ford's name, to see if Finn was okay, but my voice was caught in my throat. My lungs locked tight, refusing to draw in air, my heart thudding so hard it was all I could hear. Only the scrape of feet on asphalt, the grunt and thud of more fighting, got through my panic.

In my head, I screamed *Ford, Ford*, but I couldn't get the words out.

I worked my way farther under the Jeep, pushing my hair back out of my face. From behind me came another scrape and Finn's voice. "Stay down, Paige. West's deputies are on the way."

"What...what..." I tried to force out the words, but they wouldn't come.

"I don't know what's happening," Finn said, breathless. "Just stay down."

In front of me, Ford thudded to the asphalt, landing on his back. I thought to reach for him, but he rolled and then launched to his feet. There was a clatter—the gun tumbling to the ground only feet away. I squeezed my eyes shut, afraid it would discharge, but it had barely landed when it was scooped up. The rumble of an engine filled my ears as a car must have turned into the side lot, and then feet pounding...and everything was quiet.

"Who the fuck was that?" Finn asked, breaking the sudden silence.

"I don't know who that was," Ford said, his voice tired. "Or why he jumped me."

And while I also had no clue what had just happened, I knew in my gut that Ford was lying.

Chapter Eight

FORD

When we finally got back to Heartstone Manor, Finn was driving slower than I think he had since he was a fifteen-year-old with a learner's permit. From the adrenaline crash or general fear, I couldn't tell. I didn't think I was in shock, but I knew I was pissed. Pissed that someone had come at me and endangered all of them. Pissed that I was still paying for something I didn't do. And absolutely furious that Paige had been caught in the crossfire.

She was all I'd been able to think about all day. That kiss. I hadn't planned it. I'd been moving on autopilot: lights were out, check the breakers in the hall closet. The door had opened, startling me, and I'd pulled her into the dark without thinking. Then she was in my arms, every-thing about her soft and warm and so sweet. All my willpower deserted me, and I kissed her.

A better man would regret it—grabbing her, kissing her without asking. The conscience I'd developed in the last decade told me I owed her an apology, but I couldn't bring myself to regret it. Kissing Paige was the best decision I'd made in years, and I wanted to do it again. As soon as possible. When she'd walked into the taproom, I'd thought I was dreaming for a second. She'd been haunting me all day, and there she was, in the flesh, sitting at the bar.

I couldn't remember the last time I'd flirted with a woman. Not as easily as I did with Paige. The way she smiled, the flush on her cheeks when she was embarrassed, went straight to my head. For a few minutes, I'd thought that maybe... And then she was facedown on the pavement under Finn's Jeep, hoping she didn't get shot. I wanted to kiss her, to laugh with her, and instead I almost got her killed.

Finn slowed to a stop in front of the Manor, putting his Jeep in park with deliberate effort. All of us moved slowly as we got out, bodies aching from hitting the pavement. Griffen swung open the heavy door before I could reach for the handle, his sharp eyes scanning us, one by one. I could tell he'd settled into his professional badass mode, checking us for signs of shock.

"My office," he barked, turning and leading us down the hall. He didn't say another word until we were inside.

Hawk was already there, waiting for us. West, who had been enjoying a rare day off with Avery, followed us in, closing Griffen's office door behind us.

"Everybody okay?" Griffen asked.

"We're fine," Finn said quickly, sliding a wary glance my way. I didn't blame him. It wasn't the first time I'd let my little brother get hurt. It was going to be the last.

"We're fine," Paige echoed, her eyes on me, less wary

and more concerned—as if I needed another reminder that I had no business anywhere near her. The scrapes on her forearms were proof enough. Paige McKenna had never rolled under a Jeep in a parking lot for safety before. The memory of her terrified eyes burned deep inside me.

"We were lucky," I said quietly, trying not to think about Paige and Finn wedged behind the tires as I did everything I could to stay alive and keep the attacker off them.

"Ford took the brunt of it," Finn said.

"I can see that," Griffen agreed.

"I should leave Sawyers Bend," I said. It was the only thing that made sense. I had brought this into my family's life. Finn and Paige could have been killed. And what about the last time the guy had come after me? He'd come at us with a knife, leaving Avery in the hospital. "This is the second time we got lucky," I said. "At this point, we're pushing it. If I leave—"

"Finn, Paige, could you excuse us?" Griffen interrupted.

Finn looked from Griffen to me and nodded. On his way out, he closed his hand over my upper arm, giving me a quick shake. I forced myself to meet his eyes, expecting accusation. Instead, I saw only pity. Better, but it still made my gut twist. I didn't want to be pitied, but this was my life. I'd gotten myself here, and now I had to figure out how to get us all out.

"Wasn't your fault, man," Finn said with another shake before he let go and walked out, Paige trailing after him in silence.

The door shut behind her, and Griffen spoke into the quiet. "You're not leaving Sawyers Bend."

"Whoever he is, this guy is after me. If I go, he follows. The rest of you will be safe." I crossed my arms over my chest, resolved.

"First of all," Hawk cut in, "you don't know that leaving will make anyone any safer."

"Cole said—" I began, but Hawk cut me off with a quick shake of his head.

"You can't believe a fucking thing Cole Haywood says. He sent this guy after you—that, I buy. But the idea that he's going to leave the Sawyers alone because you're out of the picture?" Hawk shook his head again. Out of the corner of my eye, I saw Griffen doing the same.

"This guy," West said dryly, "is a shit assassin. I hate that he got a knife on Ford and Avery back in October, but that was mostly luck."

"You're sure it's the same guy?" Griffen cut in.

"Yes," I answered. "No question. Same height, same build." I shrugged, not sure how to articulate what my gut told me. "He moved the same."

West continued. "I'm sorry he got a blade on you two, and I'm sorry he roughed you up today. But his job was to kill you, and he struck out twice. I don't know where Haywood found him, but he's not exactly top-notch."

"Agreed," Hawk said. "Trap?"

West nodded. "If it was anyone else, I'd say I didn't want to endanger a civilian. But I'm assuming setting a trap would be preferable to being locked in the attic until we catch this guy."

"Or taking off and abandoning your family," Griffen added.

"A trap." The idea bloomed in my mind. There were few people I trusted to keep me alive more than Hawk, my brother, and West—though all of them had reasons I wasn't their favorite person. But they were some of the best men I knew, and they wouldn't let personal feelings get in the way of keeping me safe.

I'd risk myself in a second if it meant no one else would get hurt. I was sick to death of being the reason other people got hurt.

"What do you have in mind?" I asked West.

"I'm reluctant to expose the brewery," he said, considering. "But he jumped you in the employee parking lot, away from customers. As stupid as he seems to be, I doubt he'll make a run at you through the taproom. Too many people. I think he'll try again. We'll put you on closings. You appear to go in and out by yourself, parking in the dark lot. He'll try again."

"My guess is he's local," Hawk added, "for a few reasons. The main one being his skill set. Haywood hired him out of opportunity. If he was coming in from out of town, it's unlikely he would've waited so long between attempts—"

"Or, frankly, been this sloppy," West finished.

"I agree," Griffen said with a nod.

I didn't have their expertise. I'd take their word for it. I wondered how often I'd passed him in the street, how many other times he'd thought about coming at me and hadn't. "So, what?" I asked. "We put the word out that I'm working nights? Closing up alone?"

"Exactly. Locally, folks are still interested in Ford Sawyer serving beer," West said. "Word will spread."

I still wasn't comfortable with the attention, but I'd deal with the stares if it would help us catch Cole's hired killer.

"You think Avery will be okay with that?" I asked. "She generally keeps me off nights for that reason."

West raised an eyebrow in challenge. "She keeps you off nights for your sake, not hers. If you were working nights, she'd sell more beer, but she doesn't want her brother to be a circus sideshow, so she gives you afternoons. Plus, Dave likes the tips when he closes, but we could talk them into swapping."

"I don't think it would take more than a week, maybe two, before he makes another run at you," Griffen added.

"Do you have the manpower to set something up like that?" I asked.

West shook his head. "No. Not on our own." He looked to Hawk. "Considering the circumstances, I'd be open to a joint task force if you can spare some of your team."

"We'll make it work," Hawk said.

"And in the meantime," I interrupted, "I want you to teach me how to defend myself. I don't know why Cole hired someone who couldn't get the job done. But if I was dealing with anyone more competent than this guy, I'd be toast." I let out a frustrated breath. "I managed to keep him busy and away from Finn and Paige, but I've spent most of my life behind a desk. I'm in crap shape after the last year. I can throw a punch, and I can still shoot a gun, but that doesn't mean I know what I'm doing. I know you can't teach me everything in a few days, but there's got to be something." I exhaled again, my eyes locked on my feet. Unable to look at them, I said, "I couldn't keep them safe."

"You did," West cut in. "You got a little beat-up in the process, but Finn and Paige barely had a scratch on them."

I wanted to feel that was true, but all I could remember were their shouts, Paige's frightened eyes, and the gunshot that had gone wild. Only sheer luck had kept the bullet from burying itself in Paige or Finn.

"We can teach you," Griffen said, sharing a look with Hawk. "Enough to give you an edge. What happened to that nine millimeter you used to have?"

I looked to West. "I don't know. West's people confiscated it along with the gun that shot Prentice. I don't know where it ended up. For all I know, Haywood has it."

"I'll look into it," West said.

Griffen nodded. "We should get you time on the range. If you know what to do with it, you should be carrying it."

I shrugged. I was a pretty good shot—we all were—but my definition of *knowing what to do with it* and theirs was not the same thing. "I feel pretty useless at the moment," I admitted quietly. "I'm like a magnet drawing danger to the family, and I can't do a goddamn thing to stop it. If I left—"

"So that's it, then?" Griffen asked suddenly. "You're leaving?" His chin was set, his eyes hard.

I froze, teetering back and forth between *never* and *absolutely*. Finally, I settled for the truth.

"I've brought enough harm to my family," I said. "I can't tolerate the idea of bringing more. What if this guy gets to the Manor? The kids are here."

"That idiot is not getting through our security," Hawk stated firmly.

"Maybe not this guy," I said. "But once we get rid of this one, do you really think Cole is going to give up? If he's found a way to communicate with this guy from inside the prison, he'll be able to do it again. And the next time—"

"He'll find someone better," West finished for me. "Knowing Haywood, he wasn't planning for this guy to kill you. He just wanted to watch you dance, and if his guy got lucky, then that was a bonus. But now that he's in prison, I don't see him playing around. He has connections and cash. And my gut says he was prepared for this."

"You think he already had a backup plan in place?" Hawk asked, his dark eyes narrowed in thought.

"It would be on brand for Haywood," Griffen said slowly.

"As long as I'm here, the rest of you are in danger," I said. Stating the truth that baldly sent a bolt of fear up my spine. My gut told me I was right. Being in prison had barely slowed him down. Cole would never stop, and I didn't know what to do about that.

Griffen gave a slow nod, his arms folded across his chest. "And what do you want? Do you want to go? I know you're not without resources. You could do it. The will doesn't apply to you since Dad disinherited you. You could pack your things, take off, and start over somewhere else."

Everything inside me recoiled at that idea. When I'd lived under my father's rule, all I'd wanted was freedom. Especially after I'd gotten rid of Griffen and realized I was only more trapped now that I was alone with Prentice. But freedom no longer meant being out there somewhere, untethered from my family and Sawyers Bend. Freedom meant the chance to have a real life. If I started running, I'd never be able to stop.

"No, it isn't what I want," I said finally, meeting Griffen's sea-green eyes, so like my own. "I've made a lot of mistakes. The worst with you and Finn. I've spent a lot of my life thinking only about what I wanted, what would make me happy."

"And now?" Griffen asked quietly.

I paused, understanding this was a time I had to be completely honest, especially with myself.

"I want a second chance, even though I don't deserve one. I want to try to make up for everything I've fucked up. I want a future as a part of this family. That's what I want. I just don't think it's the best way to keep all of you safe, because as long as Cole has connections, he's going to keep trying to kill me."

"We don't sacrifice one of us for the good of the rest," Griffen said firmly. "Ever. We have shit to figure out, but not this way. Not by exiling you."

"It's what I did to you," I reminded him, guilt a cold

hollow in my chest. If Griffen wanted revenge, this was his chance.

He dropped his arms to his sides and rolled his eyes. "It's not the same thing. We were kids, and you were an asshole. As far as I'm concerned, you've paid for it, and I was better off. I don't like how it went down—that's the asshole part—but you're the one who had to marry Vanessa."

I shook my head, trying not to think about my brief marriage. Calling her a viper was an insult to snakes. I was sorry she was dead, but that was about all I could say.

"And you dealt with Dad by yourself," Griffen continued. "I think, at the end of the day, you got what you deserved. I don't need to punish you. Whatever lies between us moving forward, you're my brother. I won't throw you to the wolves. Even if I wanted to—which I do not—Avery, Sterling, and Quinn would kill me, and the rest wouldn't be far behind. Your family doesn't want you gone, Ford. We need to take a stand. If part of that means beefing up security," his eyes flicked to Hawk, who nodded, "then we'll work it out." To West, he said, "You'll talk to Avery about putting Ford on nights at the taproom. She's not going to like it, but I think she'll go along."

West agreed. "I'll let you know when we'll start."

Hawk gave a nod. "I'll go meet with the team, see how we can organize things. Might need to bring in someone from the outside, but I think we can handle this in-house."

Griffen turned his attention back to me, one blond eyebrow raised. "So how beat-up are you?"

I shrugged. "I'm a little sore here and there. I'm okay."

"Good." Griffen came toward me, slinging an arm around my shoulders. "Then let's get started. If he jumps you again, we'll make sure you can take him down."

Chapter Nine

PAIGE

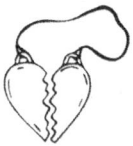

I put some antibacterial ointment on the scrapes on my forearms and changed clothes before I went to hunt down the kids, already home from school and probably having a snack in the kitchen. Now that I was back at Heartstone Manor, I was slowly processing what had happened in the parking lot. Some of it was still a blur, but of one thing I had no doubt—Ford Sawyer had not killed his father.

The man who'd shoved me under the Jeep, taking on a stranger with a gun to keep me safe, was not a murderer. Neither was the man whose first response had been "I'm leaving."

Who the hell would want to leave Heartstone Manor? He had a beautiful home in a town where he belonged, with a family who loved him, and he was willing to leave it all behind to keep that family safe. This was not a man who'd shot his own father in cold blood.

I rubbed the heel of my palm against my chest, not liking the hollow feeling I got at the idea of Ford packing his bags and driving away. It shouldn't matter. We had one kiss and a conversation between us. Barely anything. Whether he stayed or left was nothing to me.

Right?

I was a liar.

I pulled my sleeve over the cleaned and treated scrape and paced down the hall toward the stairs. Ford and I, in some ways, couldn't be more different. He was a Sawyer, with everything that came with being the son of a billionaire, who'd grown up in a castle. I was a normal girl from a normal family, raised by a single mom. I'd worked for a living since high school.

And yet, we were both kind of a mess. Ford was caught in limbo, tending bar for his sister instead of running a multinational corporation. And me—I was here in Sawyers Bend on a wild goose chase, for the first time in a long time feeling at home and without any idea what came next.

Despite all the reasons I should keep my distance from Ford Sawyer, I didn't want him to leave.

I jogged down the stairs to the lower level, hoping to find the kids at the table in the kitchen. Instead, I found them in the hall, huddled around the open door to the gym.

I didn't bother with the gym often. I was more into yoga, which I did in my room, and long walks in the woods when I had time. The gym had a few treadmills, plenty of free weights, ancient medicine balls, and a section of floor covered with mats that I knew Hawk, Griffen, and the rest of Hawk's team used for training— though I'd never been quite sure what that meant.

I came up behind the kids, putting one hand on Nicky's shoulder and one hand on August's, standing beside Thatcher, who, at fourteen, was taller than me.

"What are we looking at?" I whispered.

Finn came up behind me and said, "Tea is on the table." Then, glancing in the room, he grinned. "Griffen talked Ford into staying put. He's teaching Ford what he should have done with that guy in the parking lot."

"Oh?" That was all I got out.

Griffen and Ford strode into view, both of them stripped to the waist, and my mouth went dry. Maybe I should have been looking at Griffen. He was ripped, his golden skin tanned, muscles popping, reminding me of an action star from a movie.

Ford, in contrast, was still a little skinny from prison, his muscles rangy and his skin pale. But there was something elemental about him, an energy that vibrated under his skin. He wasn't there to play around. To him, this was life and death.

Griffen launched himself at Ford, and Ford went down hard, landing on his back with an audible *oomph* and the sharp smack of skin to mat. I couldn't even see what Griffen was doing; he moved so fast. A heartbeat later, Griffen was on his back, his arm around Ford's neck. Ford pounded his fist on the mat to indicate he'd given up.

"Fuck, that was quick," Finn said from behind me.

"I know," Thatcher agreed, breathless.

"How the hell did you do that?" Ford asked, rolling to his knees and sucking in a breath.

"Like this." Griffen was on his feet, reaching out a

hand for Ford. He pulled Ford up and broke down, step by step, what he'd done.

I hadn't realized how complicated the choreography of fighting could be as Griffen prompted Ford to step forward with his left foot, turning his hips open and aligning his shoulders, explaining where the power came from as he lunged and took Ford to the ground again. I expected Ford to protest, but he listened intently, rolled to his feet, and jumped at Griffen. His movements were clumsier and less efficient. Griffen let Ford take him to the ground, but once they hit the mat, he had Ford in an armlock again in seconds. They got back to their feet, Griffen explained the next sequence of moves, and they tried again.

I could have stood in that doorway for hours. Every move Ford made convinced me further that he wasn't the man I'd thought he was. I'd known his family didn't think he'd killed Prentice, but he'd spent a year in prison, and since he'd been living in the Manor, he'd been withdrawn. It had been easy to fill in the gaps of silence with assumptions—he was a killer, he was resentful, he was bitter. But this man, doggedly getting to his feet again and again, taking the punishment inherent in learning to fight so he could keep the rest of us safe—not only wasn't the man I thought he was, I suspected he wasn't the man *he* thought he was. This man wanted to do right.

I rubbed the heel of my palm into my chest again, the hollow space filled with a warmth, a yearning I didn't want to acknowledge.

"We should give them privacy. Did you mention something about tea?" I asked Finn.

"Probably gone cold, but yeah," he said, nodding, his eyes locked on the action on the mat. "PB&Js and some cookies to tide you guys over till dinner."

August and Nicky let me lead them away from the open gym door. Thatcher lingered.

"Be there in a minute," he said. As we walked away, I heard him call to Hawk. "Hey, can you teach me how to do that?"

"Sure, kid," I heard Hawk say. "Come on in. You've got some size on you. We'll see what you can do with Ford when Griffen needs a break."

I went through the motions of getting Nicky and August to wash their hands and sit at the table, asking them about school and deflecting when they asked why Ford and Griffen were fighting. All the while, I couldn't get the picture of Ford out of my head. His lean muscles straining under his skin, the determination in his eyes as he got up again and again. Those hands—I couldn't forget how they'd felt gripping my hips when he kissed me.

I had to figure out what I wanted and how much I was willing to risk to get it. Did I want Ford Sawyer? *Yes.* With heat in my chest, I answered with a resounding yes —I wanted Ford Sawyer.

And my father? My search for the mysterious Sarah? What about that?

I wasn't sure I could have both.

* * *

Ford didn't talk to me for five days after the attack in the parking lot. His door was always firmly shut when I went to bed, and still closed when I woke in the morning. The two times the lights had gone out in the guest wing, Ford had been working at the taproom, so I'd fixed them myself. I'd seen him every afternoon around tea, training with Griffen in the gym. Hawk had decided that fourteen-year-old Thatcher was adult enough to serve as a practice dummy. Since Thatcher wanted to learn to fight, and his mother and Tenn were okay with it, he was regularly getting tossed around on the mat and was having a blast, in contrast to Ford.

Every time I caught sight of Ford stripped to the waist, his rangy body sending heat flooding through mine, all I got from his expression was grim determination. He wanted to learn as fast as humanly possible.

By the fifth night of silence from Ford, I was out of patience. I lay in my bed, tossing and turning, trying to untangle my snarled thoughts. I shouldn't want Ford, but I did. I'd come here under false pretenses, and yet I wanted to stay. I thought I wanted to teach, but I was happy exactly where I was. Everything was a contradiction—a war between what I thought I wanted, or what I should want, and what I was feeling.

One thing at a time, I told myself. Career planning could wait. I had money in my savings account and a job I liked. I could figure out the future later. I'd come here to find Sarah Sawyer and my father. It felt like I was supposed to put Ford aside and continue with my search. The problem was, I wasn't sure there was anything to find. It didn't seem like Sarah Sawyer had much more to do with her family than my father had with me. Sarah and my father were long gone, living it up somewhere, their families forgotten. My quest, which had been filled with such purpose after my mother's death, now felt empty. It was what had brought me here, but it wasn't what was keeping me at Heartstone Manor.

The answer to why I stayed was so much simpler. I liked the Sawyers and the kids and the job. I liked the town. I felt rooted for the first time in years. And yes, I liked Ford Sawyer. He might be the last man I should want, but I was having trouble respecting all my shoulds lately. I didn't care about *should*. I wanted Ford. I wanted to run my hands over all that lean, corded muscle, to feel the heat of him, those strong fingers closing over my hips or cupping a breast. Those kisses—if he kissed like that, what would the rest be like?

And now Finn and I had almost gotten hurt. Ford was learning to fight and working nights at the taproom. It didn't take a genius to put it all together—especially considering the argument I'd overheard between Avery and West, ending with Avery saying, "I can hate this and still agree it's a good plan. But I don't like it."

"Neither do I, Ave," West had said. "But Ford wants to finish it, and this is the best way."

I hoped they were right. I didn't like the idea of it either. Even knowing there must be some kind of guard or something—Hawk's guys or West's deputies or somebody—keeping an eye out to make sure Ford didn't get hurt the next time this guy went after him.

More than just disliking Ford using himself as bait, I didn't like him shutting me out. We'd had an agreement in the taproom that this—that *we*—were going to happen. He didn't get to back out now.

I'd run these thoughts through my mind in dizzying circles for five days, and now I was done. Enough was enough. Before I dozed off, I set my alarm for 1:35 a.m., a few minutes before the time Ford usually got home when he closed the taproom. I'd planned to catch him in the hall, but I must have fallen back to sleep after I hit snooze. I jolted awake to the sound of knuckles rapping lightly on my door.

I opened the door, rubbing at my eyes. Ford stood there, his brows drawn together.

"Were you asleep? I saw the light under your door and thought you were up."

"I was," I said, shaking my head, trying to wake myself up enough to remember what I'd planned to say to him. "Come in."

I closed the door behind him and turned, absorbing the sight of him. Exhaustion was all over him in the slump of his shoulders, the dark shadows under his eyes.

"Are you getting any sleep?" I asked.

"Enough," he said.

"Doesn't look like it." I heard the rudeness in my tone, but couldn't dial it back. He shouldn't be punishing himself, but that was what this felt like. "You need tea," I said. "Sit." I tilted my head toward the armchair and ottoman in the little sitting area of my room.

"I don't want tea," he grumbled.

"You will once I brew it," I said.

The water boiled as we stood there in silence. The electric kettle was fast, but not so fast that the quiet didn't start to get awkward. I dunked the tea bag into the hot water, added some honey, and handed it to Ford.

"Give it a minute to steep," I said. "I love these little coffee and tea stations Savannah put in all the rooms."

"Except mine," Ford said, finally sitting in the armchair.

I filled another teacup with hot water and dunked my own bag of tea, taking it to sit on the love seat catty-corner to the armchair Ford occupied. "You don't have one? Why not?"

He raised an eyebrow. "Not everyone wants me here."

"That doesn't seem like Savannah, though. She's always so thoughtful."

"Savannah is loyal to Griffen and now Finn," Ford said slowly. "And while they seem to have forgiven me for the past, not everyone is as kindhearted as my brothers. Savannah knows who I am, what I've done, and she knows how to hold a grudge."

"I think it's time you give me all the gory details you mentioned the other day," I said, "because I don't get it."

Chapter Ten

PAIGE

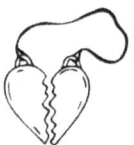

"What don't you get?" Ford asked, blowing on his steaming mug of tea.

"Anything," I said. "Why did you say Griffen would kick you out before me? Why doesn't Savannah want you here? And why do you seem to think you're the villain?"

"I think I'm the villain," Ford began, "because for most of this story, I have been." He sipped at his tea, leaning back into the soft armchair. "Griffen and I were closer than brothers when we were kids. Despite the few years between us, we might as well have been twins. Other than our hair color, we looked alike, talked alike. We both wanted to grow up to run the Sawyer empire together. We were going to do it right—not be assholes like our father—while bringing endless wealth and glory to the Sawyer family."

I could picture it exactly, even if I didn't have the same experiences to draw on. Two little boys, big dreams.

Ford looked into his teacup and sighed. "My father

was an expert manipulator. He liked nothing better than to set all of us against each other. He kept us isolated and desperate for his approval. But I can't blame him for what happened. I was weak." He rolled the mug between his palms, seeming to soak in the warmth as if he was frozen to the bone. "I hate admitting that."

I wanted to reach out to him, to squeeze his hand. To hug him. To comfort. But we weren't there yet, and I also didn't want him to stop talking. I stayed where I was.

"Griffen was two years older and always just a little more of everything. More charming, smarter, a little better with girls, sports. He was a better shot. I was still pretty fucking good at everything I did, but never as good as Griffen. And my father noticed every time I fell short. It became a secret language between us—him acknowledging my inadequacies with the raise of an eyebrow or a stray comment—and I let him get to me until the brother I loved more than myself became my only benchmark. And then he became the enemy." Ford shook his head and took a sip of tea. He stared into the mug for a long moment before his eyes rose to meet mine, the beautiful sea-green shadowed with guilt. "I thought if Griffen was out of the way, I could finally come first. I was twenty-one and so goddamn self-centered."

My heart ached at the life he'd described. "I don't have any siblings," I said slowly, "so I can't relate to that part, but I know what it's like to live with a parent who's never satisfied. I don't know who I would have become if I hadn't gotten away from her poison. I don't think I understood until she died that it wasn't about me. I was never going to be good enough. I could have made a billion dollars and cured cancer, and she still would have found fault with me." I took a long inhale of the tea, letting the herbal spice blend soothe the raw wound in my heart. It had taken me a while, but now I knew that understanding my mother didn't erase the hurt. "What happened with Griffen?" I asked. "What did you do?"

"I don't want to tell you," he said, "but you should know what kind of man I am." He set his mug on the side table with a click and crossed his arms over his chest. "My father was involved in a business deal that was going to make everyone involved a lot of money. It was with Forrest's—Sterling's fiancé's—father. In a way, it's the reason Forrest came back to Sawyers Bend."

I nodded to let him know I followed the story so far. I was vaguely aware of Forrest's past with the Sawyers, but I hadn't known that Ford had played a role.

"Griffen and I found out our father was planning to double-cross Forrest's dad, Alan, and take everything. We agreed we wouldn't let that happen and started putting together a plan—but the whole time, I was undoing everything Griffen did to protect Alan and his company. I thought that if I could rescue the deal for my father, it would tarnish Griffen in his eyes, and I could finally be number one. I didn't think he'd go as far as he did. In the end, my father exiled Griffen for trying to undermine the deal. He threw him out with only a backpack, banning him from Heartstone and Sawyers Bend. Prentice walked away with Alan Buckley's company, and I took everything that was Griffen's. His fiancée, his position in the company—all of it."

I sipped my tea, processing. The way he described

what he did without defending himself told me everything I needed to know about how much he'd changed.
"How long ago was that?"

"Sixteen years," Ford answered.

"And your father died two years ago?"

"Eighteen months," Ford said.

"And that's when Griffen came home?" I asked.

"Yep."

"So, what happened after Griffen left? What came
between sixteen years ago and eighteen months ago?" I
asked.

Ford picked up his cooled tea and took a long sip
before shaking his head—not in negation, but in what I
thought was remorse.

"A lot of wasted time," he said slowly. "I spent the
first half of it kissing my father's ass. Thinking if I could
just be more of what he wanted, then everything would
finally feel good again. I'd stop missing my brother. I'd be
happy. But nothing I did was ever good enough for Prentice Sawyer, even when I worked by his side. Even after
I'd protected him and double-crossed my own brother. To
the outside world, I was the heir to Sawyer Enterprises.
But at home, I was a constant disappointment, a fuckup,
and a failure. Vanessa was a nightmare of a wife. She's
dead now, and I feel guilty saying it, but it's true. Any
woman who would dump her fiancé for his younger
brother as soon as said fiancé was disinherited...Well, I
should've known how that was going to work out. But all
I could see was what she showed me. I was an arrogant,
selfish idiot."

He paused, and then his tone dropped lower.

"And then things got dark. My father started getting involved in business that wasn't so aboveboard. One of those deals almost got Finn killed—and I didn't stop it." Self-hatred spiked through his words, so sharp I could feel it. "I'm surprised Finn can even look me in the eyes. He's like Griffen in that. Or maybe he's just so happy with Savannah and Nicky that he doesn't have it in him to be bitter. He should hate me. Instead, he acts like everything's fine."

I was still caught on the *almost got Finn killed* part. "How exactly did you almost get Finn killed?"

Ford drew in a slow breath and let it out. Instead of answering, he said, "I came here tonight to tell you that what I said in the taproom was wrong. This can't happen. You could have gotten seriously hurt that day in the parking lot. And even once we catch this guy, we don't know that there won't be another. I'm not safe to be around."

I met his eyes, not backing down. "Then no one needs to know I'm around you."

"Telling you the truth about the time between then and now is probably enough to change your mind anyway," he said.

I doubted it. "Tell me, and we'll see."

"My father was doing business with gangs out of Mexico, moving various illegal goods—mostly arms. Nothing so 'unsavory' as trafficking drugs or humans. It was all very professional, dealing with men in suits carrying briefcases. Except when it wasn't. We were at a sticking point in our negotiations, and unaware of any of this, Finn decided to go to Mexico on spring break. He was a sophomore in college. We considered telling him that Mexico might not be the safest place for him to travel, but we didn't."

Ford drew in a breath, and his eyes, when they met mine, were so sharp with pain I had to bite my lip to keep from reaching for him.

He looked away, fixing those tortured eyes on his almost empty mug. "I think, in retrospect, my father may have dropped enough hints to point his contacts in Finn's direction. They kidnapped him, trying to use him as leverage. And my father said this was an opportunity to show them what hard-asses we were. That Finn was a liability, and he wasn't going to come to anything anyway, so he might as well be useful. He was going to let them kill my brother—his son—to get the edge in a business negotiation. He was going to let them kill Finn for money, and not even that much money. It was more about ego, about who's got the bigger dick, who's tougher. And for that, he'd sacrifice his own child."

I took a sip of tea to cover my shock. *What the fuck?* What kind of father would do that? And this was the man who'd raised this family I'd come to love? Ford carried so much guilt over the decisions he'd made—and from what I'd heard, he should—but he didn't seem to recognize that he'd been just as much a victim as Griffen or his siblings.

I knew what it felt like to be told, over and over, that you were a disappointment, never good enough, no matter what you did. If I'd had the opportunity to deflect my mom's criticisms or thought I could rise beyond them, I might have taken it too. Looking back, I was glad my only option was to leave, and so grateful for the Bellinghams' job offer my freshman year. Without them, I wouldn't be the woman I'd grown into. They'd given me a home and family, along with a job. They'd taught me what love was supposed to look like.

Ford hadn't had anything like that.

"What did you do?" I asked him. "After they kidnapped Finn?"

His shoulders rose in a scrunch and fell abruptly. "Nothing," he said. "I didn't call the FBI. I didn't intervene and make a counteroffer or pay the ransom. I did nothing."

"How did Finn get away? Did your father—"

Ford was already shaking his head. "Prentice Sawyer give in? He would have shot Finn himself before backing down. According to Finn, the people holding him got a little too drunk, and he managed to get away. He called our former chef—the one who'd taught him to cook—and Chef Guérard got him a plane ticket to France and a job when he got there. Finn never came home."

God. What an awful time they all had under this monster of a man.

"And what happened to you?" I asked.

Ford's eyes flicked up to mine. "I realized I couldn't be the man I'd turned into. I'd driven Griffen away, and Finn had escaped, but I still had siblings, and they needed me to be better. I couldn't stand it—knowing Finn had almost died and I hadn't done anything to stop it. I'd thought about it, gone back and forth, come up with scenarios, but in the end, I didn't do anything to save him. He saved himself."

That explained so much. "No wonder you're freaked out about what happened in the parking lot," I said. "He didn't get hurt, you know."

"That's not the point," Ford said between gritted teeth.

"That's part of the point," I argued. "Nobody got hurt." I paused, gathering my thoughts. "And you guys—I'm assuming—have a plan to catch this guy. You're working late in the taproom in the hopes he tries again?"

Ford glanced at me, clearly surprised. "Something like that, yeah," he admitted.

"You can't fix the past, Ford. It's what you're doing now that matters. And what happened in that parking lot wasn't your fault. Finn said it after it happened. It's the fault of the guy who tried to shoot you, and whoever hired him." I'd used my best no-bullshit voice, and it seemed to get through, just a little, given the way Ford looked at me.

"That would be my former lawyer," he said.

"Well, that sucks," I said, unable to stop the laugh that his wry comment startled out of me. "Maybe you need a new lawyer."

"I don't need a lawyer at all anymore," he said.

"Ford..." I set my mug, still full of rapidly cooling tea, on the coffee table. "None of what you've told me changes my mind."

He shook his head. "You deserve better than me."

"Probably," I agreed with a smirk. That drew an answering curl of the side of his mouth. Not quite a smile, but I'd take it. "But you already said you can't give me a relationship."

He nodded.

"And honestly, I'm not sure I want one. This is complicated—I work for your brother; we all live in the same house."

"So, what do you want?" Ford's eyebrow raised, and he looked at me with speculation, his dark mood fading slightly. "Friends with benefits?"

"Something like that," I said, standing and crossing the short distance between us.

Before he could stop me, I set a knee next to his hip on the armchair and straddled his lap.

Glad we both fit in the oversized armchair, I grinned, my mouth hovering over Ford's. "I say we try it again. Maybe you'll be a dud, and we won't have to worry about it."

"You think?" he asked, his palms landing on my thighs, sliding up and around to grip my ass.

In answer, I kissed him. It was like a bomb went off, heat rolling up inside me, fusing my lips to his. His hands kneaded my flesh, pulling me closer, his hips rocking up into me, his mouth demanding. I sank my fingers into his thick, dark hair.

I couldn't get enough. He tasted of the tea, of flowers and spice, and something darker underneath that was all Ford. I might have started the kiss, but he dominated it. My mouth moved against his, just trying to keep up.

He tipped his head back, his eyes dazed, one hand cradling the side of my face. "Paige," he breathed, running a fingertip over my lower lip. "I could kiss you all night."

Sitting up a little, he brought his other hand to my

face, holding me, his green eyes shading to emerald, fixed on my mouth. He strained forward, brushing his lips over mine, trailing his mouth to the side of my jaw and down the side of my neck, setting me on fire everywhere we touched.

His teeth closed over my collarbone in a teasing bite. "You taste so good." Then his mouth was on mine again, kissing me until my head spun.

His hands slipped under my shirt, splayed hot against my back, deft fingers unsnapping my bra. I wanted it off. I wanted everything off. I wanted to touch that smooth skin I'd seen every afternoon in the gym. I needed to see if he felt as good as he looked.

The world shifted, and he was standing, one arm hooked under my ass, bringing me with him. He crossed the room in long strides, and I landed on my back on the bed, sideways, my hips on the edge, legs draped and barely touching the floor, Ford standing between them. He reached down, grasping onto my shirt, and pulled it up. I arched my back, helping him work the fabric free. And then my shirt and my bra were gone, and he looked down at me with hot, hungry eyes.

"Paige." He came down on the bed beside me, half on and half off. I didn't have time to think as he leaned over, cupping my breast in his hand, his mouth closing over the tight peak of my nipple, sucking hard enough that it almost hurt, then kissing, licking, soothing, sucking again. Every touch sent jolts of liquid bliss straight between my legs. I was so lost in the feel of his mouth on my breasts that I almost missed his fingers at the waist of my jeans, unbuttoning, unzipping, peeling them down until I was naked.

"More." I sat up just a little to claw at his shirt, thinking about his bare chest so close to mine. I got the shirt off him and pulled him down, the little hairs on his chest scraping my nipples with a delicious friction as he kissed me again.

This was what I'd wanted—his weight and heat on top of me, pinning me down, Ford touching me until my head spun. His hand slid between my legs, fingertips circling my clit before sliding inside. It had been a while since I'd had sex, but I couldn't remember ever feeling this ready—this desperate.

He lifted his mouth from mine and slid down, kissing my collarbone, my shoulder, the peak of my breast, my belly button, before settling on his knees at the end of the bed and dropping his head to close his lips around my clit.

The top of my head exploded.

One hand plucked my nipple, the other had two fingers inside me as he sucked and licked and tasted. I slapped my palm over my own mouth as a scream rose inside me. It was so much, so fast, and it felt so good. I came in a rush, gasping his name and then just gasping as I melted into the sheets.

"Ford," I murmured. I cracked an eye open and met his smug, satisfied smile. I was pretty sure the one on my face was a match. I was feeling pretty smug myself. Propping up on an elbow, I reached for him. "What about—"

"Not tonight," he said. "Tonight, this is what I wanted." The side of his mouth curved. "No, that's a lie.

Tonight, I wanted to tell you all the reasons this couldn't happen."

"And now?"

He just shook his head. Sliding an arm under my back, he turned me on the mattress, tucking the sheets and blanket around me.

I reached up to grab his wrist. "Stay," I said softly. "Just for a little. Stay." My head was still spinning, my body aglow. I wasn't ready to be alone, wasn't ready for him to leave.

Fabric rustled and he slid in beside me—not naked, in boxers, I guessed—and hooked an arm around my waist, turning me onto my side exactly as I usually slept, though he couldn't have known that. His body fit against mine, his skin a little damp, his breath warm against my ear. I stretched, rolling my ass against the tempting bar of his erection.

He let out a low groan and pressed his mouth to the side of my neck. "Next time." Ford let out a long breath and sat up just enough to look into my eyes. "I want you to promise me something."

"Maybe," I breathed, sleep creeping up on me.

"Stay at Heartstone until this guy takes the bait. Don't leave the Manor grounds. He saw you with me. I don't want you to be a target."

"What if it takes a long time?" I asked.

"How about just for now? Can you promise me that?"

"I have to talk to Griffen and Hope first. Part of my job is driving the kids around." I heard what I'd said and hated the thought that sprang into my mind. "Do you think the kids are safe with me?"

"I'll talk to Griffen," he said. "We'll figure something out."

"If he thinks it's safer, I'll stay on the Manor grounds. But I need a promise too."

"Hmm?" he asked, his breath warm on my ear, sounding as if he too teetered on the edge of sleep.

"We don't tell anyone about this, okay? It's just between us," I said, my words starting to slur with fatigue and the release from a truly amazing orgasm. "It's our secret. I don't want things to get complicated."

"Our secret." His lips brushed the shell of my ear. "Promise."

Chapter Eleven

FORD

I should have had my eyes on the road and my mind on driving home after yet another closing shift at Sawyers Bend Brewing. Instead, all I could think about was Paige and what had happened between us the previous night.

I wasn't coming home to her after a long day of work, because that was way too domestic for whatever was going on between us. But I couldn't deny that was what it felt like.

I liked tending bar in the taproom at Sawyers Bend Brewing, and I didn't mind the closing shift. Avery didn't keep the taproom open late, and while she did a steady business, it was never jammed. But these last few days waiting for Haywood's assassin to strike were wearing on me. I wasn't used to the stress of being the bait in a sting operation. I'd been an executive. I wasn't in law enforcement. The closest I'd come was my brief stint as a felon.

I just wanted to catch the guy and maybe think about

what came next, after we found my father's killer. After this was over.

A doubting whisper in my heart asked if it would ever be over, or if I was due for a lifetime of purgatory. I hadn't felt hope in a long time—not since Finn had barely escaped the kidnapping with his life, and I'd faced the man I'd become. Since then, I'd been trying to make amends, but I was aware it was too little, too late.

And then last night, Paige listening as I laid it out. I had expected her face to twist in disgust, that she'd throw me out of her room, and that would be the end—and it would have been right if she did. I'd convinced myself it was what I deserved, and that she deserved so much better than the washed-up, morally bankrupt, underemployed black sheep of the Sawyer family.

Instead, she'd listened without judgment, had understood when I spoke about my father. She'd given me empathy but not pity, been kind, but hadn't let me wallow. It was exactly what I'd needed.

I wanted to know her story, though it hadn't felt like the right time to ask. I hated the idea of her growing up the way I had, always trying and failing to feel a parent's love. I wanted to know everything about her.

I just wanted her.

I'd drifted off in her bed, arm around her waist, her dark, shiny curls tucked under my chin. Hours later, I'd woken and forced myself to cross the cold hallway to my lonely room. I'd promised her we'd keep it a secret, and we would. I didn't want my baggage tainting Paige. She was close to my family. She loved them. They loved her.

If that changed because there was something going on between us—

I shook my head at the thought. I wouldn't be the reason Paige had less. I should turn away. I should tell her... But I wasn't going to. Despite all my efforts at reform, I was selfish enough to refuse to give her up completely.

She was a grown woman. She made her choice, fully informed.

But she doesn't understand, I thought—

And then all my thoughts cut off at the crack of a bullet and the jerk of the wheel in my hands as the car started to veer out of control.

I gripped the wheel, hitting the brakes, trying to get the car to the shoulder of the narrow mountain road before I lost control and it went off the side. There wasn't much room to pull over, but it was better than a nosedive over the edge.

There was another crack of sound and an explosion of glass followed by a thud. I ducked, the car jerking to a stop, half on, half off the road. Grimacing, I wedged myself as far out of sight as I could, broken safety glass grinding into my skin.

I couldn't see where the shot had come from, or if they were close enough to run at me.

My heart thumping wildly, I fumbled my gun out of the glove box. The weight in my hand wasn't as reassuring as I'd hoped. I could shoot in defense of my life—I wasn't worried about that—but jammed down in the seat, hiding under the dashboard, I couldn't even see who was approaching the car. West or Hawk were supposed to have me covered. I trusted them to do their jobs, but at that moment, the gun wavering in my hand, I realized how much I was trusting men who didn't like me all that much. I forced myself to breathe. It was too late. All I could do now was stay down and try not to get killed.

I guessed that the first shot had taken out a tire, and the second had exploded the rear windshield. It seemed likely that if my head popped up, a third shot would bury itself in my skull. *No thanks.* I stayed down, my eyes flicking from window to window, blind in the darkness.

I caught the sound of footsteps on asphalt. Another shot, although I didn't hear it hit the car, so it must have gone wild. I flinched. I couldn't help it. I hated feeling like a sitting duck, but this was the plan. If he struck, I was supposed to get out of sight as fast as possible and let the professionals deal with him. My ego hated hiding while someone else risked themselves to save my life. I told my ego to shut it. I was qualified to do a lot of things. Taking down an assassin—even a bad one—wasn't one of them.

Tires squealed outside—another vehicle—and shouts echoed. *West*, I thought.

A hard double knock sounded on the passenger door. *Hawk.* The door jerked open, and I stared up at him.

"You good?" Hawk scanned me and nodded to himself before I could answer.

I sat up, flicking the safety on the gun and setting it on the seat. "I'm fine. Did you get him?" I wondered how long it was going to be before my heart rate settled back to normal. I felt like I'd just finished running up a hill.

"We got him. West is slapping the cuffs on right now. You okay?"

"Yeah," I said. "Not sure about the car though."

Hawk shrugged. I was driving an old beater Griffen had lent me—the car that got passed around whenever anyone needed a vehicle. I'd sold my sports car—rather, I'd had Haywood sell my sports car for me—while I was in prison, using the proceeds to pay a chunk of his fees. It made sense at the time. I'd been facing at least a decade behind bars; might as well have gotten the value out of the car. Maybe it was time to replace it.

"Will it start?" Hawk asked, bringing me back to the moment.

"I don't know. Let's see." I turned the key and the car rumbled to life.

"Inch her forward a little bit," Hawk said. "Get it all the way off the road. I'll call the garage to pick it up in the morning."

I nodded, and he stepped back, shutting the passenger door. It only took a minute to ease the car carefully off onto the shoulder. I got out, locked it, and found Hawk standing at the side of the road, hands on his hips, watching West shove my would-be assassin in the back of his cruiser.

I recognized him as the same guy who had shot at us in the parking lot, but I didn't know him otherwise.

"Can I get a ride back to Heartstone?" I asked.

Hawk gave an abrupt nod. "You handled the vehicle well," he said. "For a second, I was worried you'd go off the mountain."

It had been close. Closer than I'd liked. "Me too. I wonder if that was his plan."

Hawk shrugged. "Hard to say. So far, he hasn't overwhelmed me with intelligence or skill." His dark eyes cut to me. "The next one Haywood sends will be better."

"I know," I said.

"We'll get that one, too," he stated with absolute assurance.

I nodded, my throat tight. I wanted to say I could handle it, but I wasn't going to endanger the people around me by being an arrogant ass. This was not my area of expertise. I'd only survived this guy because, as Hawk said, he was a dumbass.

If Cole Haywood managed to find someone who knew what they were doing, I'd be a sitting duck at best.

We rode back to Heartstone in silence.

Griffen met us at the door, his eyes scanning me from head to toe. A grim smile spread across his face as he nodded in satisfaction. "You're okay."

"Yeah," I said.

He looked to Hawk. "And West?"

Hawk's jaw tightened slightly. "Has him."

Griffen raised an eyebrow. "Yeah?"

"He won't be a problem again."

"Good." Griffen looked back to me. "You're off nights at the brewery, but you need to be careful. I don't know how long it'll take Haywood to find another, but—"

"He will," I nodded. "I know." I found myself saying words that turned my gut into a block of ice. "I need to go to the prison. I need to talk to him."

Griffen nodded slowly. "I'll go with you."

I wasn't expecting that. "Yeah. That would—" I didn't have the words.

I felt sick at the idea of walking through those doors again, even as a free man. I didn't want to do it alone. But asking Griffen seemed like too much. He didn't owe me anything. The child in me, the part that had never stopped hero-worshipping his older brother, wanted nothing more than to have Griffen at my side if I had to go back to that place.

"Thanks," was all I could choke out.

Griffen nodded once. "Tomorrow?"

"Yeah. Tomorrow."

"I'll see what I can arrange."

I doubted Griffen would have any trouble getting us in. He hadn't when I'd been locked up—the prison warden happy to acquiesce to the top-dog Sawyer. Once upon a time, that had almost been me. I was familiar with the power at Griffen's fingertips and knew I no longer wanted it. For so many years, I'd been eaten up by jealousy, by envy. Now, I knew I wanted more than tending bar. I didn't know what that looked like, but I did know I didn't want what Griffen had. Not anymore. I just wanted my brother back.

"I'm going to head up," I said, suddenly exhausted.

"I'll let you know tomorrow when we can head out," Griffen said.

I nodded and shifted to face both Griffen and Hawk. "Thanks."

"It's what we're here for," Hawk replied casually.

I shook my head, my gaze moving from Griffen to Hawk. There was no question that Hawk's loyalty belonged to my brother and to my sister Quinn. Hawk had helped me for their sakes and not my own. It didn't matter. I still appreciated it. "I know it's your job, but it's more than that. I know I'm the last person you or West want to help, but you did it anyway. So, thank you."

Griffen's hand closed over my shoulder in a tight squeeze. "I'm glad you're okay." He squeezed again and let go, shoving me gently at the stairs. "Go get some sleep, and we'll figure out tomorrow when we get there."

I nodded, trudging up the stairs and down the hall of the guest wing. The sconces were turned low, the bedroom doors shut. There was no light under Paige's door, and the stab of disappointment was sharper than I'd expected. I wanted to tell her the guy who'd almost hurt her was behind bars. She was safe, for now, and I'd make sure she stayed that way.

I wanted to touch her, strip her to the skin, and watch the light that hit her eyes when I made her come. The way she'd moaned my name—I wanted to watch that over and over, the sounds of her pleasure a balm to my bruised soul. I wanted to lose myself in Paige.

But she was asleep, and I wouldn't be the asshole who woke her up. Instead, I closed my door behind me.

I crossed mental fingers and let out a sigh when steaming water came from the showerhead. I washed off the brewery, scrubbed a towel over my hair, slung it around my waist, and stepped into my room—to find the door closed, the lock turned, and Paige tucked beneath my sheets. Her robe and what looked like a nightgown were draped over the end of the bed, her bare shoulders gleaming in the moonlight.

"I thought you were asleep," I said.

A slow smile spread across her face as her eyes traced my mostly naked body. "I was. And now I'm not. Are you tired?"

"Not that tired," I said. "We got him."

"Really?" The smile widened. "That's good news. Like, arrested and in jail and everything?"

"Exactly like that," I said, closing the distance to the edge of the bed. "I think that calls for a celebration, don't you? We're in the clear. At least, for the next day or two."

"I do," she agreed.

Dropping the towel, I slid between the sheets, desperately grateful that I'd optimistically run an errand that morning and had a fresh box of condoms tucked in my bedside drawer. If I was lucky enough to be naked with Paige McKenna, I wanted to be prepared.

She curled into me, warm and soft, the weight of her breasts pillowed on my chest.

"I've been thinking about this all day," I said, my lips closing over hers.

She answered by sliding a leg over my hip, her fingers sinking into my hair, kissing me back until my head spun, my senses full of Paige—and nothing else.

Chapter Twelve

PAIGE

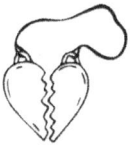

Instinct had driven me across the hall to Ford's room and into his bed. I couldn't shut off the need burning inside me, no matter how many times I tried to talk myself out of it. All those shoulds and shouldn'ts—I was tired of it. That voice in my head reminded me of my mother, overanalyzing, criticizing, breaking me down.

Maybe I shouldn't want Ford Sawyer, but I did. And miracle of miracles, he wanted me back. Maybe it wasn't a good idea, and maybe it was. I wouldn't know unless I took the leap, and I was so fucking tired of telling myself no. I was an adult, a free woman, and he was a free man. I wasn't asking him to marry me or make me any promises, but I wanted him. He wanted me. And what was wrong with that? Not a damn thing.

I hadn't had a plan in mind as I lay in my bed, listening to the clock tick, trying to find sleep, and tossing and turning in the dark. I'd heard his feet on the stairs, the way he paused in the hall before moving to his door instead of mine. After the night before, he had to know he'd be welcome, but perhaps he hadn't wanted to wake me up. Or maybe he was exhausted and would turn me away if I knocked. No way to know unless I took a chance.

I had slid out of my bed before I could talk myself out of it, grabbed my robe, and crept across the hall. I'd tried the antique crystal handle on his door, and it turned easily, swinging open to reveal an empty room, the beat of the shower pounding on the other side of the bathroom door. A smile curved across my mouth as I thought about my next move. And again, before I could talk myself out of it, I tossed my robe and nightgown across the foot of the bed and slid between his sheets. It could have been the most humiliating moment of my life thus far... But I had payback in mind, and as much as nerves fluttered in my belly, I didn't think he'd send me away.

The look on his face when he saw me in his bed told me everything I needed to know. That flare of hungry desire. The slow smile. I was coming to love every one of Ford Sawyer's smiles. As faint and brief as they were, they were real, and I treasured every one. But none as much as this one—not just curving one side of his lips, but stretching all the way across, so real and true I could see his teeth and the light of it in his eyes.

Even once he told me they'd caught the bastard who'd come after him, I could tell the smile was about me.

He reached for me, awe and lust a heady swirl in that sea-green gaze. His kiss was possessive, his hands closing over me, one cupping my chin, the other sliding down my back to rest on the curve of my ass. Strong. It was one of the things about Ford that sent heat spiraling through me every time we touched. His body, his hands, his mouth, his eyes—every part of him. And yet he didn't use that strength in force. He used it to protect, to care, to pleasure. Everything about that turned me on so much; it made my head spin.

I hooked my leg around his hip, my fingers lost in his thick hair, kissing him as if my life depended on it. He shifted, and I sensed he planned to flip me to my back. I had something else in mind. Dragging my mouth from his, I braced my forearms on his chest and pressed up, putting a few inches between us.

"Stay put," I ordered.

His mouth curled in another smile, and his eyes flamed. "For what?" he asked.

"You'll see," I said, grinning back at him as I inched my way down his long body, pressing kisses as I moved—the curve of his pec, his flat, dark nipple tightening under the flick of my tongue. He let out a short gasp, and I slid my mouth down the ridges of his abs, dipping my tongue into his belly button, closing my teeth gently over the side of his hip.

His erection pressed against me, thicker, longer with every touch of my lips to his skin. When my fingers closed around him, he sucked in a breath, exhaling my name. "Paige—fuck, Paige."

I nudged his legs apart and settled between his thighs. Ford lifted up on his elbows, something that looked like alarm in his eyes, shadowed by lust.

"I can't believe I'm going to say this," he said, "but if you do that, I'm going to embarrass myself."

I raised an eyebrow. "You can't embarrass yourself—I'm going to do all the work."

His lips quirked, and he shook his head. His eyes flicked away and then back to mine. That was definitely embarrassment, colored by lust, but still there. "I haven't been with anyone since before prison. Long before."

I dropped my head and licked, tasting the crown of his penis. He smelled of soap, and beneath that, of Ford. He made a choking sound as my mouth closed over him, and I gave a hard suck.

"Paige, I—"

I lifted my head and smirked up at him. "It's been a while for me, too. It's been so long, I'm not sure I know how to do this anymore. I might end up being the one embarrassed."

I dropped my head and gave the length of his erection a long, slow lick. He shuddered, groaning, his head tipping back.

"Feel free to practice on me, then," he rumbled, his words slurring. "Just don't be surprised if it's a short lesson. Because goddamn, you're good at that."

I didn't argue about my proficiency or lack thereof. I didn't have an extensive sexual past. God knew dating had been the last thing on my mind in recent times, but I liked being exactly where I was—with this man trembling beneath me, at my mercy.

I wanted this. I wanted to make him come, to leave him as stunned with bliss as he had me the night before. I had no doubt that he would take good care of me later.

But for now, I parted my lips, sliding them over his length. I couldn't take all of him—he was too big—and I didn't know how to go about trying to deep-throat a penis. Judging by the way his breath shuddered and the groan of my name on his lips, I was doing well enough.

After the first minute or two, I stopped worrying about technique and my lack of experience, because he tasted good. I loved the feel of him, the way he arched and moaned, one hand gripping the duvet and the other tangled in my hair—not pushing or guiding, just holding, staying connected as I worked my mouth over his erection and drew out every gasp.

He was barely touching me, but he didn't need to. Just those fingers tangled in my hair, the feel of him beneath me, the sound of him in my ears was enough. My breasts felt full and tight, my nipples hard, needy peaks. The heat between my legs grew, demanding I slide his cock out of my mouth and climb on top. I couldn't remember the last time I'd wanted a man like this. Maybe never. Maybe just Ford.

His fingers tightened in my hair, giving a sharp tug. "Paige, I can't. I can't—"

I knew what he wanted, but I disagreed. I tightened my grip, his length slippery from my mouth, and stroked and sucked until I drew the orgasm from him. His groan was long and deep. I almost couldn't swallow it all, but I managed. When he relaxed into the bed, I rested my head on his stomach, drawing lines on his hip with a light touch.

I was restless with need, and at the same time, I could have stayed there forever, curled at his side, touching

IVY LAYNE

him, listening to his breathing slow, his fingers threaded through my hair, brushing it from my face. Usually, I thought of oral sex as something I did for my partner. It had never turned me on like this before. I shifted my legs, feeling the slick heat from having him in my mouth. I traced the flare of the head of his cock with my fingertip, watching in fascination as it grew longer, hard once more. He'd never truly gone soft.

I shifted, flicking my eyes up to his.

He propped himself on his elbows and grinned down at me, the light in his sea-green eyes bright in a way I'd never seen before—as if all his worries had lifted for just these moments.

"I told you it had been a while," he said.

"So, this isn't your normal refractory period?" I asked, dipping my head down to press a quick kiss to the tip of his cock.

"Not exactly. But maybe it's you."

He curled up, his abs flexing impressively—the muscle distracting me before I realized what he was up to. Strong hands hooked under my arms, and suddenly I was on my back, my hair spread across the pillow, my body splayed out beneath him. He pushed up on his hands, taking me in—my flushed cheeks, my shoulders, my breasts, nipples still peaked, begging for his mouth.

"You are so fucking gorgeous," he said. "I feel like I'm going to wake up and you'll have been a dream. And it's not this..." He shifted his weight to one elbow, reaching down to cup my breast, running his thumb along my nipple, sending shivers down my spine. "I mean, it's partly this, because your body is beautiful. But it's this..."

He looked up, running a finger across my forehead with the sweetest, lightest touch, down my nose, up my cheekbone, tapping beside my eye. "And this. You have light inside you. You glow with it. When I'm near you, I feel like it spreads across me. You lift the dark."

His lips met mine, and my heart swelled. No one had ever said such things to me. That I was pretty, that I was hot—I'd heard that now and then—but nothing like this. I understood what he meant. Not the glow-inside-me part, but I knew it wasn't that he lifted my dark. It was different than that. My hands reached up, closing over his shoulders, pulling him down, and I kissed him, as I struggled to find the right words.

He didn't chase off my dark; he anchored me. That raw energy running through him, the strength of him, the steadiness. I'd been drifting for so long, but here... Here was an anchor, not holding me down but stabilizing me.

At that thought—possibly one of the least sexy thoughts I'd ever had—I kissed him harder, needing to feel that solid strength. It was so good.

His mouth left mine, trailing over my chin, my jawbone, and the hollow of my collarbone. He found the spot behind my ear that sent every nerve in my body flaring white-hot. I squirmed beneath him, and he chuckled, the sound drenched in lust.

"You like that, Paige?" he asked, dropping another kiss to that sensitive patch of nerves behind my ear.

I squirmed again, raising my knees to clamp on the sides of his hips. The brush of his cock, so close to where I wanted it. "Ford, please. You're killing me."

"I want to tease you," he said, lifting off of me enough

to reach for the drawer in his bedside table. "I could tease you for hours. But not this time."

He pulled out a box of condoms and rose up on his knees, his impressive erection distracting me as he tore off the plastic from around the box and pulled out a foil-wrapped packet.

"Hours?" I asked suddenly, dragging my eyes from his cock and meeting his, my heart speeding up at the look I saw there—hungry, determined, and behind that a spark of glee. My heart pounded harder. "You couldn't tease me for hours. You'd break."

I wasn't sure I wouldn't break either. Being teased by Ford was enticing, but the way I felt right now, I didn't think I could stand another thirty seconds without him inside me.

"Next time we'll find out," he promised, rolling the condom over his cock, pressing my legs farther apart, raising my knees, and baring me to his hot, hungry eyes.

A picture flashed in my head. Me, my arms tied above my head, secured to the bed, while Ford teased and tortured me until I begged him to fuck me. I trembled from head to toe, wanting that desperately. I wasn't sure if I liked being tied up. But if Ford was doing the tying—

The thought flashed out of my head at the hot press of his cock against me. It was a good thing I was so wet—I knew exactly how big he was. A gasp tore from my lungs at the delicious, almost painful stretch of him filling me inch by inch. I squeezed my eyes shut, overwhelmed by the pleasure of it—of him inside me—and then he started to move.

"Oh, Ford. Please, please—" I didn't even know what

I was begging for. Every long, slow thrust ended with a grinding pressure on my clit, sending spikes of bliss through my body. He filled me completely, our bodies moving together in perfect harmony.

I tossed my head from side to side, overwhelmed. It was too much, and I wanted all of it. He rolled, taking me with him, and I rose on my hands, looking down into his eyes, his lids heavy, his eyes bright. He cupped my breasts, thumbs stroking my nipples. I tilted my hips just enough—

One strong hand closed over my hip, holding me in place as he thrust up into me. The orgasm took me by surprise—a fast, hard crash of pleasure. I gasped his name, the world whirling around me.

I was on my back again, Ford looming over me, still inside me, not moving, his gaze absorbing everything in my face.

"You're—you didn't—"

"Not yet," he said, dropping a kiss on my lips, then another and another. Slow, easy kisses as my heart slowed and my breath evened out. My body relaxed, then heated again. When my hips rocked into him, he lifted his mouth from mine, his lips grazing my ear. "One more."

I started to shake my head. I'd never come twice in my life—not like this.

He just gave me one of those half smiles, his eyes glittering. "Definitely one more."

He rolled us again, putting me on top, curling up as he pulled me down until his lips met my nipple. He sucked, and a bolt of pleasure went straight to my clit, my core tightening on his cock.

"Oh God," I said, the words drawn from me with every pull of his mouth. "Oh...oh..."

I couldn't think. My hips rocked on their own, chasing the glory of him filling me, the base of his cock grinding into my clit as he sucked, switching from one breast to the other, his strong hands shaping and kneading me for his mouth.

"I— I—" It was rising so fast. He drew pleasure from every part of my body until it grew to more than I could take. I cried out his name, gasping for air.

We rolled again, Ford still inside me, my knees drawn up and spread wide as he fucked me in short, fast thrusts, drawing out my orgasm until I was blind with it. My fingers closed around his biceps, holding on for dear life. I'd never imagined anything could feel like this—mind-numbing in the best way, everything so good it was beautiful.

When he stiffened against me, my name slipping from between his lips, the joy on his face cracked the shell around my heart. I'd never seen him so unguarded, and all I knew was that I wanted more. We'd agreed this wasn't going to be a relationship. He'd promised me he'd keep it a secret. I wasn't ready for any of that to change.

I was playing a dangerous game, throwing myself into Ford Sawyer's arms when I'd come to his home under false pretenses. I couldn't get lost in Ford and keep this from him. Eventually, I was going to have to tell him the truth. First, I had to figure out how.

In that moment, I only knew one thing. For as long as this lasted, Ford Sawyer was mine, and I wouldn't give him up without a fight.

Chapter Thirteen

FORD

I woke at dawn, alone in my bed, the scent of Paige on my pillows. I'd expected her to run after I told her all the gory details of my past with my family and my father. I hadn't expected the best night of my life with a woman who was turning all my expectations upside down.

I'd said no relationships. I'd meant it at the time. What did I have to offer her? And now, I had even less to offer. We'd caught Cole's assassin, but I had my doubts that I'd improved my situation. Next time, Cole would make a better choice, and I'd be up shit's creek. I had no business getting involved with Paige, even as a casual hookup.

Last night had been anything but casual.

I wanted more. Not just the sex—though I'd take as much of that as I could get—but more of Paige. Falling asleep with her in my arms, her curls soft against my cheek, the rustle of her breath, the steady thud of her heart. I wanted that just as much as I wanted to take her to bed again. None of that was the plan.

I cringed at the idea of telling Griffen I was involved with his nanny. Since I'd been home, it had been made very clear that my brother did not ascribe to my father's attitude toward "the help." He expected excellence, and he treated his staff like the intelligent, competent employees that they were. No fraternization—though that hadn't held with Finn and Savannah.

That had been different. They'd known each other since they were kids, and Savannah was more than capable of telling Finn to go to hell. Comparing our situation to theirs wouldn't buy me any points with Griffen.

But Paige was a grown woman, not a child. From what I'd seen, she was smart and level-headed. She could make her own choices about what she did with her personal time. And I knew what I'd told her was true. If it ever came to a conflict between us, Griffen wouldn't give me a second chance. Not if he thought I was taking advantage of a staff member—especially not if that staff member was his daughter's nanny.

All of that should have had me turning away. Instead, I was distracted, wondering if I'd find Paige in my bed that night or if I'd have to hunt her down. I was glad she'd asked me to keep what was between us a secret. Just a little bit longer to have her all to myself. Everyone outside our secluded end of the guest wing could leave us alone. Here, it was just the two of us. Crappy lighting, dodgy electrical, questionable heat—I'd take it all to be alone with Paige.

I checked my phone. Nothing from Griffen, but it

was too early for him to have gotten in touch with the prison. Just the thought of going back there turned my stomach. I still had nightmares. The heat in the summer. The cold in the winter. The clang of the doors. Once I'd gotten out, it had taken me almost a month to relax enough to take a deep breath. Aside from my bedroom, the library downstairs was one of the only places I was truly comfortable.

I felt more like myself these days than I had in a long time. But picturing the prison in my mind, all the progress I'd made dissolved. My chest went tight, my gut tied itself in a knot. I couldn't breathe.

Fuck. I had to get past it. I had to hold it together if I wanted to get to the bottom of this.

I needed to see Cole, to look him in the eyes for the first time since I'd learned he was the one who had set me up for my father's murder. I needed to know what he had planned next. I had to face him. The only way to do that was to go to the prison. I wouldn't show him my weakness, couldn't let him see how off-balance being back there would make me. I needed to get my shit together.

With nothing but time to kill, I got up, threw on a T-shirt and athletic shorts, and jogged down to the gym. If I had any hope of putting Griffen on his ass the next time we sparred, I needed to get in better shape. I had no illusions that I was going to get into the kind of physical condition Griffen and Hawk maintained. They were both a little scary, as was the rest of Hawk's security team. But once, I'd been fit, strong, and agile. I'd let go of all of that in prison and hadn't reclaimed it since I'd been out. It was time.

Maybe I could get my out-of-shape ass back into the kind of condition I'd need to go trail running again. Heartstone Manor was surrounded by trails, and there'd been a time when I'd loved nothing more than to kill a few hours sweating it out in the cool shade of the forest. For now, I'd make do with the treadmill.

An hour later, my phone chimed. Griffen.

> We're good to go whenever you're ready.

> I'm in the gym. Need a shower. 30 minutes.

He sent back a thumbs-up. The run had burned off some of my tension. I could do this. I could go back there, face Cole Haywood, and find out what I needed to know. I could do it because, unlike Cole, I'd be going home after our conversation.

Griffen met me in the garage, standing at the door with his keys in his hand. He scanned me and gave a nod, though I wasn't sure what the nod was for. Approval at what I was wearing? I'd dressed casually in a dress shirt and pants. No tie, no suit. I didn't want the extra armor. It felt too much like overcompensating. I didn't need a suit to establish the difference between Cole and me. I remembered every moment of wearing that orange uniform. How diminished I'd felt when Cole or my family had come to visit. I wished I had the confidence to roll into the prison wearing jeans and an old T-shirt, but I wasn't there yet. I wasn't sure I ever would be.

Griffen didn't say anything as we got into the SUV,

appearing lost in thought. Silence reigned until the prison sign appeared on the highway.

"You ready for this?" Griffen asked quietly, his eyes flicking to me then back to the road.

My gut reaction was to put up a front. *Sure, yeah, I can handle anything.* I opened my mouth and snapped it shut. That wasn't the way—not if I wanted to fix things with my brother. Putting up fronts was how I'd gotten myself in this mess in the first place. I leaned my head back against the headrest and looked up at the fabric of the ceiling. "Ready to see Cole again, or ready to go back in that prison?" I asked.

"Both," Griffen clarified.

"I'm not ready for either one. I hate how I didn't see what he was. I hate that my blindness let him hurt people I care about. But it's not about Cole so much. It's going back there at all."

Griffen nodded slowly, absorbing my words. "Was it that bad?" Griffen asked.

I shook my head. "That's the thing. It wasn't, and it was. It wasn't like a movie with scary, violent shit happening twenty-four seven. I kept my head down and my mouth shut. Didn't piss anyone off and didn't make any friends, which kept me out of trouble. I'm big enough that people didn't want to fuck with me. Which is a good thing, because as you've learned, I can't fight worth shit— not when it really matters."

"Not yet," Griffen said and grinned at me. "We'll get you there. What was the bad part?"

Flashbacks of shivering alone in my bunk washed over me. "The isolation," I said. "The restriction. I went from having the world at my fingertips to having my fruit cocktail stolen off my tray and knowing I had to let it go if I wanted to hang on to the little bit of peace I could carve out for myself in there. The monotony and the loneliness..." I trailed off, realizing this was the core of what I'd been struggling with. I was lonely, and I didn't know exactly how to get back to a place where I felt normal around my own family. "I know it seems like I've been hiding away since I came back."

I glanced at Griffen and caught a short nod.

"And I have been,'" I said, "but not because I'm avoiding you guys. It's just...the Sawyer clan feels like a lot after going so many months barely speaking to anyone. Just the freedom to sit in the library and read, or make a sandwich if I want one—I can't tell you how overwhelming that was. It was only a year. I don't know how guys who're in a decade or more do it. How do you transition back to the real world? I think it would have broken me if I'd stayed much longer."

Griffen swallowed and gave another nod. "I'm sorry you had to go through that," he said, his voice rough.

I laughed, but it wasn't bitter. "You're the one person who can honestly say I got what I deserved. But you're too good to think it, aren't you?" I shook my head. "You always were the better man between the two of us."

"Fuck off with that," Griffen said with a rough laugh. "I'm not a saint. And yeah, that thought crossed my mind a few times. I still had a chip on my shoulder when I came back here after Dad died. I didn't want anything to do with Sawyers Bend. Fuck the family. Fuck the town.

You all got rid of me—well, now you can get what you deserve."

I looked at him in surprise. When he'd come to the prison to confront me after our father had been killed, he'd seemed settled, ready to fight for his family and his town, his new wife by his side. "Why didn't you just walk away?"

A slow smile spread across my brother's face, a light in his eyes. "Hope," he said. "She wasn't having it. She told me I owed this town and my family more—that I had a chance to fix what went wrong. And if I walked away, I'd be just as selfish as our father had been. And I finally realized you did me a favor. It didn't feel like it at the time, but you did. I got to live a life I never would have had if nothing had changed. I don't know that I'd be the man I am today if I'd spent all those years working side by side with Dad. I don't know how you could do that and not be poisoned by him."

"I didn't," I said, unable to keep the surprise out of my voice. "I drank his poison all on my own. You know what happened with Finn."

"Was that the worst of it?" Griffen asked, sounding more curious than judgmental.

"Yes, but there was plenty that wasn't a whole lot better." The words came more easily than I expected, and I realized I was done hiding my sins. If I wanted to atone, I had to face the choices I'd made.

"After Finn, you changed," Griffen said, considering. "I've heard from Quinn, from Royal, Sterling, and Parker —I know you were trying to fix things. You said you were investigating Dad."

"Yeah." I shifted, rolling my shoulders. "That was all true. But it feels like too little, too late."

"Nah, that's bullshit," Griffen said, flicking on his blinker at the exit off the highway, slowing to take the road toward the prison. "*Too little, too late*—it's just an excuse to not try. You decided to try, and getting caught up in Dad's crap is what ended with you being thrown in prison for a crime you didn't commit. I wouldn't say it was what you deserved. No one deserves to pay for something they didn't do. But you put yourself in a situation, and that situation landed you in prison."

"That's a fair way to put it," I agreed.

"It's just a matter of probabilities," Griffen said. "You played with fire, you got burned. And when I say I'm genuinely sorry that you had to go through that and I'm really glad you're out, I mean it."

I nodded and swallowed hard, fighting back the words that beat against my brain until they spilled off my tongue. "Can you ever forgive me?"

The silence stretched until Griffen said, "I don't think that's really what you want to know."

My chest felt hollow, but he went on.

"Forgiveness is the easy part," he said, glancing at me, his eyes seeing straight through to my soul. "I forgive you. You were a fucking kid, barely out of college. We had a toxic family. Our father was a nightmare. So yeah, I can forgive. I can forgive you for selling me out and getting me exiled and for marrying Vanessa. Jesus, I'm glad it was you and not me. We were both idiots where she was concerned."

"I was thinking with my dick and my jealousy," I

admitted. "She was so beautiful, and she always knew the right thing to say to get under my skin. Looking back, I can't believe I fell for her act so easily."

"You weren't the only one," Griffen said with a laugh. "But what I really think you're asking is if things can ever go back to how they were."

My chest felt like it was caving in as the prison came into sight. The hard-edged shape of it loomed, blocking out the sun, as I waited for Griffen to finish, knowing he was right. Forgiveness wasn't what I really wanted.

I wanted my brother back.

Chapter Fourteen

FORD

Griffen turned into the parking lot and slid into an empty space. Throwing the SUV in park, he turned and looked at me, his green eyes so like mine, searing straight through me. "I don't know if we can go back, but this is a start. All we can do is figure it out from here. So, what's our plan when we go in there?"

The pressure around my heart eased, and I took a breath. He was right. All we could do was figure it out from here.

"I have a couple of things in mind," I said and filled him in.

The process of getting in to see Cole was both amusing and a little stomach-turning. The warden kissed Griffen's ass like he was my father times two, cutting me out of the conversation, giving me the back of his shoulder, and refusing to meet my eyes. Fine with me. He didn't know what to make of a Sawyer who was also a former inmate.

I found that instead of envy at the warden treating

Griffen like the king of the universe, I felt only a faint disgust and sympathy for Griffen, who handled it well, making use of it when he needed to expedite the process of getting to Cole. As someone who knew him, I could see his discomfort with the ass-kissing. It was all part of being the head of the Sawyer family.

I tried not to flinch as the first set of doors opened in front of us, the long concrete walls narrowing in on me. My fingers curled into fists, my heart thumping in my chest until I was a little dizzy with it. Griffen shot me a concerned look and I forced a smile—more for our audience than for him—then unclenched my fingers, drawing in a slow, deep breath. I wasn't here to stay. I just had to get this over with.

Cole waited for us in the room where Griffen had so often come to visit me, sitting at the metal table, hands and feet cuffed, in that familiar orange jumpsuit. Other than the surroundings and what he was wearing, he looked exactly as he had the last time I saw him—as if prison hadn't touched him at all. Only Cole Haywood could manage to look like a model wearing a prison jumpsuit.

"Look, it's the Sawyer brothers come to visit an old friend," he said. "Nice to see you both."

Griffen sat without a word.

"Your assassin got arrested," I said, taking a seat beside my brother, propping an ankle on one knee, and leaning back in the metal chair, trying for casual and unconcerned.

"I heard you were attacked," Cole said. "Something

about a crazed local at the brewery?" He shook his head. "Troubling what the world's come to, isn't it?"

"That's one way to put it," I said. "I'm assuming there'll be more."

Cole raised an eyebrow, amusement glittering in his blue eyes. "You know what they say about assumptions. But in this case," he shrugged a shoulder, "it seems within the realm of possibilities. You made a lot of enemies over the years. Any one of them could want payback."

"The only one who sent a killer after him is you," Griffen reminded him.

Cole had admitted it when he was arrested, to both Avery and West, but clearly his lawyer brain had clicked into gear sometime between now and then.

"It's funny," he said, looking up at the ceiling before his eyes dropped to meet mine. "You'd think arresting that unfortunate gentleman at the brewery would have solved your problem. But from where I'm sitting, it's likely that only cleared the way. Even as we speak, there could be more winging their way to Sawyers Bend." He lifted a hand, cuffs rattling, miming a bird in flight, "And you're out there, trying to pick up the reins of your life. Hard to do when you're always looking over your shoulder."

He was right. I *was* out there trying to pick up the reins of my life, and it was fucking hard to do when I was constantly looking over my shoulder. But he'd confirmed one of the things I'd wanted to know.

This was not over.

It was safe to say whoever was coming next would be better than the guy West had arrested. Not great news, but not a surprise. Which left me with the only other thing I needed from Cole Haywood: any information he could give me about my father's death.

"What do you know about Prentice's murder?" I asked.

"What makes you think I know anything?" Cole countered.

"You and my father, along with Edgar, were all tied up together. I know the three of you were keeping things from me."

Cole shook his head. "Of course we were. You'd gone all Boy Scout, focused on building the business and carving off pieces for your brothers and sisters. I don't know who killed Prentice. You'd have better luck badgering Edgar—or Harvey, maybe—though he's got a little too much Boy Scout in him, like you. He missed out on a lot."

"Harvey claims lawyer/client privilege, and Edgar isn't talking," I said. I knew Griffen and Hope had confronted her uncle. When Edgar clammed up, it was like hitting a brick wall, and any mention of his business with my father was off-limits.

"Well then," Cole said, "you're shit out of luck. The only thing I can tell you—and I will, just because it isn't helpful—is that your father wasn't killed over business."

"But you know why he was killed?" Griffen asked.

Cole drew in a short breath and let it out, and I got the sense he wasn't messing with us. He was telling the truth. He was far more obnoxious when he was lying. "Fair question, because I don't. So, it could have been business. But as Ford said, I was tied up in a lot with

Prentice and Edgar. And nothing we had going would have resulted in his death. In fact, his dying when he did cost us a lot of money. Very inconvenient. And it didn't profit anyone. His death was, all around, a pain in the ass. So, while I guess it's possible that business was involved in his murder, as far as I can tell, it's extremely unlikely that was the motive. Which leads me to think it had to be personal."

"Which brings me," I said, "right back to you."

He sat back and crossed his arms over his chest, flicking his head to toss back his dark hair. "I can see why you'd say that. And to be fair, if I'd shot your father, the last thing I'd do is admit it right here. But I can truthfully tell you I didn't kill Prentice, and I don't know who did. I only know that they were there not long before I showed up. But I never saw anyone." He raised an eyebrow. "If I can offer some advice..."

"Sure, lay it on me." I stood, bracing for his parting shot before we got out of there.

"I'd watch your back, Ford." His gaze slid to Griffen. "Your brother may think you've paid for your crimes, and the state might agree. But that doesn't mean there's balance in your universe. You'll never be free of the past. And anyone around you will be in danger. That includes your pretty little wife and that baby. Those kids running tame in your house. All of you. You keep him close, and you risk what you love."

Griffen stood and shoved his hands in his pockets, his face stone-cold as Cole got to his feet, chains rattling. "He's not alone anymore," Griffen said, turning and dismissing Cole. He looked to me. "Are you done?"

"I'm done," I agreed.

Griffen signaled to the prison guard, and we left.

Cole's eyes burned holes into my back as I walked out of the room, my gut twisted tight, not ready to relax until the outer doors shut behind me. I didn't draw a full breath until I was back in the SUV, sitting beside Griffen. We pulled through the gates and out onto the road.

Griffen's voice vibrated with fury when he spoke. "Don't even think about taking off after that bullshit he laid out."

I let out a slow breath. "I think we need to have a meeting with Hawk and Sinclair Security, because I'm not going to run." I turned to look at Griffen, glad to see his jaw relax at my words. "I'm not walking out on my family," I said. "Not unless all of you agree you're safer without me."

"Not going to happen," Griffen said.

"Then I'm not going anywhere. But we need a plan."

Griffen nodded. "Already working on it."

I hoped whatever his plan was, it was good. It would have to be. Because Cole Haywood had made it very clear he was not finished with me—not even close.

Chapter Fifteen

PAIGE

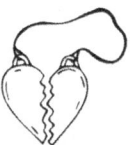

"Are we going to bring both soccer balls?" August asked. His blond brows furrowed in weighty contemplation as he studied the bin in the garage that held athletic equipment.

"I think so," I said, considering the situation just as seriously. August, seven years old and halfway through second grade, had discovered soccer that fall. Now, with the season over for the year, he was determined to practice every day until he was the best player on the team. I hadn't been a soccer player when I was in school, but I knew enough to help out.

I had baby Stella strapped to my chest, still sleepy after Hope had handed her over post-nap and feeding. She snuggled into my chest, a cozy little armful, her knitted cap pulled down over her blonde curls. I'd learned that December in the mountains could be gorgeous, but it could also be cold. Today it was both, the sky electric blue and the air icy as it cut through my scarf. I squatted down to refasten the zipper on August's jacket.

"Why don't you each take one?" I said to August and Nicky. "Nicky can play keeper, and Stella and I will ref from the sidelines while August practices shots on goal."

"I'm the best keeper," Nicky said, grabbing one of the soccer balls out of the bin.

"You're not bad, kiddo," I said, ruffling his dark hair. At six, and in first grade, Nicky didn't have the height to cover ninety percent of the soccer goal Tenn had set up in the side yard, but he had the enthusiasm to make up for his small size. Some days, Thatcher joined us for soccer practice, though today he was down on the lower level with his mom, Scarlett, in her glass workshop while she helped him make an ornament for the winter carnival at school.

The garage door rolled up, startling me. "Back up, boys," I said, reaching out to corral the kids, making sure they were out of the way of the giant SUV rolling in.

The vehicle parked, and the driver's door opened. I caught Griffen saying, "I'll call Hawk. We'll get Cooper on the line. Get to work on a strategy." He shut the door as his gaze swept over the scene in front of him, and a grin broke out across his face. "Getting in some more soccer practice?"

"Yeah," August said, holding the ball above his head.

"Looks good." Griffen closed the distance between us and reached up to run his knuckles across his daughter's soft cheek. "She looks like she just woke up."

"She did," I said fondly. "Hope handed her off a few minutes ago."

The warmth in his eyes as he looked at Stella brought tears to mine. A sheepish smile on his face, he looked at me with a half-shrug. "I want to steal her from you and take her back to the office, but..."

"You and Hope have a call," I said. "I know. She didn't want to hand Stella over either. But if you text when your call is over, I'll bring her back."

"Thanks, Paige," he said with a smile.

"That's what I'm here for."

I snuck a glance across the hood of the SUV to see Ford watching us, pensive. I risked a tiny smile, and a light flashed through his eyes. I looked away, not wanting Griffen to see the flush I felt rising to my cheeks just from looking at Ford. I couldn't help remembering the way I'd left him, a faint smile on his face, the covers pushed down to his waist, his lean, bare chest begging me to touch.

"Let's go, Nicky," August said, breaking the spell.

"I'd better get moving or these two will take off without me," I said, smiling at Griffen and flashing a last look at Ford, wishing I could say something—anything. But as far as Griffen knew, Ford and I had never spoken to each other. Why would we? Anything other than a polite nod would draw attention I didn't want. I forced my attention back to Griffen. "Just give a shout when you guys are done. I'll bring her back."

I resisted the urge to look at Ford again. He drew my gaze, my body, my attention like a magnet. For just a moment, I regretted saying that this thing between us had to be a secret. I let out a sigh as I followed the boys across the lawn to the area designated for soccer.

I was deluding myself into thinking that it would be as simple as telling everyone Ford and I were together. First of all, I didn't know that we were. We'd had sex.

Amazing sex. I wanted to have a lot more of it. But it wasn't only sex—not for me, and I was reasonably certain not for him either. But what did that even mean?

Was I ready to risk my job for a relationship this new? That would be idiotic. And on top of that, I'd come here for a reason—to find my father. I'd had zero success on that front, but if I got myself fired, I'd give up the only lead I had. I supposed I could hire a private investigator. But why blow my savings when I could hang around here, maybe find out what had happened to him, and get paid for a job I loved while I was at it?

I shook my head. *Such a weak excuse, Paige.* I was full of excuses lately.

Focus, Paige, I told myself.

August took a shot. Nicky leapt to block it, and both boys looked at me for a response.

"Nice shot, August," I said. "I didn't know you could jump that high, Nicky. Try it again."

I wasn't here to moon over my boss's brother.

I pulled my phone out of my pocket. I had the whole family in my contacts, though I rarely texted most of them. I pulled up Ford's number.

> My room after dinner?

I hit send before I could think twice and stuffed my phone back in my pocket.

I was here to watch the kids. And not just watch them, but engage, teach, and guide. I couldn't do that if I had my face in my phone and my mind on Ford. Dinner wasn't that far away—I'd survive.

The hours dragged. I dropped Stella off with Griffen and Hope for a while, then picked her back up when they both had other calls. Normally, I loved being with the kids, but I was distracted.

Stella was fussy after dinner, her teething pain back with a vengeance. I couldn't keep up with the way it ebbed and flowed. One day, she was screaming bloody murder, and the next, she was her normal peaceful self. We were all looking forward to the rest of her teeth coming in. Her pained cries were so hard to hear.

I finally made it upstairs, well after the family had finished eating. As I rounded the corner from the main stairs and entered the guest wing, a chill sent goose bumps over my skin. I shouldn't be surprised that the heat in the guest wing was struggling, considering how cold it had been all day. Along with the dodgy electricity and the questionable plumbing, the heat worked when it decided to. We had electric blankets for when it didn't, though they didn't do much good if the electricity also went out. The heat had been fairly reliable over the last few weeks, but maybe the cold temperatures outside had taxed the aging system too hard. I shivered, then thought of Ford. Under the covers, we'd keep each other warm.

I reached the end of the hall. His door was closed—no light showing beneath—but mine was cracked a few inches, the glow of the light spilling out. I pushed open the door, a welcoming smile on my face. "Hey, sorry I took so—" I cut off as he turned.

My heart fell as my eyes met his, the sea-green ice-cold, his face without expression. In his hand was the picture of Sarah Sawyer I'd found with the letters in my father's trunk.

I closed the door behind me.

"What are you doing with a picture of my mother, Paige?" he asked, his voice like stone.

"Where did you find that?" I asked. It was a stupid question. I knew exactly where he'd found it. My bedside drawer was open. "Why were you going through my things?"

I crossed the room, ignoring him, to look in the drawer. A strip of condoms sat on top of the manila envelope that held the letters and the picture of Sarah. I recognized the brand from Ford's room the night before and instantly understood. My heart twisted. He was being responsible, doing the right thing, and I'd been an idiot not to hide the evidence better. But I hadn't thought about anyone going through my drawers. I should have, but I'd been here for months and no one had—until now.

"Paige. Answer me," he demanded, his voice as cold as the air in the room, sending a chill all the way to my bones.

I pulled the envelope out of the drawer. "Is that all you saw? The picture of Sarah?"

His eyes focused on the envelope in my hand. "What else is there?"

"I…" I couldn't think of how to explain. "Sarah Sawyer's your mother?" I asked, though I knew the answer already.

He glared. "You know she is. Why do you have her picture? *I* don't even have her picture."

That sidetracked me. "Why not?" Stupid question, I

realized. I didn't have a picture of my father beyond what I'd found in the trunk.

"My father took them all," he said.

I nodded, my eyes locked on the black-and-white photograph in his hand. "I didn't have any pictures of my dad either," I said. "Not until I found the trunk that picture was in."

I looked at the envelope in my hand, then at Ford standing there with his mother's picture, so angry because I'd lied, and the guilt hit me. He'd been through so much. I wanted to yell at him for invading my privacy, for confronting me, for being angry. But where did I get off being pissed that he'd caught me? Yeah, he went in my drawer, but— I glanced back down at the open drawer. He hadn't been invading my privacy. No—that was me, investigating his family while I was working for them. It hadn't seemed like that much of a betrayal until now.

I sank down to sit on the side of my bed, looking at the envelope in my hands. I'd done enough damage with lies. For this, I needed the truth.

"When I was cleaning out my mother's house after she died, I found a whole trunk of my father's things. I never knew him. He took off before I was born. My mother always said there was another woman, that he left us for her, and he never came back to contradict her story. I didn't know anything. Going through the trunk, I learned he'd been in the army. And I learned that he'd been involved with a woman named Sarah who loved him. She wrote letters." I held the envelope out to Ford.

He took a step in my direction, only close enough to lean forward and snatch the manila envelope from my hands. When he looked at me, I felt ice skate down my spine, and a grief I hadn't expected wrapped my heart. We'd slept together once—this wasn't a great love affair— but the distance between us, the idea that this was over, left me gutted. I wanted to be in bed with Ford, under the covers, wrapped up in each other. I wanted to see him smile. And I'd fucked all that up.

He reached into the envelope and pulled out a letter.

As he scanned it, I said, "I looked up her name, realized she was a Sawyer. I wasn't going to do anything about it, but then my former nanny family had a connection to Hope. They knew she and Griffen were looking for someone, and I was between jobs, ready to move on— it seemed like fate. I needed a job, a change, and I wanted to find my father. So, I came here."

"And lied to everyone about who you are." Ford's eyes were fixed on the letter in his hand, but the fury in his tone sent a shiver through me.

"I didn't lie. I just didn't tell the whole truth. I passed the background checks because I am who I say I am."

"Who is your father?" he demanded.

"Paul Williams," I said, the name still unfamiliar. How had I not even known his real name until I found that trunk? And why had I risked so much to find a man who'd never bothered to meet me? If only I could go back — I hadn't known how much I would have to lose. I hadn't seen Ford Sawyer coming, and now it was over.

I could almost feel my heart cracking.

"Paul Williams," Ford said slowly, lifting his gaze to stare at the ceiling. "The name doesn't mean anything to me."

I forced myself to stay in the moment, to listen to him. "I'm not surprised. I haven't done much investigating, but no one seems to recognize his name or know what happened to Sarah—to your mother."

"My mother ran off with some guy and left us. I'm assuming the guy is your father."

"That's my guess," I said.

"And what did you want out of all of this? Some kind of compensation?"

"No. *No.*" I shot off the bed to pace the room, wrapping my arms around myself, rubbing my hands up and down my biceps to warm up. Could I see my breath? It was so cold. Everything was cold: the room, Ford, my frozen heart. I hated this. "No, I don't. I don't want anything except to know where he is, where they went, and why he never came back. Did you ever hear from her again?"

"No," Ford said shortly. "Postcards once a year to me and Griffen, but those ended a while ago." Ford slipped the letter back into the envelope, followed by the picture of his mother. "He never called? Sent you a birthday present?"

"No," I said. "Not that I—" I stopped, tucking my fingertips into my armpits, watching my breath bloom in icy clouds. God, it was fucking cold in here. "I don't know," I realized, speaking aloud. "My mother..."

I shook my head, trying to drive off the memory of her talking about my father. It didn't happen often, but the venom, the bitterness, tainted every memory of those conversations.

"She hated him," I said softly. "And I think she hated

me. She said I looked like him, acted like him. She never forgave him for leaving. She said she never heard from him again, but..." I gave a helpless shrug, wrapping my arms tighter around myself, too cold to let my body heat escape.

"I can't believe the heat is out again," Ford muttered.

I shook my head. I had bigger problems than frozen toes and fingers. "But maybe he did," I whispered. "I wouldn't have put it past her to lie about it. Maybe he sent me postcards." Hearing the wistfulness in my own voice, I sighed heavily. "This whole thing is stupid. It's a stupid wild goose chase. Nobody here knows anything about Sarah or my father."

"I'm taking these," Ford said abruptly, turning for the door.

"You can't!" I said sharply, moving toward him. "Those are mine. They were my father's! You can't—"

Chapter Sixteen

PAIGE

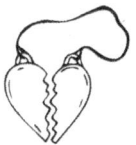

I cut off as Ford yanked on the handle of my door. He rattled the knob back and forth, twisting and pulling. He was strong—I knew firsthand how strong—but the door didn't budge. The knob turned under his hand, but it was as if a deadbolt had been flipped, though there was none.

"What the fuck?" Ford muttered. He pounded at the door, the sound echoing back at us, oddly muffled.

"What's wrong?" I asked, not getting it. "Is it stuck?"

"I don't know," he said. "There's no give."

I plucked the manila envelope from his hand and set it on the table by the door. Wrapping my fingers around the icy crystal knob, I turned and pulled. The knob turned easily, the latch clicking as it pulled back, but the door didn't budge. I yanked harder. Nothing.

"It's kind of a problem, because it's fucking cold in here," Ford said, frustration tightening his voice. "Really cold."

"The heat must be out," I said, pulling again at the door.

"Clearly," he said, "but I can see my breath in here, Paige." He turned to look out the window into the dark night beyond. "It's cold outside—as cold as it's been all year—but Heartstone is built too well for it to be as cold inside as it is out there."

He had a point, but still... "It's windy," I said. "Maybe—"

Ford shook his head, dismissing that explanation, and pulled his phone out of his pocket. "What the fuck?" he said sharply, scowling down at the screen.

Rather than asking to see his phone, I pulled out my own and saw SOS where there should have been at least two bars. We never had SOS in the house. I pulled up the Wi-Fi and tried to connect. I could see the network, but I couldn't get on it.

"Fuck," Ford muttered, staring out the window. "It's too soon, and he couldn't have gotten anyone in the Manor."

"What are you talking about?" I lifted my fist to pound on the door. As when Ford had hit it, the sound was oddly muffled.

"Haywood," Ford said, now looking at his phone. He held down a button on the side as the screen went black. "He as good as admitted there'd be more coming after me, but he couldn't have found someone new so fast, and he'd never get anyone in the Manor."

That distracted me from the door. I'd picked up enough of what was going on that I wasn't surprised Cole Haywood would send another killer after Ford. But someone who could get into Heartstone? "No one is getting past Hawk and his team," I said, pounding on the door again. "It's just really cold and the heat is out."

Ford looked down at his phone; the screen lit again. "Fuck. Still *SOS*." He shoved his phone in his back pocket. "This is more than the heat being out, Paige."

I shook my head. What more could it be? "It's been really cold all day. Maybe the heat went out earlier and the room chilled, but you were distracted when you came in, so you didn't notice."

I hadn't picked up on it at first, more focused on Ford and the picture in his hand than the icy temperature in my room. I trembled violently with cold. Crossing to grab the throw blanket at the end of my bed, I wrapped it around myself. It didn't help much, considering the blanket felt as cold as the air in the room.

"I'm going to see if turning my phone off and back on again makes a difference," I muttered, sitting on the edge of my bed and doing just that. Ford didn't bother to point out that he'd just done the same to no effect. I watched him pound helplessly on the door, the strange, muted beats echoing back at me. My brain refused to accept what was happening—the plunging temperature, the SOS on my phone, the stuck door. I rebooted the phone. Still no signal. *How?*

"Can we go out the window?" I asked, dropping my phone on the bed and crossing the room to the window. I leaned over a console table to wrench it open. It didn't budge a millimeter. It was as if it had been nailed shut from the outside.

"Does it usually open?" Ford asked.

"I don't know," I admitted. "I haven't tried."

"I don't think we're getting out of here for the moment," he said grimly.

"Well, that sucks." I pulled the blanket tighter around myself. "I'm going to freeze to death in my own bedroom."

Ford picked the manila envelope up off the table by the door and sank back into the armchair in the sitting area. He leaned forward, bracing his forearms on his knees, turning the envelope over and over in his hands.

"It seems pretty hypocritical," he said quietly, his eyes on the envelope, "to be so angry at you for lying after all the things I've done."

I sat on the edge of my bed, kicked off my shoes, pulled my feet up, and curled into as tight a ball as I could to conserve body heat, fighting the shivers running through me. "I don't know every mistake you've made, Ford, but you didn't do anything bad to me," I said softly, my voice trembling. "And I lied to you. Maybe not overtly, but I was still misleading you. I came here because of your mother."

"You should have told us," he said.

"I know," I whispered. "I didn't think it would matter. I didn't think there'd be you. Or that I'd love your family so much. I was angry and grieving, and I thought I saw a chance to find my father, so I took it. And the funny thing is, you're angry and I'm going to get fired, but I—" I shrugged under the blanket, unable to look at him. "I never even really looked for him. I asked around a little. It didn't take long to learn that no one likes to talk about

Sarah and...I've been happy here. It didn't seem as important. And now I wish I'd..."

I shook my head, looking at the carpet, my vision blurring as tears rose in my eyes.

"Now I wish I'd left it all alone. Taken the job because Janice Smith recommended me, and just let it all go." I forced myself to meet his eyes, unable to read anything in those cool green depths. "I'm sorry I wasn't honest."

"What makes you think you're going to get fired?" Ford said without accepting my apology.

"Oh, come on," I said, pulling the blanket tighter around me. "Griffen and Hawk are so tight on security, background checks. When they find out I misled them about who I was—that I took the position, in part, to use your family history to find my father? You know he's going to fire me." My throat tightened, words choking inside. I raised a hand to brush a tear off my cheek. "It's fair. But I like being here. And I—" My voice caught again, and I choked the words out. "I like being with you, and I'm sorry I ruined everything." I lowered my eyes. "And I'm even sorrier that I did it to find someone who never cared about me in the first place."

It was the hard truth, one I hadn't admitted to myself. But my father hadn't cared about me. If he had, he would have come back. I wasn't even sure what I had hoped to find out about him, now that the truth had come out. Did I want him to apologize? To love me? He'd made it clear he didn't by staying away.

"Why did you need to find him so much?" Ford asked quietly.

I considered my words. I wanted to tell him the truth, even if it hurt. "I wanted to know where I come from, other than her. She hated me so much. I could never do anything right. It was always, 'You're just like him,' 'you're a loser,' and 'you're stupid and selfish,' and whatever insult fit the moment. Everything bad about me was because of him. When I was a kid, I believed he must be a monster for her to hate him so much. And then I got older and saw that the hateful one was her. And I started to wonder—was he that bad? Or had he just escaped?" I swallowed hard. "But he didn't take me with him. If he escaped, he left me there—with her. And I have to believe he knew what he was leaving me with. He knew, and he left anyway. And then I found that trunk, and she was gone, and I thought... Maybe I came from something better than her. If I could find him, I could understand why he left. I didn't know your mom left you, too."

"I wondered the same thing when I was a kid," he said quietly, eyes fixed on his joined hands. "How she could have left us with him. Miss Martha loved her so much, and I didn't get how someone that lovable could have abandoned her children. But then I grew up with my father, and I understood what she might have done to escape. He never mentioned her—not like your mother did with your father. He took down all the pictures, removed every memory of her, and married MaryAnne a year later. It was like our mother never existed. She was just gone." He paused, turning the envelope over in his hands again before holding it out to me. "I'll give this back, but I want to read the letters. I don't have anything like this of hers."

I nodded, tears spilling over my cheeks, my heart twisting in my chest as I thought of what I would give for an envelope full of letters written in my father's hand.

"He must have written her back," I said. "But she probably destroyed them. Especially if they were hiding their affair."

"I've been going through boxes of papers in the attic," Ford said, "and I haven't seen any letters."

I nodded, not expecting there to be any. I rose off the bed slowly, crossing to the door. Only hours ago, I'd been so full of hope. I'd realized I'd been looking forward to finding Ford in my room after dinner, pulling off his clothes, drawing him under the covers. And now? Everything had fallen apart.

I turned the handle on the door and yanked. Nothing. No give, as if the door had fused to the frame. I laid my palm against it and pulled my hand back sharply at the icy burn—far too cold and wet. I stared. Frost. Crystalline blooms of frost across the white wood.

"What the fuck?" I whispered.

The chair in the corner creaked, and then Ford was beside me, running a finger down the door. "This isn't just the heat being out, Paige. Someone locked us in here." He shook his head, clearly bewildered. "The cold doesn't make any sense. I don't know how, but this is..." Gently nudging me aside, he yanked at the door again. Still nothing. "I think we should try yelling."

"I don't think anyone can hear us," I said.

He eyed the door, pounding it with the side of his fist over and over. Between strikes, he shouted, "Help! Help! Is anyone out there?"

But there was no response. Tenn and Scarlett lived in this wing of the house, along with August, and Thatcher. So did Ford's Aunt Ophelia, though she was out of town, but someone should have caught Ford's pounding on the door. Heartstone Manor was big, but it wasn't that big.

I turned to look around my room, searching for anything that would break the door down. It wasn't like I kept a fireman's axe in my closet, and these doors were solid wood. I didn't have a screwdriver to go for the hinges. We were stuck until whoever was holding us here decided to let us go.

"I don't think we can get that door open," I said. "And I don't understand why, but I don't think anyone can hear us."

Ford dropped his hands to his sides. "You're right." He eyed the door and then looked back at his phone.

"Still nothing?" I asked.

"Nothing. *SOS*, no Wi-Fi. I don't think this is someone locking us in, Paige. I think this is something... else."

I didn't want to acknowledge the possibility of *else*. It freaked me out. "What are we going to do?" I asked, watching more frost bloom over the door.

"You're shaking," he said, reaching out to lay a cold palm against my cheek.

He turned toward the bathroom, reaching for the taps, and shut them off within a minute.

"No hot water. It was worth a try." He crossed back to me. "Clothes off, and get under the covers."

"Clothes off?" I asked. The prospect of getting naked with Ford normally would have sent heat spiraling through me, but at that moment, in the icy air of my bedroom, watching frost grow on the door, I shook my head vigorously. "No way. Too cold."

"Body heat," he said. "Give me the blanket."

He took the blanket from around my shoulders and spread it across my bed, grabbing a throw from the back of the armchair and spreading that on top.

"Come on. In the bed." He reached for the hem of his sweater and pulled it over his head, baring his chest. "It's too cold to argue about this."

"Fine," I agreed, knowing next to nothing about surviving in frigid temperatures. I wasn't sure Ford knew anything either, but if I was going to freeze to death, I'd rather do it tangled up with Ford than standing here arguing. The second my shirt was over my head, my body shuddered from the frigid cold. The rest of my clothes came off faster, and I dove under the covers, Ford following, wrapping his long, icy limbs around me.

I shook as his hands moved up and down my arms, the friction generating the tiniest spark of heat.

"I'm pissed off that you lied," he said, his voice soft, without a hint of anger.

"I know," I choked out. "I'm sorry."

"I don't want your apologies, Paige," he said.

Warmth seeped from his body to mine, and I trembled harder. "I can't stop shivering. It's so cold."

"I know, I've got you." His arms tightened around me. "I'm angry that you lied, but I think I understand."

"I didn't want to hurt you. I wasn't—by the time I realized I would, I didn't know how to tell you. It didn't seem like there was anything to find out anyway, so I just thought I could let it go."

I turned in his arms, hooking a leg over his hip to stay as close as I could, the connection of our bodies creating a bubble of warmth under the covers. My face was ice-cold, but the rest of me was starting to feel a little more human. His erection pressed against the heat between my legs. Some parts of me were feeling a lot more human.

"I'm sorry," I said, looking up, pressing my palm to the side of his face, loving the scruff, the thawing in his cool green eyes as he looked back at me. "I didn't know you before. And now that I do, the last thing I'd ever want is to hurt you. I wish more than anything I hadn't lied."

The side of his mouth quirked, sending heat through my heart. "If you'd told the truth, I doubt we'd be right here. I have to think about that too. But for now..." His fingers speared through my hair, cupping the back of my head, pulling me closer until his cold lips met mine.

And I was suddenly so grateful for however we'd gotten locked in my frozen room. Maybe the end goal was to freeze us to death. Maybe this was another attempt on Ford's life, though I couldn't figure out how anyone could have arranged to jam the door and turn the room into an icebox. Still, crazier things had happened to the Sawyer family in the last few years.

I'd probably be booted out on my ass if I didn't freeze to death overnight. And in that case, I was going to make the most of the time I had left. I reached up, wrapping my arms around Ford, rolling to pull him on top of me. He settled between my thighs.

"Not cold here," Ford murmured, sliding a finger in the slick heat between my legs, dipping inside.

"Not there," I agreed.

With his chest pressed against me, skin to skin, the cold was easing away, chased out of our nest under the covers. He shifted, letting in a wisp of frozen air as he slid open the bedside table. I wasn't sure I was glad he'd found the envelope in my drawer, but I was definitely happy he'd thought to bring over the strip of condoms. A giggle escaped me.

"What?" he asked, tearing open the package.

"You brought a whole strip. So maybe we won't freeze to death."

"We're not going to freeze to death," he muttered, rolling the condom down the length of his erection under the covers and settling between my legs. "Not if I have to fuck you all night to keep us both alive."

"I'm so glad you're willing to sacrifice yourself like that," I said through another giggle.

"That's the kind of guy I am," he said, pressing inside me, sending a different kind of shudder up my spine.

I pulled his face to mine, wrapped my legs around his hips, and rocked up, taking him deeper, wanting to absorb him. If this was all I'd have of him, I was going to make the most of it.

Chapter Seventeen

FORD

The ice in the air was gone, and pale yellow morning light filled Paige's room, carrying threads of warmth. I hadn't tried it yet, but I knew if I got up and turned the handle of her door, it would open easily.

I didn't have an explanation for what had happened the night before. I stroked a hand down Paige's dark curls, her breath warm puffs of air on my neck. Lying here, with her body soft against mine, I had everything I wanted. A weird thought, considering that objectively it wasn't true.

I was still working on fixing my fractured relationships with my siblings. I was unemployed, with no clear idea of what I wanted to do with myself. I likely had at least one killer after me, if not more. And despite the fact that my name had been legally cleared, half the people in town still thought I'd shot my father. And yet, lying in Paige's bed, her sleeping in my arms, I had everything I wanted.

Fuck, I hadn't seen this coming.

I didn't know what had driven me to open that envelope in her bedside table. I'd only opened the drawer to drop the condoms in for later. But something about the envelope... I knew it was wrong when I pulled it out, but I looked anyway. When the picture of my mother fell out, the sight of her had been a stab through the heart.

I'd never seen that particular photograph of Sarah Sawyer—Sarah Fordham at the time—but I knew that face, those eyes. She'd left us before I was old enough to form a solid memory of her. I knew Griffen had a few things tucked away: an earring, a book she used to read to him. I had nothing. I'd only been two years old when she left.

Seeing that picture, knowing that Paige wasn't who she'd said she was, had sent fury coursing through me. And then my rage had fallen apart.

I didn't know many people as alone as Paige McKenna—abandoned by her father, hated by her mother. She'd spent her adult life on the fringes of other people's families without one of her own. I'd found myself in the odd position of being absolutely, morally right and not caring in the slightest.

She'd come to our home under false pretenses. Except she *was* Paige McKenna. She was a professional nanny with a degree in early childhood education. She'd omitted information, but she hadn't straight-out lied. Still...semantics. She'd been dishonest. But as I'd said to her last night, who was I to condemn her? I'd done far worse—and the things I'd done, I'd done out of greed and weakness and envy. She was looking for her father. Not the same at all.

I shifted my head on the pillow, rubbing my stubbled cheek against the silk of her curls. What I wanted was this—Paige in my arms. I wanted her close. I wanted to protect her. And I had no interest in punishing her for anything she'd done.

Which left me with a problem to figure out: how to explain all of this to Griffen. There was no way we were keeping this—our relationship, Paige's goal in finding out what she could about her father—a secret. I couldn't rebuild my family's trust by lying to them. I'd sworn I wouldn't leave, and I'd meant it. But as much as I needed to be here to mend my relationship with my siblings, I wasn't letting Paige go. If Griffen couldn't see reason and actually kicked her out, I'd go with her. If she'd have me.

She might be safer without you around. Maybe. If Cole ever figured out what she was to me, he'd go straight for her. I was going to have to gamble on Griffen's compassion. Fortunately, I knew my brother had an over-abundance of that emotion. We were going to need it.

And then there was the issue of what had happened in this room—the plummeting temperatures, the jammed door, the way we'd shouted, and the sound had seemed to bounce back into the room without penetrating the hall-way. At first, I'd thought the newest assassin had found me. But just as quickly, I'd realized that didn't make any sense. I didn't believe anyone could get inside the Manor undetected, much less set up an elaborate booby trap that could have killed us both. It had to be something else.

Paige's phone lit up, a lively tune tumbling out. She woke early since a big part of her job was helping with the kids' morning routine before she took over with

Stella. Her eyes fluttered open, landing hesitantly on my face.

I reached up to stroke the backs of my fingers down her cheek. "Morning," I said.

"Morning," she said back. "It's warmer in here now."

"I know. I doubt we're locked in anymore." I rolled to my side and tugged a loose curl of her hair.

"What happened?" she asked, moving to sit up, taking the blankets with her.

"I don't know," I said, and nodded at her phone. "You have to get up."

She let out a low groan. "Mornings are always a little crazy."

"We need to talk to Griffen," I said softly.

She gave a jerk of a nod and swallowed.

"Hey." I sat up, leaning against the headboard and sliding my arms around her to pull her into my side. "You're not going to get fired."

"Ford," she said quietly, "I would fire me."

"Yeah, well, Griffen's nicer than you," I said, knowing it wasn't true. Paige was steeped in kindness. "Don't worry about it, okay? Just put a pin in it until we talk to him. I really don't think he's going to fire you. We just need to explain."

"We?" she echoed.

"We," I repeated. "He might know something about our mother and your father. Do you trust me?" I asked, feeling like I'd never asked a question that important before.

She gave another jerk of a nod. "I trust you," she said. "I just..."

"Look, if the worst happens, we'll deal with it together."

"I'm sorry, Ford," she said, her pale blue eyes on mine.

"For what?" I asked.

"For lying."

"Are you sorry about this?" I raised my eyebrows as I tightened my arm around her shoulders.

Pink hit her cheeks, and she shook her head. "No. Maybe I should be, but I'm not. This is..." She reached up and brushed her lips across my jawbone. "This has been perfect."

"Not 'has been,'" I said, pressing a fingertip to her bottom lip. "*Is*. It is perfect. And everything's going to be okay. Just trust me."

She stared into my eyes for a beat and then let out a breath. "I do. I will."

"Then let's go see if the hot water is working," I said, sliding out of bed.

A slow smile spread across her face.

I turned on the taps in the bathroom and steam floated up almost immediately. I followed her into the shower, wishing we had time for more than just getting clean. Her skin was soft and slick under my hands as I ran them over her body. "Later," I whispered in her ear, my erection bumping her stomach as we shifted in the tight space.

"Later," she agreed. Then she dropped a hand to wrap soapy fingers around my cock, stroking until my knees went weak.

I was tempted to forget the time, but I'd left the

condoms in the other room. My promises about her not being fired wouldn't be any good if I made her late to work.

* * *

I timed my entrance to breakfast just late enough that no one would have any idea we'd seen each other that morning, but early enough that I got to lay eyes on her once more. Sometimes the kids ate in the kitchen, but more often lately, they came to the main dining room where Finn laid out a breakfast buffet in heated chafing dishes. I grabbed a Belgian waffle and a scoop of scrambled eggs. Going from prison food to Finn's cooking was the best kind of whiplash.

I took my seat at the table, pretending my attention was on my phone as I ate, though I snuck glances at Paige helping Nicky cut his waffles and pouring a refill of juice for August.

Hope came in carrying Stella. "She's going to be a handful today," she said, setting her daughter into the high chair, barely flinching as Stella let out a wail.

"Bad night?" Paige asked.

"No, maybe the opposite." Hope let out a laugh. "She slept all night. When I got her out of her crib this morning, her little legs were beating the air. I put her down, and she zoomed all over the room."

Paige grinned. "You always think you want them to walk—that first step is so important—and then you realize they were a lot easier when all they could do was roll."

"So true," Hope said, smiling wearily.

FORBIDDEN HEART

"Do you want me to take her with me when I drop the boys off at school?" Paige asked, smiling warmly at Stella who was shoving fruit in her mouth as fast as she could, smearing strawberry juice across her round cheeks.

Griffen and Hope exchanged a look. "Actually," Griffen said, "we're going to have Hawk's team do drop-offs and pickups at school for now."

Paige's eyes widened. "Because of—?" She cut off and shot a glance in my direction.

"Yes," Griffen said, catching her meaning. "I think the kids are safe at school—though we may assign someone there temporarily until this is resolved—but the drive between..." He shook his head. "We're working on getting more manpower. For now, I need everyone to stick close to the house until we've come up with a solid plan."

Paige nodded, and I couldn't help my flash of relief. I knew most of my siblings were sick and tired of the need for extra security. I pushed down the flare of guilt. Griffen had made it abundantly clear we were in this together, and I was going to do my best to listen to him.

"What does your morning look like?" I asked Griffen and Hope.

"Somewhat flexible," Hope said. "Why?"

I looked to Paige and gave a short nod.

"I need to talk to you," Paige said.

"Oh God, please tell me you're not quitting," Hope said, her hazel eyes flying wide with alarm.

Paige swallowed. "No, I'm not quitting."

Only I heard the unspoken addition: *But when we're done, you may throw me out.*

"Why don't you come to our office after the kids leave for school?" Griffen suggested.

"That would be good." Paige's eyes flicked to me, then back to Griffen. "I'll be there by eight," she said.

Stella let out another ear-piercing shriek, breaking the tension. August and Nicky watched with rapt attention as she dove her little fingers into the mound of eggs Hope had put on her tray and shoveled them into her mouth.

"She eats like a pig," August said with a giggle.

Nicky let out a little snort.

Hope grinned down at her daughter, pulling her hair back off her face and fastening it with a small band so she didn't shovel the strands in her mouth along with the eggs. "My girl doesn't like being hungry," she said with a proud smile.

"She really doesn't." Griffen beamed at his daughter.

A few minutes later, Paige rose, taking both younger boys with her. She sent a look to Thatcher a few seats down—silent as he shoveled food into his mouth and scrolled on his phone. "You about ready to go?" she asked.

Thatcher grunted in response.

"Garage in ten minutes."

Another grunt.

Good to know teenagers hadn't changed much since my time. I tried not to watch her leave the room. Griffen and Hope would know what was going on soon enough, but I'd rather wait to talk about it until we didn't have an audience.

Chapter Eighteen

PAIGE

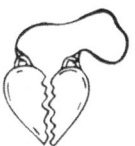

Ford was waiting in the hall as I came down the stairs at three minutes to eight, the manila envelope in my hand, my heart thudding in my chest until I was light-headed. I knew I needed to tell Griffen and Hope the truth. I wanted to come clean, but I was terrified of the consequences.

"Don't worry," Ford said.

"I can't help it," I said. "I don't want to have to leave."

"You're not going to. I promise."

"You can't promise me that," I said, following him down the hall to the office. I wasn't sure if having Ford by my side would help or hurt my case, but I was grateful he was there.

After a quick knock on the door and Griffen's answering, "Come in," I pushed it open. Hope was staring down at her phone, but Griffen's eyes widened a fraction as he saw Ford behind me. It occurred to me that if Ford hadn't found that picture of his mother, we might be having this conversation with Griffen about *us*.

I was done trying to fool myself into thinking this was casual. Every time he touched me, I only wanted him more. That wasn't changing. We would have ended up here eventually. And I would have been less nervous.

Griffen looked at the envelope in my hand. "Take a seat," he said, his tone all business. Hope looked up at his words and took in Ford and me standing together. I couldn't tell what she was thinking.

Stiffly, I sat, knees and ankles together, spine straight, the envelope clutched so hard in my fingers my knuckles were turning white.

Ford sat in the chair beside me. "Hey," he said quietly, "it's okay. Give me that." He slid the envelope from my fingers, wrapping his hand around mine.

"Why don't you tell us what this is about," Hope said gently.

"I—" I swallowed hard. "I'm not who you think I am."

Ford squeezed my fingers in his in comfort. This was between me, Griffen, and Hope. If they were angry —as they had every right to be—Ford wouldn't be able to help, but I loved that he wanted to. It meant everything.

"I mean," I clarified, "I am Paige McKenna. Everything I told you when you hired me, everything Hawk and his team looked into, is all true. But there's more that I didn't tell you." I looked to Ford, to the envelope in his hands. "Will you—?"

He nodded. "I found this in Paige's room yesterday," he said, holding up the envelope before passing it to Griffen.

"What were you doing in Paige's room yesterday?"

Hope asked sharply, her eyes narrowed on her brother-in-law.

"That's the other part of this," Ford said. "Paige and I —" He squeezed my fingers again.

"There's a Paige and you?" Griffen asked, one eyebrow raised.

"Yes," I said, "which I understand is completely inappropriate."

"And how long has this been going on?" Hope asked. Her voice was full of curiosity rather than censure, her head tilted to the side as she looked between the two of us. "I usually have a good feel for all the interesting news in Heartstone, but I missed this."

Her gaze flicked to Griffen, and he shook his head. "Me too. We'll have to ask Savannah if she knew."

"She would have told me," Hope said.

Griffen undid the prongs sealing the envelope, and opened it. The picture of his mother slid out, and he froze. After a long moment, his eyes shot to me—cold and hard. "Why do you have a picture of my mother?" he demanded.

Hope reached for it, turning it over in her hand. "Sarah Elizabeth Fordham." She let out a sigh. "She was so young."

"I found that when I was cleaning out my mother's attic," I began, explaining as I had to Ford how I'd discovered Paul Williams and the letters from Sarah. "And then Janice Smith had told me you were looking for a nanny, and it seemed…"

"Like fate," Hope finished for me.

My stomach twisted, the heavy weight of guilt

making it hard to draw a full breath. This was the moment I'd been avoiding for so long—admitting I'd been selfish and dishonest and waiting for the axe to come down.

"I'm sorry," I said. "I wasn't honest, and I understand if you want to fire me."

"He's not going to fire you," Ford said firmly from beside me. "Right?" He speared Griffen and then Hope with a sharp glance.

Neither Griffen nor Hope responded. Griffen began pulling the letters from the envelope. "What was your plan?" he said finally.

"I don't know," I admitted. "I didn't really have one. I'm not, you know, an investigator or a spy or whatever. I guess—" I let out a sigh. This was embarrassing, but the whole situation was a mess already. I might as well just tell the truth. "I thought I'd hear enough gossip to fill in the blanks. Maybe someone would know something about Sarah and who she'd run off with or where they'd gone. I didn't really get much further than being here."

I paused, gathering my thoughts.

"Then once I was here, I realized no one really talks about Sarah or why she left. It was clearly such a painful memory for everyone that I couldn't bring myself to ask any questions." I gave a helpless shrug and looked to Hope. "I love being here. I love the kids. I love your family. And I just put it aside. But that doesn't change the fact that I knew security was important to you and still came here under false pretenses."

"Do you think we should fire you?" Hope asked gently.

I wasn't expecting the question. "Do I want you to—or do I think you should?"

"Either," she said. "Both."

I drew in a slow breath and let it out. More honesty. I owed it both to them and to myself. "I'd understand if you wanted to. Of course I would. But I don't think you should."

"Why not?" Griffen asked, his narrowed sea-green eyes leaving me feeling like he could read every thought that passed through my mind, every shadow on my heart.

"I made a mistake," I said. "One that I'm very sorry for. But I'm good at my job. I love the kids. I love being here, helping care for your family."

"No one would question that," Hope said. She shared a long look with Griffen. "Is this it? Is this the sum of your secrets? That you found out your father was involved with Sarah and now you're involved with Ford?"

I nodded. "That's it. Those are my deep, dark secrets."

"I wouldn't call us a dark secret," Ford said in a murmur, lifting our joined hands to press a kiss to the back of mine.

I wanted to argue, but the twinkle in his eyes and that tiny curve at the side of his mouth had me smiling back. "Maybe not a dark secret," I said, "but definitely inappropriate."

Griffen smirked. "I'm assuming you're keeping your hands off each other in front of the children?"

I was too shocked by the question to even answer, but Hope did it for me.

"Of course they are!" she said with a teasing grin at

me. "Otherwise, we would have known already. You two were very discreet. I'm assuming this is fairly new?"

I nodded again, my throat so dry I didn't think I could swallow.

"You'll find it's nearly impossible to keep a secret long-term in Heartstone Manor," Hope said. "I don't have a problem with any of it. Assuming we keep communication clear going forward, of course."

"Absolutely," I said, letting out a breath. "I've regretted the way I handled this for months. I wanted to tell you, but...I love this job, and I was afraid you'd send me away. I feel more at home here than I have in years, and I didn't want to lose that."

I looked to Ford. He had his eyes on his brother, who was staring back at him, a small smile curving his mouth that reminded me of Ford's.

"If you do anything to drive Paige away," Griffen said to Ford, "the kids and I will murder you in your sleep."

"Understood," Ford said, his laugh a low rumble in his throat.

"Fine." Griffen nodded. "Before we look through this envelope further, I have some news of my own—from Emmett, Hawk's friend who's now at Sinclair."

I nodded, vaguely remembering hearing Emmett's name here and there.

"He's got contacts," Griffen went on, "and access to places on the dark web the rest of them don't. He found out that Cole's put out a bounty."

Ford shook his head. "What does that mean?"

"It means," Griffen said, tracing the edges of the photograph of their mother, "that he's made you a very profitable target. Hawk's coming by shortly. We're calling Cooper. We need to put together a plan. But, for the moment, our main objective is to keep you alive." He pointed at Ford. "That means you stay put. You don't leave Heartstone by yourself."

I knew from being around Griffen and Hope so much that Cooper meant Cooper Sinclair of Sinclair Security. Griffen had worked for him for years, and they considered each other as close as brothers. I hoped that extended to Cooper keeping Griffen's actual brother safe.

"Yeah, I got it," Ford said. "I'm staying for the call with Cooper."

Griffen nodded in agreement and then turned his attention back to the manila envelope. He read the first letter, and then the next, handing them to Hope when he was finished. Halfway through, he said, "This isn't right."

I watched them, letting my nerves settle.

"What do you mean?" Hope asked, looking up from the letter in her hands.

"The handwriting." He set the letter down and looked at Ford. "Do you still have any of those postcards she used to send?"

Ford's fingers uncurled from my hand, and he stood. "I'll be right back." He strode from the room, leaving Griffen and Hope alone with me.

"It seems like they were so much in love," Hope said. "But I still don't understand how she could have left her children." She looked to me. "How he could have left you."

"I wasn't even born yet," I said quietly. The pain was dull, but there, as it always was.

"Still." She laid her hand over her flat stomach, glancing over to the crib in the corner where Stella lay on her back, playing with a brightly colored toy. "I still don't understand how they could have so much love for each other and leave their children."

"Me neither," I said in a whisper, my heart aching at the thought. "But they did."

Ford came back in. He laid three postcards on the desk, pictures down, the writing facing up.

I leaned forward and read upside down:

Happy 10th birthday, Ford.
Love, Mom

"That's it?" I said. "Is that all you got from her?" It was almost worse than if there'd been nothing. The disinterest was clear. God, people could be so awful.

He shrugged. "One a year until I was in, I don't know, my early twenties. Then they stopped."

I looked to the next one:

I can't believe you're 13, my little man. Hope you have a great one.
Love, Mom

So cheerful and detached. It didn't sound like the woman who'd written the letters to my father.

"The handwriting doesn't match," Griffen said. "It's similar, but it's not the same."

"What?" Ford said from beside me. He grabbed one of the letters and a postcard and held them side by side. Up close, I could see what Griffen meant. The curve of the S wasn't the same, and the E's were narrower on the postcards. The I's in the letters were punctuated with a dot. And, in the postcards, a small circle.

"So, which are the fakes?" Hope asked. "The letters or the postcards?"

"The postcards," Griffen said.

"How do you know?" Ford asked.

Griffen shook his head. "I don't. But my gut says the letters are the real thing. Plus, the fact that they were with that picture, which probably only our mother had..." Griffen looked to me. "Do you mind if I hang on to these?"

I had the same sudden impulse I'd had when Ford had asked the same, to snatch them back and hide them away. "I know they were written by your mother, but I don't have much that was my father's," I said. "Will I get them back?"

Griffen nodded. "I'd like to get one of them checked for fingerprints, which might leave some powder on the paper."

"Okay," I agreed. I'd wanted to investigate. This was my chance. "I want to know the truth as much as you do."

"I'll be careful with them," Griffen promised.

Hope stepped back from the desk. "I'm going to take Stella up."

A knock sounded on the door. We looked to see Hawk pushing it open.

"I'll fill Hawk in," Griffen said, gesturing to the letters and postcards on his desk.

Hope scooped Stella into her arms with a coo before turning my way. "Paige, would you come with me?"

My gut sank. She'd seemed supportive, but things could be different in private. I followed her out of the room, looking back to meet Ford's eyes. He gave me a reassuring chin lift, but it didn't ease the worry twisting my stomach.

I'd made my bed. Now I had to find out if I could sleep in it.

Chapter Nineteen

FORD

I watched Paige follow Hope out of the office, trying to calm the twinge of nerves. Hope was straightforward. She wouldn't have told Paige everything was fine and then taken her off to fire her. Still, I couldn't help but worry. I didn't like seeing the anxiety in Paige's eyes as she left.

I looked back to see Hawk standing beside Griffen's chair, scanning through the letters, comparing them to the postcards.

"Definitely not the same handwriting," he said. "How the fuck did we miss Paige's connection to Sarah?"

"Because Paige didn't lie," Griffen said. "She held back some information. But there's no link between Paige McKenna and Paul Williams aside from her birth certificate, and even if we'd pulled that, it wouldn't have meant anything to us."

Hawk picked up the picture of our mother, studying it. "I've never heard the name Paul Williams before in relation to the Sawyer family or your mother."

"Neither have I," Griffen said. "But someone must know something."

"Someone always knows something," Hawk said, putting the picture down. He came around the side of the desk and sat in the chair Paige had vacated, propping his ankle on his knee. "The situation with Paige and your mother is interesting, but it's old history." He looked to me. "Right now, we have to focus on Cole Haywood. I just got off the phone with Emmett."

"Did he pinpoint who's coming for Ford?" Griffen asked.

Hawk shook his head. "Nope. But Cole has a bail hearing Monday morning."

"I thought he was denied bail," Griffen said. "He pled guilty and they put him in the state prison."

"True," Hawk said. He tapped three fingers on his knee. "But Cole knows the law, even if he's dumb enough to act as his own attorney in this. Sometimes your legal system here is a good old boys club."

Ha. Truer words, and all that. It shocked me not at all that Cole was getting special treatment.

"We're aware," Griffen said, looking at me and then to Hawk.

Hawk raised an eyebrow and met my eyes. "You would be. You've hit both sides of it."

I knew what he meant. There had been times—many of them, working with my father and his cronies—when that good old boys club had been very profitable for us. And then there were times, like me getting thrown in prison for a murder I hadn't committed, that the good old boy network could turn on you. Cole was plugged in deeper than any of us on the legal side of things, and thanks to his business with my father and Edgar, he had influence with the money people.

"So, he did what?" Griffen asked. "Finagled a new hearing?"

"Something like that," Hawk said. "Emmett wasn't clear on the specific legalities. What we know is Haywood withdrew his plea on the grounds that the first judge should have recused himself. Now there's a new judge and a hearing tomorrow, which could result in him getting out of prison."

"He admitted to murdering the jewelry designer who made that necklace Quinn found," I said, "and he kidnapped Avery and tried to kill her. He can't just make all of that go away."

Hawk shrugged. "He can't. But it's possible he can talk his way into withdrawing that guilty plea and getting out of prison temporarily."

"Did Emmett find out who the hearing was with?" Griffen asked.

Hawk thought for a second. "Judge Hemmings."

I let out a gust of air, my gut going tight. "That's not good."

"Why? Who's Hemmings?" Griffen asked.

"A friend of Edgar's and Dad's," I said. "Which means he's probably also a friend of Cole's."

"And if not friends," Griffen said glumly, "I'd bet Cole knows the skeletons in his closet."

"Yeah," I agreed. "That would be my guess."

"Well, fuck," Griffen said.

Hawk leaned forward. "Don't get distracted with

Haywood getting out. Haywood's not your problem. This bounty is your problem, and he called this in while he was still in prison."

"How the hell does Cole Haywood know how to find assassins on the dark web?" I asked, trying to merge that kind of knowledge with the suit-wearing, fastidious man that I knew.

"It seems like Haywood has his fingers in all sorts of shit he shouldn't," Hawk said. "Cooper's expecting our call. He's already talked to Emmett this morning. He's trying to figure out what he can do for us, because we're going to need a lot more manpower. Anyone who leaves Heartstone needs a guard. That means the brewery and the Inn, unless Tenn and Royal can work from home. Ditto for Sweetheart Bakery. I don't want anybody out there on their own. Fuck, I'm not even sure we should be sending the kids to school."

Griffen leaned back in his chair and looked at me. "Ford's never shown any interest in the kids, not in a way that would draw Cole's attention."

It was another gut punch—one I was getting used to— that I was the cause of danger to everyone in this house. I hated it, but I was glad for once about my lack of family involvement over the last year. It meant Cole and the people he'd sent to kill me would have less obvious leverage.

"And if we post guards at the school, we'll be shining a light on them," Hawk added.

Griffen set his phone on the desk, screen facing up, and called Cooper Sinclair, putting the call on speakerphone.

"Griffen," Cooper answered. "You just can't keep out of trouble up there, can you?"

"Not so far," Griffen said. "Can you spare us some help?"

"Not as much as you need," Cooper said, "but with the way you've got Heartstone wired, I think we have an opportunity. How many people can you keep in the Manor? Putting guards on anyone outside the gates is part of what makes this complicated."

"I'll talk to Tenn and Royal. It depends on how long this goes. I can't lock everyone down for months."

"Hopefully, we can get it wrapped up faster than that," Cooper said. "Listen, you remember Silas Creed and the team he put together?"

"Of course," Griffen said. "Silas is a fucking legend."

"Well, Silas sold me his company."

"What?" Hawk asked. "He can't sell his company. You mean the team? He sold you the team?"

"Basically," Cooper said. "We took the deal—it was too good to pass up—but the whole thing is weird."

"Why would he do that?" Griffen said. "Is he retiring? But if it's that, why not put Ryder or Miranda in charge?"

"All good questions," Cooper said. "He wasn't willing to answer them, except to say he was stepping back, and he wanted his team with someone who'd keep them together."

Hawk was shaking his head. "That doesn't sound like Silas. I mean, the keeping them together part—yeah. But stepping back? Silas Creed has never taken a vacation in his life."

"I don't know that it's a vacation," Cooper said. "He only promised that the team was clean of any trouble."

"Are they?" Griffen asked.

I could almost hear Cooper's shrug. "Clean enough. You know Silas's team—they always did the stuff that was a little too shady for us. Took bigger risks, sketchier clients."

"So why are you bringing them under your roof?" Hawk asked.

"Partly as a favor to Silas," Cooper said. "I don't necessarily believe that everything they've done is clean, but the opportunity to get my hands on the six of them was too good to pass up. We talked it over, and the decision was unanimous."

"When was this?" Griffen asked.

"A week ago. I can't say they've integrated with the rest of us yet. They're like our teams here in that everybody has a specific area of expertise. In the long term, we think they're best assigned together, but at the moment, we have them split up so they can work with the Sinclair teams that match their skill sets. I can't free up all six— some of them are out training with my people, working on bringing them into the fold—but I can send you three. If Hawk can stretch his people to cover the family, Silas's people can go after the assassins."

"Well, shit," Griffen said. "Three of Silas's crew is like twelve of anyone else's."

"They're not that much better than my people," Cooper said, sounding a little annoyed.

A slow grin spread across Hawk's face. "Considering

we were your people, we're not going to argue. But Silas's team is on a different level."

"Yeah," Cooper said, "you won't be surprised to know they took to Emmett like a duck to water. Lucas too."

"Yeah, not a surprise," Hawk murmured. "But hell, that's good news. When will they be here?"

"They're leaving in an hour, so not long."

"I feel a lot better about the idea of being murdered in my sleep," Griffen said wryly, and I barked out a laugh, despite the darkness of the conversation.

"Side note," Griffen said. "Because of course there's never enough going on around here—I need you to find anything you can on a Paul Williams. Married a woman, last name McKenna. Dropped off the map in 1986."

"I'll get somebody on it. Who's Paul Williams?" Cooper asked.

"Turns out he's the father of our nanny, Paige, and possibly the man our mother ran off with," Griffen told him.

Cooper paused, obviously taking it in. "Well, shit. That's new information."

"Yeah. Turns out Paige came here looking for him and ran into a dead end. But she found letters our mother wrote him before they both took off."

"Any interesting information in there?" Cooper asked.

"Don't know," Griffen said. "We haven't read them all yet. Paige says no, but there might be something she didn't catch. One thing we did find out—the postcards Ford and I got for years on our birthdays? Not the same handwriting as the letters our mother wrote Paul Williams. Close, but not the same."

"Interesting," Cooper said slowly, as if turning the new information over in his mind, examining it for answers.

"We thought so," Griffen agreed.

"I'll see what I can find," he said. "Meantime, keep your heads down. When the team gets there, you'll figure out a plan."

"That's the idea," Griffen said. "Talk to you later." He cut off the call.

Hawk sat back in the chair and crossed his arms over his chest, a smile playing across his mouth. "Fuck me. Silas's team is a part of Sinclair Security. I almost regret that we're not there."

"I know," Griffen said. "Not to stay. I like it here, but I'd love to watch those six try to integrate with Sinclair."

"What's the difference?" I asked, completely lost.

"Sinclair Security," Griffen said, "works for high-end clients, mostly in business and entertainment, sometimes political targets. They design security systems and provide bodyguarding services. They have a division that handles kidnappings. They work comfortably with law enforcement and generally stay on the legal side of the line, though—"

Griffen looked at Hawk, who shrugged one shoulder.

"Occasionally, we'd stray into the gray areas. But you cross those lines too often, law enforcement tells you to fuck off. Cooper, Axel, Knox, and Evers don't play that game. But Silas? He doesn't follow the same rules. His team generally works for decent human beings, but they handle things like corporate espionage. That shit can get dirty fast. And Silas's team never minds slogging through the muck."

I knew well just how dirty corporate espionage and under-the-table dealings could get.

"He found them all one by one over the years," Hawk added. "Rumor has it a teenage Ryder tried to pick Silas's pocket. Silas taught him a lesson and then brought him home. We used to joke that Silas collected the most vicious stray dogs you'd ever find, loyal only to him, and trained them until they were so fucking skilled, they're terrifying. A few of them are ex-Special Forces. Silas has always had a knack for spotting talent, even in the completely untrained. He ran his team like they were half family, half military unit. The idea that he up and sold them to Cooper is..." Hawk shook his head.

"Yeah," Griffen agreed. "It's beyond weird. Makes me wonder if he's got a terminal disease or something. He runs a business, a very profitable one, but his team is like his family. I can see him wanting them settled if he's walking away, but I can't see him walking away in the first place."

"Maybe we'll learn more when the three of them get here," Hawk said, standing. "I'm going to catch Savannah, see if I can figure out where to put three more people. I think she was working on clearing more space in the guest wing. Or there might be another room in the old servants' quarters up in the attic."

"Hang on a sec," I said, a little surprised the conversation was over. I'd been waiting for Griffen to confront me about sleeping with Paige. And even if he was going to let that go, I had something else on my mind. Hawk sat back down. "Speaking of the guest wing, last night something weird happened." I filled them in on the frozen room, the stuck door.

"That doesn't make any sense," Hawk said. "Everything was fine in the rest of the house last night. And no one heard you screaming?"

"No. We were banging on the door and yelling. And it wasn't just chilly in that room. I could see my breath. There was frost on the door."

Hawk and Griffen shared a look.

"What?" I asked.

"Nothing," Griffen said. "It's just— I'm not entirely surprised."

"What do you mean, you're not entirely surprised?" I asked.

"Since we came back home," Griffen said slowly, "the guest wing's been a problem."

"I know," I said, "the power, the plumbing, the heat, but—"

"It's been inconsistent," Griffen finished for me. "None of the tradespeople can figure out what's wrong, especially since whatever it is seems contained to the guest wing and the garage right below."

"What's happened in the garage?" I asked. I'd lived in Heartstone Manor for most of my life, and we'd never had problems with the garage. But then, we hadn't had major issues with the guest wing either.

Griffen shook his head. "Mostly little stuff. Keys being moved. The lights not always working when they should."

"What are you saying?" I asked, wanting to hear my logical, level-headed brother—or Hawk, the least fanciful man I knew—say it out loud.

Hawk shrugged. "It's an old house."

"What does that mean, exactly?" I challenged.

"That it might not be a problem with the electrical, or the plumbing, or the heat?" Hawk said blandly. "You might just have some spirits floating around."

I felt a wash of relief that someone had put into words what my brain had been telling me since the night before.

Instead of denying the possibility, Griffen shrugged. "We don't know all the people who died here—servants, family members, our grandfather, and our father."

I sat back, considering. "You think Prentice is haunting Heartstone? Or Gramps?"

Griffen leaned forward, sorting through the letters our mother had written Paige's father. "I don't know. My gut reaction is to say, of course not, that the 'it's an old house' explanation works just as well for faulty wiring and crappy plumbing. But some of the stuff that's happened in the garage—the keys moving, for example—those aren't wiring or plumbing."

"Did you guys get hurt?" Hawk asked.

I shook my head. I thought about how we'd ended up skin to skin, huddled under the covers. I had no complaints about getting locked in Paige's room.

"Then I say we table whatever that was for now," Griffen said. "Is Paige spooked?"

"I don't think so," I said. "I'm pretty sure she's in the 'faulty wiring and plumbing' camp."

"And you're sure that's not what it was?" Hawk pressed.

"I could see my breath in the room, and if none of the rest of you had problems with heating..."

"Point taken," Hawk said with a nod, standing again.

"When Cooper gets back to you about Paul Williams," I began.

Griffen gave a nod. "I'll pass it on."

Hawk left, shutting the door on his way out.

"Aren't you going to say anything about Paige?" I asked, unable to handle the tension any longer.

"What do you want me to say?" Griffen asked, leaning back and propping his ankle on his knee, an older brother smirk playing around his mouth.

"I don't know. Something. Maybe that I had no business getting involved with an employee of the family who happens to be your daughter's nanny—"

"You're both adults," Griffen said. "She didn't seem to have any objection to your attentions, and if she does, Hope will get it out of her. If that's the case, we'll have a problem."

"We're not going to have a problem," I said.

"I expect we won't," he agreed.

I stayed quiet for a beat, debating whether I could—or should—admit the fear in my heart. I remembered Griffen's words at the prison and decided to be honest. "I don't have a good track record with women," I said. "Or in general."

"Fuck that. Your track record in general is what it is," Griffen said, "and with women..." He raised an eyebrow. "Have you ever dated a woman like Paige before?"

"It's been a while since I 'dated' anyone," I said, making air quotes around the word. "There've been women—it wasn't hard to find company. I was second-in-command of Sawyer Enterprises. But dating, spending time with a woman, getting to know her with the intention of bringing her into my life—that lost its appeal after my divorce from Vanessa. There's never been anyone like Paige."

"Well then, try not to fuck it up," Griffen said and grinned at me.

"That's the plan," I said with a laugh of relief.

"I don't need to warn you off Paige," Griffen said. "I saw the way you looked at her—the way you held her hand when she was nervous. She's a grown woman. If she wants to get rid of you, she can. And if this doesn't work out and she quits, I seriously will kill you. But as long as you're both happy, it's none of my business."

Chapter Twenty

PAIGE

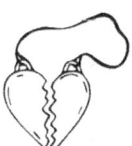

I followed Hope out of the office, nerves skittering down my spine. She'd been kind when I'd finally come clean about my father and the letters, but that didn't mean she wasn't going to bring the hammer down now that we were alone. Despite her empathy and compassion, Hope wasn't a softie. She might dislike having to fire me, but it didn't mean she wouldn't do it.

I followed her into the suite she shared with Griffen, and farther to the small nursery she'd set up for Stella. We headed straight to the changing table, where we fell into a comfortable rhythm—Hope stripping Stella down as I grabbed a diaper and wipes.

"Are you okay with the Ford situation?" she asked, shooting me a quick look. It felt like an X-ray straight to my heart.

"I don't know how to answer that," I said honestly. "It feels inappropriate—"

"You said that already," Hope said.

"Inappropriate because he's my boss's brother and we live in the same house, which is also my workplace."

"I can see that," Hope said. "But we never specifically said Sawyers were off-limits."

"I didn't think you needed to," I said.

I helped corral Stella's waving feet, smiling down at the baby as she grinned on the changing table. She was a good girl most of the time, but she liked turning her feet into moving targets when we were trying to change her. Potty training couldn't come soon enough, but it wasn't time yet—not even close.

"Then Ford came home," I said, "and I went from not even tempted, to..." I wasn't sure I could explain the attraction that had sprung up out of nowhere at my first glimpse of Ford Sawyer. "I didn't think he'd even noticed me, but—" I shrugged. "It turned out he did."

"But there was no coercion, no pressure from him?" Hope asked.

"No," I said, immediately understanding what she was getting at. "Nothing like that. Whatever's between us, it's totally consensual on both sides."

"Good to know," Hope said. "I had to check. So, are you two... Is it love? Or just fun?"

All I could do was be honest at this point. And I hadn't even figured it out for myself yet. I let out a sigh. "It's definitely fun, but it's not just fun. Not for me," I said, "and I don't think for him either. We haven't talked about it, but—"

Hope nodded, throwing away a handful of soiled wipes and tickling Stella's belly before she fastened the diaper.

"Are you upset?" I asked, bracing for her answer.

"No, not upset, just..." Hope bit her lower lip and drew in a breath, letting it out slowly.

I watched her for any sign of anger, but it wasn't there.

"Ford is complicated," Hope said slowly. "I spent a lot of years so angry at him for what he did to Griffen, for playing along with Prentice. But he changed, or he is trying to, which amounts to the same thing to me. He's more vulnerable than he seems to be. And I saw the way he looked at you in Griffen's office. He's got a strong protective streak, which I think is as much a surprise to him as it is to everyone else. But it's there. And you're one of the people he wants to protect. So, I find myself in the odd position of needing to ask you to be careful with him."

I nodded, understanding. "This isn't casual for me," I said, because it was the truth. "I can't make any promises about how things will work out. It's too new, and I don't even know what Ford wants. But I care about him—a lot more than I should, given how long we've known each other. I don't have any guarantees."

"I'm not asking for a guarantee," Hope said, "just that you take care—with both of you." She turned to me, a newly dressed Stella in her arms, and reached out with one hand to take mine, squeezing my fingers much the same way Ford had. "You haven't had an easy time of it either, Paige. If things go sideways, you can talk to me, okay? I know I'm Ford's sister-in-law, but I'm also your friend."

"I know," I said, squeezing her hand back. Her words

sent me over the edge, all the tension from the last twelve hours releasing. Tears welled up and spilled over, streaking down my face.

"Oh, Paige," she said.

"I just—oh, I don't know why I'm crying now," I said. "I was so worried you guys would fire me. I feel at home here. I've never worked for a family I wanted to leave—I've been lucky that way—but you're different. I thought I would miss the travel. I thought Sawyers Bend and Heartstone would be too small. But it's the opposite. It's always an adventure around here."

At her wry expression, I laughed.

"I don't mean the danger, or Ford getting stalked by assassins—I could do without that part. But the kids and all of you, it's just...there's always something going on. And your family, there's just so much love. I didn't want to leave, and it made me stay quiet long after I should have told you about my father and Sarah. I just didn't know how. And I'm so glad you're not throwing me out."

Hope tightened her grip on my hand and tugged me forward into a hug, Stella chortling happily between us.

"You didn't mean any harm," Hope said. "That's the important part. I guarantee you Griffen gave your dad's name to Cooper Sinclair. Maybe they can dig something up. I don't know that Griffen and Ford have dreams of seeing their mother again. They did when they were kids, but a lot of time has passed. Still, it would be good to know where they are, what they did with their lives. It might be some kind of closure, you know?"

I nodded. "That's exactly how I feel. I don't know if I want to see my father. He left me, and he hasn't bothered to reach out in all these years. Maybe they've been living on the beach in Belize for the last thirty years, or off with the Peace Corps, or— Who the hell knows? But I want to erase the question mark and put a period at the end of the sentence."

Hope nodded. "I don't think Griffen or Ford has ever looked for her. Griffen walked away from his family when Prentice kicked him out, and he did it full throttle, so I doubt he tried to find her. She left him first, after all." Hope shook her head, squeezing Stella in her arms. "I just don't understand. I get leaving Prentice. He was an asshole on his best day and a monster at his worst. But leaving Griffen and Ford—" She stroked a hand over Stella's curls, laughing as her daughter caught a finger in her little grip and squeezed, yanking her mother's hand back and forth. "I don't get how she could leave her children. And worse, she left them with Prentice. Maybe she thought Miss Martha would be the mother they needed. I know she tried, but it's not the same."

Hope dropped a kiss on Stella's head, then met my eyes.

"That's who you should talk to—Miss Martha. You probably can't go out, given lockdown and all—" Hope rolled her eyes. "But she's the only one I can think of who might know what happened when Sarah left. She might remember your father if he was ever here. Let's go see Savannah. We need to figure out where we're going to put any extra staff that's coming in for security, and she'll know better than anyone when her mother will be by next."

I followed Hope out of the room, buoyed by the idea

that I could finally ask all of my questions without worrying about being found out or dredging up bad memories. It seemed like a long shot to hope that Savannah's mother knew anything. But as Hope had said, if anybody did, it would be Miss Martha.

Chapter Twenty-One

FORD

I spent the rest of the day going through the boxes of my father's files that I'd pulled aside well over a year before, when I'd first come up with my plan to find a chink in his armor. So far, I was still batting zero.

Paige took a break while Stella was napping to come up and help me, relaying that all was well with Hope and that she was going to meet with Miss Martha the next time she came over. That settled, together we sat in ancient, threadbare armchairs, sorting through paperwork. I grabbed anything that looked like it related to business. Paige took things that looked like they had to do with the house. She found a few more invoices from the garage renovation I didn't remember from the early eighties, mixed in with other things, and a few invoices for artwork that had sold at auction in the years before my father's death.

At this point, we'd accounted for over half of the missing art. When Scarlett, Tenn's wife, had first come to Heartstone Manor, she'd tracked down some of the pieces. Formerly an art history professor and appraiser, she had more expertise than anyone else. Piece by piece, we were finding out where the family art had gone, but no one had tracked down what Prentice had done with the money from the sales.

I suspected he'd used a chunk of it to pay off Vanessa, who we'd learned had been blackmailing him after she'd discovered that the woman he'd planned to make the new Mrs. Sawyer was Cole's wife. We had no clue what Vanessa did with the money, considering she'd been broke when she died. Though the way Vanessa could spend, it was possible she'd blown it all on luxurious vacations, jewelry, and clothes. I knew from experience, nobody could run through cash like Vanessa.

Even after a few hours, Paige and I didn't find anything truly interesting in the files. No love letters from Paul to Sarah. Nothing of my mother's at all. Since I'd found the envelope with my mother's letters in Paige's room, I'd considered abandoning the search for my father's killer in favor of finding whatever she might have left behind in this house.

I wanted my name cleared. I wanted my father's killer to face justice. But as I looked at Paige, her brow furrowed, a dark curl escaping her bun as she studied the open file in front of her, I wondered if any of that was really worth it. My father was dead, and very few people had any regret about that. I wished he'd been a better father, a better man, a better husband, but I didn't wish him back at the head of the dining room table in Heartstone Manor. Maybe that made me an asshole, but I could live with that.

I wanted Stella to grow up in a house filled with love —something that would be impossible if Prentice was still alive. And Tenn had Scarlett's kids—his, now that they were married. Their father was mostly out of the picture, from what I could tell, and Tenn loved those kids like they were his own. The same went for Finn with Savannah's Nicky. My heart lightened as I thought about those children growing up in the Manor as it was now, filled with family and love.

No, I wouldn't bring my father back if I could. I didn't want the future he'd seen for us. I wanted this, what we were building here, all of us together.

I looked at Paige again, wondering. She was so natural with the kids. She'd be such a great mom. I had no idea what went into being a good father, but so far, Griffen, Tenn, and Finn were great examples. I hadn't thought much about having kids until I'd gotten out of prison and come home to a house full of them.

It was the laughter that got me. I didn't love the mess they left behind, or the noise when they were shouting back and forth to each other in the house. But I craved the laughter. I wanted it for myself. I wanted to kick a soccer ball. Throw a baseball. Take a kid fishing or camping, like I'd loved to when I was young.

I could still remember the years when my step-mother Darcy was alive. She'd brought love to this house, shining so bright she banished my father's shadow for the short years she was with us, until she died. But in that time, I'd forged my best childhood memories, rambling in the woods with Griffen, trying to ditch the younger kids so we could dam up a stream and see what happened, or build a fort out of branches and moss.

Paige and I hadn't been together long enough to think about forever, or kids, or any of it. I knew that. I wasn't rushing into anything. But I caught the curve of her cheek as she smiled at something in her hands, and I wanted more than her body. I wanted her.

"What are you smiling about?" I asked.

"Nothing," she said with a shake of her head. "Just—I found another receipt for artwork your father must have sold, and it's so god-awful ugly."

"What is it?"

"There's a picture." She showed me a pudgy marble satyr surrounded by fruit, its rounded belly and cheeks offset by a pug nose and squinty eyes.

"That is ugly," I agreed, studying the receipt. "He didn't get much for it. I wonder why he bought it in the first place." I put it aside with the other invoices from auction houses.

"I'm starting to feel like this is a wild goose chase," she said, echoing my earlier thoughts.

"Me too." I pulled my phone out of my pocket. We didn't need paperwork. We needed people. I scrolled through my contacts, looking for the one I wanted, and hit the button to call.

Miss Martha answered on the second ring.

"Ford Sawyer, what are you doing calling me? Did you get yourself into trouble again?" The smile in her voice was evident, and I was grateful. Through everything, she'd always believed in me.

"Not yet, Miss Martha. I was wondering if you were

busy. I have a few questions I want to ask you. Things you might remember about—" I didn't want to get into it on the phone. "Stuff from when I was a kid," I finished.

"I remember a lot, Ford," she said easily. "And I'm not busy right now, but I'll do you one better. I'll be there for dinner tonight. I just spoke to Savannah and it's all arranged."

"That makes things easy," I said.

Miss Martha was enjoying a well-deserved retirement, but she was around often enough since Savannah had taken over her position as housekeeper. Miss Martha wasn't just close to her daughter; she loved her grandson to pieces, and he loved her back just as much.

"I'm moving in for a bit, actually," she said.

"Why?" I asked in alarm. Visions of Miss Martha being sick flashed through my head. She wasn't a spring chicken anymore, and she was the closest any of us had left to a mother.

"Hawk and Griffen thought it was best, considering this business with Haywood," she said.

I let out a sigh of relief, feeling it flash through me. "Sorry about that. I know you love your cottage in town," I said. Griffen had offered her a place in the Manor for her retirement, but she'd said she was enjoying the alone time.

"I do, I do, but this makes sense. I don't want y'all to waste your time and worry on me, and it gives me an excuse to spend a little extra time with Nicky and Savannah, and the rest of you. If things get bad, you'll have to keep April and Kitty away, and Savannah will need a hand with the house."

207

Another good point, I realized. "Well then, I guess we'll see you tonight. Will you have time to talk after dinner?"

"I have all the time in the world for you, Ford."

"Thanks, Miss Martha," I said. "See you later." I hung up and shoved my phone back in my pocket. "Did you catch all that?" I asked Paige. She nodded as the baby monitor sitting beside her squawked with a fretful cry.

"These afternoon naps are getting shorter," she said, standing. "Little Stella's turning into a toddler."

I straightened in surprise. "She was a newborn five minutes ago."

"I know," Paige said with a grin. "It goes fast. Now she's a year old and zooming around on her feet—wait till she really starts climbing."

"Climbing?" I said, not sure what she was talking about. "She's a baby, not a monkey."

"At this age, sometimes there's not much difference. I nannied for a kid," Paige said as she walked to the door, "who could climb like nothing else—couches, bookcases, anything he could get on top of—and then he'd dive right off. I swear, for the first three years, I thought he was trying to kill himself and give us all heart attacks in the process. Stella's not nearly as much trouble." She paused at the door and smiled at me. "I'll see you later."

Before she could go, I was on my feet, crossing the room, and pulling her into my arms for a quick kiss. It lingered until Stella gave another cry through the monitor.

"See you later," I whispered against the soft skin of her cheek.

I didn't lay eyes on Paige again until just before dinner. Griffen and Hope had decided we'd all eat in the dining room—kids, Miss Martha, and Paige at the breakfast table at the far end, the rest of us around the long formal table.

We were milling around, waiting for the gong to ring, calling us all to the table, when a knock sounded on the front door. I turned to see Hawk striding that way, anticipation lighting his dark eyes. Quinn followed, her massive guard dog Ginger next to her, her hand on the dog's head.

Hawk swung the door open, his usually somber face splitting into a wide grin. "Ryder Vale! Good to see you again."

They leaned in, slinging an arm around each other's shoulders and patting backs.

"You too, man," Ryder said.

The three newcomers entered, shutting the door behind them. The one Hawk had called Ryder was taller than Hawk, with broad shoulders, his short black hair in a cut that made me think of the military, and clear gray eyes that swept the room, leaving me with the feeling he'd cataloged each of us and filed us away.

Beside him stood a petite woman. She barely reached his shoulder, slender, with sandy blonde hair in loose waves around her face and greenish-hazel eyes. She looked delicate, but something about the way she stood—hands in her pockets, eyes scanning the room the same way Ryder's had—made me think, despite her size, she was just as dangerous as the others.

And then there was the third, standing slightly

behind the woman and Ryder. He was a little shorter than Ryder, with chocolate brown hair and eyes of the exact same shade. Unlike the other two, his stance was more relaxed. He looked easygoing—the kind of guy you'd drink a beer and shoot the shit with. But if this was the team Griffen and Hawk were expecting, I knew that was as much an illusion as the woman's delicacy.

"We're about to eat dinner," Hawk said. "You guys get anything on the way?"

"Nope," Ryder said. "We figured we'd get here in time."

"You did," Griffen said, striding up. "Good to see you again."

He went through the same hug ritual Hawk had and then turned to the other two, shaking hands with a nod. Turning, he let out a loud whistle that had the entire family coming to attention.

"It'll take a minute for these three to learn all your names, but we'll go through it anyway. Sawyers, this is Ryder Vale." Griffen indicated Ryder, then the other two, as he said, "Eli Bishop and Wren Calder. They're going to be here to help us out with the Haywood situation. If they tell you to do something, you do it the same way you would for Hawk and anyone on his team, got it?"

I nodded along with everyone else in assent. I hated that we needed this, but I was glad as hell that my family was safer for them being here.

Griffen turned to the newcomers. "There'll be a test on this later, but I'll go around. This is my wife, Hope," and he began the introductions.

I had a feeling Ryder, Eli, and Wren would pass the

name test with flying colors if they were challenged to identify any of the people they'd been introduced to. But Griffen didn't ask—just led us all into the dining room.

Paige met my eye and sent me a short smile before she and Miss Martha herded the kids to the breakfast table. We rarely used it, but we'd left it just in case. Every once in a while, it came in handy.

Finn and Savannah had set up the evening meal as a buffet, similar to breakfast, making it easier for them to haul everything up in the dumbwaiter and join the family for dinner. The meal was half family talk and half strategy, though there wasn't much to the strategy at this point —at least nothing they'd shared. The plan was for Hawk to show Ryder, Eli, and Wren through the systems he had in place. They were going to run scenarios and try to figure out the most likely ways people trying to claim the bounty would come at Heartstone to get to me.

Ryder said at one point, with a heavy look at Griffen and then Hawk, "What you need is to neutralize Haywood."

"Easier said than done," Griffen replied.

"True," he agreed. "But we talked to Emmett and Lucas before we left. I have some ideas."

Griffen nodded instead of asking for more explanation. I could have asked myself, but I was distracted by the prospect of talking to Miss Martha after dinner, and I knew there would be plenty of time to learn the plan. They were the experts; I was not.

I did catch Hawk saying, "Any word from Silas?" and Ryder's solemn head shake in response.

"No. He didn't explain what pulled him away,"

Ryder said. "And he's been out of contact more than usual."

"What do you think's going on?" Griffen asked.

"We don't know. I still can't believe he sold the unit to Sinclair," Wren said, her voice as clear as a bell, dripping with indignation. She let out a short huff of breath. "Nothing against Sinclair—they're a great company, solid —but we've always operated on our own."

"That doesn't seem like Silas," Hawk said. "He didn't tell you why?"

"Not a word," Eli said with a shake of his head. "Just 'I sold the unit to Sinclair Security. Do what Cooper says. I'll be back.' Like we were kids he left with a babysitter."

The analogy made me smile. If the other three were anything like Ryder, Eli, and Wren, the last thing they were was kids who needed a babysitter. I'd gotten used to Hawk and Griffen and their ability to handle any shit that seemed to roll our way, but these three looked like they could take apart the Pentagon with a paper clip.

Since we'd talked to Cole, I'd had a weight in my gut. I wasn't so much worried about myself, but my family, the kids, Paige—so many people who were vulnerable. I couldn't keep them all safe. But with Hawk's team and Griffen, and now these three, I let out a slow breath. Having them here didn't solve the problem, but I was less worried about anything happening to my family or Paige.

Griffen, Hawk, and the new arrivals left the second they'd finished dessert, retiring to the surveillance room on the lower level where Hawk had set up his team and all their gear.

Paige met my eye from across the room, and I got the

message—she had to finish up with the kids, get them settled. She stood, prompting August and Nicky to pick up their plates to carry to the butler's pantry and the plastic bin that would bring the dirty dishware back down to the lower level. Thatcher stood beside her, not needing any reminders about clearing the table. Deftly, she hoisted Stella onto one hip and detached her filthy high chair tray with the other, crossing the room in brisk strides, quietly herding the younger children ahead of her.

A minute later, I heard the pounding feet of the kids set free from the dining room. Paige returned, grinning down at Stella on her hip as she bopped her on the nose. She went to Hope, sipping a cup of tea at the head of the table.

"Do you want me to keep Stella a little longer?" she asked.

Hope shook her head, reaching for her daughter, whose feet kicked at the air the second she was off Paige's hip.

"I think she wants to go for a walk," Hope said. "I've got her for the rest of the night. I know you and Ford want to talk to Miss Martha."

"We do, as long as you don't mind," Paige said with a quick glance my way.

"No, we're good," Hope said with a smile. "Thanks, Paige."

Hope stood, leaning slightly to the side, extending her hand down so her daughter could grab it as she took rapid, wobbly steps toward the door of the dining room, Hope walking faster to keep up with her.

"How does she do that and not fall on her face?" I asked Paige, surprised at how quickly the one-year-old could move once she got going.

"I don't know," Paige said. "It's almost like the faster they go, the less likely they are to fall. But then they do, and they scream bloody murder until they pop back up and do it again." She laughed. "We haven't had any bloody noses or stitches yet, so I'd say she's doing pretty well."

"She's going to be a handful," Miss Martha said, joining us. She looked like a slightly older version of her daughter, her hair threaded with white and more lines on her face, but still beautiful.

Savannah hovered in the doorway of the butler's pantry. "What do you three say to tea in the library?"

"You don't have to go to any trouble," Paige said.

"It's no trouble. Tea?" This time, she was asking her mother.

"If you have a minute, sweetheart, I'd love some," Miss Martha said, her love for her daughter glowing in her eyes.

"Always," Savannah said, smiling back.

I felt a stab of envy and saw in Paige's eyes that she felt the same. Savannah had been tight with her mom her entire life. That hadn't changed now that she was back in Sawyers Bend, managing Heartstone as her mother had for years.

"Is it weird?" I asked Miss Martha as we walked to the library. "Being back here so often as part of the family, with Savannah running the house?"

"A little," she said. "Sometimes I have to watch

myself or I'll start trying to organize everything. I don't want to step on Savannah's toes. She does a brilliant job. Better than I did."

"No one's better than you," I said to Miss Martha.

She smiled up at me. "Flatterer. And you're right, except for Savannah. My girl is the best."

"I won't argue with that," Paige said. "I don't know how she does it. She never breaks a sweat. She knows everything that goes on under this roof, and she keeps it all running seamlessly."

"She did learn from a master," I said, and Miss Martha smiled.

We reached the library, and Miss Martha took the seat opposite the armchair I usually sat in. I grabbed the remote and started the fireplace, grateful yet again that my father had switched some of the wood-burning fireplaces over to gas. There was nothing like the smell of a wood-burning fire, but in my mind, it still didn't beat the convenience of clicking a button and having dancing flames warm the room immediately.

"Now, Ford, what is this about?" She looked at me and then Paige in question, and I stalled, not sure exactly what to say.

Paige saved me the trouble. "There's something I didn't tell anyone when I came here," she said. Miss Martha went stiff, her eyes narrowing. Paige shook her head. "Griffen and Hope know everything now. I, um, well, my mother died not long before I took the job here, and when I was packing up her house to sell it..."

Paige explained what she'd found and why she'd come to Heartstone. While she was talking, Savannah rolled in the tea cart, a plate of shortbread beside the teapot, cups, and saucers. She might have been curious about the conversation, but she didn't linger, serving the tea and withdrawing before Paige was finished explaining how she'd found the letters and picture of Sarah.

"So, you think your father, this Paul Williams, is the man our Sarah ran off with?" Miss Martha asked, leveling a concerned look at me.

"That's what we'd like to find out," I said.

"I'm not sure how much help I can be," Miss Martha said. "Sarah and I were close." She looked to me with soft eyes. "She and your father were a terrible fit. Though, to be honest, I'm not sure who would have been a good fit for your father. Maybe that viper you married."

"Probably," I agreed. "She could have saved us all a lot of heartache if she'd just gone after him in the first place."

Miss Martha shook her head. "Normally, I hate to speak ill of the dead, but not when it comes to Prentice. The problem there is that he always liked the gentle. I always thought he enjoyed dominating them, using up all that soft and leaving them broken." Miss Martha let out a sigh, heavy with sorrow. "Your mother struggled in this house. She loved you boys so much. But Prentice was all hard edges and cruelty. Sarah needed love." She picked up her cup of tea and sipped. Finally, she said, "I knew she found someone, but not who she was seeing."

"But there was another man?" I pressed.

Miss Martha nodded slowly. "There was a lightness to her. It started not long after you were born. I didn't

216

know a Paul Williams," she said, looking to Paige. "I'm sorry. Back then, Prentice did a lot of business from the house. There were people coming and going all the time. If they stayed, I knew who they were. But those who didn't spend the night in the house, the ones who stayed in town or visited for a meeting and left again, I didn't always know. Sarah was home more often than not in those years. She didn't have a nanny or work outside the home, so she spent most of her time with her boys. If she met someone, it was probably a business associate of Prentice's. But like I said, I never had a name, just a suspicion. She didn't confide in me about that. I'd say we trusted each other, but...that's a secret she would have done everything to keep."

"Were you surprised when she left?" I asked.

Miss Martha let out a long sigh, and for the first time, I saw her years on her face. "Oh, Ford, surprise doesn't cover it. When I say she loved you and your brother, I mean she loved you so fiercely. I never understood how she could have left. But then there was your father. He made her life a misery. And Sawyers Bend wasn't like it is now, with West in charge. There was nowhere for her to go. You understand? No one to help her."

"You're saying he hurt her?" Paige asked quietly, and Miss Martha nodded.

"He did. Not so that she went to the hospital, not so that any bruises showed. Your father was a clever man, if not a good one."

"Did he ever hurt the children?" Paige asked carefully, shooting a sidelong look at me.

"No, no. Not with his hands. With his words... Well,

he hurt everyone with his words—children were no exception. But he never— Unless—" Horror washed over her face as her eyes flashed to me.

I shook my head. "Not when I was little. When we were older and could take it." I shrugged, remembering the occasional slap or hit, once a fist to the face. I summed it up with the plain truth. "All of us learned early how to stay on the right side of Prentice's fists."

Miss Martha nodded. "That was how it always seemed to me. I never would have thought she'd leave you. But I'm not surprised she didn't stay with Prentice."

"What happened to all of her things?" I asked, frustrated that we seemed to be at another dead end.

"Your father—" She shook her head. "He wanted every scrap of her burned. But I saved what I could."

A small wave of hope hit me. "Where is it?" I asked.

"We'll have to ask Savannah. In the attic, I think. Things got rearranged after a leak, but everything is still up there. We'll just have to hunt it down. I'll help you tomorrow. It's been up there for thirty years. It's not going anywhere. I don't know how much help it'll be," she said. "You should talk to Harvey or Edgar. Both of them always had a soft spot for your mother." She smiled faintly. "Everyone did except your father. They would have known who she met with, might recognize the name Paul Williams."

It was worth a try. Harvey, our family lawyer, was more likely to talk than Edgar. I knew he'd argued with both Prentice and Edgar frequently, usually trying to talk them out of some of their more cutthroat business maneuvers. But he'd always kept my father's secrets just as well as Edgar. It was hard to hope that he'd tell us anything useful.

She turned to Paige. "Are you hoping to find your father, dear?"

Paige let out a sigh and sipped her tea. "At first, I was. Now, I don't know what I'm looking for." Her eyes met mine over her teacup. "Or maybe I've already found it."

I smiled back, wanting to fall into the icy blue of her eyes, a cold burn that seared all the way to my soul. We hadn't been looking for each other. Not on purpose. But now that we'd found each other, I wasn't going to lose her. No matter what Cole Haywood had planned.

Chapter Twenty-Two

PAIGE

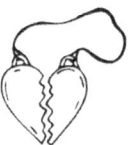

" I think I know where it is," Savannah was saying as she led us up the stairs to the attic. Griffen and Hope were right behind her, followed by Miss Martha. Ford and I brought up the rear.

I wasn't used to having so much free time in the morning. Now that Hawk's team was in charge of school drop-off and pickup, I found I missed the drive—the chattering voices on the way, the quiet and time to think on the drive back, and then hearing about their day when I picked them up in the afternoon. I hoped all of this wouldn't last too much longer. I'd heard Ford say that the new team, Hawk, and some of the Sinclair people were working on a plan to make Cole Haywood call off the bounty, but Ford hadn't heard what it was or if they even had anything solid. I was impatient to put all of this behind us. Without answers, we were stuck in a holding pattern.

Scarlett, Tenn's wife, was usually in her workshop on

the lower level first thing in the morning, creating the gorgeous glass art she sold in town and in galleries across the Southeast. This morning, she'd popped up as I was trying to figure out how to keep Stella occupied and offered to watch her while we searched in the attic. As odd as it felt to hand off my charge, I did—gratefully—still hoping, I supposed, that if we found Sarah's things, among them might be something of my father's.

It wasn't too much of a stretch. After all, I'd found Sarah's letters in my father's trunk. Maybe his were in the box of her things. Except Miss Martha had been through all of those things. She would have remembered love letters. But maybe...

I couldn't help hoping. I told myself I didn't care, that I was just solving a puzzle, and the fact that the missing piece was my father didn't matter—he'd left me, and I was over it. But that was a big, fat lie. Of course I cared. That was why I was here. And I wanted to know where he was—even if it was far too late for him to come back and be the father I'd missed all of my life.

At the top of the stairs, Savannah paused, hands on her hips, and scanned the line of connected rooms that made up the attic on this side of the Manor. "Back here, I think," she said. "Is that what you remember, Mom?"

"I think so," Miss Martha agreed, nodding with less surety than Savannah. "It's been a few years since I rearranged up here after the roof leaked. I remember that her box didn't get wet, but I switched it over to a plastic storage bin, just in case, and then I put it..." Her voice trailed off as she lost herself in memory, trying to track down exactly where she'd left Sarah's things. "I hid them. Prentice never came up here, but..."

She and Savannah led us to the room at the far end of the attic, turning sideways to squeeze through the jumble of discarded furniture—things too valuable to get rid of or throw out, but out of style or in need of repair. Here and there, were hidden treasures, like the gorgeous antique brass bed Savannah had put in my room.

At the end of the room, someone had built deep, unfinished shelves of pine running floor to ceiling. On them were rows of plastic storage bins, each neatly labeled. Miss Martha paced down the wall, scanning the bins.

"Just let me think for a second," she said slowly. She reached for a bin on the top shelf that read *Sleeping Bags*, then drew her hand back, shaking her head. "No, not that one."

A few steps later, she bent to peer at a bin labeled *Cookbooks*. She gave it a tug, but it barely moved.

"I think it's this one." Looking over her shoulder, she said, "Boys?" to Ford and Griffen in the tone of a woman who'd called them that when they were toddlers.

Neither of them objected, stepping forward to heft the heavy bin off the shelf.

"I put it in here. Your father never would have opened a bin that had cookbooks in it," Miss Martha said. "I'm not sure he knew where the kitchen was."

"Good thinking," Ford said.

As he and Griffen set it on the floor and flipped back the tabs holding the lid on, Miss Martha reached to open it. Inside, the bin was stuffed with cookbooks surrounding a smaller cardboard box.

"Is that it?" Savannah asked.

It was such a small box to hold the remains of a life. Griffen pulled the box out, the weight of it taking him by surprise as it started to slip from his grasp. Ford slid a hand beneath and set the lid back on the bin, helping Griffen set the box on top, using the storage bin as a low table. Carefully, Ford undid the flaps on the top of the box and folded them open.

"It was all I could save," Miss Martha said, reaching in to pull out a pale lavender cashmere shawl. "She got this on her honeymoon in Ireland. He took her on a tour of Europe, and she came home with this, jewelry, and more gifts. But the smile she'd worn at her wedding was all but gone." Miss Martha set the shawl aside and shook her head.

I turned and saw a chair at the edge of the jumble of furniture. I pulled it closer so she could sit. Everyone else here had been too young when Sarah Sawyer had left to know what any of her things had meant to her. But Miss Martha knew.

"Thank you, Paige." She sat and leaned over, reaching into the box again. "I wish I could have saved more," she said quietly, pulling out a tarnished sterling silver picture frame made of two sides with hinges in the middle.

Each side showed a black-and-white photograph of an infant, a lock of hair trapped beneath the glass along with the picture, one platinum blonde, and the other a deep brown. The chubby, rounded faces didn't call to mind the adults I knew as Griffen and Ford, but—

"They look like twins except for the hair," I said, reaching out to stroke a fingertip over the lock of Ford's dark baby curls.

"They did, despite the few years between them, until they were teenagers." Miss Martha looked up to Griffen and then Ford. "She kept this on her bedside table. She loved you both so much."

With a sigh, she set the frame aside and reached into the box again. There was a small leather travel case that held a few pairs of earrings and a diamond tennis bracelet. A thin volume of poems. *Shakespeare's Sonnets*. The narrow spine was cracked as if the book had been opened many times.

Ford took it, opening it to the first page. "To S, all my love, P," he read.

Griffen looked over his shoulder. "That's not Dad's handwriting."

Hope leaned in to study the inscription. "It's not." She glanced at me. "Do you know if it's your dad's writing?"

I shook my head. "I wish I did, but—" I thought for a second. "Some of the military papers in his trunk have his signature. Maybe we can see if the P matches."

"It's worth a look," Ford murmured, setting aside the book of sonnets and reaching into the box to withdraw a worn bit of blanket. He handed it to Miss Martha with a question in his eyes.

"That was Griffen's baby blanket." She let out a soft

sigh before she said, "You were still using yours when she left."

At the bottom, Miss Martha felt around and found a small red leather box. She opened it to reveal a necklace, a simple pearl hanging at the end of a thin gold chain.

"I don't remember Sarah wearing this. Maybe..." She looked at me. I knew what she was thinking.

"Maybe it was from my father," I finished for her. That would explain why Sarah hadn't worn it but had thought enough of it to keep it in her bedside drawer.

"May I?" Ford asked, reaching for the box as Martha handed it to him. He stared down at it for a long moment, then reached for the tab at the base of the piece that displayed the pearl on the chain and pulled it up. Beneath, gold flashed.

"There's something in there, under the necklace," Hope said.

"Looks like it." Ford pulled out half of a gold heart pendant, one side jagged, as if meant to fit perfectly with the other side.

My breath caught in my throat.

Ford heard the choked sound and his eyes shot to me. "You recognize it?"

"I found the other half in my father's trunk," I said. "It's with my things. I can show you later. He must have given it to her...or she gave it to him."

"And she hid it to keep it safe," Hope said. "I'd say if anyone was wondering if Paige's father was Sarah's mysterious lover, that question's been answered."

I nodded. I'd been sure, but I could understand why

they might have had questions. Now those were put to rest. I wished that had settled anything for me.

We went through the remainder of the box but found no more clues to their relationship. No letters from my father to Sarah. Nothing of his at all, except the half of the pendant and the volume of sonnets.

Griffen folded down the top of the box and placed it in the storage bin, surrounded by cookbooks. "We might as well keep this here for now, since there's nothing in it we need."

Ford nodded in agreement, and together they slid the bin back on the shelf.

Griffen shoved his hands in his pockets when he straightened. "I haven't heard back from Cooper on the search for Paul Williams, but it's almost the weekend. We may have to wait till Monday."

"What about your mother?" I asked. "Are they looking for her, too?"

Ford looked to Griffen, and Griffen shrugged.

"I asked them to look years ago, when I first joined the team at Sinclair Security. As far as they could see, she dropped off the face of the earth the day she left Sawyers Bend. They've checked here and there over the years, and no change. None of her accounts were ever touched, and her IDs never popped back up, but that doesn't mean much."

"Why not?" I asked, not understanding. Not finding a sign of Sarah in over three decades seemed pretty significant to me.

"Because if she had any intention of leaving our father, she would have known the only way to do it was to disappear," Griffen explained. "She would have made plans."

"What about a divorce?" I asked, feeling a little lost. "People get divorced all the time. Custody, alimony... People don't usually disappear."

"No, he wouldn't have let her go," Miss Martha said. She shook her head sadly. "She didn't have any money of her own. Her parents were well-off, but they were older and wanted her settled with Prentice. They were old-fashioned—husband knows best. She tried to leave—with Griffen—not long after he was born, and they sent her right back. She had no help, couldn't afford a lawyer. I don't honestly know how she could have divorced Prentice and had a hope of ever seeing the two of you again."

"Courts usually give custody to the mother. At least they did back then, right?" Hope asked.

"Back then, yeah," Griffen said, "but most husbands aren't Prentice Sawyer."

"Good point," Hope agreed. "Poor Sarah..." She looked to Griffen with a guilty expression. "I know she left you. I don't understand how she could have done that, but I can't help but feel sorry for her. Your father was a nightmare. I picture her so young, not knowing what she was getting into, and then she was stuck. I want to judge her for leaving you two, but I can't."

"Neither can I," Ford said slowly. "Especially if she'd already tried to leave before she got pregnant with me."

I hated the picture forming in my head, hated more knowing that Ford was probably thinking the same thing. If Sarah had tried to leave Prentice before she got pregnant with Ford, she probably hadn't wanted to have another child in the first place. Not with Prentice. And I'd seen enough pictures of past Sawyers to know that Ford was a Sawyer by blood. Had Prentice forced her? Or had she gone along with what he wanted, knowing she didn't have a choice?

As if she was reading our minds, Miss Martha reached for Ford's hand, letting him help her to her feet. When she stood, she didn't let go; instead, she clasped his hand in both of hers. "She loved you so much, Ford. No matter how unhappy she was with your father, she never regretted either of you, not for a second."

He pulled her into a hug, murmuring something in her ear that made her smile.

"So, what now?" I asked, wanting a clear answer, a path through the messy feelings of anger at our parents for abandoning us and sympathy for Sarah Sawyer, trapped by her love for her sons with a man who everyone seemed to agree had been a monster.

"We wait to hear from Cooper," Griffen said. "See if he can find your father. And I think we need to talk to Edgar and Harvey."

"They're your best bet," Miss Martha agreed. "They knew Sarah well—I'd say they cared for her to a degree, and they were certainly around all the time back then, even more than they are now. I don't know that much went on in this house that they didn't know about. Especially as it pertained to Prentice's business. If Paul Williams was working with Prentice, they would have known."

"They'll be here for Sunday dinner," Hope said. "I'll

ask Uncle Edgar to come early. If I do it, he won't be suspicious."

"Surprise attack?" Griffen asked, sliding an arm around his wife's waist. "I like it when you're devious."

She grinned up at him. "If Uncle Edgar knows anything, we'll find out."

"I like your optimism," Griffen said, "but I'm not sure I agree. Edgar knows how to keep secrets. My guess is we'll have better luck with Harvey."

"Well, we'll find out either—" Ford's words were cut off as the house went silent, lights flicking off. The sun streamed in through the windows on the other side of the room, but the overhead lights were out, the hum of the furnace quiet.

Griffen's phone sounded an alert. "Power's been cut at the road," he said. "Backup security systems operational."

"What do we do?" Ford asked.

"Nothing," Griffen said. "We stay put." He stared at the screen of his phone intently, brows drawn together. "Scarlett and Stella are in the safe room on the lower level, along with Finn. Hold on." He tapped his screen and held it out in front of him so the rest of us could see the feed from the security camera, in high resolution and full color. "Hawk says we have eyes."

"How is that working if the power is out?" I asked, squinting at the small screen.

"Security systems have their own power, independent of the main system," Griffen said. "Same for the network they run on."

We watched on the small screen as a figure in blue

jeans and a dark brown hoodie used a small blowtorch on the tall fence beside the gates to Heartstone.

Griffen rolled his eyes. "Good move on cutting the power where they did, but this is just sloppy. Hawk's people have the house secured," he said, reading a message that popped up at the bottom of the screen. "West is on the way. Ryder, Wren, and Eli are closing in on the gates."

The figure with the blowtorch—it was hard to tell if it was a man or a woman, given the angle of the camera and the way the hoodie was pulled up—wasn't making much progress. The gates weren't just for show. They were solid.

"They would have done better to go around and try to cut through deeper in the woods," Griffen murmured. It was almost funny the way the intruder's head snapped up as the gate swung open silently.

West's SUV came into view, cutting off the intruder's retreat. There wasn't any sound on the video, but I watched as he exited his vehicle, gun drawn, shouting at the intruder to put down the torch and get their hands in the air. The intruder turned, holding up the torch menacingly. West didn't flinch at the flare of flame. He held his weapon steady on the intruder and repeated his order.

Griffen's phone screen was small, but I could see West's expression. He didn't look scared; he looked confident, almost smug. I saw why a second later as Ryder, Eli, and Wren appeared—Ryder and Wren rounding the gate, weapons drawn. The sudden show of force sent the intruder stumbling back in surprise until their shoulders hit the bars of the fence. Eli's hands shot through and closed around the intruder's throat.

It was all over after that. The intruder dropped the blowtorch. West got his cuffs out and arrested them.

"That happened faster than I expected," Griffen said.

"The newest assassin trying to get the bounty by killing me?" Ford asked. "Or West and Ryder and his team taking him down?"

"The first," Griffen said. "West getting here so fast was lucky, but Ryder, Wren, and Eli could have handled it without him if they had to. Cleaner to have West arrest him, though. I thought we'd have another day or two before the next attempt on you."

"I'm going to go get Stella," Hope said, turning for the door. I imagined she'd feel better once she had her baby girl in her arms.

No one had gotten close to breaching Heartstone's security, but the attempt on the gate was enough. It was a stark reminder that this was an active threat and would continue to be one.

I paused before following her and turned to Ford. "Are you okay?"

He nodded, but his eyebrows were pulled together. In frustration, anger, or fear, I couldn't tell. Maybe all three. "Yeah, I guess. I'm going to follow Griffen. I want to know what's going on, even if I don't understand half the shit they say."

I rose up on my toes to kiss his cheek. "I'm going to go with Hope." Stella wasn't my baby, but I had an itch to lay eyes on her. Being separated from her when scary things were happening left me feeling restless.

I followed Hope out of the room, thinking about the volume of poetry and the pendant in Sarah's box and wishing we'd found more.

* * *

Later that night, I lay in bed, curled into Ford, dozing as his fingers combed through my hair.

"I feel like a sitting duck," he said, his voice low. "What if the guy this morning got through the fence and reached the house? He could have come across you and the kids, out there playing soccer. Or Hope, walking with Stella."

"That's not going to happen," I said, shifting to prop myself up on my elbow, craning my neck to meet his dark, worried eyes. "They didn't even get close."

"This time," he said darkly. "I've brought too much pain to my family. I can't stand the idea of anyone getting hurt because of me. Cole is doing this because he blames me for Caro's death. No one else should be a target."

"That's ridiculous." I sat up, pulling the sheet with me and holding it against my breasts. "Cole Haywood was coming after your family, even when you were in prison. And no one is going to get hurt. Hawk and the new team Sinclair Security sent are too good for that."

"I wish I had your confidence," he said, pulling me back down to lie across his chest.

I caught his hand in mine and pressed a kiss to his fingertips. "Everything is going to be okay," I promised. It had to be.

Ford went back to combing his fingers through my

hair. As sleep pulled him under, I heard him say, "I wish we could stay just like this, forever."

"Me too," I whispered, not sure he was awake enough to hear me.

Despite the danger we were in, I'd never felt more at peace. Though neither of us had said the words, I'd never felt so loved. Ford was too wrapped in guilt and worry to be at peace. I'd have to believe in happy endings enough for the both of us.

Chapter Twenty-Three

FORD

Sunday dinner was usually a production at Heartstone Manor, though not as formal as it had been when I was a child. Some of my siblings and their partners dressed up. Some of us didn't bother. Edgar and Harvey usually attended, and liked to harrumph at the presence of children at the formal dining table, but Griffen and Hope had made it clear this was their house, and children would always be an included part of the family. I suspected that while Edgar and Harvey made a show of not liking it, secretly, they enjoyed having the kids around. Everyone liked seeing Heartstone brought back to life. Everyone except Cole Haywood, of course.

Hope had called her uncle Edgar and asked him to bring Harvey and be there an hour early. Edgar had agreed, without asking why. Hope could usually get him to do what she wanted with less explanation than the rest of us would require. He'd raised her since she was a young child, saving her from her criminally neglectful parents. Edgar was gruff and not overly affectionate, but

Hope was the daughter of his heart. And while he wasn't overflowing with hugs and kisses, it was clear that in his own way, he was devoted to her.

He'd had an extra layer of smug satisfaction ever since she'd married Griffen and given birth to Stella. In his old-school way of seeing things, he couldn't have done better than to get her married off and popping out babies for the Sawyer heir. It was only icing on the cake to him that they were head over heels in love with each other.

He and I had always worked well together. Edgar and my father, along with Harvey, had been best friends. Harvey had handled a lot of their legal business—his focus had always been the law—whereas Edgar had been Prentice's business partner in many of Prentice's investments. Though they'd frequently disagreed, they'd been on the same page more often than not. While Edgar wasn't the monster Prentice had been, I couldn't say he was my favorite person. He was tougher than Harvey, more likely to think the ends justified the means. Though I knew Edgar looked at me with as much suspicion as I had for him, there'd been things over the years I'd said yes to—like the deal that had almost gotten Finn killed—that Edgar wouldn't have touched.

He was ruthless in business, but he had morals Prentice had lacked. Morals I'd ignored for longer than I liked to think about. I wasn't that man anymore, but Edgar didn't know that. Not for sure. As he and Harvey walked into Griffen's office, he gave me a cautious, borderline suspicious look, his gaze bouncing from Griffen and back to me. It didn't hurt, but only because I wasn't surprised. I wondered if he thought we were about to make an announcement about the future of the family business. That wasn't going to happen. My place there was gone, and I wasn't sure I wanted it back. I had a lot to figure out before I settled on what I was going to do with the rest of my life.

Though I had to admit, ever since Cole had put out his bounty and I'd been stuck at Heartstone, I'd missed Avery's brewery. I liked working with my siblings and seeing Sawyers Bend Brewing flourish. I had the nagging feeling of missing out on Finn's work getting the kitchen into shape. Out of nowhere, I realized I was hoping we'd have this assassin problem dealt with before Finn was ready to open. I didn't want to miss out on more of my siblings' lives than I already had.

"Well, what's all this about?" Edgar narrowed his eyes on Hope. "I don't see any champagne."

"Why would we have champagne?" Hope asked.

"I thought you were going to announce you were expecting again," he grumped.

Hope let out a laugh that was half amused and half terrified. "I can barely keep up with Stella!"

"Well, you're not getting any younger—"

"Edgar, enough," Griffen said with a shake of his head. Hope reached out to take his hand. "Everyone, sit down." He pushed out his desk chair and took a seat himself, pulling Hope into his lap. "No baby announcements, Edgar. Sorry to disappoint," he said, not sounding sorry at all.

Edgar's attention switched to me. "You're jumping back into the family business, then?"

I shook my head before he finished the question. "It's

not about that either. That's Griffen's problem now. He doesn't need me getting in the way." Griffen looked at me, surprise flashing across his face. "This is about our mother."

"Sarah?" Harvey asked, his voice soft, eyes sad. "How could anything be about Sarah? She's been gone for over thirty years."

"Do either of you remember meeting or doing business with a man named Paul Williams before our mother left?" Griffen asked.

Edgar started to shake his head. He went still as Harvey's gaze snapped to Paige's face, his eyes focused intently as he studied her features.

"I knew you looked familiar," Harvey said, an edge to his voice, "when you came in to interview with Hope. I just couldn't place you. You have his eyes. You're his daughter?"

Paige gave a short nod. "I am, but I never knew him," she said.

"How did you meet Paul Williams?" I asked.

"He had business with Prentice," Edgar said, looking between Harvey and Paige. "I guess I see the resemblance, in the eyes and the hair." He nodded slowly. "I wouldn't have spotted it unless you brought up Paul's name." He shook his head again and looked at Paige and me. "Prentice and I had gone in on some commercial real estate. A series of connected strip centers up in Johnson City. We owned two. Paul owned the one in between. We had plans to develop the whole strip, but we weren't interested in bringing on a partner. Paul didn't want to redevelop, but he was willing to sell. He and Prentice had a difference of opinion on what that sale should look like."

"And you?" I asked. "Where did you stand?"

Edgar looked up at the ceiling as if lost in memory, then met my eyes. "I'd say I was in between. Paul had some restrictions on his current leases I wasn't interested in honoring. But I felt he was more realistic on the price than Prentice. You know your father could be stubborn as hell. He had in mind the deal he wanted to make. He wasn't willing to budge on the numbers. Neither was Williams."

"How often did Paul Williams visit Heartstone?" I asked.

Edgar drew in a slow breath, putting the pieces together in his mind. "As I recall," he said, "only a few times, and he never stayed in the house." He closed his eyes for a moment, and when he opened them, he said, "Now that I think back, I don't know where he stayed. He was from Ohio, but he had business investments nearby—real estate in Tennessee, South Carolina. He traveled a lot, I know that. But how are you his daughter," he said to Paige, "if you've never met him?"

Paige sighed. "He was married to my mother, Harriet McKenna. She was pregnant with me when he told her he'd found someone else, and he left."

I studied Harvey and Edgar sitting side by side on the leather sofa, facing the matching sofa Paige and I sat on. Harvey looked uncomfortable; Edgar, thoughtful, as if he was puzzling out the bits of information we'd given him to put together the picture. It wouldn't take him long. I knew how Edgar's mind worked. And he was sharp.

"You think Paul Williams is the man your mother left with?" His eyes shot to Harvey, seeking agreement.

Harvey let out a gusty sigh. "He might have been. I don't ever recall them meeting, but he could have bumped into Sarah in the house, or even in town if that's where he stayed. She was always so focused on you boys back then," Harvey said, his eyes going from Griffen to me. "But she could have slipped away to see him."

"And that's why you're here," Edgar said to Paige, his eyes narrowing on her face as if assessing what kind of trouble she might cause.

I squeezed her hand in mine. Edgar could be intimidating, but I wouldn't let him scare Paige off.

She nodded. "I found a trunk of his things after my mother passed. Inside, I found letters from Sarah," she said, her voice calm but her fingers gripping mine so tightly I was sure her knuckles were white.

"Letters?" Harvey asked. "They wrote to each other?"

"She wrote to him," Paige said. "And from the content of her letters, it seemed like there were probably letters back from him to her, but we haven't found any."

"You've been looking?" Harvey asked, his white brows drawing together.

"Of course," I said, rubbing my thumb over the back of Paige's hand.

"They left thirty-five years ago," Edgar reminded me. "Is there a point? When was the last time you heard from your mother?"

"I stopped getting birthday postcards in my early twenties," I said.

Griffen agreed. "Same for me. Not that there was much to them in the first place, but they were something." Neither of us mentioned the handwriting issue, waiting, in unspoken agreement, to see what Harvey and Edgar knew before we told them everything.

"Were you surprised when she left?" Hope asked quietly, looking at her uncle.

Edgar shook his head, raising one eyebrow. "Surprise doesn't cover it, Hope. Sarah was devoted to her sons," he said with a glance at Griffen and then me. "I think it's safe to say you two were her only joy. That she would leave her children for a man, even one she was in love with—I never would have thought." He gave a half shrug of one shoulder. "People surprise you."

Truer words had rarely been spoken. I knew people did all sorts of things I'd never expect. I thought of Cole Haywood. In a million years, in all of those meetings we had about getting me out of prison, it had never occurred to me that Cole was the one who put me there. I hadn't known about Prentice's affair with Cole's beloved wife, or Prentice's role in her death. So many things I hadn't known and hadn't seen coming.

Everyone kept saying my mother had been a devoted parent who never would have left Griffen or me.

"How do you know Sarah ran off with my father?" Paige asked slowly.

She spoke the words I didn't want to think. Everyone looked at her in surprise.

"What do you mean?" Harvey asked.

"I mean, we know that they had some kind of relationship based on the letters and some other things we found. It seems fair to say they were in love, also based on the letters." She looked at Griffen, who had more of a background in this kind of intrigue than anyone else in the room. "But we don't actually know that they left together."

She was right, and I felt like an idiot for not considering that myself. Everyone assumed they'd run off together because no one had heard from our parents since they disappeared. But what if they hadn't run off? What if something had happened to them?

Paige and Griffen stared at one another until he asked, "How did your mother get the news? Did she ever tell you?"

"A letter," Paige said. "She got a letter."

"So, she didn't hear directly from Paul that he was running off with our mother?" Griffen asked.

Paige shook her head slowly. "Not in person, not a phone call. I know because she was aggrieved at that part —not just that he'd left, but that he hadn't bothered to tell her in person. How did you find out?" she asked, looking at Edgar and Harvey. "Who told you she ran off with another man?"

"Prentice," Edgar said, and looked to Harvey, who nodded in agreement.

"Prentice said there was a big showdown," Harvey added. "He said she told him she was leaving him, and he told her she'd never get the kids. And she said they'd see about that, and she stormed out with her suitcases."

"He never said who she stormed out with?" I asked, suddenly seeing all the holes in the story.

Harvey shook his head slowly. "Just that a man was

driving the car. If he knew it was Paul, he never said." Harvey glanced at Edgar, who shook his head. "There were those postcards," Harvey said to Griffen and me. "You got postcards from Sarah for years."

Griffen glanced at me, and I nodded.

"We did," Griffen agreed, "but we compared them to the letters, which we're very sure were written by our mother, and the handwriting isn't the same."

"What are you saying?" Edgar challenged, looking from Paige to Griffen.

I knew exactly what she was going to say. I could tell she'd gotten there, too.

"I don't know," Paige said, "but it's occurred to me that no one's found a sign of Sarah since the day she left this house."

"Cooper Sinclair has had people looking," I added, "but so far there's no sign of Paul Williams either. So—"

"Are you implying that they didn't run off together?" Edgar demanded.

"Maybe," Paige said. She let out a long sigh, leaning into my side enough to send Edgar's eyebrows up as he noticed. "I don't know. It just seems odd that there's nothing. All I've ever heard about Sarah Sawyer is how much she loved her kids, and yet she just left? Not a word, but those postcards that she didn't send. So, who sent the postcards? And my father..." Her shoulders slumped. "I can see him leaving my mother. And I could see leaving her when she was pregnant with me. He'd never even held me. It wasn't real to him the way Ford and Griffen would have been to Sarah. But I don't know..."

She shook her head again.

"All my life, I've had this idea in my head of him living a second life without me or my mother. But wouldn't he have left a footprint of some kind? He was doing business with Prentice Sawyer. He had real estate investments. I don't know if my mother was aware of any of that, or, if she was, why she didn't try to get control of assets that should have gone to her as his wife. I know she looked. And she never found anything. So where is he? How could someone just disappear?"

It was a great question. I had the same one, despite what we'd said earlier about Sarah being smart and completely erasing herself to get away from my father. Back then, you could do that much more easily. But Paige was right. Real estate investments had paperwork.

Harvey and Edgar shared a glance I couldn't read.

"I don't know how many records I have that go that far back," Edgar said. "It's ancient history. But I'll look through my files to see if I can find out what might have happened to your father's property. As for the rest—" He shook his head, regret heavy in his eyes as he glanced at Hope. "I wish I had more answers for you. But my guess is that Griffen's connections with the Sinclairs will get you more information than anything I could turn up. I can promise you I've not laid eyes on Sarah Sawyer since before the day Prentice said she walked out of this house. And aside from Prentice telling me about those postcards she was supposedly sending, I've never heard of anyone having any contact with her since that day."

Harvey let out a long, gusty sigh, his eyes sadder than I'd ever seen them. "Me either," he said. "I was always sorry she left you boys. She was such a good mother, but there was a part of me that was glad she was out there somewhere, living a better life."

"Well, was that it?" Edgar asked, bracing his palms on his knees as if getting ready to stand.

"I guess," Hope said. "If you two think of anything, you'll let us know?"

"Of course, of course," Edgar said, pushing himself to his feet. "I'm going to make my way to the dining room, help myself to a cocktail. Sad memories," he said. "A little whiskey will do the trick."

Chapter Twenty-Four

FORD

We watched in silence as Harvey followed Edgar out, neither of them speaking in words, though the looks they shared did plenty of talking.

"What do you think they know?" I asked Griffen.

He gave Hope a squeeze before he shifted his weight and stood, bringing her to her feet along with him. "My guess is they know more than they're saying, but I don't think they know where Sarah and Paul are."

"That's the read I got too," I agreed.

"Paige," Hope asked, "do you think something happened to them?"

Paige gave a helpless shrug. "I don't want to, but I'm starting to wonder if that's the only sensible answer."

"I don't like it," I said. "But I agree."

"I don't like it either," Hope said. "I'd rather imagine her neglectful and thoughtless than the alternative." She shuddered.

"Me too," Paige whispered. "Especially for my father.

My mother was a miserable person, and I was just an idea. I could see being in love"—her eyes flicked to me, then back to Hope—"and losing his head. But to never show up again? That's pretty crappy. I'd still rather he was a bad father and a selfish husband than..." She fell silent, clearly not wanting to put the other option into words.

None of us wanted to think that. I was firmly on her team. I'd much rather imagine my mother enjoying life somewhere—careless, selfish, gone. But alive.

"Look," Griffen said, "we're not going to get any answers on this today."

"It feels like the more people we talk to, the more questions we have," I said.

"Agreed," Griffen said. "For now, let's just enjoy Sunday dinner. Maybe tomorrow, Cooper's people will have dug something up on Paul Williams. Without that, I'm not sure where we look next."

"I—" Paige started to say, then stopped.

"What are you thinking?" Hope asked, leaning into Griffen's side, her arm around his waist.

Paige shook her head. "I'm not ready to say," she said, swirling her finger in the air. "I need to let things percolate a little more. I might have an idea, but it might be nothing at all." She looked up to me. "I'm up for just enjoying Sunday dinner and worrying about the rest of this tomorrow."

So that was what we did. As we'd been reminded since I'd found those letters in Paige's drawer, Sarah and Paul had been missing for over thirty years. Another day, another week, another month wouldn't make much of a difference. Our impatience to solve the mystery didn't change a thing, especially since it didn't seem like there was that much to find.

Sunday dinner was more family-style and less formal than usual, right down to the meal. Finn had made big pans of lasagna, bruschetta on fresh-baked bread, and crisp Caesar salad. With the kids in the dining room with us, the atmosphere was light and loud. Everyone lingered after the meal. Miss Martha—and to my surprise, Uncle Edgar—talked the kids into a board game, roping in Tenn and Scarlett. Hope and Griffen disappeared with Stella, and Paige and I took advantage of her evening off to hide away in my room.

It was less cozy than Paige's. To be honest, if invited, I would have ditched my room in favor of moving in with her. But given that we were just across the hall and had only been together a short time, maybe that was jumping the gun. It didn't feel like it. The idea of spending a night apart from Paige was intolerable. I'd never felt like this with a woman before—not just attracted to her, but as if she was necessary. When I could see her, touch her, even if just to hold her hand, everything was brighter and more alive.

"Are you going to do anything with this room?" she asked as I shut the door behind me.

I looked around, reminded again how much more welcoming her space was—not just because of the furniture, rugs, and artwork Savannah had hung, but the way Paige had settled in and made it her own. In contrast, I had a beat-up wooden desk with a chair, a full-size bed without a head or footboard, and an old couch. Yeah,

Savannah definitely hadn't been happy I was coming back to Heartstone Manor.

I understood. While I'd never been a jerk to her or Miss Martha, I hadn't been particularly friendly either, treating Savannah like the daughter of the help when I was younger. Savannah, like almost everyone else, had been loyal to Griffen. I'd hurt a lot of people when I'd gotten him exiled. At the time, I hadn't understood the ripple I'd create. In my head, I'd thought all of it would be temporary. Griffen shoved out so I could have a little of our father's attention for a while, so I could be number one. And then, somewhere in my immaturity and inexperience, I thought things would just mend themselves. Griffen would come back, and everything would work out. Somehow, I thought I'd still be top dog and Griffen would be second to me.

None of it had happened the way I'd imagined, because I'd been a tool, the great Prentice Sawyer manipulating me for his own ends like he did with everyone else.

"I don't know if I'll fix up my room," I said to Paige, pushing away the reminder of all the things I'd fucked up. "I guess it just feels—" I shrugged. "Temporary. I wasn't living here when I was arrested for shooting Prentice. I'd moved into a suite at the Inn."

"Heartstone wasn't big enough for the two of you to share?" she asked, her voice heavy with humor.

"It should have been," I said honestly. "But no, it wasn't. I needed to get away. The Inn at Sawyers Bend always felt like a second home. I moved in one day, intending to stay a few days while my rooms here were repainted, and I never left."

"What about now?" she asked, crossing the room, stopping in front of me to slide her arms around my waist. She tipped her head back and looked up, her pale blue eyes lit from within, filled with welcome.

I wrapped my arms around her. "I don't know. It feels too soon to make any big decisions. But for me, this room still feels temporary. I'm hoping that down the road I'll find something more permanent." I lifted my hand to tuck a stray curl behind her ear, stroking her soft skin with one fingertip. "But I don't want to rush anything. I don't want to rush you," I said, cupping her cheek in my hand and lifting her face.

I kissed her, falling into the feel of her soft lips against mine, the heat of her mouth, the stroke of her tongue—a taste that was only Paige, my Paige.

Her arms rose, her fingers sinking into my hair. She kissed me back, so filled with want. We were on the same page there. The more I touched her, the more I needed. I slid my hands under the back of her shirt, feeling the silk of her skin, and undid the clasp of her bra. Leaning back, I cupped her breasts, sliding my thumbs over the points of her nipples, breaking the kiss and running my lips along her jaw, sucking the point behind her ear that made her shiver.

"Ford," she said, stepping back, reaching for my arm to pull me toward the bed.

"Where do you think you're going?" I asked, sliding her shirt over her head along with her bra. I moved to scoop her into my arms, nipping the side of her neck just enough to make her squirm, planning to toss her on the bed and lunge after her so I could pin her down and strip off the rest of her clothes—

Glass shattered, and in a split second, all ideas of stripping Paige naked evaporated. Instead, I landed on top of her on the mattress, spread my body to cover her, shielding her from whatever had broken the glass.

I scanned the room frantically. The window was broken. How the fuck was the window broken? We were on the second floor. My eyes focused. The upper left pane of the center window was a gaping hole, shards of glass scattered over every surface in the room. "Stay still," I said.

"What? Stay still?" she said, her words muffled by my shoulder, her voice strained with fear. "You're smushing me. Are you all right?"

"I'm fine." I rolled slightly to look over my shoulder, and after a second, I saw the neat hole in the desk drawer. "I think someone tried to shoot me."

Her voice was panicked. "What? How?"

It was night. We had the lights on in here. I couldn't see a thing through the dark window, and whoever was out there could probably see us perfectly.

Could see Paige. With me. Perfectly. *Fuck.*

I couldn't do anything about the overhead light without putting myself in danger, so I left it.

"I need to call Hawk and Griffen," I said quietly. "Slide over to the edge of the bed. We're going to hide underneath." Aware I needed to get Paige out of sight, fast, we edged to the side of the bed. I risked sitting up just enough to nudge Paige down. She dropped to the floor, leaving a red smear across the white duvet that stopped my heart. She was bleeding?

"I'm under," she said.

"You're bleeding," I growled, unable to hold back my panic. I followed her under the bed, finally getting my phone out and dialing Griffen.

"Yeah," he answered.

I filled him in, using my free hand to examine Paige for injury, the tight space and darkness making it nearly impossible to see where she was hurt.

"Single shot?" he asked.

"As far as I can tell," I said.

"All right. I'm going to get Ryder's team mobilized. I'm thinking long-range sniper. One of the trees—" His voice cut off. Then, "Wren can track almost anyone. Stay there until we come get you."

I pulled Paige farther under the bed, shifting so my back was to the rest of the room and Paige was against the wall, as safe as I could make her until rescue arrived. Turning on the flashlight on my phone, I ran it over her, seeing the long slices on her bare arms and shoulders, with dots of red scattered across her chest. Flashes of light caught the beam from my phone. Glass shards had flown into the room when the bullet hit the window, slicing into Paige.

She lifted her top arm, turning it in the light. "It doesn't really hurt, Ford. They aren't deep."

Her denial sent burning rage coursing through me, followed by the ice of fear. *So close.* She'd been way too close to that bullet. She could have been killed just for being close to me.

I couldn't let that happen. I wouldn't.

"You're sure you're okay?" she asked.

"I'm sure," I said slowly. "But I'm starting to think we may need to consider a safe house."

"I thought you said you weren't leaving Heartstone," she said.

"Not for me," I said. "For you."

Chapter Twenty-Five
FORD

My phone signaled an incoming text. Hawk.

> Stay down. Active shooter.

That was it. As it should be. Hawk was doing what Hawk did best—keeping us safe. But it hammered home how much danger we were all in. How much danger I was putting everyone in.

"What did he say?" Paige asked in a whisper.

"To stay down."

Cold air filled the room, this time from the broken window. Paige's blood, warm and wet, smeared my arm. The feel of it had my stomach rolling, and I fought the urge to vomit. *Not the time or place*, I ordered myself. I couldn't help it. Bad enough that Paige was injured and bleeding because of me. Now we were stuck here, waiting.

I turned on the flashlight on my phone and scanned it over her body again. Her back had been facing the window when it shattered. The glass had exploded like a thousand tiny projectiles. I couldn't put together the sequence of events. At the time, I'd been focused on Paige, kissing her and then tossing her on the bed. We'd been moving when the bullet smashed through the window. Exactly the wrong place at the wrong time.

As far as I could tell, all the cuts were on Paige, and the blood on me was hers.

Echoing my thoughts, she asked, "Are you bleeding? Did you get cut?" She grabbed my phone, turning the light so she could shine it on my face, my arms, twisting as much as she could to get it on my legs.

"I'm fine," I said. "I don't know how, but I'm fine."

"You have a scratch here," she reached up and touched the side of my neck.

If I'd been cut, I didn't feel it. "Your back was to the window when the bullet came through," I said. "The glass got you." I caught her hand in mine. "Hold still. Moving is just going to make it bleed more."

She craned her neck to see what she could of her cuts. "They don't feel deep."

I couldn't hear her. Not the way I needed to. All I could see was the blood. Smearing across her cheek. Staining her arms, her lower leg.

"Don't move," I warned. "There's glass all over the floor, even under here."

She went still, murmuring, "I'm okay."

A spurt of fear-filled rage shot through me. Not at

her, but at the situation. At my own dumb fucking choices. My life decisions that led us all here.

"It's not fucking okay, Paige. We're hiding under a bed because someone shot at me. You could have been..." I choked the words out, feeling every one like a stab to my heart. They could have hit her. I could be holding her dead body right now. It was a matter of inches, of luck and timing. We'd been lucky. Next time, we might not be. And what would we do if our luck ran out?

I wasn't crazy about the idea of dying. If I got a say, I'd prefer to stick around for another five decades at least. But Paige? Nothing was going to happen to her. I couldn't stand the idea of it. Twice—in the parking lot and now in my own bedroom—she could have been killed, just for being near me. No. It was too high a price to pay. I couldn't allow it.

"We can't do this anymore," I said, my heart cracking in half as I put the thought into words.

"What do you mean?" Paige asked, her brow furrowed as she squinted at me in the dim light beneath the bed.

"I mean, we can't be together. You need to stay away from me. You should leave Heartstone. Go to a safe house or...shit, I don't know if Cole knows about you. You might be safe to just leave, but a safe house would be better."

"Ford, stop." Her hand came up to touch my cheek. "This is bad, okay? I agree this is not a good situation, but I'm not leaving you. I'm not running away."

"You have to," I said. How could she not get it? Her life was at stake.

"Ford, you're not thinking about this clearly," she

said, her tone even, at direct odds with the scampering fear I could barely contain. "We're all in danger, and it's not because of you. It's because Cole Haywood is a murderer and a psychopath."

"If I wasn't here, this wouldn't be happening," I argued, knowing I was right. Whether it was my fault was a different argument. I was sure Paige would take the other side. But I knew. I'd made choices. Those choices had hurt people. One of those hurt people wanted me to pay for it. I didn't think the punishment fit the crime, but I wasn't exactly in a position to parse guilt and innocence. Paige didn't deserve to pay for my crimes. "I can't stand the idea of anything happening to you." I felt her soften.

"I can't stand the idea of anything happening to you either," she said. "But I'm not going to leave you. I'm not a quitter."

Why wasn't she getting it? She was making this harder by dragging it out.

"Well, maybe I am," I said. "Maybe this is too much. Maybe you don't know what's best for you."

"I'm not a child," she snapped. "I'm an adult and I can make my own choices."

"But you don't get to make them for me," I said, keeping my tone reasonable. I had to get her to understand.

Paige lapsed into an irritated silence. I was being an ass—I knew it—but I couldn't back down. Her life was at stake.

That was all I could think of. Her *life*.

This wasn't about her being mad or thinking I was a jerk. This was about her heart continuing to beat, her lungs drawing breath, because some assassin's bullet hadn't taken her life. I'd been selfish this whole time. I understood that now. Crystal clear. I saw her and I'd wanted her. God, I wanted her so badly. The light that glowed inside her, the way she laughed, how good she was with people, with the kids, my family, me. And it'd only gotten worse when I actually spent time with her and discovered we could talk all night and never run out of things to say.

I had to make her understand.

"Paige," I said, not knowing how to explain. "I spent my entire life surrounded by selfish people, and I've been selfish too often. I love you." I hadn't thought to say the words, but when they came out, I knew they were true. "I've never been in love before," I added.

She stayed silent for one breath. Two. I found I wasn't scared of her not loving me back, of her not saying the words. I just needed her to know what was in my heart.

"How do you know you are now?" she asked, her voice quiet.

I didn't need to think. I just said what was real. What I knew.

"Because for the first time, I'm not the most important person in my world. I can't stand the idea of anything—or anyone—hurting you. And being near me is getting you hurt. I love you too much to let myself be selfish with you."

"And I don't get a say in any of this?" Her breath hitched. She forced out the words, "I don't think you can love me, because if you did, you'd listen to what I want instead of telling me how it's going to be. You're telling me what you can live with, but I can't live with walking away from you. I'm not going to abandon you just because things are hard. That's not who I am, and it's not fair for you to ask me to walk away. If you don't want to be with me, if this has run its course, then—" The words caught in her throat.

"Paige," I said, hating the pain in her voice. I reached to touch her face, but she batted my hand away, slamming her arm into the underside of the bed. Her gasp of pain sliced through me. "Be careful—"

The door to the room opened, and the light flicked off.

"It's me," Hawk said. "Ryder and Wren are out pinning down the sniper. I'm turning the lights out in here to cut the view. I'm going to cover this window. You two okay under there?"

"Paige is bleeding," I said.

"How badly? Stitches?" he asked, moving across the room.

"No," Paige answered before I could. "It's mostly stopped, I think. I'm pretty sure I don't need any stitches."

"I'm not surprised," Hawk said. "There's glass everywhere."

We fell silent, the only sounds in the room the rustling of Hawk hammering something to block the window. It felt like an eternity before he said, "Done. Give me one second to get this glass out of the way, and then you can slide out from under there. We'll go downstairs for a debrief."

Feet thumped across the floor and out into the hall. I heard the door of the utility closet open and shut, and then Hawk was back. A crystalline rattle of glass shards, the whoosh of the broom on the floor, and finally, he said, "All right, you're clear."

Hawk flipped the lights back on. When he saw Paige, he swore under his breath. I couldn't say anything, my mouth dry, lungs frozen. She was streaked with blood—smeared across her neck and down her arms. A long scratch on her arm still bled sluggishly, along with another on her calf.

"Let's get you bandaged up," Hawk said. He grabbed the robe that hung on the back of my door and handed it to me, not seemingly aware that Paige was half naked, except to offer the robe so she could cover up. She was too shaken, I think, to be embarrassed.

I reached for her arm after she had the robe on, and she jerked it away, refusing to look at me. I accepted it, even as her anger sliced through me. Couldn't she see that this was the only way? Being near me put a target on her back, whether she was an actual target or not.

Cole Haywood and whoever was trying to claim his bounty didn't give a shit about collateral damage. They'd hurt her if she was in the way—and if she was near me, she'd be in the way.

Chapter Twenty-Six

FORD

Griffen was pacing outside the door of the security room where Hawk's team monitored the cameras around the estate.

"Did they get him?" Hawk asked.

Eli leaned out of the room, his eyes dancing with adrenaline. "We're closing in on him," he said. "No one can track like Wren."

"If he took a shot from a sniper position," I asked, "what was there to track?"

"We've been studying the terrain," Eli said. "There are only so many places that shot could have come from, even with a really skilled sniper. With the mountains, you can only go so far before something gets in your way."

"If there are only a few places they could have shot from, why didn't you have them staked out?" Paige asked.

Eli looked at her and flinched, as if suddenly registering the blood on her face. "Lack of manpower," he said. "And, more relevant, there are only a handful of snipers who could have taken a shot from that position. We put sensors around the few spots we thought would work for a sniper. One of them went off twenty minutes ago. Ryder and Wren headed out to check, though we thought it was probably a bear. Last I heard from Ryder, the sniper had left his position in the tree, and Wren was right behind him. It won't be long." He looked back to Paige. "We should get you cleaned up. Make sure you don't need stitches."

"I don't need stitches," she grumbled, sounding more annoyed than anything else.

"Let's go in the kitchen," Griffen said, leading the way and flicking on the lights. "One of you grab the med kit."

I couldn't remember the last time I'd been down here so late at night. The room was quiet and still, and dishes lay on the center island ready for breakfast. It was odd seeing how neatly Finn had the kitchen organized and prepped for the next day—such a contrast to the wild and angry teenager he'd been. But this was the real Finn. He could still be wild. I was sure Savannah would have plenty to say about that. But this organized professionalism and his genius with food—that was the real man.

I'd missed so much because I'd been a selfish jackass. I'd wanted power and respect, and I'd sold my soul for them. Finn was only here because of his own resourcefulness. My selfishness had almost gotten him killed. And now there was Paige, the drying blood on her skin dark in the bright light.

Eli handed Griffen a red and black duffel bag.

Griffen unzipped the top and pulled out a pack of baby wipes. I took them and went to work cleaning her face.

"I can do it," she said, trying to reach for the wipe, but I pulled it out of the way.

"No. Let's get your arm out of the robe so Griffen can take a look at that cut. I'm not sure it's stopped bleeding."

She ground her teeth, I could tell. It was clear she wanted to argue, but was too sensible not to do as I suggested. Her hands went to the belt of the robe, and she loosened it enough to pull out one arm.

"Shit, Paige. I'm so sorry this happened," Griffen said.

He glanced at me, and I felt the accusation. I hadn't taken care of her. I hadn't protected her.

I'd done this. I might not have taken that shot, but I was the reason—the reason she was there, the reason the glass broke, the reason she was bleeding.

"Paige needs to go to a safe house," I said.

"No!" she shot back. "Griffen, he's upset and being crazy."

"I am upset," I agreed, "and I'm not being crazy."

"I'm not going to a safe house," she said. "You want me to stay away from you? Fine. I'll stay away from you."

"It's not what I want," I ground out. "It's the only way to keep you safe."

"What about everyone else in the house?" she asked. "Is everyone supposed to avoid you? Why don't we all leave, and you can live here by yourself waiting for someone to come in and murder you?"

"Now you're being ridiculous," I said. "I'm just trying to keep you safe."

Griffen's lips pressed together as he worked on cleaning her arm, and I couldn't tell if he wanted to laugh or disagree.

This wasn't funny. Not by a long shot.

"Why don't you worry about keeping yourself safe," she said. "You're the one they were trying to shoot."

"And they almost hit you," I reminded her.

"They didn't hit either of us," she shouted.

"Because we got lucky," I said, refusing to match her tone. I was the reasonable one here, dammit. "We got lucky, Paige. I'm not betting your life on luck."

"It's my life. I get to say." She lifted her chin, glaring at the wall across the room, refusing to look at me.

"Not when you're being an idiot about it—"

"You might want to shut that mouth, son," Eli said under his breath. "You are digging a hole you're not going to be able to get yourself out of."

"Shut the fuck up," I said, snapping. Why couldn't they all see that this was the only way?

Eli smirked and lifted his hands in a gesture of innocence. "Just offering some friendly advice. And though I'm not sure either of you wants to hear it, considering it's my job, I'll tell you. Paige is right. There's no point in putting her in a safe house unless you're going to put everyone in a safe house."

I opened my mouth to tell him how fucking ridiculous that was, but Griffen shot me a look that clearly told me to keep it shut.

"What about putting Ford in a safe house?" Paige asked.

"I'll get to that in a second. And also—" Eli looked at

Paige, who glared back at him. "Ford's right. I don't want to interfere in the process of young love, but you're better off keeping your distance until we shut this situation down."

Paige set her jaw mutinously but didn't say anything.

"For the record," Griffen said, "I agree with Eli." He looked to Paige, saying, "Brace yourself," and swabbed the long cut down her arm with rubbing alcohol.

Her eyes filled with tears, and she squeezed them shut, sucking in a sharp breath. "It's fine. I'm good," she said through her teeth.

"I know you are," Griffen said, calmly reassuring. He glanced at Eli. "I don't think Haywood's tracked that there's any reason to make Paige a target specifically. I think she was just in the wrong place at the wrong time."

"Agreed," Eli said.

"Do we think she's a danger to the kids?" Griffen asked.

"Not at this point, no," Eli said.

"Then yeah, I don't think a safe house is the right idea for either of you," Griffen said as he fastened a butterfly bandage in the center of the cut on Paige's arm and picked up another, preparing to place it a few inches down.

"Why not?" Paige asked, her eyes looking up to my face in alarm. "He's the one they're after. You said the sniper was unusually skilled. If there was one like that, there'll be more."

"If we put him in a safe house," Eli said, "it's just going to drag this whole thing out longer."

Fear squirmed, deep in my stomach. That wasn't an option. "No way," I said. "I want this over."

"We know," Griffen said. "Which is why we've been working on a different plan."

I forced myself to take a breath, then two, to calm down.

"What's the new plan?" I asked.

"From what we've been able to find out," Eli said, "it's pretty solid that Haywood's going to get out of prison tomorrow morning. The judge is in his pocket. It's not exactly kosher, and it might get challenged by the prosecution, but not in time to stop him from getting out, you understand?"

Meaning Cole could come after me directly. I wasn't sure how worried I should be about that. Cole was a lawyer, not a commando, but he knew his way around a gun, and he'd proven that he was resourceful. I'd seen the crime scene photos from the jewelry designer he'd beaten to death. If I'd had a doubt that Cole was dangerous, that alone was enough to chill my blood. I didn't love the idea of him out of prison and headed for me. But I wanted this over. And for that to happen, I was going to have to face Cole Haywood one more time.

"I understand," I said. "You're saying that, one way or another, he'll be free tomorrow."

"Exactly," Eli said. "Even if the prosecution gets it overturned, they'd have to find him before they could drag him back to prison. My guess is the second he's free, he'll be in the wind."

"Once he's out, what happens next?" I asked.

Eli looked to Griffen, then back to me. "This is

outside the scope of the kind of thing Sinclair Security usually does, but they knew what they were getting when they bought our team from Silas." He rolled his eyes. "We're freezing Haywood's accounts. All of them. He's going to need money—even if he has some set aside somewhere, he's going to need a big stack of cash to pay that bounty. We found all of his cards, all of his accounts, even the ones he thinks he's hidden. He's not going to be able to access a penny. We'll start putting out the word that he can't make good on the bounty."

"And then what?" Paige asked. "He's out and he doesn't have any money—"

"He'll know why," Griffen said. "And he'll come for Ford."

I got it now. I was bait. It was diabolical, but I found I didn't hate it. If it would make all this stop, I'd do anything.

"I changed my mind," Paige said, her face sheet-white. "I'll go to a safe house—if Ford comes with me." She looked to me, her pale blue eyes wide and desperate.

I shook my head. "And then what? We stay there forever? This only works if I play bait, right?" I looked at Eli and Griffen, who nodded. "Then I'm in."

The faster this was over and Haywood was out of the way, the faster I could focus on getting Paige to forgive me.

"We knew you would be," Griffen said.

"And I don't get a say?" Paige demanded.

"No," all three of us answered.

She trembled for a moment as if fighting the urge to yank her arm out of Griffen's hands and storm from the room. I thought I could feel the force of will it took for her to hold herself still and let him finish bandaging her. Through gritted teeth, she said to me, "Don't think that when this is over, we're just going to pick back up the way we were."

"Paige." I raised a hand to reach for her.

"No. You're treating me like a chess piece, like I don't have an opinion or any say in what happens. That's not love. Love is a two-way street. It's communicating and valuing the other person's opinion, not just deciding how things are."

"Well, maybe I love you enough to let you go—if it means you stay alive."

Chapter Twenty-Seven

PAIGE

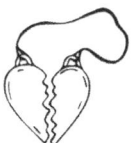

ootsteps and voices sounded in the hall outside the kitchen.

Griffen fastened the last butterfly bandage on my arm and looked to the door. I followed his gaze and saw Wren poking her head in, a grin on her face, a lock of sandy hair falling out of her stubby ponytail.

"Got him," she said cheerfully. "Ryder's dragging him into your interrogation room."

"We have an interrogation room?" Ford asked.

Griffen gave us a wry grin. "The interrogation room is otherwise known as the old storeroom. I'll be there in a second," he said to Wren.

"Cool," she replied, leaning against the doorframe. "You get shot?" she asked me, raising an eyebrow. Her voice was casual, as if she was asking if I was hungry.

"No," I said. "Glass."

She nodded sagely. "Better than a bullet."

"Are we going to talk to this guy?" Ford asked, looking to Griffen and Eli.

"Hawk and Ryder are securing him," Wren said. "They're waiting for the rest of you before they start asking questions."

Ford looked to me. "You're not going in there."

"Fine," I said, too furious to say more. I didn't want to talk to the assassin. I wanted Ford to stop being an idiot, but it looked like that wasn't going to happen.

"I've got her," Wren said easily. "I'll check the rest of these wounds. You guys go ahead."

Eli, Griffen, and Ford marched out of the room, headed, I guessed, for the storeroom. I knew it as a space lined with shelves filled with extra serving dishes and linens. Apparently, Hawk's people put it to a different use when needed.

Wren picked up the bag of wipes off the center island and came closer, taking one of my hands in hers and efficiently scanning my arm for more cuts. "I think Griffen got everything," she said. "So, what did I walk in on? Seemed tense in here."

I didn't want to talk about it, but I sensed an ally. And maybe I was too frustrated to keep my mouth shut. "Ford's being an ass," I said. "He thinks if I'm anywhere near him, I'm going to get killed. So, he dumped me."

Wren rolled her eyes. "Men. I'm assuming he didn't ask for your input?"

"Of course not," I said, mollified that she got it so quickly. "He already decided how to solve the problem, so my thoughts weren't necessary. Jackass." Sarcasm and a friendly ear didn't ease the ache in my heart, but it still felt better than staying quiet and doing what I was told.

"Well, come with me," she said, handing me the pack of wipes.

"Why? Where are we going?" I asked as I followed her out of the room.

"Just because he doesn't want you in the storeroom doesn't mean you can't watch," she said, pushing open the door to the surveillance room.

One of Hawk's team looked up from the cameras. "How come you're not in there?" he asked Wren.

She shrugged her shoulders. "I track. I don't talk. Ryder and Eli are much better at this part of it. Probably Griffen and Hawk, too. But that doesn't mean I don't want to see what happens. And I think Paige deserves to be a part of it."

"I agree," I said quietly.

Wren pulled up an empty chair and shoved it my way. "Sit," she said. "Use the wipes to get the rest of the blood off your leg."

I started to say I was fine, but she shook her head. "The adrenaline's going to wear off soon, and you're going to feel like crap. Headache, exhausted. Those cuts are going to start hurting. Anybody give you any Advil?"

I shook my head.

"When this is over, make sure you take some. For now, finish cleaning up, and we'll watch. Turn it up, would you?" she said to the guy running the surveillance system.

He nodded in agreement and hit the volume button on the keyboard.

The three of us fell silent as we watched the action in

the storage room. The guy Ryder shoved into a chair was tall and wiry, dressed in camouflage so dark it was almost black. His brown hair was cut brutally short, his eyes flat and guarded. That was really all I could make out from the way he was angled in the chair.

Ford leaned up against the wall. Eli stood by the door with Hawk. Griffen pulled up the chair across from the sniper, Ryder standing behind him.

"You want to tell us what you're doing here?" Griffen asked congenially, as if they were having a chat over a beer.

"I'm here because your people grabbed me and dragged me here," the sniper said, sounding as reasonable as Griffen.

"Fair enough," Griffen agreed. "Then why don't you tell me what you were doing up in a tree on my land, shooting into my brother's window?"

"Trying to kill him, obviously." The sniper tapped his foot on the stone floor, looking bored.

"Obviously," Griffen agreed. "It would be helpful if you could tell me who sent you."

"Bounty. But you already know that."

"It was the assumption," Griffen agreed. "Better to have it verified."

"Fine. I verified. You going to let me go? I promise I won't do it again."

"Not entirely believable," Ryder said, his arms crossed over his chest, his short hair sticking straight up as if he'd been running wet hands through it. "But how about we make that a little easier?"

"Are you going to shoot me?" the man in the chair asked, sounding for the first time a touch apprehensive.

"Too much cleanup," Hawk said curtly.

The assassin didn't seem to find that answer reassuring. "Look, I was just doing a job."

"Then you might want to spread the word that the job isn't worth it. We've stopped everyone who's come. Including you."

"Yeah, I get you," the man in the chair said. "If you caught me, my guess is nobody's getting through."

"Exactly," Hawk confirmed.

"But you've got to understand, I can tell everybody you've got Silas's team on the job along with your own people, and the smart ones will stay away. But some of us are too stupid and greedy, too arrogant. They'll still come. It's a hell of a bounty."

"Then," Ryder said, "you might want to add that the man who posted that bounty doesn't have access to any of his funds."

The man's eyebrows shot up. "Well, that is a problem."

"Yes, for you or anyone else who succeeds in killing the target. No one's getting paid. Not a penny."

"That might slow down the takers," the man in the chair agreed. "Nobody wants to go to this much trouble, risk ending up in your hands, only to walk away broke."

"Just to be clear," Griffen said, "anyone who puts a bullet in my brother isn't walking away under any circumstances."

"I heard you played on the right side of the law," the sniper said.

I thought that might get a reaction out of Griffen, and I watched with interest.

"Usually," Griffen agreed, his eyes the icy green of a frozen sea. "But you're talking about my brother. There's a lot of acres of mountain out there. Not hard to lose a body." He rolled his shoulders back and crossed his arms over his chest. "I'm already—" Griffen paused, as if searching for the right word. "Displeased," he said finally, "that one of my employees ended up bloody because of the window you broke when you tried to shoot my brother. I'm tempted not to let you walk out of here just for that. However, if you spread the word that the bounty won't be paid, and anyone we catch on our land won't ever be seen again, we're willing to let you go. Just this one time."

"Deal," the man in the chair said immediately. "I knew it was a long shot considering who you are, and that Hawk Bristol is running your security. If I'd known you had any of Silas's people here too—" He glanced to Ryder and then Eli. "I wouldn't have touched this one, even for that much money. You let me leave, I'll make sure everyone knows there's nothing here for them, and you'll never see me again."

"Fine." Ryder walked around to the back of the chair and grabbed the sniper's bound hands. He cut him loose from where he was strapped to the seat and hauled him to his feet. "Let's go. You can tell me where you left your vehicle. We'll drop you there and escort you to the county line."

We watched on the screen as, one by one, they filed

out of the room. I turned to Wren. "Thanks. I feel better, I think, seeing that."

"No problem," she said. "For the record, I can't speak for your guy. I don't know him. But civilians tend to overreact when people they care about get all bloody and cut up. Still, 'overreact' is the operative word there. You look fine to me."

I nodded, though I felt anything but fine.

"But," she said, her eyes dead serious on mine, "did Eli say anything when Ford dumped you? That you should stay away from him to keep yourself safe?"

"He did," I admitted, grudgingly.

Wren gave a decisive nod. "I'd listen to Eli." She cocked her head to the side. "I'm assuming Griffen agreed, too?"

I nodded.

"Then there you go. Your guy may be a jackass at the moment—probably freaked the hell out, considering you both almost got shot. That one—" She nodded her head at the hall, as they escorted the sniper past the open door. "I know him by reputation. He's one of the best. You got very lucky. Do what they tell you. We'll get this thing wrapped up. Then everyone can go back to living a normal life. And you can decide what to do about Ford."

Hawk ducked his head into the room, interrupting the conversation. "Ryder wants you," he said to Wren.

"Gotcha," and she was gone.

He looked to me. "You're good to go," he said. "Take some Advil before you go to bed. We'll check that cut in the morning."

"It's fine," I said automatically.

All the same, he nodded. "Keep the blinds closed on your window. Nobody's aiming at you, but we're not taking any chances. Understand?"

I nodded, suddenly exhausted. "I'm going to go to bed," I said quietly, trudging up the flights of stairs and down the long hall of the guest wing.

Chapter Twenty-Eight

PAIGE

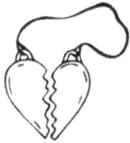

When I reached the end of the hall, Ford's door was open, his room dark. I didn't know where he was. Not that it mattered. Not anymore.

My chest felt as if it had been caved in. I wasn't sure what fantasies I'd been spinning in my mind, in my heart, over Ford Sawyer—more than I'd thought, considering how wrecked I felt to have them shattered.

He said he loved me, but I didn't feel loved. I felt manipulated and pushed aside. Abandoned.

That was it. I felt fucking abandoned.

And it sucked. I wasn't a toy to be put down and picked back up later when he wanted to play again.

I went into my room. Turning to my closet, I realized I was still wearing Ford's robe. I didn't want his robe. I didn't want anything of his, not anymore. I untied the belt and pushed it down my arms, careful around the bandages, then balled it up and threw it across the hall. It landed short of Ford's door, but he would get the message.

Closing my own door, I pulled on a T-shirt and a pair of knit shorts. At once thoroughly exhausted and too revved up to sleep, I was thinking about a cup of tea when a quick knock sounded on my door.

"Yeah," I said, lacking the energy to go open it. "Come in."

The door swung open, and Hope was there, a baby monitor playing staticky ocean sounds in one hand, a bottle of wine in the other. She walked in, Savannah following with three wineglasses in her hands and what looked like a bottle of ibuprofen tucked under her arm.

"Hey, you can kick us out if you want," Hope said, "but we come bearing wine and shoulders to cry on."

"We heard Ford's being an ass," Savannah added. "Not a surprise."

I stared at both of them, my jaw dropping. "How do you know everything as soon as it happens?"

"That's my job," Savannah said. "Hope just comes by it naturally."

"Do you want a glass of wine, or do you want us to leave you alone?" Hope asked, setting the wine on the beverage station Savannah had arranged in the sitting area of my room. "Just so you know, if you want us to go, we will. But we won't leave you alone for long."

"Why?" I asked, not sure I understood.

"Because you're family," Hope said. "I thought we made it clear—we decided we're keeping you."

"Ford will come to his senses," Savannah said. "Whether you forgive him is another matter. But this house is big enough for all of us. So, do you want us to get lost, or do you want a glass of wine? You look pretty revved up on adrenaline."

"I am," I admitted. "I feel like I could sleep for a million years and like I can't sit still."

"Wine, then," Hope said. "Just one glass?"

"Yes, please," I agreed, reeling a little at their show of support. I didn't argue when Savannah set three dark red pills in my palm. I was starting to ache all over. I grabbed my water bottle from the coffee table and took them.

Once I took the pills, Savannah went to work on the wine. She had the foil off and the cork out of the bottle with a few efficient movements. She handed me a glass, half-filled with a golden liquid that smelled of fruit and fields.

"Griffen said they have a plan," Hope offered, dropping into an armchair.

Savannah sat on the love seat, and I perched on the edge of my bed.

If you'd asked me a few minutes ago, I would have said all I needed was to be alone, to lick my wounds, and sleep for a week. But this—friends and a glass of wine— was so much better. I might have been abandoned by Ford, but I wasn't alone.

"I didn't get the details on the plan," Hope said. "Did you?"

"Kind of, a little." I told them about what Eli had said while Griffen was bandaging me, Wren pulling me into the surveillance room, and the conversation they'd had with the sniper. "Griffen was very smooth," I said to Hope.

"That's my guy," she said. "Smooth—and sometimes a little scary."

"He was definitely scary," I agreed.

"I don't know how I feel about this," Savannah said. "On the one hand, it sounds like people are going to stop trying to get to the house or shoot Ford if they know they won't be paid. But on the other hand, it means Cole Haywood's going to head straight for us. And I'm assuming Hawk and these new people will just let him in?"

"They didn't get that specific," I said, "but that was my guess too."

"I don't like that either," Hope said, "though it's not like we can all go to a safe house."

"Why not?" I asked.

"Well, for one thing," Hope said, "if we're gone too long, we violate the terms of Prentice's will, and we all get kicked out. And at the moment, that means that most of us—Tenn and Royal, Quinn, Avery—lose access to their places of business, since they're still technically owned by Sawyer Enterprises."

"Though I think," Savannah said, "more than all of that, it would mean we can't come back and live under Heartstone's roof together."

"That would break Ford's heart," I said without thinking. "I know he's been hiding away since he's been back, but it means everything to him to be here with all of you." I shook my head. "Not that I care," I added, mostly trying to convince myself, hoping Savannah was kind enough not to comment. We all knew that was bullshit. Of course, I cared.

Savannah sighed. "I feel bad that I was so annoyed he was coming back. He's not the same."

"He seems to have changed," Hope said. She took a long sip of her wine. "I'm not trying to defend him, but Ford's not trained to deal with this kind of thing like Griffen and Hawk and the rest of the security team are. He—" She shook her head. "He's tough, don't get me wrong. When I worked for my uncle Edgar, I sat in on a lot of meetings and saw Ford in action. He's an excellent negotiator, very good at understanding people—what they want, what they need, how to get them to do what he wants them to do. The fact that he's completely screwed up with you tells me how much he cares."

"Well, that doesn't make any sense," I said. "Shouldn't he have screwed up less if he cares?"

"Nah," Savannah said. "He's screwing up because he can't think straight. Griffen said you were covered in blood when he saw you downstairs. You probably gave Ford a stroke."

I wasn't quite ready for empathy for Ford, but she had a point.

Savannah let out a long sigh. "Finn said Ford can't handle his guilt. He keeps trying to apologize. But Finn doesn't want more apologies. He's fine. Everything worked out the way he wanted it to in the end. He said seeing how racked with guilt Ford is took away any need for more. He knows Ford is sorry, and they can't change the past." She took a sip of wine and sent me a long look. "I can imagine— And keep in mind, I'm not saying this to get you to cut him any slack; he can't just push you aside to keep you safe. But, I can imagine that seeing you covered in blood, thinking you could have been killed in his place, is probably fucking with his head big-time."

Hope nodded in agreement. "Definitely. Still, what exactly did he tell you? Griffen wasn't clear."

I let out a sigh. "That we have to stay away from each other, I guess. And that everyone has to stay away from him. I don't know what his plan is. To hide out in the storage room until the security team catches Cole Haywood?"

It seemed ridiculous, but what did I know? I wasn't a security expert. And they'd clearly known what they were doing by negotiating with a would-be murderer.

"I'm sure they're working something out," Hope said. "That's what they do. In the meantime, we've got your back, Paige."

Maybe sensing that I was done talking about Ford, Hope changed the subject to Stella and the tooth she thought might be coming in. Finally, maybe we'd get a break from the teething nightmare. From there, we went to Christmas, the holiday right around the corner. Savannah strategized decorations with Hope, and I sipped my wine, piping in here and there, feeling the tension and the adrenaline drain out of me drop by drop, the wine soaking into my brain cells until all I wanted to do was drift off.

I set the mostly empty glass on my bedside table and leaned into my pillows, pulling up the blanket. My eyes started to flutter shut. I felt a hand brush my hair back from my face and another tuck the covers around my shoulders.

"Sleep in tomorrow," Hope said. "It'll be the best

thing to get that arm healed up." She stroked her hand over my hair once more. "Everything's going to be okay, Paige. I promise. Come find me when you're up and about. We'll figure out the day."

"Okay," I said, my eyes heavy. "Thanks."

"Anytime," Hope said, squeezing my shoulder and giving a final tug to the covers. "You're part of the family now."

They murmured to each other quietly as they left, closing the door behind them.

I felt myself drifting, my heart still aching, my chest still feeling as if it had been caved in. I wanted Ford. I'd gotten used to not sleeping alone, and though my room was warm enough, I felt cold to the bone. And far too angry to think about forgiving him.

Chapter Twenty-Nine

FORD

The days stretched endlessly. It had been a week since I'd talked to Paige or been close enough to touch her. I'd exiled myself, avoiding the family, hiding out in my room or the attics, searching for paperwork that would point to my father's killer and coming up empty day after day. I found another invoice about the garage renovation in '86 and finally called the company to ask what they knew about it, but it was so long ago, the woman who answered said there wasn't anyone working who'd been around that long. I was running into dead ends everywhere I turned.

As predicted, Cole Haywood was let out of prison the day after the shot through my bedroom window. No one had seen a sign of him since. His funds were frozen, and it looked like his bounty was dead. Word had spread quickly that he couldn't pay. We were braced, but nothing had happened. Those of us who weren't on the security team were starting to go stir-crazy.

Avoiding Paige was painful. I was hungry for the

sound of her voice, the sight of her, of her smile. I'd take her rage if that was all I could get, and I knew she was pissed. Savannah had pulled me aside the day after I told Paige to stay away.

She'd said, "You were an asshole."

"So I've been informed," I'd responded coolly.

"Well, I'm not going to bust your chops over it. That's Paige's job." She folded her arms over her chest.

"Then what?" I'd asked.

She'd reached up to squeeze my arm. "I'm not saying you're doing the right thing, because Paige is an adult and you're not her babysitter. But I get why you did it. I can see you're thinking of her, and you hate every minute of this."

"I do," I agreed, shoving my hands in my pockets. I hadn't expected understanding from Savannah. "You know what I did to Finn."

Savannah's eyes had gone hard, but her face was soft as she nodded. "And I know that at this point it's hurting you a hell of a lot more than it's hurting him."

"I'll never forgive myself for it," I said, my voice catching in my throat.

"Maybe not," she agreed. "I honestly don't know how you could. But maybe you can accept that the person you were made poor decisions, and the person that you are now doesn't do that anymore." That idea was still settling in my brain when she added, "I've been working on a surprise for you, but you're not ready for it yet."

"What's the surprise?" I asked, intrigued.

She shook her head. "Later. After you get Paige to forgive you."

"She might not." I hated even saying the words out loud.

"I have more faith in you than that," Savannah said, reaching out to squeeze my arm again before she turned to go.

I was glad someone had faith in me. I hadn't expected it to be Savannah. I watched her leave and headed upstairs to the attics, alone. I tried to tell myself everything was better, safer, if I was on my own. But for the first time since I'd been out of prison—maybe much longer than that—I didn't want isolation. I wanted Paige, and I wanted my family. But as much as I wanted those things, I wanted this to be over.

I knew Cole wouldn't be able to resist coming after me himself. And when he did, I reminded myself, we could end this thing once and for all.

Then all of us would be free.

You'll never really be free until you find out who killed Prentice, a little voice in my head reminded me. And for the first time, I shoved it away. I might never know. The list of people who'd wanted my father dead was long and varied. We hadn't had security back then. Anyone could have walked into Heartstone. West had been looking for the killer since the day Prentice died and had come up with nothing.

I sat on the edge of an ancient trunk, digging through another box of paperwork. Three sheets down, I found another copy of the ancient, crinkled invoice for concrete in the garage renovation in '86, the one I'd already called about that had led nowhere. I could swear I'd found and filed the same invoice at least three times, and here it was again, with the same diagonal crease where it had been folded carelessly, the same handwritten notation in the margin—*pd 8/27/86*. It was way too old to have anything to do with Prentice's murder, but it was weird that I kept seeing it.

Maybe I was hung up on finding Prentice's killer because I couldn't do what Savannah had suggested—find a way to accept who I'd been, the wrong that I'd done, and figure out how to move forward. I didn't want to be the old Ford Sawyer. I wanted more. I'd spent a lot of my life doing wrong. Now I wanted to figure out a way to do right and find a way to win Paige back when this was over and she was safe.

I made my way to the bottom of the box I'd been going through. Other than that same concrete invoice—nothing. Files I was already familiar with, deals that predated me but weren't important. There was nothing here.

It was late afternoon. I'd sorted through another bin—this one of household records Savannah would probably be interested in—when my brother Royal dipped his head through the doorway.

"Hey, put that away. Come downstairs." He came in and grabbed the bin in front of me, giving it a quick glance before he dropped it on a nearby table.

"Now's not a good time," I said. "And there are too many windows down there."

"Not where we're going. Come on." When I didn't move, he propped his hands on his hips and scowled down at me. "You know you're not in prison anymore."

"I figured that out," I said wryly. "The food's a lot better here."

"Then stop acting like it. You've got yourself in solitary," he said, grabbing my arm and pulling me toward the door.

"I'm trying to prevent any of you guys getting shot or whatever the next one of them comes up with," I said, pulling my arm from his grip and following him to the stairs.

"Yeah, I get that. I appreciate you trying to keep us all in one piece."

"This is all my fault," I said.

"The fuck it is," Royal said. "Haywood used Vanessa to try to kill me while you were still in prison. He almost killed JT—Daisy's best friend—thinking he was me. You had nothing to do with that."

I shook my head. "I'm the reason. Cole blames me for everything that went wrong."

"Well, Cole's an idiot," Royal said, turning and jogging down the stairs. "And you're not the reason. Dad is the reason. Dad is the one who fucked him over and stole his wife. Dad ruined Cole Haywood's life. Not you. So, you put Dad and Caro on a charity committee together. For fuck's sake, the whole thing was supposed to do good, right? How did you know they were going to jump into bed together? Haywood's just blaming you because guys like him never blame themselves. And he's a coward, because if he wasn't, he would have just gone for Dad after Caro died. But no, he waited till he thought we were vulnerable, and then he decided to get revenge." Royal stopped at the base of the stairs and shook his head.

"Stop acting like a martyr, man. You've done plenty of asshole shit in your life—"

"Thanks," I said dryly.

"Just being honest," Royal said with a grin and a shrug. "I was there. I remember. But not this. This is not your fault."

I nodded, hearing him but unable to agree with him. Our father had been awful, but he'd made choices, just like I had. And what makes a person who he is? Choices.

Pushing the dark thoughts away, I followed him down the hall that led to Griffen's office, the library, and the family gathering room. We made a turn, and I found myself in a wood-paneled room, the windows covered from the inside, the pool table racked and ready to play. Griffen, Finn, and Tenn all waited at the side of the room. Someone had set up a tin bucket stuffed with ice and bottles of beer I recognized from Sawyers Bend Brewing.

Nash, my sister Parker's fiancé, strolled in, grocery bag handles looped over his hands. "I bought all the chips they had. And a box of cookies from Daisy," he said, looking to Royal, who grinned.

"My girl is the best," Royal said.

"Her cookies sure are," Nash replied.

"What is this?" I asked, looking at all of them.

"Guys' night," Griffen answered, shoving a beer into my hand. "We're all stuck here together—might as well make the most of it."

My shoulder blades were tight, my smile stiff, and my heart ached because they were holding the door wide open and all I had to do was walk through. "I'm up for guys' night," I said, my voice a little stiff at the rush of emotion I didn't want them to see.

"Teams," Finn said, pointing at me with the beer in his hand. "Ford and Griffen against Royal and Tenn. Nash and I play winners."

"Done," Griffen said, sending me a sidelong look. "They're totally fucked."

"Totally," I agreed. Griffen and I hadn't played pool together in decades, but when we had, no one could beat us.

"How are you still this fucking good?" Royal asked a little later as we methodically destroyed them.

I shrugged. "I like to knock the balls around," I said, and sank the final shot. "Clears my head."

"Fuck, man. Good luck," Tenn said as he passed off his cue to Nash, and Royal handed his to Finn.

Griffen just grinned at me and said, "Still got it."

"We've still got it," I agreed, and felt the smallest blooming of hope.

Both Royal's and Savannah's words echoed. Prentice had been the center of it all. Royal was right. But I'd made choices too. I couldn't undo what I'd done, but I could decide to be different going forward. I could build something new, something good and real.

I wasn't exactly sure what that meant, but I could figure it out.

Chapter Thirty

FORD

L ater that night, I lay in bed, sleep as elusive as it had been since the night I'd ended things with Paige. When I looked around, all I could see was Paige, covered in blood. I couldn't sleep in here. The memory of her bleeding haunted me.

The handle on my bedroom door turned, and the door swung open. No one was there. It had been doing this all week—swinging silently open, leaving clear the view from my bed to Paige's closed bedroom door, warm yellow light leaking beneath. My own door swung gently, as if to draw my attention, saying, *Look, she's awake. Go talk to her.*

I rolled over to stare at the wall. The door could open all it wanted, but the house or whatever was doing this couldn't make me look. I wouldn't give in to temptation. I wasn't being selfish, dammit. I wouldn't risk her just so I could have what I wanted. I knew she was angry, and it didn't change anything. I would do whatever I needed to, to keep her safe. And if that included pissing her off, I could live with that.

And once this was over, I could spend the rest of my life trying to make it up to her.

Finally, I shoved the covers back and stormed across the room, closing the door and bracing the desk chair under the handle.

When I woke in the middle of the night, it was open again.

Across the hall, Paige's light had been turned off. I imagined she slept and wished I was there with her, holding her, listening to her soft breath, the silk of her hair on my cheek.

The next day was more of the same—sticking to the back stairs, avoiding the windows, grabbing a quick breakfast in the kitchen, and hiding myself away in the attics again. More paperwork. All dead ends.

My phone rang in the silence of the attic, the blare of sound startling me. I almost dropped the file I was flipping through. I didn't recognize the number.

"Hello?"

"This Ford Sawyer?" The voice, male, was wobbly with age and unfamiliar.

"It is. Who's this?" I asked.

"This is Bailey Toms. You talked to my daughter a few days ago. I worked on the concrete job at Heartstone. The garage, both times."

A jolt of adrenaline flashed through me, and I sat up straight. "You poured the concrete in eighty-six?"

"That was me. I worked on the big garage renovation

a few years before that, and then fixed it when they tore it back up in eighty-six."

"So, you remember the job?" I asked. "The woman I talked to was sure no one would."

"That was my daughter—she runs the company now with my sons. It's been a lifetime, but I remember that job," he said, his shaky voice slow. "Doesn't matter how long it's been. Everybody remembers doing work at Heartstone."

"Well, that's the thing," I said. "I know I was young at the time, but from what I can see, the major garage renovation was a number of years before I was born. But then my father had some work done on the floor again in eighty-six. We're going through old house records, trying to organize them, and I was curious."

It wasn't entirely true, but it wasn't entirely a lie either.

"It was odd," Bailey said. "Your father didn't explain much—just said there was some water damage, the floor had to be jackhammered up. They fixed the plumbing, tried to re-pour the concrete. He said the guy they hired fucked it up and they needed my crew to finish it."

"Okay," I said. "So, what was odd about it?"

"Well, I looked, and I saw signs of some plumbing work, but then they'd tossed dirt and gravel over it and dumped what looked like hand-mixed concrete over that. Didn't make sense. And then he insisted we just fill it in, on top of what was there."

"And that's not how you'd usually handle it?" I asked, not sure what was so odd about what he'd seen.

"No. Not at all. The plumber should have filled it in

with gravel or called us to take care of it. This was sloppy, like they dumped whatever was around in the hole and bought a few bags of concrete from the hardware store. Prentice always wanted the work to be top-notch. This wasn't. And it smelled off in there."

"Like a busted septic line?" I asked.

"No. Seen plenty of those, and this was different. Like garbage that had been left out, but the garage was clean. Maybe it was whatever they used to mix that concrete," he mused.

"That is weird," I agreed, remembering my father's insistence that Heartstone be maintained to perfection. It was part of why his withdrawal in the last few years of his life had been so bizarre. The father I knew never would have let Heartstone fall into ruin the way he had. I knew now—we all did—that he'd been grieving the loss of his child and the woman he'd wanted to marry. If that woman hadn't been Cole Haywood's wife, I might have felt sorry for him.

But this was back when he was at full power, full asshole. Why would he accept a sloppy repair job?

"So, you went ahead and filled in the hole?" I asked.

"Well, a job's a job, and you knew your father. Nobody argued with him. We filled it in, smoothed it out, and got paid. Always stuck with me, though. Didn't make sense."

No, it didn't make sense. What was in the garage? I didn't want to put pieces together in the wrong order, but... "And you said this was on the right side of the garage?"

"Yep. The bay all the way on the right if your back is

to the door into the Manor. The one closest to the back-yard. The hole was right in the center of that parking space."

I stopped myself from asking any other questions, not sure I wanted to lead Bailey Toms in the direction my mind was sprinting. "Thank you, Mr. Toms. Thank you for returning my call. This is very helpful."

"Not sure how it could be," he said. "It was so long ago. But I was curious you asked, so I wanted to call you back."

"I appreciate it." Without another word, he hung up.

My mind raced. It was possible that everything Prentice had said was true—maybe he'd hired a shitty contractor to fix the hole and then replaced him with Bailey Toms's company. Maybe.

I stood up and walked down the stairs to the guest wing. Standing in the hall in between my room and Paige's, I realized that just below was the garage, and underneath our bedrooms, the spot Bailey Toms had spoken of.

I thought of my door swinging open for no reason, the plumbing and electrical fritzing out all the time, the frozen room, and the stuck door. And I couldn't stop myself from thinking that there was more than pipes underneath the garage.

Prentice had been hiding something.

And we were going to find out what it was.

Chapter Thirty-One

FORD

I knocked on Griffen's office door but didn't wait for a response, just turned the handle and let myself in. I stopped at the threshold, not expecting to see Paige lifting Stella from Griffen's arms. She froze, her eyes on me, and for a moment, everything spinning in my head stopped.

God, I was an idiot. I hadn't served any purpose in this last week apart from making both of us miserable. I doubted she was any safer. No one had tried to get to me since we'd sent the sniper off with the information that the bounty wouldn't be paid. All I'd gained was a week away from Paige—the last thing I wanted.

"Ford, what's wrong?" Hope asked, reading my face.

Paige gave herself a little shake, breaking her stillness, her eyes narrowing in sudden concern.

"I— I—" I stopped, words piling up on each other in their rush to get out. How to explain?

I looked to Paige and everything settled.

"I got a call back from the concrete contractor," I said.

Her eyes flew wide. As I'd expected, she knew exactly what I was talking about. I'd mentioned the reappearing concrete invoice more than once over the past few weeks. "What did they say?" she asked.

Realizing Griffen and Hope had no idea why concrete might be interesting, I looked their way. "I've been going through the paperwork, you know—" Griffen nodded. "And I keep finding this invoice for concrete repair in the garage."

"Dad converted that part of the Manor into garages in the late seventies, I think," Griffen said.

"Yeah," I agreed, "but this was a repair in eighty-six. Something to do with plumbing. Anyway, the invoice kept turning up." I shrugged, not sure how else to explain it. "I'd file it with household paperwork, go to another bin, even another room of the attic, and there it would be again."

"You're sure it was the same invoice?" Hope asked. "Maybe it was copies that got stuck in different boxes."

I shook my head. "It was the same invoice. I recognized the way it was folded and the note of payment in the margin. I finally decided to call the concrete company."

"You know that sounds impossible, right?" Griffen asked.

I nodded. "I know. And I'm sure it was the same. I'd put it away and find it again somewhere else."

"For a repair that was done more than thirty years ago?" Hope asked, raising an eyebrow.

"It's a little crazy, but it kept turning up and all I've been hitting are dead ends. At this point, anything feels like it's worth looking into. When I talked to them, the office manager said no one there would have any idea. I figured that was the end of it, but the contractor called me back a few minutes ago. The office manager is his daughter, and she mentioned it to him. He said no one ever forgets work they do at Heartstone, and he remembered the job."

I relayed the conversation, Griffen's gaze growing heavy with understanding by the time I finished. "There's something under the garage floor," he said.

"I think so," I agreed. "I don't know what, but I think Dad buried something there and tried to cover it up himself."

"Well, fuck," Griffen said, shaking his head. "How do we...? Hold on—" He pulled up his phone and sent a text.

Hope leaned over to read his screen. "Do we have a jackhammer? Why would Hawk have a jackhammer?"

"I don't know," Griffen said, "but if anybody around here does, it'll be Hawk, considering his sideline is managing the grounds."

Griffen's phone pinged in his hand, and Hope laughed, saying, "Hawk doesn't have a jackhammer, and he's on his way here. Clearly, he wants to know what you're up to. But I know who has a jackhammer. Billy Bob."

Billy Bob—Billy and Bob—were cousins of Savannah's and local handymen. Considering they'd also managed to clear Hawk's security checks, not an easy feat, they were around the Manor more often than not, given the rate at which things broke down around here.

Griffen sent Hawk a text. I'd bet he was asking him to

call Billy Bob and get them over here with their jackhammer. If Prentice had hidden something in the garage floor, it was probably family business. But since I didn't know how to run a jackhammer and was guessing neither did anyone else, we'd let Billy Bob handle that part.

"I'm calling Uncle Edgar," Hope said. Griffen looked at her and she explained, "If Prentice buried something in that garage and covered it with concrete, Uncle Edgar knows about it."

Hope set her phone on the desk and opened her contacts list. Before she could tap Edgar's name and initiate the call, Paige interrupted.

"Should I— Do you want me to take Stella and put her down? This is personal, family stuff and—" Her gaze flicked from me to Griffen and Hope.

Hope's eyebrows went up in surprise.

Griffen sent me a look.

I shook my head. "I think you should stay."

I'd been an idiot, pushing her away, but I'd done it because I felt so much for her. I didn't want her to walk—not now, not later, not ever—which meant I had to stop shutting her out.

"I don't want you to go," I said, "unless you want to."

She resettled Stella in her arms and shook her head. "I don't want to go."

"All right, then," Griffen said. He glanced at his phone screen. "Hawk is headed here. Billy Bob are on the way with a jackhammer. Call Edgar—let's see what he knows."

Hope stabbed her finger at the phone screen, and the sound of the ring filled the room.

"What is it, Hope?" Edgar's gruff voice said through the speaker.

"Uncle Edgar, I have a question. I'm wondering how good your memory is."

I grinned at how well Hope knew her uncle, to start with a challenge that would get him engaged.

"My memory is sharp as a tack," he said, and a tiny smile curved the side of her mouth.

"We've got some invoices," she explained. "Savannah and I are going through old household paperwork. She's found some journals. We've been trying to catalog the history of the house."

"As you should be. Wish you'd put working with Griffen aside and focus on domestic matters more. But this is a start," he said.

Griffen rolled his eyes but kept his mouth shut. Hope didn't respond to the comment and went on smoothly, "We found some invoices for concrete work in the garage in nineteen eighty-six. Nobody remembers any work in the garage in eighty-six. We were wondering if you did."

The pause extended longer than was comfortable before Edgar said, "I suppose I do. I'm surprised there are still invoices around. It was years after the big renovation. There was some sort of septic issue. They had to break up the floor, get in there to repair the leak. It smelled terrible."

"You're sure?" Hope asked doubtfully. "We didn't see any invoices related to septic repairs."

We hadn't found any related to plumbing either— only the concrete repair, but Hope didn't mention that.

"I'm sure," he said. "Nothing to remember or remark

on, especially after all this time. Not surprised you can't find the other invoices. It's been thirty-some years."

"We know, but we've been having some issues with the garage," Hope said, crossing her fingers to negate her lie. "Billy Bob is headed over with a jackhammer. We're going to dig into the floor and make sure it's not leaking again, or whatever the problem was back then."

"Well, that's just a waste of time, Hope," Edgar argued. "You're going to make a big mess with nothing to show for it. Whatever was wrong there, Prentice got it patched up good and tight. No need to go busting up the garage floor."

"You seem awfully sure about that for someone who's not a plumber or a contractor," Hope said. "I haven't even told you what the problems are in the garage."

"You don't need to. Tell Billy Bob to take their jack-hammer home. You have a problem, call a plumber."

"Maybe I already did," Hope said.

"Hope Sawyer, you listen to me—" Edgar ordered, steel threading through his gruff tone.

"I don't think so," Hope said pleasantly. "Thanks for the input, Uncle Edgar." Her finger stabbed the red button on the screen. The call cut off.

"That was suspicious," Griffen said.

"Very," I agreed. "Because when I talked to Bailey Toms, he specifically mentioned that it smelled funny in the garage. And I asked, 'like a busted septic line,' and he said no. Didn't smell like any septic line he'd ever come across, but it didn't smell good."

"I don't think Prentice buried old stock certificates or

the key to a hidden safe under the garage," Hope murmured.

"Me either," I agreed.

"Shoot." Paige interrupted, looking down at the baby in her arms. Stella's eyelids were drooping, her cheek snuggled against Paige's shoulder. "It's past time for her nap. I'm going to run up and put her down, and then I'll find you wherever you are." She rushed past me and out the door.

"What are you thinking?" Griffen asked, tapping his pen on his desk blotter.

"I don't know what to think," I said. Possibilities tumbled in my mind, and I couldn't bring myself to put them into words. Not yet. Not when we hadn't seen what was there.

"We'd better go move the vehicles," Griffen said, standing.

"Good idea," Hope agreed.

The three of us headed to the garage, meeting Hawk coming down the hall, a black vest hanging from his hand. "If you're going to the garage, put this on." He shoved the bulletproof vest at me. I took it, almost dropping it, the weight a surprise even though I'd tried it on a week before, when we'd worked out the plan if Cole came for me. I strapped it on and grabbed a jacket to cover it as Hope and Griffen put on their own jackets.

"I don't suppose any of you know how to operate a jackhammer?" Hawk asked, already dressed for the chilly December weather.

"I wish," Griffen said.

"Not me," I added.

Hope didn't bother to comment.

"Then we're going to have to let Billy Bob in on whatever's up," Hawk said.

"I think," I said slowly, "we only need them to break up the top layer of concrete." If my hunch was correct, it was going to be obvious once they got through that first layer.

"And you know where we're digging?" Hawk asked, his brows drawn together as he clearly tried to puzzle out what the hell was going on.

"I think I do," I said. "Bailey Toms gave me a pretty good description of where the hole was." I zipped up my jacket as I shouldered open the garage door, my heart thumping faster in my chest as my eyes went to the spot Bailey Toms had described.

I had no doubt there would be answers buried beneath the concrete. I just wasn't sure I was ready to discover exactly what they were.

Chapter Thirty-Two

FORD

It didn't take long for the four of us to move the vehicles out of the garage and park them in the courtyard in front of the Manor. By the time we had that sorted, Billy Bob's truck was coming down the drive, escorted by Eli and Wren in their truck, both vehicles peeling off from the main drive to take the side lane around to the garage.

"Now y'all got problems in the garage? Where in this house don't you have things falling apart?" Billy of Billy Bob asked.

Bob just grinned at us and hefted the jackhammer out of the back of their truck.

I led them to the garage bay at the far end. "Here," I said, walking in a slow circle, realizing as I did that there was the faintest depression in the concrete, hairline cracks making a loose, wide oval in front of the space where a vehicle would park.

The garage was deep and wide, considering it took up

most of the wing of the house. The spot was directly below the hall between my room and Paige's room.

"This is where we dig," I said. "Look." I stood between Billy and Bob, pointing at the area in question, about the size of a compact car. "Can you get this concrete up so we can get to the gravel or whatever's underneath?"

"Sure. Gonna take a minute, but we can get it up."

"Thanks." I patted Bob on the back as I walked away.

"Y'all back up, in case this spits concrete out. Don't want anybody to get cut," Billy said, looking at Hope.

"All right," she agreed. "We'll stay by the door."

We moved back about twenty feet. Eli and Wren hovered near the open garage doors, their eyes mainly on Billy Bob, occasionally scanning their surroundings. I noticed they worked seamlessly: Eli watching Billy and Bob, while Wren scanned the driveway, the side yard, and the woods. Then her gaze went to the men with the jackhammer, and Eli scanned their surroundings. Despite their security clearance, they didn't trust Billy Bob and that jackhammer, but it looked like they didn't trust much of anything else either.

Billy Bob worked methodically, breaking down the concrete and shoveling it out, trading off the jackhammer and the shovel until most of the space was cleared and chunks of concrete were piled on the side of the garage.

"I hope there's actually something under there," Griffen said. "Otherwise, we just made a big fucking mess for no reason."

"I don't know," I said. "I kind of hope we just made a big fucking mess for no reason."

Hope let out a sigh. The door behind us opened, and Paige stepped through, the baby monitor clasped in her hand.

"She took forever to fall asleep, but she's out," Paige said, holding up the monitor to show the screen—and a peacefully sleeping Stella. "They got that concrete up pretty fast."

"They did," Hope agreed. "I think it wasn't in great shape. We probably would have started having issues with it soon. Aunt Ophelia's car is usually parked on this side of the garage because she doesn't drive much and she's traveling so often. It made sense to put her here, but I don't think she's been examining the floor when she moves the car, and I can't remember the last time I looked at the floor on this side of the garage," she said.

"Me either," Griffen agreed. "Never even thought about it."

"All right, boss," Billy said. "Concrete's up. You want us to grab another shovel and go after this gravel?"

Griffen looked to me, and I shook my head. "Nah, we got it."

"You want us to leave the jackhammer?"

Griffen thought for a second. "We'll give a call if we need you back. Thanks, guys, for coming so quickly."

"Anytime," Bob said, and they left with a wave, Eli and Wren following them out silently.

"Okay. Well," Hawk said, holding up the shovels he'd found in the corner of the garage near the bin full of sports equipment, "here you go. I'll keep watch."

"Sounds like a plan," I agreed.

"We can help," Hope said.

"No," Griffen countered. "We only have two shovels. You two can supervise if you want to stay."

"You're sure you don't want me to leave?" Paige asked, her pale blue eyes leveled on mine.

I stopped and faced her. It was time for me to say what I needed to say, to make it as right as I could. "No. I was stupid before, and I'm sorry. This whole situation has me all fucked up. I saw you injured, bleeding, and I lost it. I should never have told you to stay away from me. I don't want you to leave. And even if I did, I think you need to stay for this."

Paige bit her lower lip, her eyes suddenly filling. "You think?"

She'd obviously had the same thought I had, which meant we were in the same boat, whether we liked it or not.

I touched a fingertip to her bottom lip. "Let's wait and see what's under there first, okay?"

A tear crested over her lower lashes and rolled down her cheek.

I brushed it off with the side of my thumb, pressing a kiss on the salty trail. "Don't cry. Not yet. Not till we know."

I didn't know what was under the concrete, but I could guess what Prentice would have wanted to hide enough that he'd buried it under layers of concrete and gravel. Still, I hoped I was wrong.

She nodded, and I stepped back. "I love you," I said quietly, the words just for her. "Everything's going to be okay."

"I love you, too." A faint smile curved her lips. "Now go dig up the floor."

"Yes, ma'am," I said, and turned to take the shovel Griffen handed me.

What followed was more digging than I'd done in a while—shovelfuls of gravel, the noise of it abrasive and deafening. It took longer than I would have guessed to get through it all. Griffen and I worked in dogged silence, side by side. Griffen's face was set in grim lines. I expected mine looked the same.

Hope and Paige watched from the back of the garage, while Hawk took Eli and Wren's former position by the doors, watching us as he scanned the field and woods on the side of the Manor. Sweat ran down my temples, but I didn't take off my jacket, not wanting to scare Paige with the bulletproof vest. It was probably overkill, but I knew Hawk would send me back inside if I tried to take it off. He didn't mind using me as bait, but he wasn't going to let me die on his watch. Since I had every intention of staying alive, I left the jacket on and dealt with the heat, shoveling until my back ached and my arms burned.

I was knee-deep in the hole when my shovel scraped against wood. A few more shovelfuls and we'd bared a section of plywood.

"What's the plywood for?" I heard Hope ask as we cleared our way to its edge, then along the border to discover there was almost a full sheet of it, at least four feet by eight feet, discolored by age and crumbling at the edges. We had the gravel scraped away in minutes.

"Probably to stabilize the surface under the gravel," Hawk answered, leaving his place at the garage door to reach down and grab our shovels. When our hands were free, Griffen and I took positions at two corners on the long side of the sheet of plywood.

"You ready?" I asked, looking at my older brother.

"No," he said, his eyes somber, "but I think we'd better see what's under here."

I nodded and leaned down, hooking my fingers under the edge. "Three, two, one, lift."

It was awkward, angling the plywood up and tipping it back, edging our way along the sides of the hole to lean it upright. My view of the hole was blocked by the plywood when I heard Hope and Paige gasp behind me and Hawk's low, "Well, fuck."

Griffen and I shoved the plywood up and out of the hole and turned to see what we'd uncovered. Beneath the plywood was, as Bailey Toms had described, a lumpy mass of concrete, clearly hastily poured. Over the last thirty years, that concrete had crumbled in places, settling into a shape that appeared to be—

I shook my head, wishing I could see something else beneath the rough blanket of concrete.

"It looks like..." Hope said, her voice fading out.

"Bodies," Hawk finished for her, his voice flat. "Two. There's an edge of fabric over in the corner there, coming through where the concrete is uneven."

Griffen said nothing, swallowing hard, his eyes on mine. He eased closer, kneeling down in the spot Hawk had pointed to, reaching out with a fingertip to touch the triangle of fabric poking through the concrete. Faded cotton, the faintest pattern of flowers in pink.

Although everything fell into sharp focus, all I could

think was that it didn't smell. The bodies didn't smell. They'd been there too long, and the air had circulated. Although we couldn't see any bones, I imagined that was all we'd find beneath the concrete, aside from the clothing. I looked up to see Paige, her eyes fixed on that scrap of fabric, hollowed with anguish. We'd had an idea of what we might find, but the reality of it was something else. Our eyes met, the pain in hers a twin to my own.

Hawk's phone beeped. He lifted it up, listened, and said, "Escort them to the garage." Shoving his phone back in his pocket, he looked to us. "This may clear things up."

Griffen straightened, stepping out of the hole. I joined him, circling around to stand next to Paige. I reached for her hand, needing the anchor. Needing her.

"I think we'd better call West—" I started.

I heard Edgar before I saw him. "You're not calling Weston—"

"Edgar, what are you doing here?" Hope asked.

"I was trying to stop you," he said gruffly, shaking his head as his eyes fell on the hole in the concrete.

Harvey came around the corner, followed by Eli, Wren, and Ryder. Harvey walked to the edge of the pit in the garage floor, his face sheet-white, shaking his head back and forth. Ryder raised an eyebrow at Hawk and Griffen, who lifted their chins in response. Ryder nodded, tapped Wren on the shoulder, and the two of them left, Eli staying behind.

It seemed clear to me that while we might be comfortable with Edgar and Harvey, our new security team didn't trust them as far as they could throw them.

"Edgar," Griffen began, "I appreciate your loyalty to

my father and the past, but I think we all know what this looks like. We have to call West."

"You can't," Edgar said.

"Prentice is dead," I reminded him, "but we're still here. It looks like we have two bodies buried—"

Edgar cut me off. "You don't know what you have—"

"Well, then tell us," Paige said, her words clipped, "since you seem to know."

"They have a right to the truth," Harvey said, his voice shattered, eyes locked on the concrete in the bottom of the hole.

"They don't have the right to anything." Edgar turned to glare at Harvey, his jaw set in a familiar stubborn line. "We don't need to get into this. It's ancient history. They should fill it back in with all this gravel and cover it up. You don't know what you're doing, Harvey."

"I do," Harvey said, his eyes blazing as he turned to Edgar. "I fucking well do, and I'm tired of keeping his secrets."

"Harvey, you can't," Edgar said, reaching for his arm.

Harvey batted him away. "It's over, Edgar. It's time. You can go if you need to. I'm telling them the truth."

"Truth is a child's concept," Edgar said, impatient. "And this is nothing but melodrama. Just let it go. We'll get the floor fixed up and it'll be like nothing ever happened."

Hope turned icy eyes on her uncle. "Shut. Up," she snapped out. "We're moving on, all of us. We're not living like that anymore. Your secrets and lies, Prentice's manipulations—it's over, do you understand?" She turned to Harvey. "Tell us— What don't we know?"

Chapter Thirty-Three

FORD

Edgar glowered at us all but didn't move to leave. Harvey crossed his arms over his chest as if hugging himself and shook his head in a slow, sad swing.

"I didn't know," he began. "You have to understand— I didn't know. Not until Prentice— I'm so sorry, boys. Paige." He scrubbed his hands over his face, his eyes locked on the concrete at the bottom of the hole. "It's Sarah buried down there. Sarah and Paul Williams."

A whimper came from Paige's throat. She covered her mouth with her hand to stop the pained sound. I slid an arm around her, holding her close—not sure if I was supporting her or using her to hold myself up as my knees turned to water. My eyes dropped to the misshapen lumps of concrete. They looked like bodies, sure, but there were no features, no distinct limbs visible. They could have been tree branches, or a weird arrangement of trash with concrete dumped on top. But Harvey said no. That was my mother under there. Paige's father.

"How? How could— I don't—" I couldn't get the words out.

"Harvey," Griffen growled, his voice rough and abrupt, "you'd better keep talking."

"I went to Prentice," Harvey said, his eyes closed as if shutting out the present so he could see the past. "The day he died. There was a trust Sarah left you boys. They'd put it together when Ford was born. It was long past the time it should have been released to you, but we needed Sarah's signature. I'd always thought Prentice knew where she'd gone, but he laughed and said he'd forgotten about it. He'd have her declared dead—then we wouldn't need her to sign."

Harvey let his eyes open, his gaze lost and pained.

"I couldn't understand the laugh, his ease with the idea of Sarah being dead. For so many years after she left, he wouldn't let anyone speak her name, and now he was laughing? I reminded him I couldn't have her declared dead when she was out there somewhere. Prentice said, 'She isn't anywhere. She's been gone a long time.' I didn't —" Harvey shook his head, his eyes fixed on the bodies under the concrete. "I didn't understand. I should have. I should have known. This was Prentice, after all. But beyond everything else, he was my friend. And I didn't want to think he could have done—" Harvey shook his head again. He drew in a long breath that hitched as he exhaled.

"What did you think he did?" Hope prompted, looking to her uncle to see if Edgar was surprised by any of these revelations. He was clearly annoyed. Nervous, maybe, but not surprised.

I found I wasn't surprised either. Edgar had always kept Prentice's secrets.

"I asked what he was talking about," Harvey went on. "And he told me. Said so much time had gone by that it hardly mattered. That he'd caught them—Sarah and Paul —that he'd known she was up to something with some-one, and finally he caught them. And then he smiled at me. He said no one betrayed him. Not a business partner. Not a friend. Sure, as fucking hell, not a wife. She thought she could have an affair and send her lover away, and come back to his bed like nothing had happened. But Prentice wouldn't bear the insult. He shot them. One bullet each, he said. They didn't deserve more. And then he dumped them in the hole in the garage floor like they were trash." Harvey's voice caught.

"He killed both of them?" Paige asked, breathless. "He shot them?"

Harvey nodded. "They weren't leaving you," he said, sounding desperate for us to understand. "Prentice over-heard everything the day he caught them. They'd decided they couldn't be together. They couldn't leave their children. They'd agreed they loved each other, but they'd realized they were spinning a fairy tale of running off together. So, they met that one last time to say good-bye. And their luck ran out."

"Why did he kill them?" Paige asked, tears spilling down her cheeks. "It was over. What was the point?"

I tightened my arm around her, my own vision blur-ring as the pointlessness of it struck me. I'd lived my entire life without the mother who'd loved me because fucking Prentice couldn't accept the ding to his ego.

"She'd betrayed him," I answered. I hadn't known my mother beyond those two short years, but I sure as hell had known my father. "Like he told Harvey, he didn't tolerate betrayal."

"Yes," Harvey agreed. "It didn't matter to him that they were calling it off, that they'd never see each other again. She betrayed him, and they both had to pay."

Paige stiffened, her eyes narrowing on Harvey. "Did you know they were having an affair? Did she confide in you?"

"No, I—" Harvey's eyes skipped around the room, bouncing off Edgar, off Griffen, skittering around Hawk, until they landed on me.

And I saw. I knew.

"You," I said. "You killed him, that day, after he confessed."

Harvey's breath caught in a sob. "I loved her," he said. "Sarah. God, I loved her so much. She never knew, but I loved her."

I tore my eyes from Harvey to glance at Edgar, who had a hand to his face, shaking his head. Edgar fucking knew everything. If he wasn't such a goddamn vault with the secrets, we might have known all of it so much earlier.

"And you let me go to prison for a year?" I demanded.

"I'm sorry, Ford," Harvey said. "I didn't know what to do. I didn't mean to kill your father."

"It seems like you did," Griffen said, "because—I'm trying to picture this—you're in his office, he confesses he murdered our mother and Paige's father, and you, what? You were packing a weapon for a simple business meeting with an old friend?"

Harvey shook his head, swinging it from side to side like a bobblehead. "I...I broke. I walked out of his office, went to my car, got my handgun from my glove compartment, and went back in. He looked up at me and said, 'You're still here?' and I shot him. I must have dropped the gun since Haywood had it later. I only remember that I walked out and drove away. No one was around—no staff in the Manor, no security, no sign I was ever there—and I went home."

Harvey's knees gave out in a slow slide that brought him to kneel at the side of my mother's grave.

"I couldn't make sense of it all," he said, tears streaming down his cheeks. "You don't understand. I loved Sarah so much. She was so perfect, so beautiful and kind. She deserved so much better than your father."

"And you two never—" Hope asked, raising an eyebrow.

"No!" Harvey said in a shout. "Never. I never thought she would have, until—" He looked to Paige. "Until your father. And then—God, a part of me hated her when I suspected she'd found someone else. But I knew it could never be me. I just wanted her to be happy. All these years, thinking she'd run off with him, that the woman I loved had abandoned her sons, that she wasn't the person I thought she was. He tarnished my memory of her when it was all I had. And then to learn that she never left you," he said, his eyes on Griffen and then me, his voice breaking. "She didn't leave. He took her. He took her from us. Didn't even give her a proper burial. All these years she's been here, and he laughed, he fucking laughed. And I killed him for it." His eyes locked on mine. "I'm sorry, Ford. I'm so sorry."

I nodded, not sure I knew what to feel. I had my answers. It should have been satisfying to know that Harvey was the one who'd shot Prentice, but the why of it rocked my reality. He'd avenged my mother out of love, but then had let me hang for it. Was I angry, given how much I'd realized about atoning for my other sins? I wasn't sure I was. I might be weirdly grateful to Harvey for what he'd done.

"You should have kept your mouth shut, Harvey," Edgar growled. "We got this one out of prison," he said, tilting his head in my direction. "Everything was fine."

"Cole Haywood got me out of prison," I reminded him. "Not you. And he only did it so he'd have an easier shot at killing me."

Edgar ignored me, focused on Harvey. "Now they're going to call West, and you'll go to jail. For what? It's not going to bring Prentice back. It can't do anything for Sarah or Paul."

Harvey just shook his head, his eyes glued on the hole in the garage floor, weeping silently.

I should have been filled with rage. This man had killed my father and, with his silence, had sent me to prison. And yet, watching his grief, feeling my own at the sight of the bodies beneath the concrete, vengeance on Harvey was the last thing on my mind.

I wrapped my arms around Paige, rocking her.

"They weren't going to leave us," she said into my shirt.

I tightened my arms, my throat thick with tears I

couldn't shed. My mother hadn't left us. There'd been no abandonment. She hadn't run off to Belize with her lover. She'd been murdered by my father.

My eyes lifted to Harvey again, his grief etched into his face, and I understood. Not the part about letting me rot in prison, but shooting Prentice? Yeah, I got that. I could picture it in my head: Prentice's callous laughter as Harvey's heart shattered. He'd spent decades following my father's orders, even when it pinched his conscience, only to find out the woman he'd loved, the woman he'd spent years disappointed in, had her life stolen.

I understood.

"We need to call West," Griffen said, his eyes locked on Edgar.

"No," Edgar said. "You'll destroy your father's legacy and make a spectacle of your family. You could bring down Sawyer Enterprises."

"Does it always come down to business, Uncle Edgar?" Hope asked quietly.

Edgar leveled his gaze on Hope, his eyes going soft. "Not always. You know that."

"Is this what you had on Prentice? Is this how you got him to change his will?" Hope asked quietly.

I wasn't sure I understood the question, but I saw that Edgar and Griffen did.

"Using the secret brought some good in the world, Hope," Edgar answered, and Hope nodded, closing her eyes for a long moment as Griffen pulled her close, murmuring something in her ear.

They'd gotten married the day Prentice's will was read. I knew Griffen had come to town planning to turn right around and leave. Instead, he'd married Hope. Because of something in the will? Something Edgar had strong-armed Prentice into adding?

"That doesn't make it right, and you know it," Hope chastised.

"No more cover-ups," I said, the words rough as I forced them through my tight throat. I cleared it and said it again. "We're done with that. They deserve a proper burial."

As I said the words, Paige jerked in my arms, a sob tearing through her. I held her closer, rocking her from side to side.

"We'll take care of it," I whispered to her. "We'll put them together, somewhere we can see them."

She nodded against my chest. "They didn't leave us. I've been so angry, but they weren't going to leave. They gave up what they wanted most." Another sob wrenched her. "And he killed them anyway," she choked out. "He deserved what Harvey did."

I agreed. Even if the aftermath meant I spent a year in prison, everyone thinking I was a murderer. In the end, Prentice had gotten what he deserved.

Hawk and Eli straightened at the same second, both of them looking at their phones.

"Incoming," Eli said, his gaze sweeping the garage. "Fuck. We have too many civilians. We've got to get them secured."

"No time," Hawk said. "Fuck." His gaze flicked to the hole in the concrete and to the door of the garage. "Haywood's on his way. Ford, you're up."

Hawk turned and shared a glance with Griffen, who

scooped Hope up, tossed her over his shoulder, and strode for the door into the Manor, Edgar tight on their heels.

Hawk's gaze slid to Paige, who looked up at me, her eyes shining with determination. "I'm not going anywhere."

Chapter Thirty-Four

PAIGE

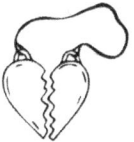

"We've got him covered," Hawk said. "He's coming in from the east, through the woods. Ryder and Wren are on him."

"What if he spots them?" Ford asked.

"He won't," Hawk said with a low laugh. "Ford, walk out of the garage." Hawk scanned the open doors and spotted the broom Billy Bob had leaned against the closest wall. "Grab that broom. Sweep the driveway. Take your time so we know he sees you. That'll draw him to you."

"And then what?" I asked. "Ford leads Haywood back in, and you guys shoot him?" I was hoping that was the answer, because this sounded an awful lot like Ford was bait. Cole Haywood had already proven he was willing to kill to get what he wanted, and it seemed clear that what he wanted was to hurt Ford.

"Paige, get in the house," Hawk said. "Harvey, you too."

Harvey shook his head, his eyes on Ford. "I'm not leaving."

"Neither am I," I added. A little voice in the back of my brain was shrieking, *Run, run, run!* But I wasn't leaving Ford. I looked down into the hole in the garage floor, at the lumps of rough concrete in the bottom. My father. Ford's mother. Tipping my head back, I stared at the ceiling, imagining I could see through the layers of plaster and wood to the hallway above. A shiver crawled down my spine at the memory of that frozen door the night we'd been trapped in the room. I thought of the lights that flickered on and off, and the problems with the heat and the water. Our first kiss in the closet when I'd gone to reset the breakers. All of it had been leading us to each other, and together, to this moment. To their bodies. They hadn't left each other, and I wasn't leaving Ford. Our parents had died together. We were going to live together. After they dealt with Cole Haywood.

"Cole isn't here for me," I said to Ford and Hawk. "I'll stay out of the way, but I'm not running for safety while Ford is in danger."

Ford looked like he was going to argue, but Hawk, his focus on the woods across the field, said, "Ford, go. Get the broom. Use it for a minute, until I give you the signal to come back into the garage. I'll deal with Paige and Harvey."

Ford pulled me close. "We have a plan," he said. "Please get inside with everyone else."

I reached up to press my palms to his cheeks, pulling him down so I could press a quick kiss to his mouth. "I love you and I'm not leaving. Go play bait so we can get this over with. I'll stay out of sight. I'm not going to mess up your plan, but I'm not leaving. Trust me."

"I love you, too," Ford said, and drew in a breath. "Please—"

Hawk interrupted with a low, "Ford, now."

"Go," I said, stepping back and giving him a gentle shove.

Ford shot a look at Hawk, that Hawk answered with a solemn nod. I expected him to toss me over his shoulder the way Griffen had with Hope, but he ignored me, turning to Harvey.

"Harvey," he began, but Harvey shook his head slowly.

Harvey edged closer to the wall beside the hole in the concrete. Grabbing one of the shovels leaning where Griffen and Ford had left them, he followed the wall to the corner by the garage door and tucked himself into the shadows. Hawk narrowed his eyes at Harvey, then glanced at Ford fiddling with the broom. His gaze flicked to the field beyond the courtyard. Cole Haywood had emerged from the woods, his cautious pace picking up speed as he spotted Ford. I worried he'd pull out a gun and try to shoot Ford, but instead he strode across the field, hands swinging free at his sides, his distant figure growing closer with every step.

Hawk looked over to Harvey. "We don't have time to argue about it. Stay there. If you get yourself killed, it's not on me. My job is to keep Ford and Paige alive."

"I owe him," Harvey said.

It seemed to be all the answer Hawk needed. Turning from Harvey, in a voice that wouldn't carry farther than the courtyard, Hawk said, "Ford, he spotted you."

Ford turned, broom in hand, and re-entered the garage, walking past Harvey's hiding spot in the corner without seeing him. As his eyes adjusted to the dimmer light inside, he spotted me beside Hawk. "Paige, you shouldn't be here."

Before I could say anything, Hawk cut in, closing a hand around my upper arm. In a low voice, he said, "Come with me," as he tugged me toward the door to the house. "Ford, stay there, in the middle of the garage. I don't want you near that hole or pinned against the back wall. We need room to move."

Ford shifted position to the center garage bay, his gaze on the figure of Cole, nearing the courtyard. Ford swept a path of floor, sparing a quick glance at the back of the garage, where Hawk led me to the alcove by the door into the Manor. Pushing me behind him, Hawk took a position at the front of the alcove and flicked off the light above us, shrouding us in the shadows. I could see past him, but Cole and Ford would have a hard time spotting either of us. And Haywood would have to go through Hawk to get to me. Apparently satisfied by the wall of man between me and Haywood, Ford turned to face Cole as he strode across the courtyard, his face set in hard lines.

Weapon drawn, Hawk kept his attention on Haywood and Ford, but took a moment to whisper to me, "Don't make me regret this, Paige."

"I won't," I promised. "Don't let him get hurt."

"Not happening," Hawk grunted as Cole Haywood

paced through the open garage door, never seeing Harvey in the corner, or Hawk and me tucked into the alcove. All of his attention was fixed on Ford.

"Cole," Ford said, sounding almost welcoming. "We've been looking for you."

"Really?" Cole asked, stopping in the middle of the garage, less than ten feet from Ford. "I won't take too much of your time. Unfreeze my money and I'll leave you alone." He paused and narrowed his eyes. "Everyone who took the bounty got the message. You're too hot a target. You'll stop me from being able to pay anyone who takes the bounty, and they'll end up in jail—or worse. Understood. Fine. I give up." He crossed his arms over his chest and lifted his chin. "Give me back my money."

"What makes you think I can do that?" Ford asked, curling his fingers around the top of the broom handle as if he had all the time in the world. "We've known each other for years. You know I'm great with a spreadsheet, but I'm no hacker."

"Don't fuck with me, Ford," Haywood snapped out. "I know you're behind this." Hawk shifted, keeping his gun focused on Haywood as he took a step closer to Ford, fury twisting his handsome face.

"And hypothetically," Ford went on, his tone conversational despite the threat in front of him, "if I *could* unfreeze your money, you'd take your cash and disappear, never darken my door again? That kind of thing?" Ford had one eyebrow raised, and I swore I saw a shadow of amusement in his sea-green eyes. Was he enjoying this?

My stomach was in knots. Cole's hands were empty. I

couldn't see that he was carrying a gun, but despite his anger, he seemed too in control not to have the upper hand in one way or another.

"We both know you have access to some of the best hackers in the world through your brother and Hawk," Haywood said. "Don't waste my time. Tell them to unfreeze my money and I'll walk away."

"So basically," Ford said, spinning the broom against the concrete in a very believable show of nonchalance, "you're asking me to trust your word that you'll leave me alone? Trust the man who's tried to kill me, repeatedly? Who's hired people to take shots at not just me, but half of my family as well? If I did have anything to do with your accounts being frozen, I don't think it would be very smart of me to unfreeze them. You've got a lot less leverage when you're broke and desperate."

Cole scowled. "I may be temporarily broke," he said, "but I'll never be desperate."

Ford shrugged, as if it didn't matter to him either way. "I have a different proposal," he said. "I think you should leave Sawyers Bend and never come back. Stay off the dark web, cause trouble somewhere else. I don't care where. Just disappear."

"And, hypothetically, if I took your advice and left town, what about my money?" Cole asked.

"I don't really see where that's my problem," Ford said. "It's still your money."

"But I can't access it," Cole ground out.

Ford shrugged. "I'm sure eventually you can sort that out."

"And when I do," Cole said, and this time he added a sneer, "you know full well I'll come straight for you."

Ford's lips pressed together in a hard line, and he gave a decisive nod. "Exactly. So why would I make that happen any faster? We both know you're never going to stand down. I don't think you're capable of it. Your life went to shit on your own watch, and you want to blame my father? Fine. He was a bastard."

Ford glanced over at the gaping hole in the concrete.

"My father was more of a bastard than you know. But he's dead. You missed your chance there. The rest of us— We didn't have anything to do with his bullshit, and you know it. I may have fucked over some of my own family, clients, and business partners, but never you. None of us here has ever hurt you. The people who did are dead, but for some reason, you can't let it go. I could unfreeze your accounts and write you a big fat check—and it wouldn't make a difference. Am I right?"

Cole narrowed his eyes on Ford. Then, with a sigh, he propped his hands on his hips, looking for just a moment every bit the lord of the manor with his perfect hair waving off his face, those sharp cheekbones, and vivid blue eyes. He was almost blindingly attractive, but so cold, and weirdly triumphant considering that his negotiation with Ford hadn't been going his way.

I felt a chill in my gut as he cocked his head to the side and reached up to unbutton his black cashmere overcoat.

Chapter Thirty-Five

PAIGE

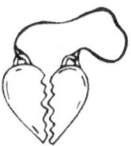

"Fine," Cole said evenly. "I was trying to do this the easy way. You give me my money, and I leave you a gift you wouldn't find until it was too late. But on the chance you weren't prepared to be cooperative—"

Haywood undid the last button and spread wide the lapels of his overcoat.

"I brought the gift with me," he finished, revealing a vest beneath, covered with blocks of—

"Fuck me," Hawk said.

"What is that?" I whispered, not understanding. White clay and wires, with a small rectangular screen in the middle. On it, 4:00 flashed on and off in glowing red.

"C-4 on a timer," he said, turning his head a fraction so I could hear his nearly silent words.

"C-4?" I asked under my breath.

"Explosive. He has enough to fucking blow a hole in the entire estate. If that goes off, there'll be a crater where

Heartstone Manor once stood." Hawk tilted his head and said—I assumed into the earpiece connecting him to the rest of his team, "Kane, evacuate the Manor. Cole has a bomb. Keep it quiet. Get everyone past the gatehouse." To me, he added, "Paige, go back in the Manor and leave through the front door."

I ignored Hawk's order. I needed to know what Cole's plan was for the bomb strapped to his chest. And I wasn't leaving Ford.

"You have three options," Cole said. "Option one was to unfreeze my money. This is option two."

Ford swallowed visibly. "Does option two involve you taking whatever that is far away from Heartstone Manor?"

Cole grinned. "In a way. Option two is that you leave with me, you make a phone call and get my funds unfrozen, then I let you walk, and you never see me again."

Ford crossed his arms over his chest. "I don't think that thing even works. It looks like you threw together some spare wires and blocks of play dough."

"You don't believe I'd blow up Heartstone Manor?" Cole asked, stroking a hand over the bomb on his chest.

Unlike Ford, I absolutely believed that thing worked.

"No," Ford said, "I think you'd blow up Heartstone Manor and every single Sawyer in it if you could. I just don't think you'd go down with us. You're way too much of a narcissist to take your own life."

"I don't know," Cole said. "I wouldn't call myself a narcissist. Just confident. But I should be. I'm Cole Haywood. I don't want to die, but if that's the cost of destroying every last member of your family in one fell swoop, it'll be worth it."

Ford shook his head. "I don't believe it."

"So, you're not going to leave with me?" Haywood asked, his eyes dropping to the mess of wires and white blocks on his chest as if he was seeing it for the first time.

Ford agreed. "No, I'm not."

"Then I guess we're on to option three. We all go down together." Cole's hand flew up, and he slapped the flat of his palm against the numbers on his chest. A second later, they flashed 3:59.

"Fuck," Hawk growled. "Timer's live. 3:58 remaining. Get the Manor clear."

Before Hawk could make a move, Harvey erupted from his hiding place in the corner, gripping the handle of one of the shovels he'd taken from where it had leaned against the wall. As he sprinted across the garage, he cranked the shovel back and swung, the flat metal blade whacking Cole Haywood on the side of the head with a low thunk.

Haywood went down hard, landing on his back with a whoosh of breath. He rolled with a groan, lifting a hand to his head. Before he could sit up, Harvey skidded to a stop beside him and slammed the digging edge blade down on Cole's neck, just below his chin. The blade went through skin and bone with a sickening crunch, Cole's head twisting to the side as it separated from his neck, blood spilling out in a flood of red, his open eyes fixed on Ford as they slowly went dim. Harvey lifted the shovel in both hands and brought it down a second time, severing whatever was still holding the head on its neck.

I closed my eyes with a shriek, unable to erase the vision of Cole Haywood's head rolling free of his body, ruby red blood pooling around him in the same shade as the numbers that flashed on his chest.

I didn't think Cole would be a problem anymore, except—

"Is that fucking timer still going?" Hawk asked, striding into the room, stepping around Cole's dismembered head to crouch beside his body. Hawk spread Haywood's arms wide, revealing the numbers on his chest counting down: 3:36, 3:35—

"Fucking hell. Eli, get your ass in here," Hawk said. "Harvey took care of Haywood, but the bomb is still live."

I followed Hawk to where Ford stood, his eyes glued to the body of his former friend. Reaching his side, I slid my arms around his waist.

He held me tight, rubbing a hand over my back. "Did you see that?" he asked, his voice rough with emotion.

I nodded into his chest, swallowing hard.

"You okay?"

I shook my head, my forehead pressing into his shirt. "Are you?" I whispered.

"Don't know yet," he said.

Hawk looked up. "Paige, Ford, Harvey, get the fuck out of here."

Before we could tell him we weren't going anywhere, Eli sprinted in, skidding to a stop at Cole's side and dropping to his knees. He scanned the device connected to Cole.

"Did he fucking go on the internet to figure out how to build this thing?" Eli muttered as he examined the device strapped around Cole's torso. He dug in a side pocket of his cargo pants and pulled out a multi-tool. "Everybody say a prayer," he said, leaning down with sharp pliers and cutting through one wire, then another.

I didn't say a prayer, but I was holding my breath, my arms tight around Ford. As the second wire fell in half, the screen shut off, the numbers vanishing. I felt a hot tear streak down my cheek as I drew in a long breath.

The door from the Manor into the garage flew open, Griffen sprinting in. He came to an abrupt stop as Eli flicked out a blade on his multi-tool, cut the vest off Cole, holding it gingerly. "I'm going to take this into the field to finish disarming it, just in case."

Hawk stood, pulled his phone out of his pocket, and tapped the screen. "West is on the way," he said when he was done. He looked up to take in the rest of us. "None of you listen worth a shit. If I tell you to evacuate, you fucking evacuate."

"You were still here," Ford countered, his arm tight around my shoulders.

"It's my job to be here," Hawk snapped back.

"And you're my brother-in-law," Ford reminded him. "What am I supposed to tell Quinn if something happens to you?"

Hawk shook his head, muttering, "You're all fucking crazy."

"Kane has everyone on the way out," Griffen said, standing on Ford's other side as we all watched the pool of blood spread under Cole Haywood. "I wasn't leaving you or my brother in here to deal with him."

Ford, keeping his arm around my shoulder, turned to

face Harvey, standing a few feet from Cole's body, the bloody shovel still in his hands.

"Harvey," Ford said, his voice sharp, cutting through Harvey's daze, "keep your mouth shut about shooting Prentice."

Harvey's eyes flickered. He shook his head. "I owe it to you to tell the truth. I should have come clean a long time ago, should pay for killing him. It was wrong."

"I don't need you to come clean," Ford said. "Tell West what you know about my mother and Paige's father. Tell him what Prentice told you, but don't tell West you shot him."

"Ford, I can clear your name—" The shovel tumbled from Harvey's hands to clatter on the concrete floor. "I can fix all of this—"

"At what price?" Ford asked. "I'm free. My name is clear according to the law. The people who matter know I didn't do it. I'm home. I have my family." He looked down to me, reaching up to stroke the backs of his fingers across my cheek. "I have a future. I don't want you to lose yours."

"I'm going to jail anyway," Harvey said, looking down at Cole's body.

"No, you're not," Hawk said. "It'll either be defense of others or self-defense, considering how close you were to the bomb. I bet West goes with self-defense. Either way, this isn't a homicide."

"I agree with Ford," Griffen said. "Tell West what you know about our mother and Paul. They deserve justice. And Prentice got what he deserved when you shot him. No one wants you to pay for that."

Harvey closed his mouth and nodded.

After a few minutes, Eli returned, carefully carrying the remains of the bomb Cole Haywood had built. He set it aside by the corner in the garage where Harvey had hidden with his shovel. "No one touch that." He shook his head as he took in Cole's head a foot from his body, an island in a sea of blood. "You can learn all sorts of shit on the internet." He raised his eyes to Hawk and Griffen. "It was a crap design, but it would have worked."

A siren wailed in the distance. West's SUV, followed by two more Sawyers Bend official vehicles, drove up less than ten seconds later. After Griffen and Hawk quickly explained what happened, including that Harvey was the shovel-wielder, I was surprised when he put Harvey in handcuffs.

"We'll get it all cleared up at the station," West said calmly, and Harvey nodded, his eyes dazed.

Harvey drove off with a deputy, crossing paths with the crime scene van. I hoped they were going to put the body into that van and take it far from Heartstone.

West took our statements and, finally, as the crime scene team got to work, kicked all of us out of the garage. We met the rest of the family in the dining room. Everyone was milling around, looking shell-shocked. Ford, his arms still around my shoulders, led me over to where Hope stood with Savannah and Finn. Griffen pulled Hope into his arms, murmuring into her ear. She held him back, her voice soothing, though I couldn't make out the words.

"It's over?" Finn asked Ford.

"It's over," Ford confirmed, meeting Griffen's eyes over Hope's head.

Griffen agreed. "I think it is. We still have to wait out the terms of the will, but I don't think anyone else is coming after us. All of this was Haywood, and he's dead."

I couldn't stop seeing Cole's head rolling from his body. It would be a long time until that wasn't featured in my nightmares. On the other hand, I couldn't deny there was something very satisfying about the danger being ended in such a decisive manner. We'd never have to worry about him getting paroled or putting bounties up on the dark web from prison, because Cole Haywood was very, very dead.

"There's always a chance someone else has a grudge against Dad," Ford said. "He pissed off a lot of people. But I don't think there's another Cole Haywood waiting in the wings. I think maybe it's time we all get to just live our lives together."

"I like the way that sounds," Griffen said.

"Me too," Ford agreed.

"What about you?" Ford asked, turning to me. Sliding his arms around my waist, not caring who was watching, he asked, "Did we scare you away?"

"Not a chance," I said.

"Then we're going to stop pretending that we're not seeing each other, because I love you and I want everyone to know."

I grinned at him. "I love you, too," I said. "And after today, I don't want to pretend. I just want to be with you."

"Sounds good to me," Ford said.

I reached up, slid my hands around his neck, and pulled him down for a kiss. In the background, I heard the kids let out a whoop as Ford's lips met mine, but the rush of my heartbeat drowned them out.

Finally, we had answers, and we had each other. I couldn't ask for more.

Epilogue

FORD

It was a novelty to lie in Paige's bed with her so long after sunrise. Up until now, lazy mornings had been saved for Sundays—the one day she had completely off. Christmas break had finally arrived. The kids of Heartstone Manor had been set free from the shackles of school for two weeks, and Paige's call time was much later, now that she didn't have to get them up and off to school. The Manor was at ease for the first time in my memory, as if the entire household had let out a breath we'd been holding for decades. Prentice was gone, and discovering how he'd died, and why, had swept his ghost from the Manor. While no one had suspected Harvey of killing him, the family was agreed that justice had been served.

Ryder, Eli, and Wren had bid us farewell, heading back to Atlanta along with Kane Black, who'd been on loan from Sinclair Security. Hawk was hanging on to the rest of his team, at least for a while. While Griffen was confident that it was over and we were free to live our lives like normal people—or as normal as a Sawyer could get—Hawk was too paranoid for that. He preferred to downgrade security gradually. He'd said that if anyone was watching and decided to take a shot at the Sawyers, he'd be ready for them.

I appreciated his caution, but I was with Griffen—there wasn't anyone else out there who wanted to come for the Sawyers. It was finally over.

West had cleared Harvey and sent in a team to process the crime scenes—both the one caused by Cole Haywood's death and the older scene of my mother and Paul Williams's murder. Once West was done, Bailey Toms's concrete company did us a favor and squeezed in the garage floor repair before they closed for the holidays. Fortunately, the weather had cooperated. The days were filled with bright sunshine and blue skies, the chill in the air mostly burned off by midday. We wouldn't have a white Christmas, but we sure as hell would have a cheerful one.

There were clouds here and there. Paige and I were both adjusting to our new understanding of our parents. There had been a part of me that had hated my mother for leaving me, that had always wondered why I hadn't been enough to make her stay. I knew Paige felt the same about her father. And now, I couldn't escape the grief of knowing that Sarah's life was stolen so young, that she'd been killed by the man who'd vowed to cherish her. It was both better and worse to know she'd been willing to give up love for me, that Paige's father had planned to turn away from his heart and go home to his daughter.

When I let myself think about it, I liked to imagine that if my mother had lived, maybe when we were a little older, we could have found a way to leave Prentice together. She could have had her freedom—maybe she could have found her way to Paul. But then again—I looked at the woman sleeping in my arms, her lashes dark fans on her cheeks, her long legs tangled with mine. Paige, as my stepsister, would have been a problem, considering I hadn't managed to keep my hands off her as an adult. As teenagers? Nope, not thinking about that.

All we had was the present. And when it came to Paige, it was hard to regret anything that had come before when it had led me to landing here, with this woman in my arms.

We'd been together such a short time, and yet, it felt like forever. Life before Paige was dull and faded. And finally, with Haywood gone—our parents soon to be properly buried in the Sawyer family plot together—we could have a life.

A future.

And that thought reminded me of what I had planned for the morning.

"It's going to be okay," I heard, and a soft fingertip traced a line between my furrowed eyebrows. I rolled my head on the pillow to see Paige smiling at me, her face sleepy and soft. "It's a great idea. And Griffen's smart, he'll see that."

"I hope so," I said. I had a plan for what to do with the rest of my life now that I had one. But I couldn't do it by myself. I needed Griffen's buy-in. I caught her hand in mine and kissed her fingertips, "Whatever happens, I'll figure it out."

"I know you will," she said, her pale blue eyes so satisfied they seemed to glow with it. "What time is it?" She stretched her arms over her head with a lazy smile.

"Eight-something," I said, easing down to bury my face in the curve of her neck, drawing in her warm, sweet scent.

She turned to face me, trailing her hands over my back. "We don't have to get up yet."

"Not yet," I agreed, closing my fingers over the curve of her ass and pulling her into my erection.

"Mm, you feel so good," she said, rolling to her back, one leg coming up to wrap around my hip. She smiled up at me, her eyes still sleepy but now fogged with lust. "This is my favorite way to wake up."

"Mine too." I leaned to nudge open her bedside drawer and pulled out a condom. I had them stashed everywhere. Her room, mine, the shower. Anywhere I thought I might get her naked. Now that life was somewhat settled, we'd been putting them to good use, disappearing every night after dinner for an early bedtime. We spent plenty of time in bed, not a lot of it sleeping. I pressed her back into the mattress, pulling her hands over her head and dipping my head to tease the tip of her breast. I was on a mission to taste every inch of Paige, and I wasn't close to satisfied.

Later, I carried her to the shower. Neither of us was surprised when the water steamed on demand. Since the day we'd found our parents' grave, we hadn't had a single problem with the plumbing or the electrical in the guest wing. No one thought it was a coincidence.

We emerged from Paige's room to find the leftovers of breakfast still laid out in the dining room. Finn always did a buffet in the mornings during the holidays. I didn't mind getting the scraps. Finn's overwarmed eggs and cooled biscuits were a hell of a lot better than anything I could have made myself.

"Are you going to talk to Griffen after breakfast?" Paige asked over coffee.

"That's the plan," I said.

"Come find me after. I'm doing a project with the kids in the kitchen."

"I will," I said. I pushed my chair back, nerves twisting in my gut.

"It's a great idea, Ford," she said.

I nodded, my throat tight with a combination of love and gratitude that stole my voice. I hadn't thought I deserved anything after the way I'd spent most of my life, and to have this woman look at me like that, glowing with feeling for me—it was more than I deserved. I'd make sure she never regretted it, not for a moment.

I knocked on Griffen's office door, pushing it open at his brisk, "Yep?"

"Ford," Hope said, surprise on her face as she noticed the file folder in my hand. She glanced at Griffen, eyebrows raised.

"Is now good?" I asked. Griffen had said they didn't have anything on the schedule, but I knew how quickly things could change.

"Yeah, come in." He looked at his wife. "I meant to tell you Ford was stopping by this morning," he said to Hope, "but then I got—" He paused, and something in his look had Hope's cheeks flushing. "Distracted," he finished.

I didn't bother to hide my grin.

"Oh," Hope said. She cleared her throat and looked to me, giving me a bright, professional smile that belied the very personal blush on her cheeks. "What's up? Is this a business meeting or a family thing?"

"It's both, actually," I said. "I've been doing a lot of thinking about what's next."

"The last time we talked about this," Griffen said, "you were determined to find out who killed Dad."

I sat back, crossed my ankle on my knee. "I was."

"And you did," Griffen said. "I can't say I saw that coming."

I shook my head. "Me either. All these years Harvey was pining for our mother, and then..."

"And you're really not mad?" Griffen asked, his eyes narrowing on my face. "You spent a year in prison."

"I know," I said. "Believe me, I know." There were nights when I still couldn't shake the memories—the loneliness, the heat. But the nightmares would fade, and I was here. In my home. With my family. With Paige. Prison felt very far away.

As a family, we'd talked about Harvey killing Prentice—minus West—and had agreed to keep what we knew to ourselves. None of us wanted to see Harvey in prison. West knew we were keeping something from him, but so far, he seemed content to let it go. I suspected

Avery had played a part in that. But I hadn't talked about it with Griffen.

"Here's the thing," I said, "he lied. And I went to prison for it. And yeah, that was miserable. But if he turns himself in to West for shooting Dad, he'll be locked up for the rest of his life. I don't want that. And knowing Harvey, the guilt he's feeling is worse than anything the legal system can do to him." I looked at Griffen. "Do you want Harvey to go to prison?"

He closed his eyes and sat back, thinking for a long moment. Hope reached out to take his hand, squeezing hard. Griffen was usually more compassionate than me, but it seemed like in this one case, he was having a hard time letting go. He squeezed Hope's hand and opened his eyes.

"No," he said. "You make a good point. Part of me wants him to bear some responsibility for what he put you through, but not if that means he spends the rest of his life in prison. I can understand why he snapped. I feel like I can see the whole scene in my head. Prentice laughing, admitting he'd murdered the woman Harvey loved—our mother—like it was a joke."

I could picture it, too. All too easily.

"I'm glad Harvey did it," I admitted. "Maybe that makes me a terrible person, but I don't care. I'm glad he shot Prentice. It doesn't bring our mother back, but it's some kind of justice."

Griffen met my eyes in perfect accord. "I agree."

"Well," Hope said into the heavy moment, "I uninvited Harvey and Edgar from Christmas."

"You uninvited Uncle Edgar from Christmas?"

351

Griffen asked slowly. Hope had learned how to set boundaries with her uncle, but he was still her only family, and I knew she'd never turn her back on him.

"Griffen," she said, "he lied. For years. To us, to Harvey. He knew. He knew where your mother was this whole time." Her voice caught. She lifted her hand to cover her mouth, her eyes filling with tears. "I can't. I'll be able to live with it eventually, but I can't right now. I know Uncle Edgar is no innocent, but that's just too much. And I know you don't want to see him across the table at Christmas dinner."

Griffen shook his head slowly. "I really don't. I was willing to put up with him for you, but I need time, too."

Griffen looked to me, and I sent Hope an apologetic look. "I know Edgar thought he was doing the right thing —he always does—but all those years he watched us living without her, thinking she'd left us, and never said a fucking word. It's going to be a while until I want to share a table with him."

Hope nodded. "We can talk about it later, when we're ready." She paused, gave herself a little shake, and then smiled at me. "So, what did you want to meet with us about?" she asked. "What's your plan now that the question of your father is settled?"

"You're aware that Prentice started a charitable fund a few years ago?" I asked.

Hope's cheeks flushed again, this time in embarrassment. "That's been my project. We came across it not long after your father died. We've been meaning to do something with it, but we were getting a handle on the business, and then there was Stella, and it's been on the back burner, I'm sorry to say. Prentice had a few things set up. There are some donations from when he was alive that were questionable," she said. "We stopped anything like that when Griffen took over, kept the regular donations to the food bank, Laurel Country Day, and a few others. Why do you mention it?"

"I want to run it," I said. "There's enough money in there that, if properly invested, we can make it grow while still deploying it. And there's a lot of need here in the community, locally, and abroad. I'm good at making money, but so are you and Hope and Royal, and I don't want to step on your toes."

"Ford, we'd make room for you at Sawyer Enterprises if you want to come back," Griffen said, and for the first time since we'd been together as adults, I knew he meant it wholeheartedly.

If I wanted a seat at their table, they'd make one for me, and knowing that meant everything. I shook my head. "I appreciate that. But if you don't have an objection, I'd like to put my focus on the philanthropy fund. Dad used it as a tax shelter, but now it's ours, and we can use that money to do some good. Here are some things I've been thinking about." I opened the file folder I'd brought and pulled out the presentation I'd thrown together, highlighting local charities I thought could use a boost.

With me at the helm, I could bring both funds and media attention, letting us rope in other donors. I had a lot of plans. I just needed the go-ahead. Once, it would have burned that I had to ask Griffen. Not now. We were a family. We decided together.

When they were done going through my charts and spreadsheets, Griffen held up the file folder and said, "Can I hang on to this?"

"Sure. What do you think?" I kept my tone light, but nerves twisted in my gut. If he wanted his revenge, now would be a great time to smack me down.

But that wasn't Griffen. And that was the old me.

He grinned. "I think it sounds great. It's a perfect fit for you."

"I'll put some more plans together," I said, not trying to dim the smile that spread across my face. "We can go over them after the new year." I stood, suddenly eager to leave the office.

"Tell Paige hi from us," Griffen said with a smirk as I walked to the door.

It should have annoyed me that my older brother knew exactly where I was going. I shot him the middle finger as I walked through the door, but I did it with a grin on my face, because he wasn't wrong. I'd been headed down the stairs to the kitchen to find Paige and tell her my new life plan was a go.

I was starting over—a little late in life. But this time I knew I was going to feel good about my work. And maybe, if I could hang around long enough, I'd leave the world a better place than I'd made it up until now.

I found Paige and all the kids, even Thatcher, sitting around the table in the kitchen. The room smelled of citrus and spice. I watched as Finn pulled a cookie sheet out of the oven, covered in—

"Are those oranges?" I asked. I could smell them, fragrant and sweet, but the skin looked darker than I would have expected. "Did you bake a bunch of oranges?"

"I dried them," Finn said. He set the tray down and gingerly transferred the oven-hot oranges to a dish, picking one up and knocking his knuckles against the side with a low, hollow thump. "They've already made their way through one batch." He lifted his chin to the box sitting at the end of the kitchen island.

I looked in to see it half full of oranges studded with cloves, tied with red ribbons. "You guys are making pomanders?" I asked. "I haven't seen these in an age, except in the gift shop in town and at the Inn."

"Miss Martha remembered having them when you guys were kids," Paige said. "She mentioned them to Nicky, and we all thought it sounded like fun."

"Can I help?" I asked, sliding into the chair next to Paige.

Her smile was blinding. "Of course. Here, watch what Nicky's doing."

I watched as the first grader carefully applied tape in lines around the orange.

"That's where the ribbon goes," he said. "You have to put the tape on first, or you put the cloves in the wrong place and then the ribbon won't stay."

"Makes sense," I said. "I'm impressed." I watched the kids work for a minute. "How many of these things have you guys made?"

"A lot," Thatcher said. "I'm covering this one in cloves."

"I don't think you can use that many," his younger

brother August said, looking at the pile of fragrant cloves in front of Thatcher doubtfully.

"Want to bet?" Thatcher challenged.

I caught Paige's grin. Part of why she was so good with the kids was that she genuinely loved being with them. The more time I spent watching her work, the more I understood why. They were good kids. And hanging out with Paige, watching her craft beside them as she gently guided them—helping cut ribbon, sort cloves—I looked at the kids and thought I wouldn't mind having one. Maybe more than one. I might actually be able to figure out how to be a good father. I had examples all around me now. And if I ended up with a kid as cool as these three were, and if they had a mom like Paige...

"What are you thinking about with that smile on your face?" Paige asked me in a low murmur, leaning in close.

"You." I dipped my head to sneak a kiss. "And the future," I added, after I pulled my lips away.

"This is going to be a good Christmas," she said.

"It really is," I agreed.

Savannah found us an hour later, just as we were tying up the last of the pomanders.

"Who wants to help me decorate?" With a shriek, the kids evaporated, sneakers pounding down the hall. Savannah laughed. "I wasn't expecting any help—not after I roped them into putting up pine boughs everywhere the other day. I'm amazed you got them to sit still for this long," she said to Paige.

"It accomplished two goals," Paige replied with a grin. "We got all the pomanders made, and they'll hide from the rest of us all day in fear of more crafts. It's a win/win."

"Before I start setting these all around the house," Savannah said, hefting the box on her hip, "I have something to show you, Ford. Do you have a minute?"

"Sure," I said, curious. I reached for Paige's hand, and she followed along.

"I've been working on something," Savannah said as we climbed the stairs. "I should have done it a long time ago."

As we reached the top, she turned toward the family wing. My sister Parker stood at the end of the hall, beaming at me. "I feel like we've been waiting forever," she said. "This way."

I slowed when I saw where she was heading: the door to my old suite. But she passed it and stopped at the rooms that had been Griffen's. When our father had thrown Griffen out of Heartstone all those years ago, he'd had the rooms emptied and everything painted white, as if he could erase Griffen's imprint on the Manor. No one had touched it since.

Parker stopped, her hand on the door. "I found a lot of things when I was working on the cottage and the gatehouse that I thought would be perfect for you. You seemed adamant about not using your old rooms. But we talked to Griffen and—"

Parker opened the door to the room and stepped inside. Savannah, Paige, and I followed.

I knew Parker had been redoing the most outdated areas of Heartstone Manor, but I hadn't thought she was working in the family wing. She'd completely redone the empty suite, painting the walls a deep forest green, the trim a warm cream. The combination was both crisp and welcoming. The view of the back gardens and the mountains beyond looked like a painting. Savannah had set up half the main space as a sitting room with a long leather couch, armchairs with ottomans, and a huge flat-screen against the wall. The other side of the main room had a desk big enough to really use, with a matching cabinet that I imagined could hold a printer and office supplies. I crossed the room and opened the antique corner cabinet to see a snack and beverage station stocked with a mini-fridge, kettle, coffee, and baskets of cookies and the chips she knew were my favorite.

I wandered into the bedroom to find a king-size bed with an upholstered dark leather headboard, made up in crisp white sheets piped with dark green that matched the walls. Parker must have done some remodeling, because I didn't remember Griffen ever having a walk-in closet or a bathroom this big.

I realized as I walked through the rooms that there was space here not just for one, but for two. When I was done, I turned to Parker and Savannah.

"When did you both have time to do this?" I asked.

"Here and there," Savannah said.

"I understood why you didn't want to go back to your old rooms," Parker said. "And if you'd rather stay in the guest wing—" She smiled at Paige before looking back to me. "That's okay, too. But we wanted you to have this. We're all so glad you're home." Parker rushed forward and threw her arms around me.

I hugged her tight. "I love you, Parks."

"I love you, too." She pulled away and wiped a streak of moisture from under her eye. "We'll give you guys some privacy to look around." Parker grabbed Savannah's hand and tugged her out of the room.

I watched them go, closing the door behind themselves. Sometimes it was hard to believe how things had worked out and how blind I'd been.

"Are you going to move in here?" Paige asked.

"I don't know. This is really thoughtful. I wasn't expecting—" I looked around at the comfortable, masculine, classically styled room that was a perfect fit for my personality and my taste. "Parker is amazing," I said. "And Savannah might as well have a furniture store up in the attics."

"Everything in this room looks like it was well made for you," she said. "I think you should move in. Let them welcome you home."

"You want me to move over here?" I asked, raising an eyebrow. "I wouldn't be across the hall."

"True," she said, walking up and sliding her arms around my waist.

"I'm assuming," I said, pulling her close, "that it's too soon to ask you to move in with me."

Her mouth curved in a smile that tempted me to kiss her. I didn't wait, running my thumbs along her chin to tilt her face to mine, her full lips a soft invitation.

"Maybe a little too soon," she said when I broke the kiss, "but I could leave a few things over here, just so I'm not sneaking around the halls in my robe." She leaned back out of my embrace and swept the room with her gaze.

"It's big enough for two," I said.

"It is," she agreed.

"Eventually," I said, and kissed her again.

"Eventually."

And I could see it all—our future laid out in front of me: Paige, family, everything I never thought I'd have, never thought I deserved. It all started with the woman in my arms.

I'd been waiting my entire life for her. Now that we were together, life was just beginning.

The Will

GRIFFEN

THREE YEARS LATER

"Are you ready for this, Griffen?" Hope asked, sliding her arm around my waist and leaning into me, her head against my chest.

"I'm ready for anything," I said, "as long as I have you right here." My heart fell for the trillionth time at the sweetness of her smile, the spark of lust in her warm hazel eyes. Life was good. But even when it hadn't been, the days that I spent with Hope at my side—loving me, loving her in return—could never be truly bad.

But I knew what she was really asking.

"No," I admitted, a little surprised by my answer. To Hope, I could say the thing that had me off-balance. The vulnerability I didn't want to admit, but could to her. "What if they all leave now that they don't have to stay? It's been five years, and sometimes even a house as big as Heartstone feels a little crowded—especially now that there are so many kids and pets running around."

"You wouldn't have it any other way," she said with a smile, "and neither would I. The truth is, some of them will leave, and some of them won't. Savannah is still working on getting Miss Martha to move in. The lure of a new granddaughter is pretty strong. Sterling and Forrest will move into their house in a few weeks. He gave his tenants notice months ago. And Parker and Nash—that place he built up the mountain is like a work of art."

"I know," I said, seeing in my mind the plate-glass windows overlooking the mountains, the long lines of cedar and black metal. It was modern and bold and very much my brother-in-law, but Parker, with her more classic elegance, somehow fit right in—just like she did with Nash. "They're only a few minutes up the mountain, though," I reminded Hope and myself.

"With a toddler and an infant, they want more space and privacy. I get it."

"So do I," I said, and I did. "But I wish they could all stay."

Hope let out a knowing laugh. "You're going to be a nightmare when the kids leave for college, aren't you?"

"Definitely," I agreed. "To be honest, I'm a little anxious about Thatcher leaving next year, and he's my nephew, not my son. But still, it feels like yesterday he was this gangly teenager, angry at the world, fiercely defending his mother, and now he's ours."

"Well, you know Tenn and Scarlett aren't moving out."

I did. They too had a baby, and it was a running joke that Thatcher would miss his infant sister more than the rest of us when he went off to college in the fall. Tenn, Scarlett, and their brood had taken over a good chunk of the family wing of Heartstone, and Tenn had asked a month before how we felt about them staying once the terms of our father's will expired. I'd been surprised he even asked. I thought I was clear with my siblings that there was room in Heartstone Manor for all of us.

"I know we're spreading out," Tenn had said, resting his ankle on his knee as he sat across from me in my office.

"Are you and Scarlett going to try for another?" I'd asked. I wouldn't have been surprised if he'd said yes. Tenn had taken to parenting August and Thatcher as if he'd been with them since birth—and had been just as excited when Mandy was born a year ago.

"I don't know. I'd be up for it. I'm not sure Scarlett is. It's a lot more work on her end," he said with a grin.

"True," I'd agreed.

"It's just that this is home for all of us. And more than that, the boys are anchored here, and I think they need it." His grin had faded. "They need their family around them."

"They talk about their dad much?" I asked. Their father was a deadbeat, lowlife criminal, so it was better if the answer was no, but better didn't mean easier.

Tenn shook his head. "They don't talk about him. They don't hear from him."

"You're a great dad," I assured him.

"I try," Tenn said. "They make it easy. But we know —it still sucks when your dad sucks, right?" He shot me a sideways grin. We knew all about dads sucking. "I don't want to uproot them again. I never thought I'd say this about Heartstone, but there's a lot of love here."

"I know what you mean," I said, "and there'll always be room for you in the Manor. One way or another, we'll figure it out. I mean, hell, if we cleaned out the attics, there's practically a whole other house up there."

"Good point," Tenn had said, and that had been one problem solved.

"No," I now confirmed to Hope, "Tenn and Scarlett definitely aren't going anywhere. And Nash's mom is staying, since Ophelia is, and they're hoping to snag Miss Martha."

We'd all found it amusing when Nash had attempted to build living quarters for his mother in the new house he and Parker had designed, and she'd sweetly turned him down. Heartstone was only a few minutes down the mountain from his and Parker's new place, and Nash's mother had been another family member who'd dropped into my office to make sure it was all right she stayed, considering we were only very loosely related now that Parker and Nash were married. But all of us had grown to love Claudia Kingsley, and while I couldn't say she was like a mother to me, she felt like part of the family. I knew my aunt Ophelia felt the same and would have been disappointed if her friend had moved up the road.

So, we were losing Parker and Nash and their two boys, but keeping Nash's mom, which meant the Kingsleys would be at Heartstone more often than not, anyway.

"And Savannah and Finn aren't going anywhere,"

Hope reminded me. "After that addition we put on the cottage, they won't need to."

"You know, if Finn wanted to go, he would have gotten himself completely out of the kitchens at Heartstone by now. He lets Greg run things most of the time," Hope said, referring to the apprentice chef Finn had been training. He'd come up with an interesting system of mentoring new chefs interested in working with the now-renowned Finn Sawyer. They shadowed him, learning at Heartstone and at the restaurant he ran at Sawyers Bend Brewing. When they'd learned enough, he put them mostly in charge of our meals at Heartstone, swapping back and forth as needed. By the time he set them free, he was ready for another mentee. We'd been through two chefs so far. It was fun to watch Finn teach them the way Chef Guérard had taught him when he was a teenager.

"Same for Hawk and Quinn," Hope had said. "Parker just finished renovating the gatehouse last year. You'd have to blow it up to get them out of it."

"True," I said. "They've got the perfect setup, odd as it is."

The gatehouse spanned both sides of Heartstone's drive. Built in a porte cochere style, when entering the estate, you basically drove through Hawk and Quinn's house. It had been abandoned for years by the time Hawk moved in—happy to share the space with mice and spider webs if it meant he didn't have to live in Heartstone with the Sawyers.

These days, he shared the gatehouse with my sister Quinn, their enormous dog and monster cat, and their infant daughter, whom he carried around in a baby wrap, scowling fiercely at anyone who tried to get too close. It made everyone laugh—their daughter a carbon copy of her father, right down to the dark-eyed scowl. Parker, knowing that Hawk and Quinn loved the gatehouse but needed more room with a baby on the way, had redesigned the unused side of the building—a mirror to the space Hawk and Quinn had been living in.

Once we'd cleaned the other side of the gatehouse of the old broken furniture and junk the former groundskeeper had stored there, Parker had transformed it, turning the first floor into a huge family room and the upstairs into a bedroom suite perfect for two parents who sometimes needed a little space from their kid. The second floor on each side of the gatehouse, connected by the part of the building that spanned the road, so, with the new design, Hawk and Quinn would have privacy but also easy access to the baby once they moved her into her own room. Given Hawk's newfound devotion to fatherhood, I had a feeling the baby was not going to be an only child, but the gatehouse now had three bedrooms, so they had room to grow.

I rested my chin on top of Hope's head, rubbing it back and forth. The apple scent of her shampoo drifted up, comforting and familiar. "Ford said he and Paige are staying," I said.

Hope turned in my arms and looked up at me, her eyes bright with surprise. "Did you think he was going to leave? For one thing, Paige wouldn't like the commute."

Despite their marriage and toddler, Paige was still the family nanny. She'd thought long and hard about what she wanted and came to the realization that the only change she was looking for was Ford. Otherwise, she loved taking care of the kids. She said that maybe, when all the Sawyers were done having babies and hers were in school, she'd think about going back to school herself or substituting in the classroom. But for now, she wanted to chase around her own two-year-old. And if she was doing that, she might as well take on the rest, too.

Ford had turned one of the former gallery rooms near my office into his own workspace and had done exactly what I expected him to when he took over the Sawyer Philanthropy Fund: he made it a force to be reckoned with. If you asked him, he'd probably say he still had a lot to atone for. But from where I was standing, he'd already brought more good to the world than he ever did wrong. He'd found ways to grow the fund while deploying it generously to charities that made a real impact. He had his fingers in everything from food banks to legal aid, rent assistance, and job training. These days, he'd left any trace of prison behind, the pallor and thin frame replaced with the healthy glow of a guy who spent as much time as possible outdoors, hiking, trail running, and playing soccer with the kids.

Hope, Royal, and I had made him another offer two years ago to come back to Sawyer Enterprises, and he'd turned us down, saying he had exactly the life he wanted. We didn't argue. I would have loved working with him again, but having his office next door was good enough.

"Avery and West are going," Hope said. "Is that what you're really bummed about? That your best friend is moving out?"

"Maybe a little," I admitted.

Having West living in Heartstone with Avery had been an added layer of fun. We'd had sleepovers now and then when we were kids, but nothing was quite like wandering in to play a game of pool with my best friend on a random Tuesday night.

"It makes more sense for both of them to be in town, and he's got a great house," I said. Both things were true, and they'd only be ten minutes away, but I still found myself wanting to talk them into staying. I kept my mouth shut, reminding myself that life is change and I'd see them all the time. "Are you okay with your BFF moving out?" I knew Hope had loved it when Daisy moved into Heartstone to be with Royal. They were married now, and not planning on kids. They liked being in the Manor, but it wasn't exactly convenient.

"I guess," Hope said. "Daze has to be in the bakery before dawn. And they found that great place right between the Inn and Sweetheart Bakery, and only a few blocks from Grams. They can both walk to work. It's just..."

"You're going to miss her," I finished.

"I am. It's silly, because she's right in town, but still. I loved having my family here."

"Me too." I turned, dipping my head to kiss her. When Prentice threw me out of Heartstone Manor all those years ago, I never thought I'd end up back here, madly in love with Hope and secretly wishing my family would live at home forever.

Her phone dinged in her pocket, and she leaned

back, breaking our kiss. "It's time," she said. "Do you think they're going to be disappointed?"

"Honestly, I don't think anyone's expecting anything."

When my father died five years ago, he'd left behind a complicated will, filled with secrets and irritating requirements. Ford had been cut out entirely; our father sure that Ford had been plotting against him. Considering he'd been right, Ford said he didn't care. It wasn't his money anyway, and he had enough without any inheritance. Technically, he didn't even have to be here, but I told him I needed him here. He might have been disinherited, but today wasn't about our father. It was about us.

We walked down the hall to the dining room, my fingers twined with Hope's. I thought how funny it was, all those years ago, driving to Sawyers Bend from Atlanta to hear the reading of Prentice's will. I'd planned to be in and out in an afternoon, and when I left Sawyers Bend, I was never going to return. That plan hadn't lasted long.

After the funeral, Harvey, our family lawyer, had pulled Hope and me aside and informed us that unless we married and stayed that way for five years, the entire Sawyer empire would fall apart. I wouldn't have had a problem with that, considering my father had thrown me out years before, but I did care about all the people who would lose their jobs if Sawyer Enterprises folded. So, Hope and I had married. The will that had been a weapon of my father's spite ended up being the greatest gift of my life.

I walked into the dining room to find Harvey already

there. He was semi-retired these days. After he killed Cole Haywood, he'd wound down a lot of his business and closed his office in town, and worked out of his house when he worked at all. He said his main job these days was to be an honorary grandfather. And he was a good one—more affectionate than Uncle Edgar, the only other grandfatherly figure around on a day-to-day basis. Harvey always had a hug, was always willing to play with LEGOs or kick a soccer ball.

With the admission that he was the one who'd shot our father, that he'd done it out of rage when he'd learned Prentice had murdered Sarah, things had changed. At first, there'd been distance. Not only had Harvey shot Prentice and set all of this in motion, but he'd also allowed Ford to spend a year in prison, falsely accused of killing his own father. Of all of us, Ford had let it go first, but one by one, we'd forgiven Harvey. The first time Hope invited him back to Sunday dinner, before she'd extended the same invitation to her uncle, Harvey had come to us a different man, the distance he'd been holding between us erased, a layer of formality stripped away. These days, Harvey wore his heart on his sleeve when it came to his family. Because, in the end, that was what we were. Family.

He'd never married, never found a woman to replace my mother in his heart, and I wondered sometimes if the attention he lavished on her grandchildren was a way to keep his love for her alive by sharing it with the grand-children she'd never know.

Most of us had moved past Prentice's death and Harvey's role in it, but I had to wonder if today would be awkward and uncomfortable. Here we all were, gathered this time in Heartstone's dining room instead of Harvey's conference room. Five years later, we were a much bigger group now that everyone had paired up.

"All right," I said to my siblings and their spouses milling around in the dining room. "Let's get this over with so we can have a party."

"Party?" Tenn asked. "Who said there was a party?"

Finn, down the table, leaned forward and grinned. "I've been cooking, Daisy brought goodies, and Savannah's got it all set up. As soon as we're done with the boring stuff, we can kick back and have some fun."

Scarlett looked at the time on her phone, her red hair curling wildly around her face as her eyebrows drew together. "We have pickup from school in an hour." She looked to Paige, who often took the afternoon run.

Paige's glance skipped over to Hawk, who assured Scarlett, "It's covered. No worries."

"All right, then," Scarlett said. "I'm down for a party."

I was scanning the room to see who we were missing when the front door opened and a second later, Forrest ducked his head in.

"She's not here?" he asked me about Sterling.

"Not yet," I said.

"I'll go get her. She loses track of time when her head's full of code." Considering the whole household knew how true that was, no one was surprised.

Forrest was back a few minutes later, Sterling in tow.

"Sorry, sorry, sorry," she said. "I got an idea, and..." She shook her head. "You know how it is." She and Forrest slid into their seats, and we were ready to go.

"All right. This doesn't have to take too long," I said. "Harvey, you want to do the formalities?"

I looked at Harvey, who picked up a manila file folder and opened it. "This is a lot more fun than the last time we went through this."

"No video will from Dad?" Royal asked wryly. The first time around, our father had left a video reading of his will, full of sarcasm and spite. Nobody wanted a redo of that.

"No video will this time," Harvey said seriously. "Not much of anything, honestly. I can officially state that the five-year period outlined in your father's will, requiring you to live in Heartstone Manor if you wanted access to Sawyer properties or any hope of inheriting your trust funds, has now elapsed."

A cheer went up.

Covered by the noise, Harvey turned to me. "Your part of the will has also been satisfied."

I looked to Hope and winked. "Here's your chance. You can get away."

"Really?" Her eyes sparkled back at me. "Just pack my things and go?"

"If you want," I said. "But be warned. I'll chase you down and bring you back."

"Well, then I might as well just stay," she said. "If you insist."

"I do." I took her hand and raised it to kiss the backs of her fingers. I was kidding, but I wasn't. I would never give Hope reason to want to leave me, but if she ever did—

"And what about the trusts?" Sterling asked. "Officially, I want to know if I win my bet with Forrest."

"What's your bet?" Harvey asked.

"My bet is that dear old Dad left us all a big fat goose egg of nothing. Because honestly, I can't see him doing anything else." She flipped her platinum ponytail over her shoulder, her vibrant blue eyes bright with amusement.

"What did Forrest bet?" I asked.

"Forrest bet that he left us all a token amount, like five bucks." Sterling rolled her eyes at the thought. "So, which is it?"

I looked at Forrest, who met my eyes, one brow raised. My brother-in-law was an optimist. He'd had to be, to win over Sterling. I knew he didn't care about the cash. Forrest had plenty of his own, and these days so did Sterling. He just wanted her to feel like her father had cared, if only a little bit.

"Sterling wins," I said, expecting to see shoulders slump and disappointment spread across my family's faces. I should have known better. I was met with an array of expressions that ranged from Sterling's smug grin of triumph to Parker's amused head shake.

"I told you no one would care," Hope said, leaning in to whisper in my ear.

"Not even a dime?" Forrest asked. "Damn, he was a bastard."

"You're not wrong," I agreed, remembering how furious I'd been the day the will was read. My father had always known how to twist the knife he'd stabbed in my back. "But I wouldn't take it personally. A lot of the will was a big fuck-you to me."

"Vintage Dad," Sterling said. "That's why I was so sure the trusts were empty. Because in that dumbass video will, he told you to drain our trusts if you needed money. But he was trying to punish you, too. So why would he give you access to a pile of cash?"

"He didn't," I confirmed. "He gave me the Manor and the company, but almost every penny of his personal funds went into the trust to maintain Heartstone Manor."

I looked to Harvey, who slid a folder my way, his face bright with anticipation.

I held up the file. Prentice's will might have been intended as a fuck-you to me, but finally, I got to make it right. "Now that the terms of the will are up, Harvey was able to execute a few things on my behalf as the head of the family. I decided to make a few changes to the way things are run. Harvey has some paperwork that some of you will need to sign, but we can do it tomorrow. Today is for fun and celebration. I'll keep it short. Tenn and Royal —the Inn at Sawyers Bend is yours. Quinn, your guide business is yours," I went on. "And Avery, you and Finn need to discuss how you want to handle the building the brewery is in, considering his restaurant takes up almost as much space as your brewery these days. But whatever you decide, it's yours."

Avery sent me a blinding grin and said, "I think we can work it out."

I looked down the table to where Daisy sat beside Royal. "The building that Sweetheart Bakery is in now belongs to you and Grams equally."

"Griffen," she said, her dark brows flying up in surprise, "you didn't need to do that. I'm not your family—"

"A sister-in-law is as good as a sister," I said, meaning it. "And Grams would have bought the building years ago if Prentice had been willing to sell. I couldn't do anything about it until the terms of the will were up, but now I can. And I did. So, it's done."

"Thank you," she whispered, her dark eyes misty.

"We've also made a few other changes. Dad did create trust funds for all of you, though he failed to fund them. Whether or not he would have added to them later, we'll never know. But I did. Nobody's running off to buy an island in the South Pacific, but there's enough in all of them to give you some padding. And if you're smart with it, it'll be plenty to cover your growing families. We also created an educational fund so none of the kids need to worry about tuition for college, trade school—whatever they want to do."

"Griffen," Sterling interrupted, "This is too much. If Dad didn't leave anything in our trusts, how are you paying for all of this?"

I should have known Sterling would want the details. I wasn't going to tell her of the sleepless nights Hope and I had shared as we tried to get a handle on Sawyer Enterprises, our only source of income. Things had been easier once Royal had come on board, and slowly, we'd not just stabilized the family business, we'd made it thrive.

"That brings me to the next thing we need to talk about," I said, sending Sterling a wink. "Dad left me

Sawyer Enterprises, but no ready cash, assuming I'd run it into the ground when I took over."

"He was such an asshole," Quinn muttered, shaking her head.

"True." I grinned at her. "And, in this case, he was wrong. Sawyer Enterprises is thriving, and Hope, Royal, Harvey, and I put a lot of thought into how to handle the profits. Ultimately, all of you have a share of the company. There are hoops to jump through for anyone who wants an active role, but in terms of profit sharing, everyone gets a cut. A portion of that cut will be diverted into your trust funds and into the educational fund. The remainder of your share goes straight to you. It's a family business, so it should be a family business."

Royal sat back, his arm around Daisy, and shook his head. "Damn, brother, when you go big, you go big."

I didn't have an answer for that. I looked around the table, seeing my family—my siblings, their spouses. We'd gone from mistrust and betrayal to this. These people would have my back, no matter what, and I'd do anything to protect them, every single one.

My father had raised us to hate each other. I hadn't truly known love, not completely, until Hope. For me, she was the beginning. And this was what we'd made together. A family. Not just Stella and Alexander, the sleeping baby strapped to her chest, but everyone here—my brothers and sisters, their husbands and wives and children. With Harvey, who, with one act, had taken our father and set us free.

"Before we pop the cork on this bottle of champagne," I said, tipping my head to the bottles chilling in ice that Savannah had set up before we began, "I just want to say how much I love you all."

My throat got tight, and I swallowed. *Keep it together,* I ordered myself, because before we celebrated this day we'd been waiting for, I had something to say.

"I know some of you are moving out, and I guess I'll learn to live with that." I smiled, trying to soothe a very real sting at the idea of any of them leaving. "But I want you to know—all of you, you and yours, will always have a home under this roof. No matter where you go and what you do, this is home, and we're family. When I came back here five years ago, I never imagined that we would have this." I spread my arms, encompassing the room. "And as much as I know we've all cursed the terms of this will many times over the last five years"—laughter scattered around the table—"I've come to think of that will as a gift. Without it, I never would have come home. I never would have married Hope." I looked down at my wife's beautiful face and smiled. "And I wouldn't have all of you. So, on this day—the day we're all set free—I'd like to make a toast."

I popped open the champagne bottle, grinning as the cork flew to strike the ceiling far above. I passed the bottle and popped another, sent it down the other side of the table, and waited until every glass had been filled.

"I'd like you to raise your glasses. To our family. Together, we can do anything."

"To family," every voice rang back.

And all of a sudden, I couldn't wait to see what happened next.

Fractured Promise

SNEAK PEEK

CHAPTER ONE
Sylvie

Don't leave us hanging, Sylvie - when is the next season coming out?

I stared down at the comment on the post for the latest episode of my podcast, my finger hovering over the screen on my phone. I debated whether to respond. I loved talking to my listeners on social media, but I hated letting them down. And the truth was, there was one episode left of my current season, and I had no idea when the next season was coming out. I'd thought I had a plan, had felt the story taking shape in my mind, but the more I investigated the murder of Emily Shaw, the more questions I had. So far, I'd found very few answers. I scrolled away from the comment, removing the temptation to give a vague promise about *soon*.

Usually, I loved nothing more than diving into a cold

case, hoping I could uncover something new and find answers for the dead and their families. I'd been intrigued by the first reports I'd found of Emily Shaw's murder—a car bomb in suburban Tennessee—and further interested by the way she'd disappeared from the news as quickly as the unusual story had hit. Too quickly.

Murder was my bread and butter. I paid attention to the rhythms of the media. You can learn a lot by the way things are reported, and this one was pinging my radar. I'd dug in—and was getting nowhere.

I sat back in my chair, feeling unusually claustrophobic in my van. Normally, the compact living and working space felt snug and comforting. Today, everything felt like it fit too tight. I got like this when I was frustrated. Restless. I'd come to Atlanta following a lead, and that lead had thrown up a stone wall.

Another message illuminated the screen of my phone: *Only one more episode left of this season. I can't take the suspense.*

That one made me grin. I led a solitary life, pretty much a one-woman show, but my listeners always made me feel like I was part of something bigger. Maybe because I'd started out as one of them. I'd been a true crime junkie since I was a kid, sneaking books off the shelf at the library. Aside from hiding my reading material from my mother, I'd been a rule follower back then. A good girl fascinated by darkness, by serial killers and criminals. In my real life, I dotted every I and crossed every T, got straight A's, and was respectful to my elders, but I couldn't quench my curiosity about those who walked outside the lines—and those who tracked them down and brought them to justice.

The second I discovered podcasting, I'd given up my books for endless episodes, digging into the minutiae of unsolved crimes, listening to shows that followed the crime all the way to conviction. I was captivated, but had the single worst day of my life not happened, I probably would have spent my entire life being the good girl, listening to my murder podcasts, and not doing anything about the stories that haunted me.

Being a good girl couldn't save me from being in the wrong place, at the wrong time. A life shoved brutally off course had turned into something new. I hadn't planned to spend my life in a camper van chasing justice for murdered women, but the woman I'd become didn't see any other path. I'd never get the justice I needed for myself, but I had a shot at getting it for someone else. Even then, filled with grief and a need for justice, I never thought about taking up the microphone myself.

Not until Carol Stevens.

Five years before, I'd come across her case in a compilation episode of one of my favorite podcasts. Carol Stevens had been working the dinner shift in a restaurant; she'd had the job for a few years, knew most of the customers, was close with the staff. One night, she picked up her purse, changed her shoes, and walked out through the kitchen, waving goodbye to the line cook still cleaning the grill. The door was propped open to the parking lot, lit by a single streetlight that Carol had carefully parked beneath.

The line cook had watched her open the door to her

car and lean down to get in before he'd turned back to the grill. When he looked up again a few minutes later, Carol's car was still there, the door hanging open, her purse on the ground beside it. Carol was nowhere to be seen. Her body was found three weeks later, less than a quarter mile away, in a drainage ditch.

I don't know what it was about Carol Stevens' case that got to me. Maybe it was that I'd waited tables to put myself through college and I knew what that was like—feet aching at the end of a long day, sweaty, the grease of the kitchen on my skin, my stomach growling, wanting nothing more than a hot shower and an equally hot meal, desperate to put my feet up and not feel obligated to smile at anyone for at least a few hours. I remembered what it was like to walk into that empty, dark parking lot. The way I, too, had always been careful to park under a light, as if that would protect me. The way the scuff of a foot on asphalt would have me spinning around in alarm.

The world was quiet in those empty places in the night: stairwells and parking lots. And I couldn't get what happened to her out of my head. Had someone been waiting in the car? Had they come up behind her? Did they have a gun or a knife? I could guess at what they'd threatened her with, given what we knew of the condition of her body when she was found.

Barely understanding why I was doing it, I'd taken the day off work and driven to the restaurant where Carol had worked. I don't know why her co-workers talked to me, what they saw in me that made them want to share what they knew, when I could tell they were tired of the media, of the endless questions. But they'd shared Carol's story with me, and I'd found what I was put on this earth to do.

I didn't find answers for Carol. In my frustration, I recorded what would end up being the first episode of my podcast. The first step into a new life. Episode one was a mess, mostly stream of consciousness ranting. No structure, no polish; I had no clue what I was doing, recording my thoughts only to get the frustration out, so I didn't feel like I was carrying it alone. I posted it for the same reason. And it felt so good to get everything out of my head and into words that I did it again. And again.

It didn't occur to me that anyone might be listening. Not really. But someone did, and then someone else. By the time I posted episode five, I had an audience—a small one, but they were there. I got a little more organized and posted a few more episodes. I never found Carol's killer. But the renewed interest in the case, and a few pieces of evidence I uncovered, had caused the local police to reopen the investigation. That felt better than anything I'd done in my life thus far.

There was no guarantee they'd find whoever did it, but they were looking, in part because of me. They hadn't given up on Carol. And it was an awakening. I'd done as much as I could for Carol Stevens. But there were other victims, other killers who'd gotten away. Maybe I could help someone else.

It didn't take long before another case popped up on my radar. And I was off, investigating, for what would become season two of *Evidence & Echoes*.

Somewhere along the line, my audience grew big enough to attract sponsors. My episodes got a little more organized and easier to follow, which didn't hurt. I'd learned a lot more than I realized through my years of binge listening. It helped that, along with loving research, I was enough of a tech geek to set up a recording studio, edit, and produce my own episodes. The second I could justify it financially, I'd quit my day job, poured my savings into kitting out my van, and hit the road, traveling all over the country, investigating cases and recording episodes.

Season two hadn't resulted in any answers—not even a reopened investigation, the police refusing to "waste" time looking into the disappearance of a murdered sex worker. I wanted more for the victim, but at least I brought attention to her story.

Season three blew everything wide open. By then, I was in a very pared-down version of my current van, living on ramen, wondering if I was going to have to sell plasma to pay for gas. My full-time job had seriously restricted my ability to investigate, but the income had been nice.

But then, season three: the murder and kidnapping of a teenage girl. The police had a prime suspect—a family friend and neighbor, everyone said, was such a nice young man. But there had been a few stories that had raised questions: an ex-girlfriend who wouldn't talk to the cops and seemed terrified, a guidance counselor who mentioned anger management issues. But no one had any evidence to tie him to the crime.

Until me.

It was part good luck, and part dogged determination to tie the smug asshole to the girl he'd murdered. I got him to talk to me—though of course he admitted nothing —but looking in his flat blue eyes, I knew he'd done it. And he knew I knew he'd done it, but we were both aware there wasn't any proof. He'd laughed as I'd walked away, recorder in hand, knowing I had nothing, and more determined than ever to nail his ass to the wall.

The police had warned me to be careful. But the detective suggested I press on the guy's ex. They hadn't been able to get her to talk to them, but maybe I would have better luck. Often, I was an annoyance to the police. Fair enough. I got it—I was a civilian with a microphone getting in the way of actual police work. But sometimes, like this case, they were willing to use me to get something they couldn't, and I was more than happy to be used.

I wouldn't make a good cop—I definitely get too involved emotionally. I wanted answers and justice for all of the women I investigated. But this one, Hillary Atkins, fifteen, dead far too young...

I wanted someone to pay for her loss.

And, somehow, after long conversations and slowly built trust, I got the ex to tell me what she knew. It wasn't a smoking gun; she didn't have proof or first-hand knowledge of what Troy Baker had done to Hillary. But she mentioned a name, a friend of Troy's. And it turned out Troy had bragged to that friend. And, like hopscotching stones to get across a river, I followed one clue to the next until we discovered where Troy had hidden the trophies he'd taken from Hillary after he killed her.

By the end of season three, Troy Baker was sitting in a jail cell, and I was a household name.

That was a year ago. The household name part didn't last very long—better for me. It's hard to investigate when everyone knows who you are. But it had been enough to propel me into a different level of notoriety and the ability to support myself through sponsors. No more ramen, no worrying about selling plasma for gas money. I wasn't a millionaire, but I had enough to keep doing what I loved.

And I did love it, even on nights like tonight when I was frustrated and getting nowhere.

I pulled my sweater tighter around me and stretched my legs, grimacing when I bumped my desk. I liked my little vehicular nest with everything I could need, but it was tight quarters. I had a queen-size Murphy bed that folded up into one side. When it was up, I could pull out my desk and swing out my wide monitor on an arm. The monitor did double duty as a TV when I had the bed folded down. Between the seats in the front and the bed/office area, I had a tiny kitchen and an equally tiny shower-bath.

I didn't mind clocking my elbows on the wall when I washed my hair if it meant I had my own private bath-room. Sometimes I stayed in campgrounds where I could hook up to utilities. And sometimes, like tonight, I found a moderately legal parking spot and hoped I'd be able to spend the night in one place. I was currently parked on a side street in Midtown Atlanta, grinding my teeth after another frustrating day of dead leads. The closest camp-ground was a haul outside the city and, in the cold, dark drizzle, I didn't feel like making the drive.

My stomach growled. I leaned back to stare at the

wood-paneled ceiling of the van, considering what exactly I was going to do about that. I'd been holed up in here for hours, debating what to do next, and had, as I often did, forgotten to think about food until my stomach was yowling for it.

I didn't bother to check the Dometic fridge drawer or the cabinets above the small sink. I had ramen. I always had ramen. Canned tuna. A half-empty jar of peanut butter. Probably some yogurt of questionable age. I didn't want any of that.

I thought of a hot, greasy burger and fries with a strawberry milkshake. I'd passed a place a couple of blocks away. It would be a wet, dark walk in the rain, but I glanced at the clock: 7:48 p.m. Definitely still open.

Drawing in a breath, I let it out in a gust, staring at the monitor in front of me, the cursor blinking in my notes file. My very empty notes file. I'd come to Atlanta chasing a lead that had turned into a brick wall, as everything about Emily Shaw's death seemed to do.

From the beginning, her murder had been smoke and mirrors: a freelance data analyst died when her car exploded in the driveway of her suburban townhome. Cars don't just explode on their own, not like Emily Shaw's car had exploded. And the fact that she looked at data for a living left me wondering if she'd seen something she shouldn't have. It was all weird enough to catch my attention. And interesting, because the news reports had been so vague about her professional background, the lack of detail seemed deliberate. I couldn't stop asking myself—who was Emily Shaw? People died by murder all the time—I knew that better than anyone. A gunshot, a stabbing. These were the crimes I ran into day after day. But a car bomb? That was rarely a crime of passion or one of opportunity. A car bomb implied premeditation.

But if Emily Shaw was a simple freelance data analyst, what had she seen, and who would kill to keep her quiet? And then the stories had disappeared from the media. Nothing, not another word. No one knew what had happened, and it was over. Unsolved, case closed—that had drawn me back, and I couldn't stop wondering: who was Emily Shaw, really, and who had decided she had to die?

A cold flutter in my gut told me this case might be more than I could handle. The more I dug in, the more I was simultaneously attracted and repelled. Attracted because I loved a puzzle, and repelled because there were too many pieces missing in this one. Too many dead ends. It was either a waste of time, or I was in over my head.

I was okay with wasting my time. That happened. Not every case that caught my attention could sustain a season of podcasting. Sometimes I had to move on because there just wasn't enough. Maybe Emily Shaw was one of those. But something told me there was more. And I wasn't ready to give up yet.

Emily Shaw had lived a quiet life in the suburbs of Knoxville, Tennessee. She'd worked from home and hadn't been living in her townhome long before her car had blown up with her in it. But I'd gone to her prior address and found a neighbor who'd traded cookie recipes with Emily and had mail she'd left behind after the move. She'd said Emily had planned to come back and pick it up, but she never did. And in that mail, I'd found a bill from an unpaid Peach Pass toll, which told me Emily had been in Atlanta only a few days before she'd died.

I thought I might know why, because along with the bill, mixed up in the stack of junk mail, there'd been a handwritten note. On it were the two scrawled letters, SS, a street address with no city or state, and a phone number with an Atlanta area code. I'd looked up the phone number. It was the main line for a company called Sinclair Security. Their website told me Sinclair Security handled high-end security, protection, and problem-solving. I didn't know what the last meant, but once again, I got the feeling I was in over my head.

It didn't help that ever since I'd seen the neighbor, I'd been getting phone calls. Hangups, always from unknown numbers. Twice, I'd gotten out of the van with a crawling sensation between my shoulder blades, as if there were eyes on me. I'd received threats before; it came with the territory. But nothing that had seemed legitimately dangerous.

This felt different. Emily Shaw's murder had me spooked.

I didn't want to give up on finding answers for Emily. But if I couldn't get anything out of Sinclair Security when I went to see them tomorrow, I might have to move on. I had one more episode of my last finished season, the fourth. I hadn't found answers for the young mother I'd been investigating, but I had dug up a few things the detective on the case thought might get them a new search warrant for their prime suspect. My listeners were going to love it.

But season five was supposed to be Emily Shaw. And if I couldn't find anything solid in the next twenty-four hours, I was going to have to let this go. There were a lot of great true crime podcasts out there. If I couldn't deliver a season five in time, my audience might move on, and I'd be back to ramen and wondering how I was going to pay for gas.

I rolled my shoulders back and stood, glad, as I often was, that I was only average height and build. If I'd been tall, the van would have been a nightmare. But as it was, I fit almost perfectly.

My stomach rumbled, clenching almost painfully on the nothing inside. That was it. I couldn't think straight without a burger and a milkshake. I wasn't going to figure out the course of the case or my career tonight. I was going to eat a good meal, come back to the van, tuck myself in for a good night's sleep, and start the day fresh in the morning by getting Sinclair Security to tell me why Emily Shaw had their number.

Grabbing my bag, I shoved my phone in my pocket, pulled on my raincoat, flipping up the hood, and made my way to the front of the van, sliding into the driver's seat and reaching for the handle.

I let out a huff of annoyance when I realized a big box delivery truck was double-parked beside me, blocking me in. The passenger side door wasn't an option, a tree just on the other side that would stop it from opening wide enough for me to get out. I eyed the space between the side of my van and the box truck. It would have to be enough. I was starving, and they could be there for an hour.

Wrapping my fingers around the edge of the door as I eased it open to keep from crashing it into the side of the truck, I wiggled my way out into the dark, closing the door behind me. I squeezed my body down against the side of the truck and ducked around the front, crossing the street, jogging through the light mist toward the burger place I remembered from earlier in the day.

I ended up eating inside. I learned from experience that if I brought the burger and fries back to the van, I might have a comfortable dinner, but I'd be treated to the smell of French fries and burger grease for the next few days. That was why, even though the van had a basic kitchen, I rarely cooked for myself unless I was in a camp-ground and could do it outside. I love the smell of a burger and fries, but I didn't want to smell it in my dreams.

I relaxed in the restaurant, watching people come and go: college students, people on the way home after working late. The burger place was basic, but the food was delicious, and they attracted a varied crowd. I inhaled my burger and took the lid off my shake, dipping fries in the frozen strawberry treat, savoring the salty and sweet indulgence as I let the details of the case shuffle in my brain.

Emily had come to Atlanta three days before she was murdered. I thought she'd come to talk to someone at Sinclair Security. A phone call told me that the recep-tionist at Sinclair was no dummy. She'd neither confirmed nor denied that Emily Shaw had been there, stonewalling me completely. My plan for tomorrow was to just show up, but it was a long shot and I knew it. I'd driven past their sleekly modern office building in Buck-head earlier in the day and doubted I'd get past the front door. I was going to try anyway.

My phone buzzed on the table. UNKNOWN. I wasn't answering that. The last thing I needed on a dark, rainy night was to creep myself out by answering calls from UNKNOWN. I already knew what I'd hear on the other end. Nothing. What was the point of calling if they had nothing to say?

The rain was coming down even harder when I finally left the burger place, my crossbody purse tucked under my raincoat, feet squelching in my wet sneakers as I wished I'd traded them for rain boots. I came around the corner and caught sight of the black gleam of my Sprinter van a couple of hundred feet away, letting out a breath of relief when I didn't see a ticket on the windshield. It was late enough now that I might actually be good to stay in one place all night. I stopped before the curb, ducking into a doorway with an overhang while I waited for the light to change so I could cross the street.

Cars passed through the intersection, clearing my way to cross, as a shadow separated from the back of my van, melting out from beneath the rear bumper and rising to full height before taking off down the street at a rapid jog.

Someone had been under my van. Doing what, I had no idea. Planting a tracker, maybe? Chills erupted over my entire body.

"Hey," I yelled, sprinting after them, my eyes locked on their dark form as they turned a corner and disappeared.

Not knowing exactly what my plan was, I picked up the pace, determined to catch up. Just before I reached my van, a roar of heat and sound struck me, lifting me off my feet, throwing me back into the narrow alley opposite where my van had been. In an instant, the van I'd built from bare metal into a home was gone. In its place was a fireball.

The heat licked at my skin, the air acrid with smoke. Thoughts skittered across my mind.

I should move.

The gas tank might still blow.

Who would want to blow me up?

I didn't have any answers. The best I could do was a crab walk deeper into the alley, far enough that the heat from my burning van didn't threaten to set me alight. My face stung, the rain dripping down my skin, burning, falling in pink drops onto my hands. I was bleeding. I noted it absently, along with the cold wet of my jeans.

I don't know how long I sat there watching the shell of my home burn. Everything I owned was in there. I had my bag, like I always did, with my wallet, passport, and tablet. I had my phone. That was it. Everything else was in the van. My clothes. My computer and podcasting equipment. The award I'd won for helping to solve Hillary Atkins' murder. The collar from my childhood dog, that I'd kept as a good luck charm. All gone. I'd run every wire in that van, sanded each piece of wood for the paneled ceiling. It was insured, but...

My brain wouldn't work. The light from my burning home flickered, illuminating the street and the opening of the alley. Sirens wailed in the distance, and in a split second, the little I knew about my case flashed through my mind. Emily Shaw. Car bomb. The phone calls. That itch between my shoulder blades. And now my home, blown up.

I had to make a choice. I could stay there, wait for the police and the fire department, like I was supposed to. But I couldn't forget Emily Shaw's unsolved murder, closed so quickly. The cold flutter in my gut started up again as the sirens drew closer. I was alone. And right now, whoever blew up my van might think I was dead. If I stayed and waited for the police, they'd know I wasn't.

I could ask the police to protect me... As soon as the thought formed, I shoved it away. Too risky. I didn't know who to trust. And sitting there, the rain dripping down my face, soaking into my clothes, the sirens wailing louder and louder, I knew there was only one place I could go.

I wobbled to my feet, slowly backing away from the mouth of the alley and the sight of my burning home. I had to find a place to hole up for the night. Somewhere I could go unnoticed. Stay off the radar. Stay alive long enough to get to the only lead I had. Because there was no fucking way I was walking away from Emily Shaw's murder. Not now.

Not when I was pretty sure whoever had killed Emily had just tried to kill me, too.

CHAPTER TWO
Eli

"If Silas was coming back, he'd have turned up by now."

Ryder's words landed between us like a stone, sinking the mood in the room. What had started as a simple team meeting had taken a turn. Cooper Sinclair, my new boss, sat at the head of the conference table, looking at the rest of us, a light of amusement in his ice-blue eyes at Ryder's flat tone.

He was amused because, in my opinion, he still wasn't quite sure how he'd ended up with the team from Creed Global folded into his own company, Sinclair Security. Neither were we. The team—consisting of me, Ryder, Miranda, Maddox, Wren, and Shade—had worked for the last decade or so under the leadership of one Silas Creed. Creed Global wasn't all that different from Sinclair Security. Not really. We handled similar business: protection, investigations, and, as the Sinclair Security website put it, problem-solving. It's just that Creed Global solved problems with a little more edge than Sinclair Security. We worked in parallel lanes, and while we'd always shared mutual professional respect, that was it.

Then Silas had disappeared, telling us only that he'd sold Creed Global to the Sinclairs, and we should move over there and take orders from Cooper, while Silas tied up some loose ends from his old life. He'd dodged all our demands for more information, promising that he'd be back. That was months ago. Since then, there'd been no sign of Silas Creed.

If Silas was coming back, he'd have turned up by now.

Ryder's words ping-ponged in my head, and I watched as the amusement left Cooper's eyes once Ryder's flat tone penetrated.

Leaning forward, Cooper tapped the tip of his pen on the conference table, drawing all eyes to him, before he said, "You don't know that, Ryder."

Ryder didn't reply, but pushed the sleeves of his tactical shirt up his arms, the green contrasting with his tanned forearms. Shade leaned forward to catch Ryder's gaze, her dark, sleek ponytail sliding over her shoulder. "Silas has gone undercover for longer than this. He told us to trust him. Maybe it's taking longer to tie up those loose ends than he expected."

"I don't buy it," Maddox said in his low rumble, rubbing his wide palm over the back of his shaved head. "Loose ends can be slippery, but there hasn't been a trace of him. I looked. I asked Emmett to look—" He flashed a glance to Cooper, maybe waiting for a protest, but Cooper only gave him a short nod.

"Emmett didn't find anything either?" Cooper clarified.

"Nothing," Maddox said with a quick shake of his head. Emmett was one of several extremely talented hackers at Sinclair Security. Maddox was good—maybe as good as Silas. I knew my way around a keyboard, though explosives were more my thing. But Emmett? Emmett was the guy everyone went to when they knew what they needed was out there and they just couldn't fucking find it. Emmett could find almost anything. But he hadn't found Silas.

"So, what are you saying?" I asked Ryder as he sat back. "You think he took off on us, or you think he's dead?"

Miranda flicked me a worried glance. I avoided her eyes. She always saw too much, and I knew why she was worried. From me, you were more likely to get a joke than a blunt confrontation, but I never minded laying it out when I had something to say. And I didn't see the point in avoiding reality. Because Maddox was right. Silas going undercover for a few months wasn't out of the realm of possibility—especially if he was tying up loose ends from a life he'd walked away from decades before. But to do it and drop out of sight so completely? That didn't fit. There were any number of ways he could have communicated with any one of us and still stayed off the radar. A simple proof of life would have been enough. If he wasn't going to contact us because we were practically his fucking family, he at least should have done it because it was company policy.

I'd been over it in my head, going in circles trying to come up with an explanation, and in the end, I kept coming to the same conclusion. The only reason Silas wouldn't have contacted us was if he couldn't.

I swallowed at that thought, pushing away the cold nausea turning my gut. Silas wasn't dead. Silas couldn't be dead. It wasn't a possibility I was ready to face. Silas was the guy who'd saved my unit when everything had gone to shit, turning up in the dark out of nowhere with a vehicle and firepower exactly when we'd needed it. He'd told me he'd been watching me, had been impressed, and he was helping because he didn't want to lose my talent to some bullshit mistake. After we'd gotten ourselves out of that mess, he'd offered me a job. I'd seen Silas make the impossible possible too many times over the years to imagine something had gone that badly wrong. But nothing about this had made sense from the beginning.

Why had Silas sold Creed Global to Sinclair? It was one of the things I couldn't work out, and the unanswered question nagged at me. He should have put Ryder and Miranda in charge. Ryder had been working with Silas the longest, and second was Miranda. She had the logistical skills to run the team. Hell, she practically ran it for Silas until he disappeared.

And if Silas was coming back, why sell his company? As the thought unrolled in my mind, I felt it leave my lips, directed toward Cooper. "I still don't understand why he sold Creed Global to you and your brothers."

"You ready to jump ship so fast?" Cooper answered, which wasn't an answer at all.

"No," I said, looking out into the array of partitioned desks opposite the conference room. Our setup at Creed Global had been a little more low-key—a converted warehouse kind of thing. This was— I rolled my neck, stretching out the stiffness. This was corporate. Cooper was wearing a suit for fuck's sake. I could wear a suit if I had to, and we did corporate work at Creed Global. It just felt—I don't know—more relaxed, the way we did it. "I don't love the cubicle farm, but I'm not looking for an out. Not yet, anyway."

"Fair enough," Cooper said, setting his pen on the table and sitting back in his chair, propping his ankle on his knee. "Look, I don't know why Silas sold us Creed

Global instead of turning it over to Ryder and Miranda."
He shifted his gaze to Ryder and then Miranda, sitting
side by side. "You've been here a couple of months now.
You're familiar with our people. You've seen how we
work. Do you want out?"

"Are you offering us an out?" Miranda asked, one dark
red eyebrow raised in an arch. She was cool, Miranda—
her expression pleasant but giving away nothing.

"I'm keeping the client list and the contracts," Cooper
said, "and I'll hold you to the NDAs, but you're all at-will
employees. I signed a contract with Silas, not with each of
you individually. And frankly, given the nature of what
we do, if you don't want to be here, I don't want you to
stay."

A jolt of panic hit my chest, the unexpectedness of
the emotion taking my breath for a split second. Yeah,
Sinclair Security wasn't where I thought I'd end up, but it
hadn't occurred to me that any of the team might jump
ship. We'd worked together for years. They were my
family. I clamped down the panic, forcing myself to take
a slow breath and look around the table—really look.
When I did, calm chased out the nerves.

"None of us are going anywhere," Maddox said,
sitting back, mimicking Cooper's posture down to the
ankle on his knee, his chair creaking under his broad
frame. "Not saying I'm going to retire here, but you run a
good shop. I like most of your people. Your cases are a
little more straight-edge than what we're used to, but you
know, I can adapt. Maybe you can adapt, too."

Cooper acknowledged that with the slightest nod.
"Alright, then." He put his foot down and slid closer to

the table, braced his elbows, and said, "Then what do you want to do about Silas?"

"What do you mean?" Wren asked, tucking a sandy blonde strand of hair behind her ear. She was doing her unassuming girl thing: no makeup, hair in a messy, stubby ponytail, flannel shirt, and jeans. Like this, she could disappear almost anywhere in America, unnoticed, which was a load of bullshit, because she was one of the toughest, most dogged investigators I'd ever known. We could drop her in the woods or a city, and she could track anyone. Despite her size, she fought like a demon. And when she wanted to, she could look like an innocent kid a few days out of junior high.

"Obviously, you've looked into where Silas is, if you've tapped Emmett?" Cooper said. Maddox nodded.

"So, what do you want to do?" Cooper repeated. "Do you think he's out there, up to something, or do you think—"

He didn't say it, and I was glad. I couldn't get my head around the idea that Silas might be dead. We'd all seen enough death. I'd seen more than most. But I couldn't—wouldn't—consider that Silas wasn't coming back.

"It depends," I said, slowly. "There are a few options here: he could be out there tying up loose ends and just isn't done yet. Doesn't explain why we can't find a trace of him or why he hasn't contacted anyone."

"It's possible he can't contact anyone," Wren said, the hope in her tone begging me to agree with her. We both knew better than to hope in a situation like this. We needed to see what was, not what we wanted to see. "What if he needs our help?"

"It could mean that," Maddox said and crossed his arms, his biceps stretching the sleeves of his faded black t-shirt. "Or it could mean he's dead."

"He isn't dead," Wren ground out between clenched teeth.

I found myself agreeing. "Not Silas."

"Everybody's ticket gets punched eventually," Maddox said evenly, his chin lifted.

"So, you're just willing to give up on him?" I demanded, irritated with Maddox's dogged pessimism.

"We're not doing ourselves any favors by hiding from reality," he shot back.

I wanted to argue, but I'd been telling myself the same thing only minutes ago.

"So that brings me back to my question," Cooper said. "Are we looking for Silas, or do we give him more time to deal with his loose ends?"

"You would, wouldn't you?" Miranda asked slowly, her unwavering calm washing over me. "If we wanted to open a full-fledged investigation, you'd put aside the resources?"

"Not everything's about business, Miranda," Cooper said. "Silas is a friend. The six of you are assets, and I'm glad to have you at Sinclair. Silas's going missing is a big deal. Especially after selling the company he spent half his professional life building. To deal with loose ends? I want answers, too."

"I think we're worrying too soon," Ryder said quietly. "He's not a kid. He knew what he was doing. He clearly had a plan. He's still executing that plan. Just because you're all getting antsy doesn't mean he's done with whatever it was he had to do."

"Maybe," I agreed. "I'd like to think you're right, Ryder. I think you could be. And I don't think he's dead, but—"

"What if he's in trouble?" Wren asked. "Even Silas runs into trouble now and then."

"We need to find him," I finished for her.

Cooper's icy blue eyes met mine. "I've had the same thought. Silas and I are square. He doesn't owe anything. Didn't promise me he'd be back. But if he's out there and in a jam—"

"So, we're agreed," Ryder said. "We keep looking?"

"Emmett did find one thing," Maddox said. "He dug it out this morning." He reached into his back pocket and pulled out a folded piece of white paper. He opened it and slid it into the middle of the table.

I leaned forward and snatched it up, staring down at the lines of numbers and symbols on the page. I raised an eyebrow and shoved it back at Maddox. "What is that?"

"Encrypted code. It popped up on one of Silas's old networks—nothing anyone's used in years. But this was recent, after he left that note and dropped off the face of the earth. They matched data packets coming from a device belonging to one Emily Shaw, who died when her car exploded in her driveway. Two days after...this," he pointed at the paper on the table, "indicates that she and Silas were communicating."

"Who set the bomb?" Ryder asked, getting straight to the most crucial question we needed to answer.

"No idea," Maddox said. "It hit the papers for a day or two—big splash, as a car bomb in a suburban neighborhood would be, then nothing. Closed, unsolved. Evidence is still sitting, unprocessed."

"So, who was Emily Shaw?" Cooper asked, picking up the pen he'd left on the table, and flipping it between his fingers. I noted it had gold trimmings. The guy was classy. And rich, I reminded myself. Not that any of us were hard off. Silas had made sure of that. But Cooper Sinclair was a step above comfortable. Several steps.

"That's an interesting question," Maddox said, tilting his head to one side. "According to the papers, she was a freelance data analyst who worked from home, which begs the question of where she was going when she got in the car that day. Emmett and I looked into her."

"And?" I prompted.

"And she seems to be what the paper said she was. But the information we found was—" he looked at the ceiling, as if searching for the right words in the bright lights above "—curated," he finally said.

"Like everything fit into a perfect picture?" Miranda prompted, and Maddox nodded.

"Exactly. Too perfect. As if the Emily Shaw we were seeing was exactly who she wanted us to see."

"Which is outside the skill set of your average freelance data analyst," Ryder finished.

"And that's our only lead," I said. "A dead woman and a car bomb. Nothing on those old servers of Silas's since then?"

Maddox shook his head. "Nothing."

"Well, I guess we keep looking then," I said. "And if

403

we find out he's in a jam—" I looked to Cooper, who nodded. "Then we ride to the rescue."

There was a quick triple rap on the door, and it swung open. Alice, Cooper's wife and the Sinclair Security office manager, poked her head in, her short, dark bob swinging, her sky-blue eyes bright with intrigue.

"Hey, sorry to interrupt, but we've got a walk-in." She raised an eyebrow. "She insists it's urgent."

I knew already after my short time working here that walk-ins were not the usual at Sinclair Security. At what they charged, people didn't just wander in off the street. For one thing, you needed a referral to even find them. Us.

"What aren't you saying?" Cooper asked, reading something in his wife's face. Even I could see the grin she was trying to repress.

"You're not going to believe this, but Sylvie Calloway is sitting in our lobby. She's working on a case, and she wants to talk to us."

I had no idea who Sylvie Calloway was, but Cooper appeared to. I looked around at the rest of the team, who seemed equally clueless.

"Who the hell is Sylvie Calloway?" Ryder asked what we were all wondering.

"She's one of Alice's favorite murder podcasters," Cooper answered with a grin at his wife. "She helped solve a cold case last year."

"You mean one of those true crime people?" Miranda asked.

"Pretty much, yeah," Alice said cheerfully. "Eli, you're up."

I started to shake my head, but Cooper sent me a grin that was almost a smirk. "Sorry, man, but she's right. Maddox is with Emmett on that other thing, which works since they're also digging into Silas. Miranda's working on some project assignments with Ryder and Alice, so I can't spare her. Ditto for Ryder. And Wren and Shade are both due time off."

"I don't need time off," Wren said, but Shade elbowed her and shook her head.

"Can it," Shade said. "You know we both need a day or two. You promised me we'd go to the movies. Popcorn, extra butter."

"Yeah, but I want to meet the podcaster," Wren said under her breath.

"Nah, make Eli do it. It'll irritate the shit out of him." The grin I got from Shade was definitely a smirk.

"Fine," I said. "But if she has a microphone, I'm chucking it out the window."

"As long as you don't chuck her out after it," Alice said, following me down the hall.

I wasn't making any promises.

ARE YOU READY FOR ELI & SYLVIE'S STORY?

Visit IvyLayne.com/FracturedPromise
to see what happens next!

Never Miss a New Release:

Join Ivy's Reader's Group

@ ivylayne.com/readers
&
Get two books for free!

About Ivy Layne

Ivy Layne has had her nose stuck in a book since she first learned to decipher the English language. Sometime in her early teens, she stumbled across her first Romance, and the die was cast. Though she pretended to pay attention to her creative writing professors, she dreamed of writing steamy romance instead of literary fiction. These days, she's neck deep in alpha heroes and the smart, sexy women who love them.

Married to her very own alpha hero (who rubs her back after a long day of typing, but also leaves his socks on the floor). Ivy lives in the mountains of North Carolina where she and her other half are having a blast raising two energetic boys. Aside from her family, Ivy's greatest loves are coffee and chocolate, preferably together.

For More Information:
www.ivylayne.com
books@ivylayne.com
Facebook.com/AuthorIvyLayne
Instagram.com/authorivylayne/

Also by Ivy Layne

WHERE PROMISES LIE

Fractured Promise (July 2026)

Deadly Promise (November 2026)

Dark Promise (2027)

Shattered Promise (2027)

Last Promise (2028)

THE HEARTS OF SAWYERS BEND

Stolen Heart

Sweet Heart

Scheming Heart

Rebel Heart

Wicked Heart

Wild Heart

Broken Heart

Reckless Heart

Forbidden Heart

Made in United States
Orlando, FL
05 December 2025

73500312R00233